£2.
50

BEST OF ALL POSSIBLE WORLDS

A NOVEL

GARY ANDERSON

WORDSWORTH
GREENWICH
PRESS

ALSO BY GARY ANDERSON

ANIMAL MAGNET:
A NOVEL

WHAT PEOPLE ARE SAYING
ABOUT GARY ANDERSON

Goodreads voted Anderson's *debut* novel, *Animal Magnet,* among the **"Best Books of the Decade"** and **"Best Literary Books of All Time."**

"Reminiscent of John Barth's *Sotweed Factor* – and equally accomplished, Gary Anderson's *Best of All Possible Worlds* is a sustained comic delight. Masterful, outrageous, teeming with exotic incidents and characters.... An astonishingly fine novel. Don't miss it." ★★★★★ **Terry Richard Bazes, Novelist, Author of** *Lizard World*

"In *Best of All Possible Worlds* Gary Anderson recreates Voltaire's narrative style, but with a conceptualist's eye. He takes a small fragment from *Candide* and builds a rich story upon it that is full of comedic turns of phrase... I continue to be impressed with Anderson's literary genius and highly recommend *Best of All Possible Worlds* to anyone looking for a critical and fresh look at the world."
★★★★★ **Jacqueline Valencia, Author of** *Tristise*

"*Best of All Possible Worlds* is a literary *tour de force* of real genius. The narrative voice is one of a kind: witty, shrewd, captivating, hilarious. Its satirical quality rivals Voltaire in *Candide*. Anderson's brilliant imagination for his story line knows no bounds and signifies his indelible mark as a story teller. This ambitious epic genuinely is the best of all possible literary novels – read this masterpiece." ★★★★★ **David B. Lentz, Author of** *Bloomsday*

"This work (*Animal Magnet*) is a knockout and is the most original piece I have read since the early 90's." ★★★★★ **Jessica Visconti, Goodreads**

"I love this book (*Animal Magnet*). As soon as I finished it, I wanted to start it, again. The sort of book I wished I could forget so I could read it again for the first time. It is one of the best novels I have read in a very long time and I look forward to reading Mr. Anderson's next book, which I hope will come out soon. In this era of dull derivative novels isn't it nice to stumble across a book that makes you go "WOW!"? Do yourself a favour and read this book!"
★★★★★ **Chico Picante, Goodreads**

FOR MY SON, CALEB

Foreword

HOW CANDIDE MADE HIS ESCAPE
FROM THE BULGARIANS, AND
WHAT AFTERWARDS BECAME OF HIM

There was never anything so gallant, so spruce, so brilliant, and so well disposed as the two armies. Trumpets, fifes, hautboys, drums, and cannon made music such as Hell itself had never heard. The cannons first of all laid flat about six thousand men on each side; the muskets swept away from this best of worlds nine or ten thousand ruffians who infested its surface. The bayonet was also a sufficient reason for the death of several thousands. The whole might amount to thirty thousand souls. Candide, who trembled like a philosopher, hid himself as well as he could during this heroic butchery.

At length, while the two kings were causing Te Deum to be sung each in his own camp, Candide resolved to go and reason elsewhere on effects and causes. He passed over heaps of dead and dying, and first reached a neighbouring village; it was in cinders, it was an Abare village which the Bulgarians had burnt according to the laws of war. Here, old men covered with wounds, beheld their wives, hugging their children to their bloody breasts, massacred before their faces; there, their daughters, disembowelled and breathing their last after having satisfied the natural wants of Bulgarian heroes; while others, half burnt in the flames, begged to be despatched. The earth was strewed with brains, arms, and legs.

Candide fled quickly to another village; it belonged to the Bulgarians; and the Abarian heroes had treated it in the same way. Candide, walking always over palpitating limbs or across ruins, arrived at last beyond the seat of war, with a few provisions in his knapsack, and Miss Cunegonde always in his heart. His provisions failed him when he arrived in Holland; but having heard that everybody was rich in that country, and that they were Christians, he did not doubt but he should meet with the same treatment from them as he had met with in the Baron's castle, before Miss Cunegonde's bright eyes were the cause of his expulsion thence.

He asked alms of several grave-looking people, who all answered him, that if he continued to follow this trade they would confine him to the house of correction, where he should be taught to get a living.

The next he addressed was a man who had been haranguing a large assembly for a whole hour on the subject of charity. But the orator, looking askew, said:

"What are you doing here? Are you for the good cause?"

"There can be no effect without a cause," modestly answered Candide; "the whole is necessarily concatenated and arranged for the best. It was necessary for me to have been banished from the presence of Miss Cunegonde, to have afterwards run the gauntlet, and now it is necessary I should beg my bread until I learn to earn it; all this cannot be otherwise."

"My friend," said the orator to him, "do you believe the Pope to be Anti-Christ?"

"I have not heard it," answered Candide; "but whether he be, or whether he be not, I want bread."

"Thou dost not deserve to eat," said the other. "Begone, rogue; begone, wretch; do not come near me again."

The orator's wife, putting her head out of the window, and spying a man that doubted whether the Pope was Anti-Christ, poured over him a full.... Oh, heavens! to what excess does religious zeal carry the ladies.

A man who had never been christened, a good Anabaptist, named Jacques, beheld the cruel and ignominious treatment shown to one of his brethren, an unfeathered biped with a rational soul, he took him home, cleaned him, gave him bread and beer, presented him with two florins, and even wished to teach him the manufacture of Persian stuffs which they make in Holland. Candide, almost prostrating himself before him, cried:

"Master Pangloss has well said that all is for the best in this world, for I am infinitely more touched by your extreme generosity than with the inhumanity of that gentleman in the black coat and his lady."

The next day, as he took a walk, he met a beggar all covered with scabs, his eyes diseased, the end of his nose eaten away, his mouth distorted, his teeth black, choking in his throat, tormented with a violent cough, and spitting out a tooth at each effort.

HOW CANDIDE FOUND HIS OLD MASTER PANGLOSS, AND WHAT HAPPENED TO THEM

Candide, yet more moved with compassion than with horror, gave to this shocking beggar the two florins which he had received from the honest Anabaptist Jacques. The spectre looked at him very earnestly, dropped a few tears, and fell upon his neck. Candide recoiled in disgust.

"Alas!" said one wretch to the other, "do you no longer know your dear Pangloss?"

"What do I hear? You, my dear master! You in this terrible plight! What misfortune has happened to you? Why are you no longer in the most magnificent of castles? What has become of Miss Cunegonde, the pearl of girls, and nature's masterpiece?"

"I am so weak that I cannot stand," said Pangloss.

Upon which Candide carried him to the Anabaptist's stable, and gave him a crust of bread. As soon as Pangloss had refreshed himself a little:

"Well," said Candide, "Cunegonde?"

"She is dead," replied the other.

Candide fainted at this word; his friend recalled his senses with a little bad vinegar which he found by chance in the stable. Candide reopened his eyes.

"Cunegonde is dead! Ah, best of worlds, where art thou? But of what illness did she die? Was it not for grief, upon seeing her father kick me out of his magnificent castle?"

"No," said Pangloss, "she was ripped open by the Bulgarian soldiers, after having been violated by many; they broke the Baron's head for attempting to defend her; my lady, her mother, was cut in pieces; my poor pupil was served just in the same manner as his sister; and as for the castle, they have not left one stone upon another, not a barn, nor a sheep, nor a duck, nor a tree; but we have had our revenge, for the Abares have done the very same thing to a neighbouring barony, which belonged to a Bulgarian lord."

At this discourse Candide fainted again; but coming to himself, and having said all that it became him to say, inquired into the cause and effect, as well as into the sufficient reason that had reduced Pangloss to so miserable a plight.

"Alas!" said the other, "it was love; love, the comfort of the human species, the preserver of the universe, the soul of all sensible beings, love, tender love."

"Alas!" said Candide, "I know this love, that sovereign of hearts, that soul of our souls; yet it never cost me more than a kiss and twenty kicks on the backside. How could this beautiful cause produce in you an effect so abominable?"

Pangloss made answer in these terms: "Oh, my dear Candide, you remember Paquette, that pretty wench who waited on our noble Baroness; in her arms I tasted the delights of paradise, which produced in me those hell torments with which you see me devoured; she was infected with them, she is perhaps dead of them. This present Paquette received of a learned Grey Friar, who had traced it to its source; he had had it of an old countess, who had received it from a cavalry captain, who owed it to a marchioness, who took it from a page, who had received it from a Jesuit, who when a novice had it in a direct line from one of the companions of Christopher Columbus. For my part I shall give it to nobody, I am dying."

"Oh, Pangloss!" cried Candide, "what a strange genealogy! Is not the Devil the original stock of it?"

"Not at all," replied this great man, "it was a thing unavoidable, a necessary ingredient in the best of worlds; for if Columbus had not in an island of America caught this disease, which contaminates the source of life, frequently even hinders generation, and which is evidently opposed to the great end of nature, we should have neither chocolate nor cochineal. We are also to observe that upon our continent, this distemper is like religious controversy, confined to a particular spot. The Turks, the Indians, the Persians, the Chinese, the Siamese, the Japanese, know nothing of it; but there is a sufficient reason for believing that they will know it in their turn in a few centuries. In the meantime, it has made marvellous progress among us, especially in those great armies composed of honest well-disciplined hirelings, who decide the destiny of states; for we may safely affirm that when an army of thirty thousand men fights another of an equal number, there are about twenty thousand of them p-x-d on each side."

"Well, this is wonderful!" said Candide, "but you must get cured."

"Alas! how can I?" said Pangloss, "I have not a farthing, my friend, and all over the globe there is no letting of blood or taking a glister, without paying, or somebody paying for you."

These last words determined Candide; he went and flung himself at the feet of the charitable Anabaptist Jacques, and gave him so touching a picture of the state to which his friend was reduced, that the good man did not scruple to take Dr. Pangloss into his house, and had him cured at his expense. In the cure Pangloss lost only an eye and an ear. He wrote well, and knew arithmetic perfectly. The Anabaptist Jacques made him his bookkeeper. At the end of two months, being obliged to go to Lisbon about some mercantile affairs, he took the two philosophers with him in his ship. Pangloss explained to him how everything was so constituted that it could not be better. Jacques was not of this opinion.

"It is more likely," said he, "mankind has a little corrupted nature, for they were not born wolves, and they have become wolves; God has given them neither cannon of four-and-twenty pounders, nor bayonets; and yet they have made cannon and bayonets to destroy one another. Into this account I might throw not only bankrupts, but Justice which seizes on the effects of bankrupts to cheat the creditors."

"All this was indispensable," replied the one-eyed doctor, "for private misfortunes make the general good, so that the more private misfortunes there are the greater is the general good."

While he reasoned, the sky darkened, the winds blew from the four quarters, and the ship was assailed by a most terrible tempest within sight of the port of Lisbon.

TEMPEST, SHIPWRECK, EARTHQUAKE, AND WHAT BECAME OF DOCTOR PANGLOSS, CANDIDE, AND JACQUES THE ANABAPTIST

Half dead of that inconceivable anguish which the rolling of a ship produces, one-half of the passengers were not even sensible of the danger. The other half shrieked and prayed. The sheets were rent, the masts broken, the vessel gaped. Work who would, no one heard, no one commanded. The Anabaptist being upon deck bore a hand; when a brutish sailor struck him roughly and laid him sprawling; but with the violence of the blow he himself tumbled head foremost overboard, and stuck upon a piece of the broken mast. Honest Jacques ran to his assistance, hauled him up, and from the effort he made was precipitated into the sea in sight of the sailor, who left him to perish, without deigning to look at him. Candide drew near and saw his benefactor, who rose above the water one moment and was then swallowed up for ever. He was just going to jump after him, but was prevented by the philosopher Pangloss, who demonstrated to him that the Bay of Lisbon had been made on purpose for the Anabaptist to be drowned. While he was proving this à priori, the ship foundered; all perished except Pangloss, Candide, and that brutal sailor who had drowned the good Anabaptist. The villain swam safely to the shore, while Pangloss and Candide were borne thither upon a plank.

As soon as they recovered themselves a little they walked toward Lisbon. They had some money left, with which they hoped to save themselves from starving, after they had escaped drowning. Scarcely had they reached the city, lamenting the death of their benefactor, when they felt the earth tremble under their feet. The sea swelled and foamed in the harbour, and beat to pieces the vessels riding at anchor. Whirlwinds of fire and ashes covered the streets and public places; houses fell, roofs were flung upon the pavements, and the pavements were scattered. Thirty thousand inhabitants of all ages and sexes were crushed under the ruins. The sailor, whistling and swearing, said there was booty to be gained here.

"What can be the sufficient reason of this phenomenon?" said Pangloss.

"This is the Last Day!" cried Candide.

The sailor ran among the ruins, facing death to find money; finding it, he took it, got drunk, and having slept himself sober, purchased the favours of the first good-natured wench whom he met on the ruins of the destroyed houses, and in the midst of the dying and the dead. Pangloss pulled him by the sleeve.

"My friend," said he, "this is not right. You sin against the universal reason; you choose your time badly."

"S'blood and fury!" answered the other. "I am a sailor and born at Batavia. Four times have I trampled upon the crucifix in four voyages to Japan; a fig for thy universal reason."

CHAPTER ONE

When Jakob Onderdonk forwent the cleansing ordinance of baptism for the third time in as many months, he sloshed ashore and, collapsing into a heap, imagined his flesh melting into pink puddles on the searing griddle of Hell's floor. He lay almost despondent at the thought of it, until at length he rose with unsteady resolve to utter the words, "It's not the right time."

They were familiar words to his companion. Bonifaas Quackenboss waded from the river and retrieved a bar of bracken soap. "One of us is going to be washed clean today," said the preacher. "Sin or dirt, no matter to me."

Jakob felt sorry and a bit ashamed. For he had correctly discerned that Bonifaas Quackenboss grew weary of the young man's non-committal ways—although it should be said that *discerned* may be the wrong word, as no ambiguity existed that Jakob might need discern anything. Neither was *weary* completely accurate, since Bonifaas was more *frustrated* than weary. Each failed attempt had ended the same, with Jakob making a similar pronouncement about his state of readiness—or lack of readiness, to be precise.

And so it was that as Jakob slipped from the clinging gossamer frock into his clothes, he wondered if Bonifaas suspected there was a real reason for the disappointing routine. No sooner had he thought it than the flesh of his cheeks swirled red—redder than usual, that is—for Jakob knew there was a reason, a real reason he did not care to discuss with Bonifaas. As kind and compassionate as the preacher was, Jakob doubted that he would understand how sin can hook the insouciant man like a stupefied fish. For Christ was not the only fisher of men. And sin is the deadliest and most devious predator of all—devouring the sick and lame of the fold. Or in Jakob's case, the depraved; at least, so thought Jakob. In any case, though a sinner he might be, Jakob Onderdonk counted himself a believer. And with or without the saving ordinance of baptism, he was one of them: an Anabaptist.

With a somewhat guarded wave of his hand, the young man bid

his companion farewell and started down the hard clay road that led home to Leyden.[1] The *Oude Rijn* River floated over the land in a foggy dream of the North Sea. On the horizon, the summer sun lay tangled in the sails of a slow-meditating windmill. This being the Sabbath, the resplendent green hills of South Holland rang out with a prolonged chorus of *hosannas* and *hallelujahs*.

There was simply no end to God's grandeur, it seemed.

Crossing the stone arch of *Kanaalbrug*, he wound down the lane that would lead him to a modest flat above a cobbler's shop.[2] Pulling a watch from his vest pocket, he checked the time.[3] 6:15. Jakob stepped up the pace.

It should here be said that Jakob Onderdonk was a compulsive checker of time—a chronologist, of sorts. That is, the kind whose world revolves around the tick-tocking of the clock. For there were certain eventualities he hoped to avoid in his day-to-day existence. (*Eventuality* being the correct term in this case, encompassing not only possibility but also consequence.)

Jakob was about to duck into the doorway when a familiar voice boomed behind him—"Good evening!" Here was one eventuality he had hoped to avoid, the consequence of his tardy arrival home: Pastor Hogarth.

"Good evening, Pastor. I trust your evening service was a monument to the mind and will of God," said Jakob.

"Never mind that, Meneer Onderdonk. Did you seal your fate in perdition this day?" The man of God peered inquisitively from beneath the wide brim of an imposing black hat.

"No, Pastor. I'm afraid not."

---

[1] A sign post stood at the foot of the bridge with one arrow pointing down the road and another pointing north along the river. On the former was written *Leyden be here*; on the latter was written *Oude Rijn runs there*.

[2] Jakob passed the following shop signs on his way to his flat above the cobbler's shop: *Bakehouse; Lars Berg: Potter; Leyden Habberdashery*.

[3] Engraved on the back of Jakob's watch were the initials JAO [Jakob Ambroos Onderdonk]. Below it was the following: *Time is neither ally nor foe, but 'tis the battlefield on which all wars are waged*.

"How many balks is that now? The lapsed Franciscan of Bolsward must be writhing in his grave."[4]

"It is not the right time," said Jakob.

The penitent tone of this utterance was like strong drink to the pastor, invigorating him with a heady supremacy. "Not the right time? Ha! Your perpetual shilly-shallying may be the one thing that saves your mortal soul from the inferno below," said he. And with this, Pastor Hogarth swished away in the holy robes of his employ, certain that he had made his point convincingly.

Jakob stood in the pastor's gusty wake with his head hanging slightly lower than before. Even the warm greeting of the calico Gertrude did little to comfort him.[5] Jakob ripped a crust from a loaf of bread and cut a slab of soft ripe cheese. Sitting at the table, he took alternating bites, washing each down with a quaff of *bier*. His manner was anxious, troubled even. Like a prisoner awaiting judgment. But then, this was nothing out of the ordinary. This too was a weekly occurrence for Jakob Onderdonk—the moment he dreaded every Sabbath eve. Another eventuality. When he, the insouciant man, was snagged like a stupefied fish by sin.

Jakob flipped his pocket watch open: 8:30.

Across the lane, a pale light appeared. His anxiety from only moments before turned instantly to tingling excitement as the faint light swelled and grew, finally teeming into the street. He froze in his seat, his eyes fixed on the buxom figure in the window. From the

---

[4] The pastor was here referring to Menno Simonszoon, the leader of Dutch Anabaptism, who was believed to have attended the Franciscans monastery in Bolsward.

[5] Gertrude's mother ran afoul of a brewer's trolley only months after giving birth to an unusually small litter of kittens—of which only one survived. Finding the mother calico on the cobblestone road, lifeless and bleeding from the eyes and ears, Jakob carried the cat to the woods and buried it under a towering elm tree. On his return he noticed a small kitten— a calico in the selfsame image of its mother—sniffing at the bloody stones and squeaking noisily. He scooped up the tiny orphan and, swathing it in his coattail, took the kitten home.

darkness of his flat, Jakob watched the customary ablutions of the pastor's wife with a kind of profane reverence: the rolling flesh upon her back, the drooping gray buttocks, and the thick fur pelt of her pubis. And then there were the low-hanging breasts with their delectable meat-pie nipples. Jakob allowed his ravenous eyes to feast upon them for a time.[6]

It was precisely at this ticklish moment that Gertrude chose to spring into his lap. (Another eventuality he did his best to avoid.) Sweeping the feline away, Jakob flipped open the buttons of his breeches with an eager hand. Presently, he was fully in the grips of sin. A full-fisted, unrelenting grip, that is. Moments later, he let out a slight gasp at the issue of his *zaad*. An issue which Gertrude sniffed before walking away with a stiffly vibrating tail.

Jakob slouched before the window and sighed. "The worst of all men is what I am," said he to no one.

The next morning, the clippety-clop of hooves over cobblestone rang through the quaint lanes of Leyden—a familiar sound, proclaiming men to be about the work of a new day, a new week. Jakob awoke from a fitful slumber. His surrender to sin the previous night had made sleeping difficult. The deep but dreamless state had proved to

---

[6] As was her habit, the pastor's wife indulged in the extravagance of a hot bath while her husband stayed late at the church after evening mass. Being a woman of formidable proportions, preparations for the routine ablutions took no small amount of time and planning. A raging fire was built and pot after pot of water boiled. The steaming hot water was offset by leaky pails of fresh cool water, which her maidservant dutifully hauled from a spring over a furlong away.

After preparations were completed, the maidservant helped the pastor's wife to disrobe, itself no small feat due to the rotund woman's propensity for absurdly constrictive corsets. By now, evening was fast falling, so lighting a lantern, the pastor's wife stood for a time before the unobstructed window— being iniquitously proud of her immense, low-pendulating bosoms and knowing that the young manufacturer above the cobbler's shop secretly admired her—before flopping with a great splash into the great iron tub.

be wholly unsatisfying. As if sin had washed every image from his head and replaced them with a blackness that amounted to a kind of restless emptiness.

He rose to find a scrap of dried cod and tossed it to Gertrude. Making ready a bowl of boiled oats, he spooned it into his mouth with a clear lack of relish. And when he shaved, Jakob did not so much as peek at himself in the mirror. Nor did he brush his breeches and jacket before dressing himself. It wasn't until he left the flat and breathed in the cool morning air that Jakob's spirits began to rise, for he knew that a vision awaited him. A vision much different than the lurid exhibition he had witnessed the previous night. What awaited him today was loveliness, pure and simple. It was what he lived for these days.

Jakob arrived at the factory ten minutes early—7:20 sharp—as was his habit. The dankness of the room led him to prop open windows. As he did, he noted how the abandoned carpet looms were not unlike the ribbed hulls of shipwrecks lying at the bottom of the sea. He thought it strange that he had never noticed this before. The looms' skeletal shafts and beams reminded him that he may well have escaped just such a fate. For as his father had always said, "The sea never loses." But for Jakob Onderdonk, the sea had indeed lost. And he had found the Lord and had been found by the Lord. Two cosmically synchronized events that had changed everything, that had changed him.

Unlocking the office door, he dropped down behind a spare desk and shuffled some papers.[7] At one time, it had been the best he could afford—in the early years. Now he had the means to purchase better, something more befitting a young manufacturer, but still Jakob chose to keep the desk as a reminder of his humble beginnings.

And it was from behind that very desk that he whiled away his days admiring his beloved Heleen through the glass. Her nimble fingers braiding colored strands of wool or passing the shuttle to

---

[7] On the front left corner of the desk was business stationery with the following letterhead: *Jakob Onderdonk: Mercer and Manufacturer, Leyden, South Holland.*

thread the warp. Her delicate hands trimming and hemming. Her bouncing knees beneath a stuff gown producing a working rhythm, the beat to which she marched diligently from one end of the working day to the other. Truly, she was a sight to behold.

Yet it should be said that the *beloved* in question knew nothing of her young master's affections for her. From the start, Heleen had attributed his acts of kindness to a profound good-heartedness in Jakob and not to any real matter of the heart. Although it must also be said that she did admire him greatly—his good-heartedness, that is. Or so she told herself.

The factory door rattled open and in she walked. 7:25. Five minutes early, as was her habit. Five minutes to make tea. But this day, Heleen stood in Jakob's office doorway, her hands pressed tightly together, not making tea. She wore a gray traveling gown and her black hair was tucked into a linen hood tied loosely beneath her chin. Although pensive, her visage looked pleasingly bright, despite a forced smile that produced petite dimples on either cheek. These, Jakob held to be the best of all her womanly charms.

"Meneer Onderdonk—" She stopped, tearing up.

"Heleen!" Jakob hoisted himself onto two unsteady lower limbs. "What is it? What troubles you?"

"I must leave for Lisbon this very morning. I am sorry."

"But what has happened?"

"My *tante* is sick. And my cousins have been conscripted by Prussian forces.[8] I must go and attend to my family."

"But when will you return?" The urgency of the question was very nearly overcome by its apparent underlying plea.

"I do not know." She took a step back then turned to leave.

---

[8] Atílio and Marcelo Monteiro were stooped over in their field of sweet potatoes, plucking musk thistle, when three dragoons clubbed them and dragged them away. When the two brothers regained consciousness, they were in Madrid wearing the navy blue jackets of the Prussian Army. On the other side of Serra de Estrela, their mother still clung to her torn dress.

Jakob summoned every scrap, every shred of courage that lay in his sickened soul and spoke: "Heleen, wait."

"Yes, Meneer Onderdonk?"

"Might I, that is, what I mean to say is would I be presuming too much if I asked you to receive my letters?"

Heleen's smile returned, this time a more natural version of the first. "You want to write?"

"Yes, I want to write."

FROM THE JOURNAL OF JACOB ONDERDONK

September 12, 1746
Son of Batavia docked in its home harbor today with her hold full of black
powder and tea from the orient. Father seemed especially eager to report to
the office of Opperhoofd Kunst and made it clear that Robrecht and I were to
accompany him without comment or question. It is not uncommon for the
ship's officers to accompany the captain to VOC headquarters; however,
Robrecht and I are, in fact, low-ranking officers, and thus, leaving First
Mate Bloothooft and Second Mate Merteens behind on company docks to
see to lowly ship matters was an unprecedented oddity. Needless to say, both
Robrecht and I knew something was afoot, although we knew not the exact
nature of it. I think it would be fair to say that Robrecht was annoyed by
what amounted to an inconvenience, at least to his way of thinking, for it
was clear by the way Able Seaman Dag, Robrecht's wilfully abiding sidekick,
lurked about the ship's quarterdeck that the two of them had plans to slink
into the brothels of Glodock. For my part, I was simply curious as to what
would call for such unusual proceedings.

Opperhoofd Kunst welcomed Robrecht and I into his office with a
familiarity that would suggest we had been long and close acquaintances,
which was not the case, although such was indeed the case with father and
the opperhoofd. Father sat at Opperhoofd's bidding, while Robrecht and I
remained standing. At this point, father was beaming like a topmast sun in
equatorial waters. Without delay and with no amount of conspicuous
ceremony, Opperhoofd Kunst informed us that effective immediately,
Robrecht and myself were to be moved up in the ranks of Son of Batavia:
Robrecht to third mate and I to first. I am sure that the surprise which
registered on my face in that moment was clear to both Opperhoofd and my
father. And in truth, it appeared that the two men took some small measure
of amusement from my reaction. However, if I was clearly surprised,
Robrecht was likewise disgruntled. For it occurred to me only later that my
younger sibling truly believed the rank of first mate should have been
rightfully his.

I do not wish to here question the judgment of Opperhoofd or my father,
but I must simply say that after some consideration, I believe Robrecht may
be right. For in my years at sea (which are now just above six) I have

discovered that some men are accepting of, or perhaps suited for, the chaos and lawlessness of life at sea, while others are continually trying to force order and array upon something which by its very nature incites disorder and disarray in everything and everyone about it. Clearly, Robrecht is a man of the former ilk, while I am a man of the latter. Yet even as I write this I know that father would ardently contend that the sea needs more men of the latter ilk and less of the former, for although the sea cannot be tamed, it must not be allowed to wreak havoc upon Man and his worthy endeavors. How am I to respond to such well-meaning platitudes? How is any man to respond? Although Robrecht, I feel certain, would brave a simple and direct response, as he is known to do, and bellow, "Hogwash!"

CHAPTER TWO

Mevrouw Onderdonk stood before the mirror as her maid draped a lace *fichu* over her shoulders and pinned it snuggly around her neck. Being a capable woman, Mevrouw Onderdonk could fasten her own *fichu*— without the aid of a mirror—if she had a mind to. Quite simply, she did not have a mind to, or even half a mind to, for that matter. As far as she was concerned, some things were better done by others, even when one was capable of doing those things for oneself. "It adds value to the act, especially to those acts that otherwise have little value of their own," she had once told Jakob when he asked about that very thing.

Mevrouw Onderdonk stepped away from the mirror and to the window. *Hooglandse Kerk* looked old and unbecoming in the plain light of day. She had always said as much. "An eyesore," she had once called it. To which Jakob had responded with some ridiculous tale about God's temple and dwelling therein. Although she said nothing at the time, she correctly surmised that her son's story alluded to the brooding Gothic structure whose immensity, she felt, should itself be viewed as something of a transgression.

In her forty-nine years, Mevrouw Onderdonk had breached the sprawling archway of the cathedral's entrance precisely five times— at least, such was her claim.[9] Four could be easily accounted for— three christenings (one being her own) and a marriage (also her own). The fifth was not so easy to account for, mainly because it did not involve a ritual in which some poor soul was doused, drunk, or eaten. It involved her seeking solace in the House of God. (*Solace* being the correct term in this case, suggesting both grief and diversion, the importance of which we shall soon see.) When Mevrouw Onderdonk thought about it now, she found it deeply troubling. For in her mind, religion and the religious were simply institutional renderings of a foolish master and his foolhardy

---

[9] At the base of the archway was a foundation stone with the following carved into it: *In the year of our Lord, 1314.*

followers. And in either case, each existed only for the other and neither could exist alone. It was a farce *par excellence*.

Still the fact remained that Mevrouw Onderdonk did once enter unbidden into the house of the Lord following her husband's death. At the time, she had sniffled and said, "Cornelis Onderdonk," listening to how his name echoed within the ribbed vaults of the cathedral's ceiling. The pleasing combination of largely apical consonants and open back vowels produced what she thought to be an angelic ring. Although it should be said that Mevrouw Onderdonk was not quite herself at that precise moment. (How else would one explain her being there in the first place?) Not to mention the monk's meal's worth of provincial French wine she had consumed at dinner. And so it was that in this peculiar state of mind, Mevrouw Onderdonk had lifted her eyes to the life-sized marble crucifix at the front of the church and gazed upon the stark white Christ, shining like a bright beacon in the oppressive squall of her sorrow. She rose and walked up the aisle, stopping to stand before the figure then dropping down to the front pew.

There could be no doubt that the crucifix was splendid. And Mevrouw Onderdonk could not look away from the long sinewy limbs, the taut midriff, the feminine bearing. Or the draped loin cloth that barely concealed the deistic privates. It was then that she detected—or *believed* that she detected—a look of longing on the Christ figure's face. In truth, it was more a look of misery than longing—an understandable mistake, given the grieving woman's diminished capacity and distant perspective.

The strange attraction that Mevrouw Onderdonk right then felt for the Christ figure, ostensibly naked and tolerably handsome, would stay with her in the years to come. It would also explain her intentionally false claim that she had entered the church only five times in her life. For the truth was she would enter the church regularly, if secretly, after this peculiar episode in order to sit in adoration at the Lord's feet (although *adoration*, in this instance, may be a nuance or two shy of expressing the complex feelings that Mevrouw Onderdonk felt for the statue).

Just then, the maid stirred behind her. "Your son arrives, my

Lady."

The slight stiffening in both her form and demeanor was almost undetectable, but there nonetheless in her response: "Fine," said Mevrouw Onderdonk. "I shall be down presently."

He had locked up at 8:00 and trudged to the *herenhuis*. Heleen's loom sat idle the entire day, as if a vital organ within the factory had suddenly stopped, resulting in unexpected malaise. Jakob felt forsaken. Doubly forsaken. First by God and now Heleen, too. It occurred to him as he strolled mindlessly down the lane that her abrupt departure may have been the work of the Almighty; that is, punishment for the sin of onanism. After all, it would not be the first time. For had God not struck down dead deviant Onan? thought he.

Jakob succumbed to the sudden urge to rake his palms.[10]

He halted at the door of the Onderdonk *herenhuis*, taking a moment to compose himself before knocking. Such dark thoughts around his mother would not do. She had a way of drawing them out of him. "Like poison from a wound," said he with a mutter to no one. He recalled how she had divined the sad news of his father's death the moment he had stepped from the gangplank. She had even correctly supposed the cause of death: "cholera" was all she had said, not waiting for confirmation before gushing tears onto the briny planks of *Lands Dok*.

The Lady's maid showed Jakob to the dining room. As always,

---

[10] Jakob had first witnessed self-abuse while still a cabin boy on *Son of Batavia*. It was, he would quickly learn, common practice among sailors at sea to fire their *zaad* broadside from the open ports of the gun deck anytime of the day or night, in public or private, drunken or sober. But finding the whole production distasteful, Jakob had never acquired the habit while at sea. This, however, would change once he had settled on land as a full-fledged landlubber. Pleasuring oneself while sitting in the privacy of one's private premises seemed to him much less distasteful. Indeed, it seemed even less than distasteful, bordering very nearly on acceptable. By the time he learned that it was a sin (although it must be said that he had had his suspicions all along), the habit was already a time-hardened vice.

Oma Onderdonk sat stooped in the corner, murmuring to herself. It was then that he noticed the muslin gown and lace *fichu* worn by his mother. It struck him as too fashionable for the occasion. "Have I forgotten something?"

"Whatever do you mean, Jakob?"

"A special occasion?"

"I have invited Captain Schoonhoven's *nicht*, Anneke, to dine with us. Did I not mention it?"

"No, you did not." He fingered the buttons on his jacket.

"Well, my memory fails me now and then."

"I am a grown man," said Jakob, making no attempt to conceal his agitation. "I am fully capable of finding my own mate."

With an impressive burst of energy, Oma Onderdonk jumped to her feet, clutched her dress in two crumpled fists and raised it over her head. "*Coïteren! Coïteren!*" she squealed, performing an immodest pirouette that had the Lady's maid scrambling to the rescue and settling the old woman back into her chair.

"Please, Jakob! You know how such words affect her. If I didn't know better, I would say that was a deliberate provocation."

"I'm sorry. It's just that I don't need help finding a—you know what."

"Really? Twenty-eight years old and living alone—wifeless, childless. And you need no help? Perhaps if you spent less time with those religious fanatics—"

"Those religious fanatics helped me to find Christ the Savior."

"Oh blah! If you want to find Christ the Savior, cross the street to *Hooglandse Kerk*. He's always there hanging from that big cross of His."

"You know what I mean. If it weren't for them I might still be sailing aimlessly around the world on a three-masted ship looking for any and every iniquitous port." As soon as the utterance had slipped from his lips, Jakob regretted it, wished he could take it back.

"Is that some veiled reference to your brother? You know I forbid you to speak of him in this house." She sat down and took the skeletal hand of Oma Onderdonk. "Jakob, you are not like him. If not for all this religious nonsense, you would be sitting comfortably in an office in Batavia, just like your father. God rest his soul."

"I'm tired of all this trifling with my life! Sometimes I feel like storming down to the docks and returning to my former life as a . . ."

"No, Jakob, don't! Don't you say it—"

"Seaman!"

Meisje Schoonhoven arrived late, as was fashionable for young ladies of the day.[11] Jakob recalled Heleen's habit of five minutes early and marveled at how a risible social convention had so easily brought his beloved to mind. Jakob missed her already.

---

[11] Anneke Schoonhoven traveled from Guelders to Leyden on the day of her sixteenth birthday. Having been discovered in the stables by her father in the arms of the stablemaster's son, she was sent posthaste to live with her father's brother in Leyden. Promiscuity was one thing, but promiscuity with the servant class was quite another. And as if to underline this particular point, her father died the very next day from a massive heart attack.

Anneke's *oom* was a stranger to her, he having always been at sea or stationed overseas with the VOC. And, in fact, he would remain a stranger to her, for Captain Schoonhoven was not in Leyden when she arrived, nor would he be there in the years that followed, even up to the death of his wife. Her *tante*, on the other hand, was like a second mother to her. Having no children of her own, for that would require a husband who was both present and moderately amorous, Mevrouw Schoonhoven showered the girl with affection, to the point that Anneke would find herself looking for ways to avoid the tender and watchful gaze of her loving *tante*. And so it was that when an old family acquaintance, Mevrouw Onderdonk, invited Meisje Schoonhoven to dine with her and her son, Anneke could not have been more willing. In fact, the word *yes* jumped from her throat before she'd even conferred with her *tante* upon the matter. That is not to say that she was not interested in making the acquaintance of Meneer Jakob Onderdonk—she was. It was simply that lately, her *tante's* increasingly unpredictable moods had made spending time with her something akin to a prison sentence. Any occasion that would require her to leave the Schoonhoven *herenhuis* was an occasion not to be missed as far as Anneke was concerned. Thus it was that, when the carriage of Mevrouw Onderdonk came calling, Anneke jumped to her feet, pecked her *tante* on the cheek, and pattered with tight staccato steps to the front door.

Meisje Schoonhoven—Anneke—looked older than her eighteen years. Jakob attributed it to a worldliness that aged her disproportionately. Admittedly, she looked handsome, fetching even, in her stiff-bodied mantua. Upon a swell of blond curls sat a miniature cream-colored cap. A matching ribbon around her neck drew one's gaze to the sculpted isthmus bridging mind and body, and to an alabaster bosom that rose and fell with a mesmerizing lilt. For Jakob it was all a bit too much. And immediate action was required to quell the sinful uprising that rallied below before it escalated into something of a raging revolt. So Jakob turned his thoughts to Oma Onderdonk, which produced the desired quelling effect.

Much of the dinner conversation revolved around Meisje Schoonhoven's *oom* in Batavia, *Opperhoofd* of Batavia in the *Vereenigde Oost-Indische Compagnie*, the VOC. Captain Schoonhoven had been promoted to the head position shortly after his sometimes-friend and long-time-acquaintance Cornelis Onderdonk had succumbed to illness—also shortly after Jakob had forsaken the sea and returned to Leyden. Everyone knew, or more precisely, everyone *believed* that the promotion would have gone to Captain Onderdonk had he lived. Everyone in Batavia, that is. In South Holland, Mevrouw Onderdonk had thought little about it. With her husband gone, it seemed a moot point to her. Besides, the business of the VOC had never interested her—even when Cornelis was alive. And Jakob had never found any reason for bitterness where the promotion was concerned. Clearly, Captain Schoonhoven could not be blamed for his father's untimely passing. And thus was there no blame to be laid nor fault to be found. As far as Jakob was concerned, the position of *opperhoofd* rightly belonged to Captain Schoonhoven.

That is not to say the death of his father had not been an unexpected and unmitigated tragedy. Of course, it had. But it had also been an event to stir young Jakob's soul. Watching the life drain from the once venerated captain of the VOC had planted a seed of yearning within him. Although for what Jakob yearned, exactly, was unclear to him at the time. But it would become clear soon enough. Upon his return to South Holland, Jakob met Bonifaas Quackenboss, and the Anabaptist preacher had helped him to realize that what he yearned for was life eternal with his personal Savior, Christ the Lord. And so Jakob gave up everything—his life past, present, and future with the VOC—for that chance.

By any standards of culture and refinement, dinner this night was a resounding success—stimulating conversation, refined tittering, and a savory meal of Indian-spiced mutton. The only glitch came in the form of a booming gastric offering by Oma Onderdonk during the main course. At the moment in question, the polite tinkle of silverware ceased and chitchat ground to a halt. Jakob did his level best to ignore the odious intrusion.[12] Mevrouw Onderdonk, on the other hand, was openly aghast with the indiscretion and had Oma Onderdonk removed at once and set upon the *privaat*.

But the intrusion was quickly forgotten, as these things usually are. Windows were opened and, as a fresh air of decorum filled the room, the conversation found renewed footing.

"What is your opinion of the war that brews all over Europe?" asked Meisje Schoonhoven.

"I find it morally reprehensible," said Jakob. "I am a pacifist."

"Now dear, no need to bring up that," said Mevrouw Onderdonk.

"A pacifist? How novel of you. I don't believe I've ever made the acquaintance of a pacifist."

"It is a phase, nothing more," said Mevrouw Onderdonk. "It flares up with the summer heat. He will be through it before the season's change."

"It is no phase, Mother. It's my firm belief. I object to war."

"But why would you object to war?" said Meisje Schoonhoven. "Is it not waged for a noble and good cause?"

"'Jesus answered, my kingdom is not of this world: if my kingdom were of this world, then would my servants fight, that I should not be delivered to the Jews: but now is my kingdom not from hence.'"

---

[12] Jakob would later describe the stench as something that "would have caused a pack of famished hyenas to turn up their snouts and turn tail for the sterile deserts of the Dark Continent."

"Jakob, really! Must you always drag Jesus into it? Does He not have enough problems of His own to contend with?"

"I find it refreshing to meet a man who stands firm in his beliefs," said Meisje Schoonhoven. "Perhaps I should learn more of this pacifism."

To this, Mevrouw Onderdonk responded with confidence and without hesitation: "Jakob would be delighted to acquaint you with the principle, wouldn't you dear?" Aside from Mevrouw Onderdonk herself, no one noticed the flawless, if manipulative, turnabout she had just then executed, a point that relieved her more than pleased her.

"Well, yes, of course. Perhaps Meisje Schoonhoven would care to join me at a meeting of the Anabaptists?"

"Indeed. I would care to very much."

"Then it is settled," said Mevrouw Onderdonk, not without a triumphant clap of her hands. "Jakob would be pleased to take you this coming Sabbath day. Wouldn't you dear?"

"Why . . . yes, of course," said he. "I would be happy to."

When he had first begun to attend meetings with the Anabaptists, Jakob purchased a calash carriage and chestnut gelding especially for the Sunday outings. These days, he rarely used it for anything else. Jakob was not one to make a show of his wealth. Not that his wealth was staggering. But he had more of it than most young men of his age and social standing. Despite this worldly success, Jakob possessed a modesty that quite frankly baffled his mother. "My God, you live like a travelling friar," she would often say to him, poking a finger into the threadbare elbows of his jacket. That he had inherited his frugal nature from his father was lost on the Onderdonk matriarch.

Jakob helped Anneke into the carriage and took his seat beside her.

For their part, the townsfolk of Leyden admired the oldest Onderdonk son, frugal or not, for he was truly a self-made man. Upon his return to land, he had used his carefully accrued savings to buy the factory where he manufactured his pleasingly exotic carpets. For Jakob, the thrill of owning something solid and unmovable—

something enduring—had not diminished one iota since the day he first opened the factory door and walked into the world of manufacturing. Every day, he pushed open that very same factory door, and every day, it sent a rush of pride coursing through him—not the sinful kind, mind you, but the kind that comes with accomplishment. And every day, pausing there in the doorway, Jakob would repeat his mantra, which over the years had acquired a scriptural solemnity not unlike that of the Good Book itself: "For who can own a parcel of the sea? Who can say this wave or that wave is mine and mine alone?" The implicit answer of course being "no one, save God himself." Thus, implicit within Jakob's daily ritual was the assertion that he did indeed own something now, something real.

It was this very realization that never failed to send a rush of pride coursing through him, much like the rush of steam he had once witnessed erupting from a great geyser off the island of Sumatra while still a cabin boy. He yet recalled the magnificent plume of water and steam that had blasted from the earth and soared for the heavens before floating back down over the shoreline in a mist of color that mixed with the jade froth of the sea as it battered black volcanic rocks along the coast. There had been something miraculous about that rush of steam. Something about it had made young Jakob think that anything was possible in this world.[13] It was the same feeling he now felt whenever he thought

---

[13] Only moments before Jakob had witnessed the miraculous rush of steam, he had been enraged, finding nothing miraculous about being drenched by a high-looping stream of *pis* spilling from the Crow's Nest. This particular rush—a rush of rage—was indeed the sinful kind.

Just prior to the time in question, *Son of Batavia* had cleared the Mentawai Islands on starboard side and Padang harbor on portside and was following a due south course through the waters of Mentawai strait set for Java. Jakob was swabbing the deck when his father appeared at the rail of the quarterdeck and asked after his brother. The young cabin boy raised his eyes to see a tricorne hat eclipsing the noonday sun. Reluctantly, he informed his father that Robrecht was fast slumbering below. Furious, Captain Onderdonk ordered the first mate get his second son into the crow's nest immediately.

about Dutch flat-weave carpets and how far he had come in just five years.

Jakob snapped the reins and clicked his tongue, sending the carriage jolting forward. Meisje Schoonhoven let go a girlish squeal and clasped his arm. He swiveled in his seat and spoke to Oma Onderdonk: "Hold fast!" Not surprisingly, his mother had insisted on a chaperone. "It is only right and respectable," she had said. But of course, she herself had declined, sending the mentally diminished septuagenarian in her stead.

A characteristic Sabbath calm presided over the streets of Leyden this day. Buildings shoulder to shoulder with row upon row of windows. Some with gables and tall chimney pots. Some with barbed iron spires. Some of mottled brick. Some painted in bright colors. Up ahead, grand *Pieters Kerk* stood stoically, defiantly, beneath the faraway sun. Outside the city, they loped through *Grote Polder*, by shallow furrows of creeping velvet grass and, of course, *Pesthuis*, with its perfectly squared angles built to intern the plague's afflicted. Beyond that, a yellow speckled field of false flax and a green pasture where a flock of sheep grazed. A light breeze blew sweet with the season's bloom—blue bugles, red chamomile, St. Benedict's herb; together comprising a heady concoction to rouse the

---

When Robrecht appeared on the spar deck, being dragged roughly over the timbers, Jakob dropped his head and turned away, as if to shield himself from his brother's indicting glare. With a stern hand, the first mate sent Robrecht up the main mast to the lookout perch. Scarcely had the officer disappeared, when Jakob heard the loud patter of pis on the spar deck, and then felt the pungent warmth of it falling on his head and shoulders. Taking cover, he tipped his gaze up, but even as he did, he knew from whence the pis came. The look on his brother's face was half delight, half derision. An infuriating sight, to be sure. A rush of rage surged through Jakob. It wasn't that his brother had thought to pissen upon his head from a height of fifty feet, it was the look—*that* look. Jakob dropped the swab, curled up his fist and raised it high to bawl a fraternal curse. But his curse was drowned out. His muted words floated unheard into the ether, smothered by a thunderous scour and the earsplitting rush of steam.

senses.

Bonifaas Quackenboss welcomed them with an outstretched hand. His combed hair lay flat on his head and the long whiskers of his grizzled beard had been clipped for the Sabbath. As always, a white cotton shirt and black fustian trousers and jacket comprised his Sunday-best. And as always, the firm grip of his handshake attested to his blacksmith trade. Jakob shrank slightly before the preacher this day, for the failed baptism of the previous Sabbath still troubled the young manufacturer's conscience.

The simple meetinghouse had been raised by the congregation no more than a feeble-armed stone's throw from Bonifaas Quackenboss's forge. Jakob ushered Anneke and Oma Onderdonk to the front pew, just as Katrine Quackenboss started in on the fortepiano, pounding out "A Mighty Fortress is Our King" with painful gusto. The congregation was immediately on its feet singing praises to God in an impressive polyphonous show of piety.

Jakob joined in, sang unabashedly. For this fervent display of devotion in song never failed to move him. The enthusiastic raising of voices to heaven was what he most admired about the Anabaptists. A community of devout souls seeking communion with their maker. And with each other.

At that moment, Anneke's hand brushed his own, circling like a scorching comet around the sun, pulled ever closer by the invisible force of gravity, until finally, inevitably, she slipped her hand into his.

Jakob froze. The music stopped.

"We must invite the Lord Jesus Christ into our lives," said Bonifaas Quackenboss from behind the pulpit. "There is no other road to salvation. There is no other way. We must say to the Lord"(and here his voice rose sharply): "COME, COME, COME!"

The crowd stirred and cried back: "COME, COME, COME!

"Say it with me again," said the preacher. "COME! COME! COME!"

"COME! COME! COME!" cried the crowd.

If the sheer volume of their invitation to the Lord Jesus Christ were any indication of their desire to one day see His face, then it would be fair to say that a more eager group of Christians could not be found in all the land. Despite this, Jakob remained silent. For it was as if the hand that now held his own had a firm grip on his tongue also. In fact, so preoccupied was Jakob with that hand that he neglected to see Oma Onderdonk fidgeting in her seat.

"COME! COME! COME!" said Bonifaas Quackenboss.

"COME! COME! COME!" echoed the crowd.

Finally, Oma Onderdonk, the old matriarch on the front pew, stopped fidgeting in her seat and shot to her feet. Then raising her dress overhead, she squawked lustily: "*Coïteren! Coïteren! Coïteren!*"

Although every jaw dropped and twice as many eyelids rose, the disturbance was handily brought under control by Jakob and tardy Bonifaas, and the sermon continued without further incident. Still, Jakob inwardly berated himself for the remainder of the service for not having turned a more watchful eye to his oma. And so when the last of the Anabaptist congregation trickled from the meetinghouse, shaking hands and bidding one another farewell until the next Sabbath, Jakob approached Bonifaas Quackenboss. "I must apologize for my oma's outburst," said Jakob. "She is highly excitable. Not always, mind you. Just at the mention of certain words." Jakob pushed a weak smile onto his lips and turned to the old woman, who was now docile as a newborn calf. "They bring back memories for her — unpleasant memories."[14]

---

[14] Jakob had only ever heard tell of the "unpleasant memories," for that was the extent of the explanation that was offered to him. In truth, it was not unpleasant *memories* but actually a single *memory* — a story, to be precise, which had never been recited to him in full. What Jakob could not have known was that every time his oma raised her dress as if she were the May Queen executing a bawdy Morris dance the story took on renewed significance; that is to say, it reared its ugly (and tragic) head.

Katinka Naaktgeboren married Heike Onderdonk in the village of Woubrugge in 1704. Heike, a robust peasant, was a well-known cheese maker whose goat cheese was highly-prized throughout the entire county. Little wonder, then, that he possessed a remarkably positive outlook. Or so went the thinking of the Woubrugge villagers.

True to his name, Heike Onderdonk (*Onderdonk* meaning literally "under the hill") lived in a cottage at the base of a grassy hillock and near to a

"Unpleasant?" said Bonifaas. "But Oma Onderdonk seemed to be overflowing with joy. How could these unpleasant memories result in such exuberance?"

"Yes, well, perhaps they are not entirely unpleasant for her," said Jakob, "only for the rest of us." His smile drooped, now even less convincing than before.

"Never mind. Your oma is welcome to join us here any Sabbath." Bonifaas took Oma Onderdonk's hand in his own. "And so is your delightful Meisje Schoonhoven."

---

stagnant green pond. It was to the hillock that Heike took his new bride so that they might lie down together as man and wife. There among the indifferent sheep and goats, the newlywed couple tasted that which has been called the greatest of all earthly pleasures. Katinka hoisted her bride's dress, and Heike, crawling atop her, began to gently thrust his buttocks up and down, high and low, in and out. For the young couple, it was love and lust, pain and pleasure, all mingled into one quivering sensation. Truly, it *was* the greatest of all earthly pleasures.

But a mischievous black goat named Idioot took an interest in the musky odor rising from the general region of their sexual congress. The shepherd groom responded to the intrusion with a kick to Idioot's head. And the billy goat responded in kind with a sound thump to the shepherd's skull. Heike cursed the filthy beast, spat blood, and then dropped dead on the lacey breasts of his wife. Katinka screeched, tore at the grass all around her, and finally broke down and wept into the clotted hair of her dead husband. They found her three days later with her beloved still clutched to her breast, atop her still, his rigid blue member still inserted into her burst maidenhead.

A child was born to the widow Onderdonk nine months later—a son, Cornelis, who would grow strong and proud, a son in whom she would take great delight and find warm consolation. But the emotional trauma Katinka experienced at the moment of her son's conception—that is, at the time of the untimely and unusual death of her Heike—lay dormant within her, the seeds of dementia. Finally, in her autumnal years, the seeds bloomed into blossoms of full-blown lunacy. Her vivid memory became her undying affliction. And the slightest hint, the most diluted mental whiff of coitus would carry her away—transport her back to the hillock where first she had hoisted high her dress and eased open her pale maiden's legs to the cheese maker she so dearly loved.

"*My* Meisje Schoonhoven?" Jakob felt his face redden, as his gaze instinctively swung to the young woman who had escorted him here, sitting at the Silbermann fortepiano with Katrine Quackenboss. "No, no. I think you misunderstand. Not *my* Meisje Schoonhoven. She is simply a guest—she is interested in the precept of pacifism." Jakob realized that this had the insincere ring of a forced apology.

"But it is no sin to let one's heart out of its cautious cage, Jakob. Especially if the time is right."

It occurred to him then that Bonifaas had been witness to Anneke's earlier—and unexpected—display of affection. "No, no. There is no cage. And no caution. And, no, the time is not right, not right now anyway—" But before Jakob could put this all together into a more coherent rebuttal, Anneke appeared at his side—close at his side—where she slipped a gloved hand into the crook of his arm, an act that nullified everything that had just then prattled from Jaokob's mouth.

"Well then, we will see you both again next Sabbath," said Bonifaas.

And Jakob thought it best say nothing.

That night Jakob sat stiffly at his table before a blank piece of paper, deeply troubled. What troubled him was Meisje Schoonhoven—Anneke. He could not deny that her touch had been pleasant. Although it must be said that any touch other than his own would have been pleasant to Jakob. But there was something quite singular about her, something so naked in its appeal. Jakob wondered at how she had beguiled him. He had, after all, agreed to see her again. But then what else could he do? At what level of intimacy is one obliged to call again upon another? A touch? A kiss? A hand hold? Jakob did not know.

He crumpled the paper in his fist and tossed it on the ground. He had been toiling over the letter for better than an hour. Gertrude inspected the remnants of Jakob's foiled correspondence, pawing it to make certain it was not some edible scrap of food.

How could a simple letter be so difficult to write? he wondered. He would simply tell her how he'd missed her so. For it was true—

he had missed her sorely. And what more need be said than that?

Jakob managed to convince himself that Meisje Schoonhoven's display of affection at the meeting of the Anabaptists had been innocent enough. Certainly no reason not to write to his beloved Heleen, thought he. "Beloved." He spoke the word aloud. His *beloved*. It sounded somewhat foolish to him as he did. For Jakob was well aware of the fact that no level of intimacy at all had been established between Heleen and himself. No physical intimacy, that is. Yet he believed there had been something more. And although he would not have dared to call it a mingling of souls, he knew that something deeper than physical intimacy had existed—still existed, he desperately hoped—between Heleen and himself. Something pure and simple, something which defied the profane tricks that the senses can play on an unsuspecting soul.

Jakob picked up the pen, dipped it in ink, and began to scribble.

This time the words came easily. This time he was set to open up, "to let his heart out of its cautious cage," as Bonifaas had said. Jakob felt a sad longing like a sharp pain in his chest—starting as if the lone buzz of honey bee trapped in a mead jar but soon multiplying to the frenzied hum of a swarm set to burst from the confines of its hive. He scribbled faster and faster, the words now dripping fully formed from his pen.[15] But then the longing within grew suddenly silent and his pen grew still. For in that moment, Jakob detected the faint glow of a lantern across the lane. It grew brighter, until there in a lusty halo of golden lamplight appeared the familiar figure of the

---

[15] Jakob wrote the following:

Dear Heleen,

It seems ages since last I saw your face peering back at me through the glass. Ages of agony, for there is much I have not told you, sweet Heleen. From the very first moment I laid eyes upon you, covered in wool and gritty perspiration as you were, I was wholly smitten. And I remain so to this day. For I can never forget the trill of your voice as you made work merry and the single tear perched like a frozen waterfall at the corner of your eye as you shared the story of your fair mother's demise. I knew then that I had found you—you, the one that I should one day wed if I were to ever experience a true moment of joy in this lifetime.

pastor's buxom wife. Jakob sighed and resigned in that moment to sin again then sin no more. A promise, it should be said, he had made and broken on many a Sabbath eve before.

"The worst of all men is what I am," said he.

And Gertrude mewed.

FROM A LETTER ADDRESSED TO
CAPTAIN CORNELIS ONDERDONK,
BATAVIA, DUTCH WEST INDIES

August 12, 1747

My Dear Cornelis,

Do I not miss you? Do I not want to be by your side? Oh Cornelis! How could you ask me such things? The tenor of your last letter cuts me to the quick. Of course I long to be by your side now and forever; it is simply that I do not wish to be by your side on some Godforsaken island now or forever. I am sure it is as you say — an adventure on par with that of Odysseus's — but you know that I am no adventurer, and certainly no Odysseus. I have, however, hoped to be a siren, instead, singing you to me, where you will drown happily in my turbulent affections. But certainly my trope lacks the wit and intelligence you are accustomed to there in the far-flung wilds of the kingdom, does it not?

Dear husband, when first we met I knew you were destined for a lifetime at sea. For what else could there be for a young man of such sterling character? In love with the sea first and me second. But did you not know then that I was a women fond of the comforts of home? A Penelope, of sorts. Did you not think that I may not wish to spend my life toiling in the heat and fighting off infestations of insects and avoiding visitations from other ungodly creatures? Not to mention the natives, whose savage ways beat out a hollow rhythm lacking all civility and decency. How, Cornelis, could I ever get along in such a place?

You ask if I do not miss our sons, but you know as well — perhaps better — than I do that only one of our sons is worthy of my thoughtful concern. Please do not try to make mournful excuses for the other, as you always do; for he is dead to me, or at least he would be had I a more steely resolve and a less feminine sensibility. Better that he had slid still and harmless from my womb into this unsuspecting world! Harsh words? Indeed! But why should I wish to be the one who bore a person such as he? He being an affliction to all around him and to everything that is good upon God's Earth. Surely you must have some inkling as to the truth of my words. For you are with him day in and day out. Do you not see his foul deeds at every turn? For rumors of just such deeds are here lisping on the lips of every VOC wife and dropping into my ear like a slow poison. Like constant death.

Oh, Cornelis! Now you see that even fleeting thoughts of him put me in a fractious mood. There shall be no more talk of it. And I shall not come to you either, my dear. Not now and not ever. And that, it would seem, is the end of that.

> *Your Loving Wife (Fuming and All),*
> *Marijke*

CHAPTER THREE

The swell of a temple gong thrummed through the room, rattling the *tokkuri* by his head and causing a pleasant tingle in his scrotum. Robrecht hoisted one eyelid, then the other, just in time to bid farewell to a pair of porcelain-white breasts disappearing into a *susoyoke*. The makings of a weak smile curled on the lips of the young woman dressing before him. Robrecht was surprised and aroused. The previous night was a blank, although he did recall drinking saké and sneaking from Dejima early in the evening. After that it got foggy.

Just as he was about to snag the berg of that drifting recollection and pull it astern, something moved beneath his armpit. A head of long black hair rose from his side and tipped back. The pale face that appeared there belonged to a young man. Robrecht was reminded of the story an old Chinese merchant in Macau had once told him about the mythological Country of Men, where men gave birth to other men through their back or sides. The young male *yūjo* jumped to his feet, knocking over the ceramic tokkuri and spilling rice wine. Then he spoke tersely to his companion, a young female *yūjo*, who slipped into her kimono and frantically tied the sash.[16] The gist of the young male's communication, Robrecht correctly surmised, stressed a quick and silent retreat. Pulling on a loose *fundoshi*, the *yūjo* gathered a kimono up into his arms and scrambled to the door. The sunrise

---

[16] Being unable to discern even the most apparent variations in the Yamato people's physiognomy, Robrecht believed the male and female yūjo to be brother and sister. Not surprisingly, his assumption was based mainly on the observation that they had a similar physical carriage (that is, slight) and that they both possessed black hair and brown eyes. In actual fact, the yūjo with whom he had spent the night were not brother and sister at all but lovers who had drunkenly decided that Robrecht resembled the front piece woodcut of poet Samuel Butler (whom they wrongly believed to be Don Quixote) in *The Life and Notable Adventures of that Renown'd Knight Don Quixote de la Mancha* by Edward Ward, a favorite book which had been gifted to them by a Dutch officer educated in England.

behind it lit up the panels of paper and wood like a wall of golden bars. As the door slid open, sunlight streamed in. "You must go," said the *yūjo*. "Quickly!"

Robrecht blinked painfully.

"Do not let the shogunate catch you here." Then the two vanished as if into thin air, whisked away in a scented breeze of incense and cherry blossoms.

Robrecht's journeys had brought him to Japan before. And each time he had left Dejima without incident, that is, without being discovered. He knew there would be severe consequences for both him and the *opperhoofd* if he ever was. But Robrecht cared not a damn about the *opperhoofd* of Dejima. (Here it should be said, as we will soon see, that Robrecht cared not a damn about many things.) As always, he would rely on good fortune and his own instincts to get him out of the present predicament. For it was true that they had yet to fail him.

In fact, it was this very thought which occupied his mind when first he detected the padded footfall of a shogunate samurai approaching the tea room. Dropping to the floor, Robrecht rolled himself in a *tatami* mat, hoping to be mistaken for a besotted Japanese merchant abandoned to his vices. Through the woven rice straw, he watched the samurai step into the room. The warrior drew his *katana* and crept over to the *tatami* mat. Then raising the sword, the samurai made ready to strike. Believing that some less cautious course of action was now required, Robrecht tensed his legs and made ready to sweep the warrior from his feet. This, however, proved to be unnecessary, as the temple gong sounded again, startling the samurai, who then spun too quickly in his *zōri* and, slipping in the spilt sake, fell with a groan onto his *katana*. The impaled man squirmed and kicked, trying to escape this mortal mishap. In the meantime, Robrecht rolled from out of the mat. If it was true that he cared not a damn about many things, then the reverse was also true—he cared a damn lot about a few things. One of those things was finely crafted weapons that would bring a good price in trade. So, he pulled the *katana* from the *samurai's* belly and watched the wounded warrior bleed out. Soon the dead man's eyes went cold and a gurgling of red breath spilled from his lips. One final tremor attested to the end. Robrecht watched silently, unmoved but not uninterested. For death held a boundless fascination for the first mate of *Son of Batavia*. And it goes without saying that he had witnessed it many times before.

He bent to wipe the blade on the samurai's sash. "A bit of good fortune, that was," said he to the dead man.

Robrecht returned to the man-made island of Dejima in the back of a laundry wagon pulled by an old man crooked over like a fish hook. Once across the bridge, he slipped the *katana* inside his redingote and strode for the dock, just as the ship's bell clanged its seafaring intent.

Robrecht took his place on the quarterdeck amid a flurry of nautical preparations. Catching the eye of an able seaman, he motioned for a word with the sailor. "Take this to my quarters," said he, handing the sword to the shifty-eyed deckhand. "It should bring a decent price in Canton."

"Aye, sir. Correct old Dag if he be wrong," said the seaman with clear delight, "but it would seem some samurai came to a bad end."

"A bad end can come to any man, Seaman Dag. It's the fortunate man who is there when it does." said Robrecht. "Some will die and others live to benefit. It is natural law."

Seaman Dag's eyes were screwed tight with concentration, as if committing the utterance to memory. "Aye, sir. A mighty truth be that."

"The captain wishes to see you in his cabin." It was Meneer Bleeker. "He awaits your call now."

Robrecht was keenly aware that the second mate harbored no small amount of ill will for him. Meneer Bleeker, as well as others among the sailors of *Son of Batavia*, felt that Robrecht had moved quickly through the ranks because of who he was. Or more precisely, who his father was. Like his brother, Robrecht had first come aboard as a cabin boy in his youth. And it was true that under their father's command both he and Jakob had moved quickly through the ranks of *Son of Batavia*. By the time Captain Onderdonk had taken ill, Jakob was first mate of the ship and Robrecht third mate. But it was Jakob's baffling abandonment of the sea shortly after their father's death that proved to be most beneficial for Robrecht. For it had left the position of first mate open, a position that had fallen to Robrecht.[17]

Robrecht knocked at the captain's door and waited. "Enter," said a voice from within.

"You wanted to see me, sir?"

"Yes, Meneer Onderdonk. There is some talk among the men of an officer going ashore last night. Do you know anything about that?" Captain Roorback raised his eyes from the map spread out

---

[17] Robrecht's taking up first mate on the *Son of Batavia* was not a foregone conclusion—far from it. However, with Jakob out of the way, Robrecht was determined to seize the position; that is, he devised a rather devious scheme in order to snatch it away from the second mate, Meneer Bleeker, whom, it was assumed by the rank and file of the ship, would rightfully assume the post. To make certain that this would not be the case, Robrecht enlisted the help of Able Seaman Dag.

It was a simple but effective plan. Slipping a silver bar from the ship's hold into his tarred tunic, Dag stole into the officers' cabin and placed it in the second mate's cabin trunk. Then Robrecht knocked upon the door of the Captain's quarters and, affecting his best rendition of a man torn between duty and camaraderie, reluctantly told him of the second mate's habit of thievery. When the accusation came to light, Meneer Bleeker adamantly denied it, prompting Robrecht to demand that the second mate show the Captain the contents of his cabin trunk. Of course, Meneer Bleeker was unable to account for the silver bar in his trunk. The Captain refrained from taking punitive measures. The harsh punishment that such a crime would normally demand was waived—mainly because Captain Roorback had his doubts concerning the veracity of the thievery charge. Yet, on the other hand, he did not wish to call into question the character of the accuser. For although Captain Onderdonk had recently passed on, his legacy yet held great sway among those at the helm of the VOC, and it goes without saying that Captain Roorback did not wish to do anything that might impede his own rise through the ranks. In the end, the Captain vied for a simple solution. He would move the third mate up to fill the vacant first mate position, and the second mate, Meneer Bleeker, would stay put.

before him.

"Ashore? You mean off Dejima? But it's forbidden by the shogunate, sir."

"Precisely. *Opperhoofd* has caught wind of it. Needless to say, he is not pleased.

"Yes, I would imagine as much, sir."

"Such incidents could spell the end of us in Japan."

"I will keep my eyes and ears open, sir. Rest assured we shall get to the bottom of it."

"Good. I'm counting on you, Meneer Onderdonk." The captain dropped his gaze, adding: "You know there are men aboard this vessel who still claim that you've only risen to second-in-command because of who you are."

"Who I am, sir?"

"Your father, Meneer Onderdonk. May he rest in peace. Surely you've heard whisperings of the like."

"Quite frankly, sir, I haven't."

"Well, never mind that. What I'm trying to say, Meneer Onderdonk—Robrecht—is keep up the good work."

"Thank you, Captain. I intend to."

He returned to the quarterdeck just as *Son of Batavia* weighed anchor and budged from its berth. As in a well-played final act, the *dramatis personae* of this well-rehearsed scene each gave all to his part. Meneer Bleeker barked orders at the coxswain, who then barked orders at the boatswain, who in turn barked orders at the deckhands, the same who jumped to and set about the task of busily tying off sails and securing equipment. However, what each of them failed to notice was the small procession of VOC officials, including the *opperhoofd* of Dejima himself, rushing for the docks, arms waving, voices straining to be heard. For his part, Robrecht watched them shrink into the harbor as the vessel cut the black waters and headed for open sea.

That night when the sun dropped below the blue meridian of the western sky, Robrecht crept from the officers' cabin, careful not to awaken the second mate. Outside, Third Mate Buskirk, propped against the gunwale of the spar deck, softly rumbled in sleep. On the poop deck, the helmsman, entranced by the gleaming scythe of the moon, stood stock still. Had he not been accustomed to it, Robrecht may himself have noticed the bark of taut timber and the constant thwack and patter of canvas as the ship rose and fell, pushing farther into darkness.

The lower deck was dim but not for lack of activity. A group of sailors huddled around a table in the mess galley gambling away their wages. Behind them, the cook sang a rum-infused tune, scraping equal parts potato peel and equal parts knuckle into a bucket. Beyond the mess galley, sailors lay motionless in their berths, exhausted by the preponderance of preparations necessary to launch. And as always, the lower deck was heavy with smells. The very timbers exuded the odor of brine, piss, rum, tar, gun powder, and sweat—all mingled together into one offensive olfactory broth.

Robrecht drew a deep breath and exhaled loudly.

Navigating the lower gun deck, he neared the bow of the ship, directly below the forecastle. There, Able Seaman Dag stood stooped among the chickens. The sailor had a copper-red laying hen by the neck and was about to impale it on his stiff *pik*.

"Dag!" said Robrecht.

"But, sir! See how she goads old Dag with an impish eye. One look, sir, and ye'll see she is a wanton bird."

"Wanton or not. You're on watch."

"Aye, sir." Dag dropped the hen. "Old Dag'll be back, me precious. Rest assured, he'll come looking for his little vixen."

They descended to the hold, where Robrecht pulled back a tarpaulin, exposing the corner of a sizeable stack of silver bars from Japan. Dag snapped one up and ran his tongue along it top to bottom. Then side to side. This lustful display caused Robrecht to shake his head. "Put it back" said he. "And wipe it first."

The bars of silver would be traded for tea in Canton and cinnamon and silk in Pulicat, goods that were the lifeblood of the Oriental trade. Goods that had made the VOC the most powerful chartered company in the East Indies. But more than herbs, spices, and textiles were being traded in this largely uncharted part of the world. Every officer had his scheme and each hoped to amass his own personal booty. And Robrecht was no exception.

He slid behind a pyramid of cast iron cannon balls to a dome-top trunk. "Make sure this one is offloaded in Canton."

"Aye, sir. And if someone's the wiser?"

"No one'll be the wiser. There is no reason for them to wonder about an old trunk."

"Aye, sir. Ye can count on old Dag."

Son of Batavia cleaved the point cities of Hong Kong and Macau, clearing the islands that peppered the mouth of Pearl River. Steering north to the river's head, the ship dropped anchor at Canton, several miles downstream from the Thirteen Factories.

As first mate, Robrecht oversaw the offloading of goods from the hold. He had made it his business to become acquainted with all harbormasters at such trading ports. Not surprisingly, a large part of that involved passing bribes, something which Robrecht had proven to be particularly accomplished at. However, the Manchu official waiting for *Son of Batavia* to dock on this day looked unfamiliar to him. This, the first mate knew, could spell out trouble for him and his scheme.

The bars of silver were offloaded by a gang of coolies and each bar was examined and weighed. Robrecht peered over the harbormaster's shoulder as the scrupulous little man scratched squiggles and lines into a ledger and fiddled with the beads of an abacus. Finally, Dag descended the gangplank shouldering the dome-top trunk with an unsteady gait.

"Stop," said the harbormaster.

Dag hesitated, looked at Robrecht.

"Open," said the scrupulous little man. "Put down! Open!"

Dag set the trunk down, and Robrecht retrieved the key. Just as he was set to open it, a rogue breeze caught the poorly fastened mainmast and the mainstay snapped, sending the block and tackle swinging through the air in an unrestrained arc. Robrecht heard the hefty wooden apparatus whir by his ear and thump the brains from the harbormaster, leaving the scrupulous little man sprawled headless on the dock. The pages of his ledger flipping open in the breeze, taking flight like meat-spattered seabirds.

Robrecht nodded to Dag. The seaman hoisted the trunk onto his shoulder and disappeared into the gathering crowd.

The opium dens of Canton were dingy sanctuaries of sin. Light, natural or otherwise, had no place in them. The filth was lifelike, animated. And the partitioned rooms always looked to have escaped incineration a time or two. All in all, they were his kind of place, and Robrecht longed for them during those interminable crossings of the South China Sea.

Able Seaman Dag had first introduced Robrecht to the mysterious pleasures of poppy tears. He was scarcely a young man at the time, only recently moved up from cabin boy to deckhand. The two of them had stolen ashore in Macau, away from the paternal gaze of Captain Onderdonk and the fraternal stare of Jakob, and spent the evening drinking strong millet alcohol in a hovel near the harbor. Robrecht, already having consumed great quantities, believed himself capable of taking on more liquid ballast. So, speaking with the bravado of youth, a volatile mix of fearlessness and foolishness, he declared himself to be in dire need of more drink. Able Seaman Dag eyed the young man, sized him up. Finally he spoke: "This way, then, young seaman," said he, motioning with a sinewy hand. "Sure as the sea's got salt, old Dag's got the cure for what ails ye."

Robrecht ducked into the unlit doorway. Behind him, Dag blathered nonstop about the day's events—namely, the discerption of the harbormaster's most upper corporeal jurisdiction. Seeing them enter, the Chinese proprietor floated through the opiate haze for the front door. "Mena On'e'dong. Nice see you. You usual, sir?"

"Yes. And I'll be needing female companionship. My friend here will be needing some companionship of the four-legged persuasion. Can that be arranged?" Robrecht slipped a Dutch ducat into the proprietor Kwon's smooth palm.

"Oh yes, sir. I half-skin mongrel bitch chained up in alleyway. I soon to butcha for dog stew feast, but feast can wait one more night."[18]

Dag licked his chops.

"Yes, that'll be fine," said Robrecht.

He took his place in a screened-off chamber complete with a robustly horned caribou coat rack, lumpy wooden cot, oil lamp and marble-top commode after the fashion of the French. He slipped from his redingote, kicked off his shoes and loosened his cravat. Before long, he was reclined and circling a long porcelain pipe over the open flame of the opium lamp. He inhaled deeply then exhaled a plume of smoke into the black nostrils of the caribou overhead. The creature melted into a deep brown infinity. Robrecht dropped his gaze and inhaled again. The dragon on the screen began to dance its convoluted dance—a twisting green flame looping in and out of existence. All around him, the sounds of the den weaved together to

---

[18] The mongrel bitch had been hanging around the narrow lane behind Kwon's establishment for several weeks before he took any notice of it. Stray dogs were no strange occurrence. They wandered the streets in unruly packs. But what Kwon did find odd was the *mŭquăn's* apparent attraction to pigs. He would often find it sleeping in the small bamboo pen behind his establishment, it's brown snout nestled into this or that sow. Each time he passed by he remarked: "You want live like swine, you die like swine. One day Kwon butcha you for dog stew feast."

But each day came and went, and the *mŭquăn* remained alive, unharmed, and living with Kwon's pigs. In fact, more and more, Kwon found himself amused by and even attached to the peculiar beast. Until a few months later, when a young gilt birthed a single runt that bore a striking resemblance to the *mŭquăn*. Kwon swore the piglet had a shiny brown nose, white paws, and a long straight tail. The plain fact that the *mŭquăn* was a mongrel bitch—a female—was somehow lost on Kwon. He was livid, enraged. Not only was he enraged that the gilt had not birthed a full litter, he was now terrified that the *mŭquăn* had done something unnatural to the gilt, something that would rain down bad luck upon him and his establishment. Kwon knew there was only one thing to do. And the more painful the better. Cursing loudly, he caught the mŭquăn and strung it up. "You live like swine, you die like swine," said he, setting a butchering knife into the fire.

form an impenetrable armor of isolation. Robrecht dropped his head onto his arm. This journey was exhilarating, even more so than anything the sea had to offer. He let the opium lap at him like a coming tide, suck him into a maelstrom of bliss. Soon his eyes grew heavy with narcotic dreams, and finally, he succumbed to their call.

He awoke to snarls and growls from the mongrel bitch next door. His eyelids rolled up like millennia-old papaya scrolls. From the adjacent chamber came the unsettling yelps of the half-skinned canine and the gruff curses of Seaman Dag. Robrecht sat upright, only then noticing the young woman sitting there quietly, waiting. "Ji-Sum," said he. "How long have you been here?"

"Since you friend start humpa-humpa Kwon's dinner." She undressed. Her small breasts pronounced an almost boyish bearing. She came from a northern province where her father had sold her into sexual slavery before she'd reached puberty. That was all Robrecht knew about her past life—all he cared to know.[19]

---

[19] In actual fact, Ji-sum had not been sold by her father into sexual slavery but had been inadvertently discarded and later sold by her general lover.

The last of twenty-three children, Ji-sum was born to peasant parents in a *shāncūn* of northern Xinjiang. She was the last only by minutes—three minutes and forty-two seconds, to be precise. Ji-sum's slightly older brother, her twin, preceded her into a world of strife and hardship and several months later would precede her out of it also. After returning from the village and finding the infant boy lifeless on her back, Ji-sum's mother directed her husband to dispose of the body. Seeing both twins lying motionless side-by-side and believing both to have died, Ji-sum's father scooped up the two tiny bodies and taking them to a nearby mountain crevice dropped them in—with only the slightest hesitation, it should be said, for he had made this very trip eleven times before.

Baby Ji-sum was saved by a goat herder who happened to hear her spirited wail, even over the bleats and bells of his hirsute charge. The man, Chien Yán, ascended the mountain crag to retrieve her, finding her atop her dead brother in a slough of broken blue shale. The goat herder swaddled the young infant girl in a wool blanket and carried her home to his hut.

Chien Yán, at thirty-two, remained single, largely due to the disfiguring curse of a cleft palate. He was neither a good nor a bad man, particularly. However, having suffered much in his life, he viewed the event as a sort of

"How you want?" said Ji-sum. "Mouth? Bushy? Plato cave?"

"All of the above." Robrecht grasped her sharp hips and pulled her down to the cot.

"You miss Ji-Sum?"

"Yes, of course."

"So long time you no come see Ji-Sum."

"I'm a sailor. Many ports to visit."

"Many ho to humpa-humpa."

---

karmic compensation. Thus had it never crossed his mind to do anything other than keep the infant for himself.

Ji-sum grew up believing that Chien Yán was her real father and that her mother had been murdered by marauding Qing soldiers. Her life with Chien Yán was a relatively happy one until she reached the age of sexual maturity. At that time, the goat herder, who it must be said had lain with more goats than women in his lifetime, found himself unable to keep his goat herder hands off Ji-sum. For her part, Ji-sum vigorously fought off the advances of the man she believed to be her father, to the point where the barrage of kicks he took to the *wài shèn* in all likelihood rendered him sterile. Deciding that the young girl was too feisty for his particular needs, Chien Yán traveled to a nearby garrison and sold her to the commanding officer for two laying hens and a jug of rice wine.

Ji-sum worked as the commander's servant girl until the stern Qing Manchu took her as a lover, one of six other concubines. The competition drove Ji-sum to redouble her efforts to prove herself the best concubine in the garrison. She bathed in rainwater and peppermint and slept on a bed of plum blossoms. She trained her young slender body to do things that no other concubine could—or would. And these efforts did not go unappreciated. The Manchu commander showered her with plundered riches, if not with affection.

And so was Ji-sum's euphoria great when her Manchu commander bid her travel with him to Guǎngzhōu—known as Canton to the Europeans—in Guǎngdōng Shěng province, where he would trade his ill-gained booty for Dutch gold and silver. But once in Guǎngzhōu, she quickly realized that she was the crown jewel of her Manchu's booty, and she too was traded for silver and gold. Thus, still months shy of her fourteenth birthday, Ji-sum found herself broken-hearted and working as a common whore in a rickety opium den perched on edge of Zhū Jiāng—Pearl River.

"But this is my favorite ho to humpa-humpa." He was about to demonstrate the point when a mighty roar filled the den. Screens flew and commodes crashed. "Where is she?" bellowed a sailor in a rumbling cockney brogue.

"I go now," said Ji-Sum, jumping up. When a strapping English sailor appeared at the chamber's entrance, Ji-Sum scampered back onto the cot, taking cover. "Hold, Seaman," said Robrecht in an authoritative tone.

"That rice cunt gave me the clap," said the sailor.

Robrecht rose up onto his elbows. "Surely there's been some mistake."

"No mistake, mate. She's drippin' with it." No sooner had the brute stepped into the chamber than he screeched fiendishly and clawed at the air around his ears as if being swarmed by his own demons. In truth, he was being swarmed by a single, very real demon. In the dim light, Robrecht could just make out the figure of Dag. The able seaman had his teeth clamped into the thick neck of the Englishman, who responded with a wallop from his savage fist then slammed the would-be Jenglot into the wall. The force of the blow knocked Dag unconscious and sent the caribou head rattling to the floor. The brawny sailor, now turning his attention to Robrecht and Ji-Sum, dropped his head and charged wildly. With not a moment to waste, Robrecht snatched up the caribou head and held it fast, just as the Englishman plunged onto its pronged rack.

A pained moo gushed from the sailor's punctured lungs, sounding a guttural death rattle. The rage that had moments earlier contorted his block-like features drained away in a gurgling stream of pale blood. The sailor dropped his sizable head onto Robrecht's chest and draped his arms like broken-necked swans by his sides. With some effort, Robrecht rolled the dead man's body onto the floor, where it landed with a final thud.

The following day, *Son of Batavia* set sail for Java. Driven by prevailing southwest winds and cutting a wide berth around the Indochinese peninsula, the ship was swept past the point of Cà Mau in a week's time. The Thousand Islands of Java Sea protruded from sparkling green waters like the tufted humps of a submerged mythical beast. The sun hung overhead, unrelenting in its blazing intent. When land came again into view, Robrecht spied the palm trees of Batavia. He breathed in the odor of spices—cinnamon and pepper with a hint of nutmeg—and watched the locals toiling in their masters' orchards.

When the ship docked, Robrecht disembarked and set out in the direction of VOC headquarters. He strolled by the imposing stone walls—white and twice the height of a man—to an ornate iron gate. A voice called after him. "Meneer Onderdonk, sir. A nip of rum to wet yer whistle?"

"Another time, Dag. I've someone to see."

Robrecht marched down the whitewashed hallway towards the office of the *opperhoofd* of Batavia. He had marched down this same hallway to his father's office countless times before, usually accompanied by Jakob. At those times, they would march shoulder-to-shoulder, Robrecht inevitably lengthening his stride, inching forward slightly. And although Jakob had been oblivious to the significance of this act, it was Robrecht's symbolic coup, his way of silently defying his brother's authority over him as first mate of the vessel. Robrecht recalled how they had been marching down this very hallway years earlier, prior to his father's death, when, sensing something afoot, he had first approached Captain Schoonhoven and the two of them had become business partners shortly thereafter, remaining so to this very day.[20]

---

[20] On the day in question, Robrecht and Jakob were only strides away from their father's office when the door swung open and a man, hatless, with periwig askance, stormed out and brushed passed them. Robrecht recognized the man as Captain Schoonhoven, a friend of his father's and a longtime family acquaintance. When the two brothers entered the office, their father sat slumped behind his desk in a huff, clearly agitated. Robrecht asked what had taken place to set Captain Schoonhoven on his way in such a perturbed state. The Onderdonk patriarch railed about Captain Schoonhoven's scheming, calling him a blackguard, the likes of whom would surely spell the demise of the VOC. Captain Onderdonk rose and tugged on his sleeves, then slipping into his jacket, apologized and excused himself, as he had business to attend.

The two brothers watched their father disappear out the door before
themselves retreating the way they had come. Halfway down the hall,
Robrecht pulled up short, claiming to have left something behind in their
father's office, then turned on his heels and retraced his steps down the
hallway. He rounded the corner and halted before the office of Captain
Schoonhoven. Without further hesitation, he rapped on the door and, upon
hearing the word *enter*, turned the doorknob and went in.

For his part, Captain Schoonhoven had been surprised to see Robrecht.
What business the younger of the two Onderdonk sons could possibly have
with him, he did not know. Nevertheless, he greeted the young man civilly
and bid him sit. Choosing to stand, young Onderdonk spoke curtly, saying he
had just come from his father's office and that Captain Onderdonk had been
upset over something that had passed between the two men. And now he
wondered what exactly that was. Captain Schoonhoven took a moment to
size up the young man—standing too confidently, with an air of impertinence
about him. Perhaps sensing Captain Schoonhoven's reluctance Robrecht
added that he had hoped he might "be of some assistance."

"Does your father know you have come to see me?"

"No, sir, he does not. I have come of my own accord. If I may ask, sir,
what difference would it make? I am here now."

"You're father and I have been acquaintances—friends—for many years."

"Yes, sir, I am aware of that."

"Are you also aware that he now regards me as something of a
scoundrel?"

"I believe he referred to you as 'Hendrik the Blackguard,' sir."

Here, Captain Schoonhoven chortled. "Blackguard? And you, do you
believe I am a blackguard?"

"A man who schemes to advance his own station in life is no blackguard.
He is a realist. That is how I see it."

"A realist. I like that. Yes, a realist is what I am." He picked up his pipe
and lit it. "And did your father tell you what exactly this scheme was?"

"He did not." The young Onderdonk shifted on his feet. "Sir, may I be
frank?"

"By all means, yes. Be frank."

"My father is a man for whom the world is black and white. He is an
idealist, not a realist. I am not my father. I am not like my father in this
respect. I, too, am a realist. I, too, am a man looking for a scheme to advance
my station in life."

Robrecht knocked on the door and entered without waiting for a response. The *opperhoofd* of Batavia sat behind a sprawling oak desk, jacketless and collarless, poring over a ledger. Aside from a slightly expanded paunch and a few added lines crisscrossing his pasty brow, *Opperhoofd* Schoonhoven looked much as he had when Robrecht first called upon him—*Captain* Schoonhoven—years earlier.

"Meneer Onderdonk, first mate of *Son of Batavia* reporting, sir."

Opperhoofd rubbed his head, which without the concealing benefit of a periwig, resembled the smooth exterior of an exotic melon. "Never mind the formalities. I trust the excursion went well. By that, I mean as planned."

"As planned, sir." Robrecht took a ducat from his pocket. He ran a finger over the coin which had been minted in Amsterdam but counterstamped at the VOC mint in Batavia.[21] He flipped it to *Opperhoofd*.

"Your contact in Canton gave you the going rate?"

"Yes, sir. Six gulden, twelve stuivers per ducat—in Portuguese reals. Two stuivers commission on each for the trader."

"And the reals?"

"Tucked neatly away in a warehouse, sir."

"Where is the next exchange?"

"I've a contact in Pulicat."

"Excellent work, Meneer Onderdonk. Your father would be—" *Opperhoofd* stopped mid-sentence.

"What, *Opperhoofd* Schoonhoven? Proud? Hardly."

"No, I suppose not."

Robrecht, suddenly agitated, paced to the window overlooking the warehouse yard. Dark-skinned *pribumi* stacked cinnamon tree

---

"I see. And you come to me in hopes that I may have the scheme for which you search."

"Precisely, sir."

Captain Schoonhoven exhaled a plume of smoke. "Sit down, then. Please. Let me tell you of something I have recently discovered."

[21] The single four-letter word *JAVA* had been counterstamped on the coin.

boughs in long neat rows. "We set sail for Pulicat in two weeks."

"Unfortunately, that may have to wait. Some complications have arisen—elsewhere."

"Complications? What kind of complications?"

"The nutmeg planters of the Banda Islands are having problems with the locals. They refuse to bring in the crop."

"And how does that affect the itinerary of *Son of Batavia*?"

"I need you and Captain Roorback to get down there and quell this thing before it turns into a full-scale rebellion, God forbid."

"And how do I go about doing that?"

"You'll think of something. I have every confidence in you, Meneer Onderdonk. Just get those *pribumi* to bring in the crop."

"Do I have your full authority to do whatever is necessary?"

"You have it. Do whatever is necessary. Just do it quickly." *Opperhoofd* eased himself into his chair. "If you put the matter to rest expeditiously, there will be a promotion in it for you."

"Then consider it done, sir."

FROM THE JOURNAL OF ROBRECHT ONDERDONK

February 12, 1746
Father threatens to put me ashore with the savages of Papua for good if I do
not keep a more meticulous record of my daily dealings and innermost
thoughts in a journal. Innermost thoughts! Ha! He says—with as much
authority as he can muster—that I shall never don the stripes of a captain
in the VOC if I do not. Am I to assume, then, that only the most thoughtful
and organized men of the VOC will rise through the ranks and find
themselves in the exalted post of captain? 'Tis pure folly! For the sea is rife
with mindless thugs who man the poop decks of vessels both far and wide.
Their only concern is the whereabouts of the next warm cunt they will plug
with their proud pricks.

Thoughtful and organized! Ha! Here is a daily dealing for you. Yesterday
father ordered a schedule to be drawn up for swabbing the decks, a schedule
that all deckhands were to adhere to—strictly. Yet the following day,
deckhands flipped stuivers to willing cabin boys in order that they might
swab the decks on their behalf. The schedule be damned! There is his
organization!

Were it not so painfully piteous, I might be amused observing Father as
he attempts to impose his order upon the sea—all to no avail, of course. He
is like the vessel whose bow and hull leave their wake upon the water for
only the space of a moment; and after that moment, all traces of its existence
are gone, washed away in the eternal sea.

Who is Father to say what I shall or shall not do? For I will make my
own way in this world, as I have already proven myself capable of doing.
Even at the youthful age of twenty and one, as I now am, I have witnessed
more, experienced more, accomplished more than most men do in a lifetime.
But Father does not see this as a badge of honor but simply as the
circumstances of being—acts unfolding in the sturdy march of Time. To his
mind, all worthy acts and experiences must be tempered by reason and
morality. Those that are not are simply unaccountable circumstances that
belong to no one. However, I say, if this be the case, then no man, living or
dead, save perhaps Father himself, can rightly be said to have accomplished
anything in this world. For what man measures and gages the morality of
every act that manifests itself before him as an opportunity. To be taken or to

be lost — that is the only measure a man may make.

FROM A LETTER ADDRESSED TO
MEVROUW MARIJKE ONDERDONK,
LEYDEN, SOUTH HOLLAND

March, 1740

Marijke, Dear Wife,

How you must be worried about your boys. How you must dream of them in their tiny plush velvet breeches and their pressed white nightshirts. I believe, dear wife, that you think it a secret, how you cried the night before they shipped out with their father for the first time. But I was there, too, remember? Lying next to you as your silent sobs shook our marriage bed, and wondering if you would ever forgive me for what I was about to do. But you must know that I only did what I believed best for the boys, and the only thing that I know how to do. When we were wed, you brought the wealth of your family to our union and I only the wealth of my good name—Onderdonk; an honest name I was determined to forge into greatness upon the high seas. So it is to the high seas that I must always return and it is there that I must usher our sons from childhood to manhood.

And manhood is not far off; for they grow strong and sturdy at sea, like the very vessel they man. Perhaps it is the rivalry between them that pushes them both on—that rivalry of opposites. For Jakob is quiet and thoughtful and Robrecht brazen and impulsive. And although I make efforts to treat them equally, I fear there are times when my great concern and my desire to guide and instruct are oppressive to Robrecht. He believes me oblivious to his bitter feelings towards me; yet how can I not take notice of the indignant and wrathful looks he levels at me from time to time. For now, all I can hope it that in time he will see that I had only the best intentions where he and his brother were concerned. Jakob fares better and is a goodly Christian boy, but, to my great chagrin, has little influence over his younger sibling. And so it is that I struggle daily to find equal affection for them both. Forgive me, dear wife; for I am trying.

Yours from across the Sea,
Cornelis

FOUR

J akob reached into a drawer and removed a piece of stationary. *Dear Heleen,* he wrote then paused. He looked to the loom where once his beloved had labored, trying to imagine her there. The certainty and grace of her movements. The curve of her spine, the bend of her arms, the flutter of her fingers. How he had adored them all in secret. How he had adored her, still adored her.

He recalled their first meeting on her father's farm. He had called to find out why the agreed-upon wool from Funske Bonk had not arrived at the agreed-upon time on the agreed-upon day. What he found was Heleen, knee-deep in fleece, having that very morning single-handedly shorn a small flock. Wearing only a head kerchief and a coarse peasant's gown, she was the most comely maiden he had ever laid eyes on. She straightened up and, with blade shears still in hand, wiped away the silver beads of sweat glistening on her brow. Jakob stepped into the shed, where he scooped up a handful of fleece and perfunctorily inspected it.

Together they packed the wool into jute bags. Jakob delighted in her tuneful vitality, as a bouncy melody filled the shed, making labor light. Her voice was sunshine infusing a stained glass sky. Between refrains, they talked. Or she talked, mostly. Of her family, mainly. Her mother had been a casualty of the Black Death, she had told him—a young life burst and drained away like so many black pustules of that fearful pestilence.[22] She had been raised by her

---

[22] Alda Helena Almeida Nasi married Funske Bonk in a small *dorpskerk* south of Leyden. The marriage was the product of long-distance matchmaking orchestrated by the bride's grandmother, whose family of Sephardic Jews had migrated to Amsterdam in the declining years of the Dutch Golden Age. Alda Helena, a handsome enough maiden, possessed a distinctly Sapphic bent that made the prospect of marriage improbable if not impossible. Finally, Oma Nasi took matters into her own hands, and within weeks, her seemingly unmarriageable *kleindochter* was on her way from Portalegre to South Holland, where she was to meet a man whose own Agathonean bent had also made marriage an unlikely prospect for him.

Funske Bonk shepherded a flock of two hundred merino sheep and twenty-four head of scrub goat. By peasant standards, he was a wealthy man, a king among shepherds. Despite this, his "lover-of-men" reputation had essentially nullified his eligible bachelor status in the county; thus, any marriageable maidens who may otherwise have flaunted their conjugal virtues before him simply did not. Thus, when Oma Nasi approached him with the promise of a Portuguese bride, one who knew nothing of his reputation, Funske was both pleased and grateful. What he did not know was Oma Nasi had approached her Alda Helena in a like manner; that is, by telling her that she might yet be able to capture a Dutch bridegroom who knew nothing about her and her questionable proclivities. By the time Oma Nasi had finished playing matchmaker, the wedding was an ineluctable reality. And much to the relief of all involved, it went off without a hitch.

The wedding night was another story entirely. Of course, nothing happened. In fact, the newlyweds kept their distance, or at least as much distance as was possible in the diminutive cottage of Funske Bonk. To be fair, it should be said that the cottage was diminutive not because Funske could afford nothing larger, but because he had not anticipated sharing the one-room dwelling with another sentient being, ever. Consummation occurred several months later purely by accident when the two quite literally bumped into each other in front of the fireplace one winter's eve.

On the night in question, Funske had been absently fantasizing about a young, broad-shouldered tinker in the village, unaware that his arousal had become apparent, not to mention unfettered from his wool undergarment that was missing several strategically significant buttons. For her part, Alda Helena knitted furiously, as was her habit when feeling anxious (although it should here be said that the sight of Funske unfettered arousal was doing a great deal to make her so), and having inadvertently snagged the drawstring of her nightgown with a knitting needle had left the garment entirely without support. Thus it was that when she stood up and bent to place firewood in the fire, her normally modest gown dropped to her ankles. And at that precise moment, Funske, who had decided to cool off with some fresh air, bumped into his bride's exposed bottom with his liberated member. If Funske had been an archer and not a shepherd, it might be said that he hit the bull's-eye with enviable precision on that particular shot. The whole thing was over in an instant, with only the slightest whimper from Alda Helena. But so embarrassed were they both by the incident that husband and wife quickly re-clad themselves and never spoke of it again. At least, not directly. For when Alda Helena began to show, it became difficult to ignore. And father, whose unpredictable bouts of illness now made it difficult for him to run the affairs of the family farm without being cheated by Catholic and Protestant alike. An only child, she was. "At least, it seems as if I am," she said. "My two half-brothers being both born idiots." For fifteen years, the twins had roamed the fields and forests surrounding Leyden much like wild beasts. Until followers of Menno Simons converted them and swept them away to Friesland in a tide of Christian zeal.[23]

---

whenever one caught the other gazing at the growing lump of life beneath her linen frock, they would blush in unison a rich carmine color more precious than all the buffed red rubies of the orient. It was, perhaps for the first time in history, truly an accidental conception.

A child was soon born, a girl which they would name Heleen. But the babe had only suckled at the young mother's breast for seven months when Alda Helena was seized by the Black Death. The symptoms appeared first in her armpits and then her groin. A physician was hailed and the buboes were burst with sharpened quills from the feathers of a blessed laying hen. But the treatment mattered little. For soon Alda Helena's pale body burned and her mind raged. The delirium was terrifying and the convulsive regurgitations foul. Finally, there was nothing for Funske to do but hope for a more expeditious end. And this would come, but not soon enough. One night, Alda Helena closed her eyes and slept, never to awaken again.

[23] The Bonk brothers were, in fact, well known around Leyden—although *well known* may not fully convey the terror the twins had once instilled in the hearts and minds of the villagers. Before the conversion, that is. To say they were *notorious* would be closer to the truth.

Funske Bonk remarried shortly after Heleen's mother had passed on, his former Agathonean bent having now seemingly disappeared and all but forgotten by the villagers. Maaike Wulheizen bore Funske twin sons, Erwin and Filibert, before running off with a Dutch Flamenco guitarist who claimed to be one-thirty-second Gitano. Although the twins were physically sound and sturdy boys, it soon became apparent that they lacked mental fortitude. As Funske would come to uncharitably put it—"They are idiots, dullards, dunces, and muttonheaded halfwits." By the time they were five years of age, Funske could no longer manage the boys. They came and went as they pleased, uttering half-cogitated gibberish to their half-sister, Heleen, while snapping and snarling threats at their father. As they grew older, they

That left only her, Heleen.

At this point, had any other soul right then been sitting with them, cross-legged in the straw of the shearing shed, it would have been painfully clear to said soul that Jakob was smitten. Wholly smitten. It would be fair to say that Jakob was in love. Yet even in such a flustered state did he feverishly consider the various ways that he might keep her close to him, in the end concluding that the most

---

returned home less and less, until finally, they stopped altogether. At that point, it was understood by all that the Bonk brothers had made the wooded area around the village their home. At times, they could be seen coming and going. But mostly, their presence was made clear by the carnage left in their wake—headless chickens, disemboweled sheep, rats with their innards nailed to trees, goats with their teats chawed. In a word, the Bonks soon became the terror of the countryside. Not that they had ever attacked anyone—aside from Funske—but the villagers began to fear them and to fear the forest, particularly after dark.

It was about this time that a group of Menno Simon's followers passed through the village on their way to Friesland. The leader among them, a man named Emil Gygax, took an interest in the Bonk brothers, firmly believing that the light of Christ was in all sentient beings, even idiots, and that they could be brought to Christ just as any other person could. To that end, Gygax lured the Bonk brothers with fresh carrion and lay in wait for them at the outskirts of the village. When the boys came loping up and snorted at the goat carcass, Gygax and the Mennonite men laid hands on them and tied them fast with ropes. What followed was a continuous, week-long prayer session in which the Mennonite brothers spelled each other off praying for the lost souls of the Bonk brothers. When at last it appeared that their prayers had been answered, Emil Gygax ordered the boys untied and dressed like "proper Christians," after which they were taught "A Mighty Fortress is Our God." Although Erwin and Filibert were only able to memorize snippets of the first stanza of the hymn, and despite the fact that they mistakenly sang the opening line "The mighty tortoise is more God," Gygax viewed their conversion as nothing short of miraculous and thereupon conscripted the boys into his humble platoon of roaming saints. Funske and Heleen bid them farewell, the twins Erwin and Filibert in collared shirts and ill-fitting suits, sitting on the back of a bouncing Mennonite wagon singing spiritedly the one line from the one and only hymn they partially knew.

effective might simply be to extend to her an offer of employment. So he did—he asked her to work for him in his factory. "There seems nothing to stand in your way," he had said, adding that the job paid well enough to support her and her father. Heleen had hemmed and hawed, squinting her blue eyes as she considered it. Then she agreed.

The memory brought a smile to Jakob's lips. He put down his pen then rose and sauntered over to the glass. After that he made tea. And although he could scarcely bear the thought of it, he knew he would have to find a replacement for Heleen, sooner or later. For the loom would not weave carpets on its own. But he just couldn't think about it now. For Jakob knew that he should instead be thinking about the dinner he was to attend that very evening with Anneke's *tante*, Mevrouw Schoonhoven. As he considered this, it struck him that fortune had played a rather underhanded trick on him. For no sooner had Heleen disappeared from his life than Anneke had appeared.

Jakob had been hesitant about the dinner, reluctant even. He wondered if his friendship with Meisje Schoonhoven was progressing too rapidly toward something more serious. But somehow, his mother had gotten involved and convinced him to go. As Jakob well knew, Mevrouw Onderdonk was gifted that way. At times, he bemoaned the fact that he was largely the focus of her attentions. But then, she couldn't reasonably be expected to turn all her attention to Oma Onderdonk. After all, wondered he, how long could the increasingly enervated multiglandular functions of the septuagenarian constitution hold one's imagination? Not long, he conceded.

Anneke met him at the door. She clasped his hand tightly and pulled him in to the sitting room. Jakob had made the acquaintance of Mevrouw Schoonhoven once before, while still a young boy (although he was aware of his mother's occasional calls upon the Schoonhoven *herenhuis* over the years). Mevrouw Schoonhoven was known about town as a handsome woman. Of course, having had no sense of what renders a woman handsome—or unhandsome, for that matter—at such a tender age as he was at the time of that first meeting, Jakob could neither confirm nor deny the rumor. However, he now discovered the rumor to be gospel truth.

When Mevrouw Schoonhoven entered the sitting room, Jakob was immediately struck by the seemingly apparent familial resemblance to her *nicht*. She had the same delicate features as Anneke but slightly sharper. Like erosion in reverse. Instead of softening her edges, time had honed them to pleasing lineaments. However, it should be said that whatever similarities Jakob believed he saw were the product of his own imagination, since no blood relation existed between Mevrouw Schoonhoven and her *nicht*, although so striking was the resemblance—or so thought Jakob—that he assumed the opposite to be true.

Jakob greeted his hostess with a formal bow. Mevrouw Schoonhoven responded with an appropriate curtsey, before tittering as a young maiden might and brushing a drooping blond curl from her forehead, allowing Jakob to catch his first un-obscured glimpse of the red blob hanging just beneath her hairline. At first, he took it to be something akin to a sizable blob of fruit jam. But upon closer inspection, he realized it was an unsightly tumorous growth. He could scarcely take his eyes from it. Jakob had visited enough seaports in his sailing days to recognize the late stages of syphilis when he saw it. He was astounded that Anneke had not mentioned this to him. For if she had, he might not be standing dumbfounded, his mouth agape. But then it occurred to him that Anneke may not be aware of her *tante's* condition. It also occurred to him that Mevrouw Schoonhoven herself may know nothing of it.[24]

---

[24] In actuality, Mevrouw Schoonhoven had known about her condition for some time—since her last trip to Amsterdam, to be precise. She had been making the regular if not secret trips for more than two years. There, she would stroll arm-in-arm down Zeedijk Street with her robust *kuiper*. He was much younger—and handsomer—than her Hendrik, but if one were to take her squeals of pleasure as an accurate indication of his sexual know-how, it would be fair to say that he *knew well* how to please her. That is to say, in pleasure-years, Kuiper was a wizened old man. By the same standards, Hendrik Schoonhoven was nothing but a boy. At least, that was how Mevrouw Schoonhoven saw it. According to her, Hendrik knew nothing

"Meneer Onderdonk," said Mevrouw Schoonhoven, "I must admit something to you," The three of them sat down in unison.

"Certainly, I'm all ears."

"I was, well, anxious about this meeting—"

"*Tante*, perhaps not now."

"For surely you have heard tell of my charms."

"Yes, indeed I have, Mevrouw Schoonhoven. And I must say that the rumors are all true."

"But you are too kind, Meneer Onderdonk. For how could the hideous blemish that mars my beauty escape your notice?"

Jakob was not prepared for such frankness. He felt the blood burning in his cheeks.

"Look, *tante*. You've made him blush. Now is not the time to discuss such matters."

"Perhaps not. But you must agree that it is hideous, is it not, Meneer Onderdonk?"

"Truthfully, I hadn't noticed."

"Truthfully? Truthfully, how could you NOT notice?" With this,

---

about women. She had once complained to her Lady's maid that he rode her like a friar rides an ass. And she couldn't remember the last time that had happened. He had, after all, been stationed in the East Indies for coming up on two decades. These days, she might set eyes on his ruddy round face once in every five years. And so it was that she carried on an illicit affair back home. On the night in question, returning from a stroll to the *herberg*, Mevrouw Schoonhoven disrobed and submitted to the fierce advances of her lover, letting herself drift off into a kind of erotic trance. Her hips moved to the rhythms of Kuiper's frantic lunges and thrusts, until she felt him stiffen and collapse upon her. It was when he rolled onto his back and began with a soft-rumbling snore that she noticed the open red sore on his floppy member. At the time, she had leaned in for a closer look, all the while wondering how she had not noticed the lesion before. Alarmed by this troubling discovery, she set a lamp and a maiden's hand-mirror upon the floor and, squatting over it, inspected herself. Mevrouw Schoonhoven left that night without so much as a goodbye, and resolved to never see her lover again. She would be fine, she had tearfully told herself, as the first rays of dawn shot across the sky.

Mevrouw Schoonhoven shot to her feet and tore the hair from her head. To Jakob's great surprise, the flaxen mane came unstuck, revealing a dry powdered orb beneath. Mevrouw Schoonhoven shook the wig as if she had right then snared it and was about to butcher and bleed it. She pointed to the gumma. "LOOK! LOOK! See how it mocks the goddess Aphrodite."

"*Tante*, no!"

"This hell-rot that crumbles the brow of Aphrodite! Where is my Adonis? Save me, my fair Adonis!"

Anneke wrapped an arm around Mevrouw Schoonhoven's shoulder and led her weeping from the room. Jakob was stunned. He remained standing long after their departure. And not wishing to sit, he wandered about the sitting room, eyeing this and touching that but, in truth, was unable to take his mind off the earlier scene.

At length, Anneke returned. "You must forgive *tante*. She is troubled."

"Of course, yes. But perhaps if she is troubled, a physician's care is in order."

Anneke's eyebrows pointed up like two finely plucked peaks. "But why would you say that? She is not mad."

"Oh no, of course not. I simply meant a physician might be able to ease her condition. Perhaps even cure her. I've heard such things are not impossible."

"Condition? Cure? Honestly, Jakob, whatever do you mean?"

"You know the—" Jakob gestured to his forehead.

"That? That is nothing but a spot. Surely that does not warrant the care of a physician. It will heal on its own."

Jakob realized then that Anneke had not a clue about the disease. "But how long has the spot been on your *tante*'s brow?"

"I don't know. Four weeks, perhaps."

"Four weeks?"

"No, three weeks seems right. She is fine. No need to worry."

Jakob simply could not bring himself to tell Anneke the truth. It was simply too disagreeable.

"Come, let us dine. We mustn't let *boerenkool met rookworst* go to waste." said Anneke, leading Jakob by the hand back into the dining room. And thus, retaking their seats, did they make a valiant attempt to salvage the evening.

Jakob sawed off a slab of sausage and pushed cooked cabbage onto his fork. Although he was partial to *rookworst*, he wondered if it might be the culprit behind the slight bulge that had recently become noticeable in the region of his midriff. He also wondered if this might be the very reason that Anneke had forgone the sausage plate and now sipped *erwtensoep* from a spoon. The tiny slurp of her pressed lips was something to admire, if not for the apt display of decorum that it was, than simply for the raw feat of it.

It put him in mind of the day he had first met Heleen. How she had greedily bitten into her *droge worst* and, lapping at her fingertips, smacked her lips loudly. When he had chuckled, she raised her head, revealing a greasy grin beneath two scarlet cheeks. It was the one time that they had been alone together — the first and last. The only time he had ever seen her outside the four walls of the factory.

As this pleasing image of Heleen sat squarely on his seat of thought, a piercing screech shattered the necessary lull in the conversation that chewing one's food constitutes. Jakob shot to his feet.

"It is *tante*," said Anneke. "She sometimes awakes in a fright."

"Is she in need of assistance? Is there something to be done?"

"No, there is nothing to be done. A warm cup of St. John's wort will ease her back into deep slumber. The maid will take care of her." Anneke smiled.

Jakob slid back into his seat and took up his knife and fork again. But the image of Heleen sitting cross-legged on the floor of the shearing shed, eating sausage, returned again to his mind like a homing pigeon to its cage. He placed his hands on the table, fork and knife raised upright, and spoke. "There is something I'd hoped to bring up. And now seems to as good a time as any."

Anneke stopped sipping her soup and sat upright, as if a gallant knight had just then called up to her castle window from fifty feet below.

"Yes, Jakob. What is it?"

"Well, I don't quite know how best to say this, so I will just say it frankly. I am very fond of someone —"

Anneke jumped to her feet, sending the spoon rattling across the table and, dragging a sleeve through the *boerenkool met rookworst*, clasped Jakob's hands in her own. "I, too, and fond of someone," she said.

"Yes, but —"

"Say no more." She placed two fingers to Jakob's lips. "Say nor more, lest we break the spell and the magic be forever lost. Just tell me when I will see you again."

Jakob floundered. Her misplaced self-assuredness had caught him wholly offguard. "Sunday?" said he.

Anneke retook her seat and smoothed out the lap of her dress. "I would be delighted to see you Sunday."

FROM THE JOURNAL OF CORNELIS ONDERDONK

June 10, 1749

Today, we docked in Dejima. It sticks like a grotesque appendage from the southern tip of Tsukushi-no-shima. There was a time perhaps when I felt the daimyo rather foolish for devising such a place for fear of the influence of Europeans. However, today when I met with the opperhoofd of Dejima, I was no longer certain of my earlier conviction, as, according to Opperhoofd Jansen, there are rumors of unsanctioned, that is unofficial trade taking place here. I am not so naïve as to believe that no unofficial trade takes place in the VOC; however, Opperhoofd tells me that this trade appears to be well-organized and ongoing. When I asked about the exact nature of the trade, Opperhoofd said it was best if he revealed nothing more until he had definitive proof. At the time, I believed that Opperhoofd's reluctance to tell me more meant he suspected one of my own men, my own officers even; however, I was in no position to make demands, so I pressed the issue no further.

I have known Opperhoofd Jansen since he was Captain Jansen of Sint Servaas and I am taken to believe that he is a just and moral man. Clearly, the daimyo, and perhaps the shogun himself, trust Opperhoofd to judiciously administer to trade between the VOC and the shogunate. On a related matter, Opperhoofd Jansen told me of the shogun's recent remonstrations concerning VOC seamen illicitly leaving Dejima and asked me to look into it among mine own men. Of course, I agreed to give the matter my upmost attention, but I was somewhat taken aback at these charges, for there have always been rumors of men going ashore, but I have always believed them to be false. And in truth, I felt the shogun's insistence on our complete segregation rather duplicitous; for he wishes to benefit from the exchange between us yet at the same time does not approve of the VOC's Christian heritage. Nevertheless, I am bound by duty to ensure that the dealings of Son of Batavia and all those sail beneath her masts be infallible, inerrant, and beyond reproach. And this, I will do, to the very best of my ability.

FROM A LETTER ADDRESSED TO
CAPTAIN CORNELIS ONDERDONK,
BATAVIA, JAVA, DUTCH EAST INDIES

August 8, 1746

Dearest Husband, Cornelis,

In your last letter you asked about your mother. Oma Onderdonk is well, although I do believe she misses her summer walks with you. Sometimes she has spells of forgetfulness, and she asks where you are. At those times, I hardly know what to tell her, for the forlorn look that follows is enough to break Hrungnir's heart. Perhaps she can join you there next summer? I'm sure it would mean the world to her. Yet I know that it is impossible, even as I write this. For how can a VOC captain find the time to take care of his own ailing mother? It seems the only one oma misses more than you is your father. On rare nights, I hear her calling out to him into the darkness: Heike! Heike! It is a chilling wail, dear Cornelis. And by the time I reach her she is clawing at her nightdress, having very nearly torn it from off of her frail frame.

Please understand that it is not my intention to alarm you—for most days are calm and quiet and Oma Onderdonk wiles away the time sitting on a bench in the garden, talking to the bluebirds and robins. And she is not without her mischievous moments. For lately, she finds it greatly amusing to break wind in my presence. Perhaps she knows how it displeases me so. Yet, like an impish child she plays upon my nerves with her windy pranks! Forgive my impassioned digression—I do not mean to speak ill of Oma Onderdonk. In truth, I find her to be pleasant company, on the whole. Especially since I have none other near that I can call family. As you know, my sister in Paris never gives me a thought—except perhaps in passing moments to despise me. But, dear Cornelis, am I to be blamed that our father loved me best? And why would he not, the way she slinks around La Rive Gauche with dramatists and poets. I would gladly make her an equal beneficiary of father's fortune if she would simply come to me in kindness and humility. But such is never to happen—I know it and she knows it. So we shall continue on as we are now. Ah, but why do I trouble you with such affairs? You have, after all, made it clear in the past that I should do as I like where it concerns my sister, my only remaining family. I do apologize, but I

*find myself thinking more of family and how I seem to have so little left
these days. When will you next set sail for home? This year? Perhaps next?
Dear Cornelis, I do hope it is sooner rather than later. I long to see you, as
does your dear mother. Please think of me fondly, as I do you.*

Your Loving Wife,
Marijke

FIVE

The sun shone high above the verdure of the commons, sending rays of light leaking through the cracks of his shuttered windows, the same which Jakob had not bothered to open for the simple reason that he was already late. He checked his watch. 10:15. With great haste, Jakob slipped into his jacket and stepped to the door. Gertrude waited, circling impatiently. He exited his flat and started on foot for the stables. Another week of work gone, another Sabbath arrived, thought he. Another eventuality to be avoided.

"Meneer Onderdonk!" The voice of Pastor Hogarth boomed behind him. Jakob felt his jaw tense and his back go stiff. It was a natural reaction, or at least, it had come to be a natural reaction over years of similar encounters. However, it should be said that his weekly encounters with the pastor were not always so thorny; although, it was true they were never pleasant. And in fact, Jakob was not the only villager who took measures to avoid the pastor. There could be no question that Pastor Hogarth was a pillar of the community. Much like the grand *Pieters Kerk* itself, towering over the shops and homes that surrounded it, the pastor viewed himself as a formidable shepherd of souls, around whom the chosen gathered, to there be edified in the shadow of his goodness. Yet it should be said that the pastor's goodness was not the natural kind, the inborn kind. It was more a hard-wrought goodness, if *goodness* can be thought the appropriate word at all.[25]

---

[25] It would be fair to say that Willem Wilhelmus Hogarth was not born for the ministry. In actual fact, he was born to a fishmonger who had escaped from Salzburg to Amsterdam at the time of the *Emigrationspatent*. Being the youngest of three sons, and having a feminine disposition and a sickly constitution, young Willem was spared work in the fish market. Eventually, he entered divinity school, where he promptly established himself as a distinctly middling student who made up for his unexceptional intellect by instigating theological debates he was incapable of winning, only to then deploy a battery of rhetorical fallacies, until such a time as his opponents threw up their hands and he became convinced that the victory was his.

Jakob turned to address the portly priest. "Pastor Hogarth, how are you this fine Sabbath?"

"Never mind that. Where are you off to?"

"Why, I'm off to worship our Lord and Savior."

"But that's impossible, Onderdonk. One can only worship the Lord and Savior in the one true house of God. And I have yet to see you show your face there."

"Ah, but the one true house of God is in here," said he, placing a hand over his heart, "is it not?"

"Don't be absurd! How can the sinful flesh be a house of God?"

It was a good point. But Jakob was ready for it. "Is sin not washed away with the renewal of each Eucharist?"

"Hogwash! Sin is washed away through absolution from Christ's duly called and confirmed representatives on Earth."

"I see. What of those heathen souls who know no confirmed representatives of Christ the Lord on Earth?"

"Why, they shall smell their sizzling flesh and bones for all eternity. The same as all others who die in sin."

"I see. Then I must ready myself in the event that you are right."

Jakob turned and strode quickly over the cobblestone. To say that Jakob grew weary of the pastor's claim to exclusivity was an understatement of colossal proportions. He was well aware of the pastor's views on Anabaptism, and by extension, his opinion of the lay preacher Bonifaas Quackenboss. And Bonifaas was as lay as a lay

---

To his father's great pride and pleasure, Willem joined the ministry and was given a congregation in Slooterdyk. There, Pastor Hogarth preached fire and damnation with great relish for five long years before being forcibly removed from *Petrus Kerk* and sent to Leyden. According to the official church report, Pastor Hogarth's re-assignment had been routine and of no real significance, other than it was the Lord's will, of course. However, less official sources said he had told a fornicator—a young man who happened to be the son of a wealthy parishioner—that he would have a better chance of "storming the pearly gates" if he were to "lop off the fleshy sprig" that was his offending member "and toss it into the North Sea."

preacher could possibly be.[26]

"There is still time for you, Onderdonk," said Pastor Hogarth. "But take heed! Do not wait until it is too late."

The carriage lunged and lurched for the fields of *Grote Polder*. This

---

[26] The Anabaptist preacher Bonifaas Quackenboss was called to the ministry of God one summer's day by a blob of molten metal. Not coincidentally, the call happened at a time when Bonifaas was searching for answers to big questions—*the* big questions.

Repairs to the trolley wheel were almost complete when he spied the glowing drip of molten metal on the floor of the forge. The smithy dropped the hammer and tongs onto his workbench and crouched down to get a better look. He eyed the blob of metal and thought it very curious. Then cooling it in water, Bonifaas picked it up held it in his palm. The hardened blob was still warm. There was something oddly familiar about it and he stared at it until a spark of recognition sent a flare of zeal smoldering down his spine. Could this be the sign he had been looking for? he wondered, finally concluding that it must be. For what else could it be but a miracle—a sign?

Of course, Bonifaas had immediately gone in search of his wife and found her toiling in the kitchen with a scrub brush and pail of gray water. "Look, dear wife," said he. "It is a miracle!"

Katrine Quackenboss jumped to her feet at the mention of a miracle. "Are you sure?"

"See for yourself," said Bonifaas. He uncurled his fist and held out the blob.

"Why, it looks like—a goat? No, wait. It looks like a goat wearing a *shtreimel*."

"A goat wearing a *shtreimel*? No, no, look closer. It is a woman on an ass." He drew in the air above the black blob, as if to sketch out the defining lines of his perception.

"A woman on an ass?" Katrine Quackenboss narrowed her eyes and crinkled up her nose. "Perhaps, yes."

"But you must see it! It is as plain as day."

"Yes—yes. I think I see it now," said she, smiling weakly. "But what does it mean?"

"It is the Virgin Mary riding into Jerusalem. Don't you see? It is a miracle! A sign! I have been called by God!"

due to the shoeless gelding's lop-sided gait. Jakob had bought the "ball-less wonder" cheap, on account of its stubborn refusal to be shod.[27] Anneke sat close to Jakob, perhaps closer than what might be thought respectable. Yet Jakob said nothing, did nothing. For he could not deny that he enjoyed the nearness of her. Of course, Oma Onderdonk was none the wiser. She drooled unintelligible mutterings into her lap, as was her habit.

At length, Bonifaas Quackenboss appeared in the distance, standing at the turnoff, waving to the congregation as they passed. A stalwart soul and a man of God, thought Jakob. A good shepherd herding his flock to the safety of salvation through Christ the Lord. Right then a sparkle of admiration glinted in Jakob's eye, and he recalled how he had first met the lay preacher in *Neuwemarkt*.[28] What was there not to admire about Bonifaas? thought Jakob.

---

[27] In actuality, it was the farriers who had refused to shoe the old hack. In its youth, the beast had staved in the head of a young smith for a careless nail pricking and had yet to live down its murderous reputation. And so it loped lopsidedly into the future, destined to pay for the mistakes of its youth.

[28] At the time in question, Bonifaas had set down a wooden box in *Neuwemarkt* and was preaching about the ordinance of adult baptism. Jakob had stopped dead in his tracks when he heard the words "wash away your sins" echo over the chatter of the market. It was as if the words had been spoken directly to him. And for Jakob, who had only recently returned from years at sea, the idea of washing away one's sins was the same as making a new start. And to make a new start was precisely why he had abandoned the sea. He approached the preacher standing on his wooden box with his eyes closed tightly, a Bible in one hand and a black blob in the other. Jakob listened for a time, until Bonifaas, finally noticing that he was preaching to an audience of one, stepped down from the box to introduce himself.
"What's that in your hand?" asked Jakob.
"What does it look like?" asked Bonifaas.
"It looks like a blob of hardened metal."
"But look closer. What do you see?"
Jakob had stared intently into the palm of Bonifaas Quackenboss. "A woman riding on a donkey," he said.

Jakob, Anneke, and Oma Onderdonk doddered up the aisle of the meetinghouse, largely due to the fact that Oma Onderdonk refused to be rushed, swinging her bonneted head left and right, and snapping her eyelids open and shut as if she recognized faces in the crowd—which, it must be said, she did not. When at long last—a seeming eternity to Jakob—they reached the front of the meetinghouse, Bonifaas ushered them to their seats on the front pew. Katrine Quackenboss banged out a hymn, which, although unfamiliar, stirred feelings of piety in Jakob. Unlike the feelings of arousal that Anneke simultaneously—not to mention, shamefully—stirred in him. That is to say, the spirited melody hailed his inner Christian soldier, while the brush of Anneke's leg beckoned the lecherous sailor in him. Jakob fought the rising tide of desire that inched toward his *roede*, threatening to hoist that member-mast to the next passing wind of desire. But before any such thing could happen, Bonifaas stepped behind the podium and tore into his sermon.

"The apostle Paul said to the Ephesians: 'So ought men to love their wives as their own bodies. He that loveth his wife loveth himself. For no man ever yet hated his own flesh but nourisheth and cherisheth it, even as the Lord the church. For we are members of his body, of his flesh, and of his bones. For this cause shall a man leave his father and mother, and shall be joined unto his wife, and they two shall be one flesh.'"

Jakob cringed at all the talk of body members and all the loving of one's own body and the cherishing of one's own flesh. A brooding cloud of guilt gathered at the periphery of his consciousness. For what Jakob well knew was the pull of onanism upon him had in no way abated. In fact, and not surprisingly, it had increased since his meeting Anneke—exponentially, it seemed to him now. The flesh is weak, he concluded, dropping his head.

Jakob wondered if there were not others in the room who were as riddled by sin as he. Had he not felt the millstone of his shame so heavily around his neck at that moment, he may have raised his head and scanned the room, looking for others whose shoulders drooped under the weight of their sin.

Engrossed in his shame and indicted by his sin, Jakob mistimed the congregational "Amen!" that rattled the rafters and so found himself the recipient of a roomful of unwanted attention. And things took a turn for the worse, where unwanted attention was concerned, when Bonifaas Quackenboss handed him a tin basin full of water for the holy ordinance of footwashing. It should be said that it was an honor to be singled out for this holy ordinance of the Anabaptists, and Jakob had on other occasions wished to be called upon. However, this particular Sabbath day, he did not feel worthy to lick the dung dust from the hooves of a distemperate swine. Yet there stood Bonifaas, with his preacher's smile and his prophet's beard, holding out the basin. Jakob had no choice but to take it.

He dropped to one knee and, removing Anneke's shoes, dribbled silver droplets of water onto her feet. The young woman responded with an impious giggle, drawing the gaze of those within earshot. Determined now, to make the best of the situation, Jakob sunk both hands into the water. But his desire to stroke the smooth white knobs of Anneke's ankles was overwhelming. He caught himself trying to peek at the shapely shank that extended upward into folds of Antwerp *pottenkant* and imagined running a hand over that silken extremity. Aroused as he now was, Jakob desired nothing more in this world than to stick her toes into his mouth and, probing between those delicate digits with his tongue, bring her to a hee-hawing climax.

Needless to say, all the imagining, fancying, and desiring had caused Jakob's *roede* to grow fat, something that to his great horror Anneke had clearly noticed, for she sat staring intently at the swollen mound in his breeches. Of course, being Jakob, he flushed a deep red, which seemed only to encourage her, as she flashed him a less-than-coy smile. Jakob looked away, excited and confused, all the while wondering if her smile were an innocent or libidinous one.

In fact, so engrossed was he in the oddly arousing ordinance of footwashing that he hardly noticed the pronounced mutterings and random noises coming from next to him. There, Bonifaas Quackenboss, having taken it upon himself to wash the feet of Oma Onderdonk, pressed a cloth to the old woman's heels, eliciting a breathy moan and a nasally bleat from the septuagenarian that made it clear to everyone present that she was enjoying the ordinance in a way that the blessed founding father had never intended it to be enjoyed. Needless to say, Jakob began to worry. And when another, much louder, moan wheezed from his oma's lungs, he knew it was only a matter of time before she drew up her dress and revealed the pale folds of her sagging rubber thighs.

It was at this point that Katrine Quackenboss wisely—or perhaps *unwisely*, as we shall see—decided to intercede, much to Jakob's relief. Abandoning her post at the fortepiano, the preacher's wife scurried to the front pew, where the scuffle that ensued was quick and assertive, with Katrine Quackenboss handily overpowering the old woman. But for anyone who cared to notice, the look Oma Onderdonk's face made it quite clear that the battle was not over. She would not be defeated so easily—that is, she refused to be put down like some poorly planned peasant revolt.

And so it was that just when it looked as if order had been restored, the septuagenarian blasted the good preacher, who was still on bended knee, with a gusty flatus. The foul and noisome zephyr rumbled and boomed on the wooden pew. Jakob stopped abruptly the sensual foot ablutions, which had up until that moment brought with them such pleasingly licentious thoughts, and gasped. Anneke, on the other hand, squeaked and brought a hand to her nose, which she tried to plug in a decidedly ladylike manner. But it was Bonifaas Quackenboss who clearly fell furthest afoul of Oma Onderdonk's voluminous *scheet*.

The preacher dropped to the floor, where he convulsed and gyrated, and jabbered the gibberish of dotards and halfwits. He croaked out words, streams of guttural dissonance that sounded painful to utter.[29] Here it should be said that Jakob had heard about

---

[29] Although unaware of it himself, Bonifaas Quackenboss had been mildly epileptic since he was very young. Before the Anabaptist meeting in question, he had had only one other seizure, a mild one when just a boy. Having slumbered with his head near the rump of a particularly gassy Poitou ass, he awoke later, feeling dazed and sore, but having no idea what had actually happened. The same methanethiol and hydrogen sulfide that had triggered

enthusiasm before, and he was well aware of the fact that the Anabaptists were known for it. What he did not know and what he had never considered was that enthusiasm could be so intense and strenuous, so galvanic.

As Jakob pondered this very thing, Katrine Quackenboss threw her arms up in the air and cried out, "Hallelujah!" And the congregation responded with an exuberant "Hallelujah!" of its own. Jakob stood dumbfounded among them. To say this was a side of the Anabaptists he had never seen before would be tantamount to saying that a man who takes a horse's hoof in the *testikels* falls down—both being seriously understated, self-evident truths. Quite simply, it was something to behold, a spectacle. From the corner of his eye, Jakob spied Anneke raising her arms to heaven. And not to be excluded, Oma Onderdonk raised her own hands high, each with a fistful of her taffeta dress, and, prancing around the prostrate preacher, yawped "*Coïteren! Coïteren! Coïteren!*" Admittedly, a long and confused pause ensued before Jakob finally raised his own hands high in the air and shouted, "Hallelujah!"

---

this early seizure were also present in particularly large doses in the flatus of Oma Onderdonk. As he washed the septuagenarian's feet, the close proximity of Bonifaas's olfactory organ to the emission point resulted in an epileptic seizure, the same which was hailed by the congregations as a manifestation of enthusiasm, or more specifically, an instance of speaking in tongues.

FROM THE JOURNAL OF JAKOB ONDERDONK

December 24, 1746

Today, we dropped anchor on the west coast port of Cochin, despite Father's concerns about the unrest routinely caused by warlords in the area. To be sure, there are times when the men need to dig their toes into the soft soil of the earth, if only for a short spell, regardless of outlying circumstances. And it turned out this was one of those times.

The distance between Robrecht and I is greater now than ever, even six months after our promotions. Clearly it is a more than a simple point of contention with my brother—he being advanced to third mate and I to first—but runs much deeper into the depths of his exclusion. I do not envy Second Mate Bleeker, caught as he is between us, like a wharf continuously butted by two ships docked on either side.

Still, in an unusual turn of events, we ended up exploring the harbor market side-by-side. In actuality, not side-by-side but with Robrecht slightly forward, as is his habit. In the midst of our exploration, an ox and cart rolled by with a bloody mass of flesh on its bed. Then behind it came another carrying a great head with gray ears and a flaccid trunk that dragged in the dust. Two ivory stubs were all that remained of the beast's tusks. Its mouth, like a small red sliver, hung open for all to see. The sight of it caused a profound sadness to settle over me. Clearly, it was one of the Moghuls' elephants, hacked to pieces on the battlefield and now being towed away to be devoured by half-starved peasant-soldiers. As we stood there, another procession of carts passed by us—each with a bloody body part and each body part unidentifiable, save for the head. Robrecht seemed to take great delight in the gruesome spectacle and a smile flickered there on his lips.

We made our way farther into the market, looking for curios and keepsakes, and came upon a booth selling inkwells of every kind. On some were men with many hands and on others were women with many heads. Still others depicted men and women in ardent embrace, attempting coitus from every imaginable angle. As I examined these, Robrecht picked up a finely crafted inkwell of a strangely human-looking elephant. He turned it around and around in his hands, examining it closely. Clearly, he was fascinated with it. A small brown man appeared: "Ganapati, Ganapati. Good, good!" he kept saying. But Robrecht seemed not to notice the man executing an enthusiastic merchant's dance before him.

It occurred to me then that it was Christmas Eve day; and I decided I would like to purchase the inkwell for Robrecht. Although I knew he would never accept my charity, I believed that he might accept a Christmas gift from me. So I pushed three stuivers into the little man's hand and wished Robrecht a Happy Christmas. He turned and looked at me like I'd just then told him the stars were dropping into the sea. And just as he was set to refuse my offer (it was quite clear in the look of consternation that set his nostrils aflare), the grisly seaman companion of his, Dag, appeared. Caught off guard, as he was, Robrecht slipped the inkwell into his pocket and sauntered away with Able Seaman Dag without so much as another word. I do not know what ever became of the inkwell, for I have not set eyes upon it since that day. However, at the time, a great sense of satisfaction settled over me and I went on my way through the market alone. I had given my brother a Christmas gift.

FROM THE JOURNAL OF ROBRECHT ONDERDONK

May 30, 1748

"What makes one man behave with such cruelty and haste towards another?" These were my father's exact words upon hearing that last night one deckhand stabbed another through the hand while in the throes of a winning game of Landsknecht. That the question was directed at me and not my brother came as no surprise. Perhaps father knew I would have my say anyway. "The fool tried to take what was not his to take," I said. "Who would not do the same and stab the thieving buzzard?" Of course, even as I said it, I knew that father would not, nor would my brother. Here the second mate, Bleeker, piped up: "Even so," said he, "stabbing is rather a harsh retaliation, is it not?" Of course, I was not surprised that Meneer Bleeker saw fit to contradict me, for he is a lickspittle of the worst sort, hoping to find favor with father by seconding his every fart and fancy.

The premise of the impromptu gathering this morning was to determine what action should be taken concerning the two deckhands. Father undoubtedly saw this as a moment to test his officers' wisdom and resolve in maintaining order upon the decks of Son of Batavia. To that end, he asked us each for our judgment. Jakob said that the deckhand willfully harmed another aboard a VOC vessel and should be made to run the gauntlet as punishment. To this he added, "And his rum rations should be cut." Father nodded gravely and looked pleased with this judgment. Then he turned to the second mate. Meneer Bleeker said the seaman's actions called for a flogging — "Twenty lashes," said he. Father hummed thoughtfully, as if flogging were also reasonable punishment. At this point, I did not hesitate, nor did I wait to be called upon. "Forty lashes," I said. "Forty?" repeated Father. To which I replied: "Forty lashes to the fool who laid his hand upon the money of another." I must admit that Father's reaction was amusing. I thought he might choke upon the gall of his own displeasure at hearing me say such a thing. "Forty lashes for the deckhand who was stabbed?" said he. "Indeed, yes," said I, "for he got off lightly." Ha! It was priceless! A moment to savor! Jakob shot to his feet like some sanctimonious windbag priest and protested loudly, but father wished to hear me out. "Was the deckhand's foolishness not at the root of it all?" I said. "It is he that should be punished, not the seaman who was protecting what was rightfully his."

Father was silent for a time; he looked upon me and yet he seemed not to see me at all (in truth, it is a look I have become accustomed to). Finally, he spoke: "To punish the deckhand who acted foolishly is to reward the deckhand who showed no restraint and caused bodily harm to another." I could not help but smile at such fallacy, such moralistic bosh. "But is the opposite not also true?" said I. Father sighed deeply. "Very well," said he. "Flogging for both men." Surely the smug look upon my face was evident to all present. As I made to rise and take my leave, father placed a firm hand on my shoulder. "Third Mate Onderdonk," said he. "You will personally see to the flogging of the stabbed deckhand. And in so doing, I hope you will come to realize that words have consequences, too . . . your words." Such stale platitudes! Such didactic bunk! For the consequence is the very meaning of the word, and there can be no other. There are only consequences, Father. And that is truth! There is the loophole in your knot of existence! Of course, I said nothing of the sort. For although he is my father, he is also my superior, my captain. Instead, my response was quick and simple: "As you say, Captain, sir."

SIX

The events of this Sabbath seemed unlikely, even for someone who had essentially been brought up within earshot of a ship's bell and all the clang and clamor that accompanies it. Not surprisingly, Jakob was having some difficulty processing the events rationally, finally placing them into one of two mental compartments: *improbable* or *enigmatic*. It would be fair to say that this day he experienced feelings of doubt concerning Bonifaas Quackenboss and the Anabaptists. Try as he might, Jakob simply could not imagine his Lord and Savior rolling spasmodically on the ground, slobbering half-masticated speech from His blessed mouth. It weighed heavy on his mind as he returned from the stables. Only as he rounded the corner did the very real possibility of having a run in with his pastor neighbor strike him. He checked his watch. 6:04. When Jakob spied the considerable figure of Christ the Lord's earthly representative up the lane, he very nearly turned and retreated the way the he had come. That is, until he noticed that the lavishly robed pastor was haranguing a young stranger dressed all in blue — a tattered uniform, it would soon become clear. Thinking he might slip by the pastor unnoticed, Jakob continued down the lane to his flat but could not help but overhear the exchange.

"Answer me this, friend, then we shall see about a scrap for you," said the Pastor. "Do you hold the Pope to be the Antichrist?"

"But, good sir, I know nothing of the Pope." said the stranger. "I only know that I am in need of bread, or I soon perish," One look at the lanky youth with no discernible girth and Jakob knew he spoke the truth — he would soon perish for lack of food.

"You, scoundrel, are no Christian! Away with you!"

With this remark, Jakob could simply no longer remain quiet. It was one thing to be braced for an encounter with the pastor — and it should be said that Jakob always maintained a certain state of readiness where the pastor was concerned — but quite another to walk into a theological ambush without the necessary provisions for evasion. Jakob stopped and turned on his heels. "But good Pastor Hogarth," said he, "perhaps a scrap of bread to sharpen the young man's wits. Then you might tell him of the Antichrist, as you see it."

"Ha! As *I* see it, says he." The pastor leveled a jeweled finger in Jakob's direction. "This coming from the Anabaptist who has not even the resolve to follow the effortless, nay heretical, path of adult baptism to a false salvation of men."

"It is true that I lack resolve and that I have only recently come to the fold of Christ the Lord. But is not charity due every featherless biped possessing a soul?"

"Fool! Blasphemer! Charity is goodwill extended only to believers in the one true Christ and his duly appointed representatives. This rascal is no believer! Now away with you both!"

Jakob turned to the young man and was about to offer some consolatory words when the shutters above them flew open and a vile stew of *rioolwater* rained down upon the stranger.

"Perhaps that will sharpen your wits, then," said the pastor's buxom wife in a fit of Christian zeal.

"Indeed!" said the pastor, the look upon his face swinging back and forth between indignation and amusement like a watchman's lantern.

The young man spit, wiped *schijt* from his eyes. Behind the mask of *poep* and *pis* Jakob discerned a soul in need of help. And despite the dousing, the stranger's crystalline eyes retained a still blue spark of hope. His long straight nose registered integrity. And his slender lips bespoke virtue.

"What is your name?" asked Jakob.

"I am Candide," said the young man.

Jakob placed a hand on the young man's shoulder. "Come inside, Candide. We shall get you cleaned up and fed, Christian or not."

"Then you are not one of those who holds the Pope to be the Antichrist, kind sir?"

"No, I am not one of those. I am an Anabaptist. You may call me Jakob."

Sloshing *bier* into a tankard, Jakob watched Candide devour a wedge of cheese and a loaf of bread. Candide gulped back the *bier*.

His appetite sated, the young guest recounted a tale of unequalled woe that had brought him here.[30]

When it was over, Jakob, feeling a deep fraternal tenderness for

---

[30] Having been turned out of the castle of Baron Thunder-Ten-Tronckh on the toe of the noble baron's boot for a slight indiscretion with the fair Cunégonde, Candide had wandered a spell through Westphalia, until he found himself in the unremarkable town of Wald-berghoff-trarbkdikdorff. There, finding an Inn, and believing that all was for the best, he was conscripted into the army of Frederick the Great, King of Prussia. Through a rigorous regiment of training and abuse, Candide proved himself a worthy soldier, being thereafter viewed by his brothers-in-arms as a prodigy, of sorts.

However, all of that changed when, deciding to exercise his prerogative as a human and member of a bipedular species, Candide one day embarked on an excursion into the countryside. Before he had passed two leagues, he was seized by Prussian soldiers and charged with abandoning his post. At his court-martial, Candide was given the choice of running the gauntlet thirty and six times or being shot through the head with a dozen lead balls. Exercising his divinely wrought right to free will, Candide chose to run the gauntlet. However, after running it twice, with the flesh hanging from his back, the young man begged to be shot through the head with a dozen lead balls. Complying, the commanding officer ordered the prisoner blindfolded.

Just as it appeared to be over for Candide, the King of Prussia himself happened by and asked what circumstances had brought this young man to stand quivering before a firing squad. Candide was allowed to speak, and it immediately became clear to the King that the young man was a philosopher, and thus wholly ignorant of the ways of the world. The King pardoned Candide on the spot. Three weeks later, Candide, having recuperated from his wounds, marched side-by-side with the others into noble battle. By the end of that particular noble battle, thirty-six thousand men had been butchered in every conceivable way. But Candide, being a philosopher and not a soldier, had hidden himself in a bloody heap of heroic corpses until in the aftermath he took the opportunity to flee the carnage.

And so, he wandered from village to village, each razed to ruins and cluttered with dismembered body parts until at length he arrived beyond the theater of war in neutral Holland. There, with holes in his pockets and a void in his heart that only his fair Cunégonde could fill, he hoped to impose on some good Christian soul for a small share of Christian charity.

the young interloper, decided that he would do whatever he could to help.

"It is a terrible tale for one as young as you to tell." Jakob rose and went in search of clean clothes. "Here," said he. "You'd better put these on. You'll not want to be seen in a Prussian uniform." He took two coins from the pouch tucked inside his trousers. "And take these. You may need a gulder or two."

"I don't know how to thank you enough for your kindness," said Candide. "Master Pangloss was surely right when he said that everything is for the best in this world."

It then occurred to Jakob that the advent of his guest's unexpected arrival might prove fortuitous for them both, for the young man looked able-bodied. "I am a factory owner who manufactures carpets after the manner of Persia," said he. "And it happens that I am in need of a loom operator. Do you know anything about weaving carpet?"

"I do not. But I assure you that I have a strong back and I am willing to learn, good Anabaptist," said Candide.

"It's settled then. You can start tomorrow."

As the two shook hands, a terse rap came to the door. Jakob jumped to his feet and mouthed a single word to his young friend: *authorities*. Only as the word silently crossed his lips did it occur to Jakob that his act of charity may have put him in harm's way. He motioned for Candide to be still. A part of him hoped it was the blowhard pastor simply wishing to reiterate his earlier point with another pot of *rioolwater*. But when he cracked the door, he saw neither the authorities nor the pastor. Instead, a scruffy boy handed him a note. Jakob closed the door, leaned his back against it and, unfolding the parchment, read it:

Must see you, tonight. It is urgent. Bonifaas

Jakob left quickly—so quickly, in fact, that his young friend Candide scarcely had time to bid him farewell. By the time he reached the outskirts of Leyden, twilight had begun to smear the edges of the sky. Jakob could not imagine what had happened that would cause Bonifaas to send such a message. Another unprecedented act this day, thought he—first the ordinance of footwashing and now this. By the time Jakob's carriage veered into the dirt lane that led to the cottage of Bonifaas Quackenboss, he was consumed by curiosity. No sooner had he halted the ball-less wonder than the preacher appeared from out the darkness—seemingly from nowhere—and rushed him inside. It is fair to say that at this point Jakob was apprehensive—although *apprehensive* may not be entirely accurate, as Jakob'a present state of unease combined with the uncommon events earlier in the day might warrant something closer to *alarmed*. However, it soon became clear that his alarm was unfounded. For Bonifaas was glowing with delight. Clearly, whatever had prompted the preacher to send him an urgent message was no grave or jeopardous circumstance. Bonifaas was animated in a way that Jakob had never known him before, not even in the throes of a particularly inspiring sermon. Thus, despite his curiosity, Jakob could not keep himself from grinning.

Bonifaas spoke feverishly: "I've had a vision, I tell you, Jakob, a vision! It was marvelous! Can you believe it?"

"A vision?" said Jakob. "But how? Why? I mean, when?"

"It was all because of your Oma Onderdonk. Like the oracle of Delphi sniffing the fumes of the slain python, I sniffed the rotten fumes of Oma Onderdonk's tremendous *winderigheid* and was struck with a vision from God. It's a miracle, I tell you. A miracle."

For Jakob, the unsavory detail concerning Oma Onderdonk caused a cognitive stumble as his mind raced to keep up with Bonifaas's rather oblique explantion. He wondered if he had heard Bonifaas correctly. Finally, he stammered: "Oma Onderdonk? My oma?"

"Yes, isn't it wonderful? The old woman is surely an instrument of the Almighty."

"But there must be a mistake. Could it not have been something else you sniffed? The butcher's feet, perhaps?"

"There's no mistake. Praise the Lord! God has seen fit to communicate with me a lowly mortal of flesh and blood through Oma Onderdonk's blessed *aars*."

"Yes, praises to God," said Jakob with a tone and gesture meant to demonstrate some modicum of conviction yet falling pitifully short of it. "What, then, was this vision?"

"In this vision, I saw the whole of Europe awash in blood. There were blue uniforms and red uniforms. There was fire and destruction, with every act of cruelty known to man being wantonly committed." A tear leaked from the preacher's eye as he spoke.

"But Bonifaas, the land has been plagued by just such a war for the past decade. And another is in the making at this very moment. Have you not heard? Why, this very day I took in a deserter from the ranks of the Prussian army. He was flogged to within an inch of his life. And he has seen the cruelties of war firsthand."

"No, I had not heard."

Jakob was dumbfounded by this revelation—not the supposed revelation that had issued forth from Oma Onderdonk's blessed *aars* but the revelation that Bonifaas was ignorant of the war that had raged for years across the land. It was true that the Dutch remained largely neutral in these matters, but it seemed unlikely—nay, impossible—that the preacher could have heard nothing of the conflict. It was, after all, one thing to be opposed to war and quite another to be entirely ignorant of it.

"But isn't a vision from the Almighty meant to forewarn or perhaps to instruct?" said Jakob. "What is to be made of your vision, then? What could it mean?

"I don't know what it could mean. But it is enough that God has chosen to speak to me. The details will sort themselves out soon enough."

If the events of this Sabbath day seemed unlikely to Jakob before, they had now taken an abrupt turn towards the peculiar. The mystery of it all lay as unilluminated as the road through *Grote Polder*, from which the ball-less wonder very nearly veered several times upon Jakob's return to Leyden this moonless night. He found Candide slumbering soundly with Gertrude curled up on his chest. The young man hailing from the flatlands of Westphalia looked oddly angelic slumbering there. Jakob extinguished the lantern and sat at the table. A glut of blackness filled the room. He heard the faint rhythm of an alternating wheeze and purr.

There was much to think about, consider. It had, after all, been an eventful day. But it would have to wait. For he was tired and the workweek lay ahead. Jakob kicked off his brass buckled shoes and tugged at his white stockings. He rose and readied himself to retire to bed. Pouring water into a basin, Jakob splashed his face and looked into the mirror at his unspectacular mug. He was no prince, to be sure. But neither was he a toad. It was then, in the corner of the mirror, that he detected a yellow tongue of light lapping at the corners of the room across the lane. With all the uncommon events of the day, he had forgotten what night it was.

Jakob felt a sudden, strong repulsion for the pastor's buxom wife and even more so for his own weakness. For it seemed to him that that weakness lurked in the shadows of his every coming and going, waiting for any opportunity to step out into the light of day and be seen—a constant reminder of his sinful state. In that moment, Jakob realized that he was indeed a slave to his sin. Onanism was no longer the pleasant pastime it had once been. It was now something beyond his control, something that demanded his attention, no matter the time of day or night. It was a need, a millstone. What Jakob could not have known was that on this Sabbath night—as on every other Sabbath night—when the pastor's buxom wife disrobed and stood before the window, she was iniquitously proud of her immense bosom and pleased to present it to the world outside.

Jakob's pulse quickened with a blaze of desire in spite of himself. To the point that he feared the sound of his own heart beating might awaken slumbering Candide. And although his soul was sickened by the prospect of another onanistic orgy of one, he knew that he stood powerless before it. And so, admitting defeat with the greedy grip of his *roede*, he dropped down onto the bench and, turning his back to his sleeping guest, went about his sinful ways.

FROM A LETTER ADDRESSED TO
MEVROUW MARIJKE ONDERDONK,
LEYDEN, SOUTH HOLLAND

October 4, 1741

Dearest Mother,

It seems that I have been to sea so long! And so long since I have seen you, even though it was only fourteen months ago that Robrecht and I bid farewell to the landlubber's life. Such a strange word, "landlubber," and an unkind word, too. Father says a "lubber" is a lazy lout. But why is the man who lives upon land thought to be lazy? Does he not toil for his bread, just as the sailor at sea? Unfortunately, dear mother, it is a word which often crosses the lips of seamen. And I am afraid it is far from the worst word I have heard cross the profane lips of these men upon the Son of Batavia. At times, it seems they have nothing else to say and nothing better to do than to curse Heaven and Earth and all things in between (as father says). Dear Mother, sometimes I wish to silence them with a brave rebuke, but I fear I am too young to protest. Robrecht does not seem bothered by the seamen and their churlish ways; and in fact, he oft times seems to aspire to their level of depravity. But do not worry, Mother, for father keeps a close eye upon us both.

I have learned much about life at sea, thanks to father. Implicitly, I have learned that the sea is the most mysterious of all God's creations. It is deep and fathomless and can no more be known to men than the stars above. Already, I have seen the many different faces of the sea and have learned which of those faces one must shudder before. Yet there are times of unparalleled calm and quietude (again, as father says) and it is those times that a young deckhand such as I am comes to cherish.

In fact, two nights previous was just such a time — that is, until we soaked the night air with cacophonous canon fire. "Were we faced off for broad fire against our French foes?" you ask. No, not that. Were we in hot pursuit of Arabian pirates? No, again. For the cannon fire was in your honor — forty-one lead balls blasting from sulfurous clouds and landing in the night sea, there sinking and bubbling to some unknown end. Forty-one lead balls for forty-one years — the same years you have graced God's Green Earth. Surely, you did not think we would forget, did you? In this way did we honor you, dear Mother. Although I knew it could not be so, I imagined each shot reverberating around this magnificent orb and chiming in your ear.

I do hope that on the anniversary of your birth you spent a pleasant evening with Oma Onderdonk. For she is all the family that remains close by your side. Rest assured, we were all thinking of you as the cannons fired one by one into the starry blackness. And we are thinking of you still. So Happy Birthday, dear Mother! Perhaps fate will have it that we shall be there for your next.

Your Loving Son,
Jakob

FROM A LETTER ADDRESSED TO
CAPTAIN CORNELIS ONDERDONK,
BATAVIA, JAVA, EAST INDIES

April 5, 1743

Dearest Cornelis,

Surely you will be shocked and disappointed to learn that our fair Leyden has been turned into a cirque de rédemption in this season when the Lord was reputed to have risen from the grave. The Papists and Reformists are at each other's throats day and night, like two sisters fighting over the same handsome suitor. The only time they loosen their deadly grip upon one another is to clasp arms and attack the Anabaptists. Surely this is not the way God in heaven would have them act. Indeed, Menno Simons's Rebaptists are a peculiar lot (I have heard they writhe and shiver and speak with the tongue of Lucifer himself in their secret meetings), but surely they do not need further persecution to drive the point home, as it were.

Myself, I am afraid to venture across the street to pay my respects to our Lord and Savior, for fear of getting caught up in some mob of Zwingli's thugs. I know, dear, I can hear your righteous rebuke reverberating in my ears from halfway around the globe. I can hear you say that I always have an excuse for what in truth is simply my lapsed faith. Perhaps it is true — my faith has lapsed. I admit it. Try as I might I simply cannot bring myself to enter the monstrosity that lurks so precipitously about the herenhuis. Were it not for the christenings of our own flesh and blood I would not have ever breached the shadowy vault of its archway (not even those few times when common courtesy and family commitments made my appearance there obligate).

I must apologize, dear husband, but you know by now that I am not the church-going sort. My father forbade it on the grounds of common sense. You, on the other hand, believe the provenance of common sense to be God, Himself, and thus, common sense dictates that one worship God in His own Holy House. But I wonder how often you find yourself able to set foot in the House of God? Surely, they are few and far between in the heathen lands you wander so purposefully about. But of course, you would say something such as God would have you worship in whatever way you can upon the deck of your Christian ship. Although undoubtedly, dear, you would put it much more eloquently than I could ever hope to do.

Forgive me, but I must keep this correspondence short, for Oma Onderdonk and I have been invited to an Easter feast at the Schoonhoven herenhuis. (I do not fear any confrontation with a man of the cloth there, but I must admit to wondering if I might inadvertently bump into one of her many young stallion suitors. Oh, forgive me again—my wicked tongue at times gets the better of me! 'Tis only an idle rumor among VOC widows.) It seems that I encounter Mevrouw Schoonhoven once a year, and at such times we both feel strangely obliged to dine in each other's presence, if only to reassure ourselves that misery does indeed love company.

At least she has no sons at sea to cause her worry. And I must say that I have often wondered why she and Captain Schoonhoven have never seen fit to bless their union with offspring. Aside from a nicht who visits from time to time, as far as I can tell, no child has ever set foot in the Schoonhoven herenhuis. 'Tis strange indeed. But if rumors be true (which I'm sure they are not), perhaps theirs is a marriage in name only. What do I mean by such a thing? I hear you spouting your objection like a poor soul sickened by plague. Dear husband, not every union is fired by the usual passions of men and women. Oh, yes, Mevrouw Schoonhoven is yet young and beautiful, and undoubtedly draws male attentions aplenty (if rumors be true)! However, Captain Schoonhoven strikes me as a passionless man, a gelding or eunuch, one wholly ignorant of what tickles and pleases a woman. Oh, Cornelis! 'Tis no sin to speak of such things to one's own husband! For you are a man who knows the inlets and coves of a woman and how to arrive at those secret spots on schedule and with cargo intact. Need I say more than that? Yes, 'tis enough said but not enough done, unfortunately. For how I do miss you and your pleasure rides! Please do come home soon! It is all that I am living for. 'Tis the reason I am here, dear Cornelis.

Your Loving (and Lonely) Wife,
Marijke

SEVEN

The previous night's *bier* and spirits thumped in Robrecht's temples. He cracked his eyes like two clackers being shucked and raised himself onto his elbows. A bleating nanny goat brought him to his senses, and the previous night's debauchery started to become clear to him. Dag and the nanny were crammed in a wooden tub, sharing a hot bath, and it should be said that the seaman's stringy hair and beard made him look remarkably like his companion. With bleary eyes, Robrecht followed a trail of silk garments that ended at his bed. The Chinese *biǎo* looked much older in the light of day than in the dim enclave that was the brothel—although *older* may not fairly describe the aged and slatternly woman that Robrecht saw before him. And although it would be fair to say that the *biǎo* was old enough to be his mother, it should be duly noted that his mother was neither Chinese nor a whore.

"Good morning, sir," said Dag. "Ye remember Agnes, don't ye? From last night?" Uncertain as to whether the sailor now referred to the elderly Chinese whore in his bed or the nanny goat in the tub, Robrecht grunted in a way that could be interpreted in neither the affirmative nor the negative. He was not surprised that he had once again landed outside the city walls—in Glodok. The truth was every time he returned to Batavia, Robrecht ended up in Glodok. Not that he minded greatly, or at all, for that matter. He was, in actuality, partial to the seedy Chinatown. And despite the fact that VOC officers typically shunned the splendidly licentious quarter, it was Robrecht's kind of place.[31]

---

[31] Robrecht was a few months short of ten years old when he had first ventured into Glodok. Their father had, of course, always made it clear that the quarters were off limits to him and Jakob. But the way that other sailors spoke of it (particularly, Able Seaman Dag), with an oddly gleeful sort of reverential awe, had caused young Robrecht to form a larger-than-life image of the place. So much so, that the young cabin boy became determined to see it for himself. He had even tried to convince Jakob to join him in his

determination—going so far as to argue that firsthand experience was the
only way to know anything for oneself. But when the time came, just as
Robrecht suspected, Jakob would not go against their father's wishes.

"Hurry up before they close the gates." Robrecht had said, flapping his
arms.

"We'll be locked out," said Jakob.

"Yes, we will. Now, come on."

"I'm sorry. I cannot. Father forbids it."

"Father will never find out." Robrecht spied a VOC guard marching for
the gate. He ducked behind the wall and listened to the dry grind of the gate
swinging closed. His brother's loud whisper, "Father forbids it," still hissed in
Robrecht's ears as he stole away from the city walls to Glodok. He would
experience the forbidden precinct alone.

He wound up and down the narrow streets until he came upon a temple.
There he paused to regard the curled up corners of the structure, which made
it seem like a friendly place—even a happy place. This in contrast to its
glaring red clay tiles that looked angry in the setting sun. Robrecht stepped
forward, hesitated, then turned and shuffled off down the street.

Returning to a tea shop that he had earlier passed, the boy pushed
through a small-paned door and took a seat on a backless chair. Here, he
would begin his experience, thought young Robrecht. A Chinaman in a red
silk robe appeared, eyed him suspiciously, and finally spoke. The words came
fast and sounded nasally. The man's wispy beard shifted unnaturally with the
rigid movements of his jaw. Robrecht responded by making a drinking
motion. The man held out his hand, palm up, waiting—a gesture that
prompted Robrecht to shrug his shoulders. "I have no money."

The man turned and walked away.

"Something to drink! Please. My father is an important man in the VOC."

This time the Chinaman shrugged his shoulders and left. A few minutes
later, a porcelain jug and cup sat before the young boy. Robrecht put his nose
the jug and the fumes made him light-headed. He took a gulp. It burned his
throat and dropped like a blob of fiery lava to his stomach. He took another
and another. Until he felt his body swaying on the chair.

The Chinaman grinned proudly when Robrecht stumbled from the tea
shop back into the street. He had said something and laughed, shedding the
weight of his prior stoop and standing straight in the doorway. Robrecht
could still hear him chortling as he rounded the corner and walked headlong
into the bare and sunken chest of another Chinaman. The jolt turned him
immediately sober. The boy's eye traced the jagged scar running from the

Dag toweled himself off then scooped Agnes from the gray suds. "Sir, may Old Dag offer ye some tea?"

Robrecht nodded. Dag poured then wrung a splash of milk from the nanny's teat. "Last night, sir, ye mentioned a new assignment for which Old Dag's assistance would be needed. 'Invaluable assistance,' were the words ye used."

"Yes, well, I was into my cups by then."

Dag frowned. Robrecht rose and dressed. "Nonetheless it's true. I'll be needing your assistance once we get to the Banda Islands— Bandanaira to be precise."

---

man's chin to his ear, the same ear which looked to have had a bite taken out of it. Before he could flee, the man latched on to him. Robrecht fought wildly, managing to wiggle free, only to have his sleeve snagged by a bony hand. One final tug tore the sleeve, sending the Chinaman flailing backwards to the ground.

Robrecht turned and raced away without looking back. When he finally stopped, he found himself once again outside of the temple. This time he entered the strangely exotic-looking place. The air inside was heavy with sweet smelling incense. Gold statues lined the walls. Against the back wall sat a large Buddha, its golden belly swollen as if a gleaming bubble of hope. Robrecht approached it, took a crimson-black plum from the wooden bowl set before it, and crawled under the pedestal table. The plum was sour, but he was hungry. And when it was gone, he ate another. Then he let his eyelids slide shut and he dropped off into sleep. He awoke to the sound of soft swiping feet on the wooden floor. When a bald-headed monk in a yellow robe tried to offer him a bowl of rice, Robrecht pushed by him and ran out into the street. And he kept running—all the way from Glodok to the gates of the city. But somewhere between the Chinatown and Batavia, the boy's fear turned to an almost delirious excitement. For he had experienced something in Glodok that changed his youthful view of the world. Not all was as it seemed, he realized in the simple rendering of a child's comprehension. Not all was good and honorable in this world. And for young Robrecht, there was something thrilling in this simple fact. For him, it was as if on that morning long ago the colors of the sky and earth—the dirt road, the brick and plaster buildings, the gleaming sea—had suddenly become not just brighter and more vibrant but also richer—the deeper shades of a complex and multifarious world.

"Bandanaira, sir?"

"Yes, there's some trouble there we need to take care of. Local trouble. We ship out at high tide. Finish your tea. Then gather the others and start preparations."

"Aye, sir. But might I have a moment to bid my Agnes farewell?"

"As you like," said Robrecht. He stepped for the door, taking a last glance at the soundly slumbering middle-aged *biǎo*. He patted his pockets as in search of a guilder or two.

"Don't ye think twice about it, sir. The *hoer* is on old Dag."

"Thank you, Dag. Very good of you."

"Make no mention of it, sir."

The Banda Islands lay scattered amidst the Spice Islands, over a thousand nautical miles to the east of Batavia. The nutmeg grown there was not only the finest in all of the Orient, it was the sole source of the highly prized spice. And the VOC guarded the islands like a jealous lover.

Robrecht had heard tell of the Bandanese locals' scarcely contained hatred for Dutch *perkeniers*. In fact, Captain Roorback, stately on the quarterdeck with his hands clasped behind his back, looking seaward, was presently articulating that very point.

"It is a mystery to me, Meneer Onderdonk, this hatred that stirs the locals to rise up against their masters. For the fathers and grandfathers of the *perkeniers* whom they are so quick to abuse were allotted land for their plantations from Governor-General Coen himself. It goes against every pretense of reason and order in this lawless land."

"Truly, it boggles the mind," replied Robrecht, but his interest was feigned and his mind elsewhere. The truth was the first mate knew very little about the VOC's attempts to solidify its monopoly of the nutmeg and mace trade—although *attempts* may be understating it.[32]

---

[32] Governor-General Coen gathered the Bandanese *pribumi* leaders, or *orang kaya*, in the early seventeenth century and with flint-lock barrels nestled firmly against their spines forced them to sign an impossibly one-sided treaty. When, predictably, the *orang kaya* failed to live up to their end of the bargain,

Himself, Robrecht had never been beyond Fort Belgica on the shores of the main island, Bandanaira. He knew little of the islands' land-dwelling *pribumi*, and he cared even less about the *why* or the *how* of their present circumstances. He only cared about getting them back into the orchards. And he was prepared to take harsh measures to do so. If he had to burn down a village or two, if he had to spill some blood to do it, he would. It was that simple.

"Land ahoy!" came the cry from the crow's nest.

"Land ahoy," said Second Mate Bleeker, inciting a flurry of activity on the spar deck. The captain snapped a spyglass open and held it to his eye. "Just as I feared," said he.

"What is it?" said Robrecht.

"The *pribumi* have overtaken the fort. Drop Anchor. Arm the men and dispatch the whaleboats. I'll not risk the ship to the likes of heathen."

"Drop Anchor! Ready whaleboats!" cried Second Mate Bleeker. "Take arms! We're going ashore!"

Captain Roorback stood at the helm of the foremost whaleboat, while Robrecht took his place at the helm of a second, cutting slightly arrear to the first. The captain's rally cry of "Onward, men!" punctuated the grunts and groans of rowing sailors drenched in sweat, as the boiling sun beat down mercilessly on their bare backs.

Coen had readily reacted with a mighty show of force. Sailing to the Islands, ships teeming with VOC soldiers and Japanese mercenaries, he cried out, "Despair not, spare your enemies not, for God is with us," and proceeded to slaughter the local *pribumi* in truly Biblical fashion until less than a thousand remained. In the end, the *orang kaya* were beheaded by the Japanese mercenaries and their heads were mounted on bamboo spikes outside the walls of Fort Nassau. The Dutch *perkeniers* were finally allotted the land that was rightfully theirs yet were then faced with the problem of a shortage of slaves to work in the nutmeg orchards. Coen addressed the problem as he did all others, with a show of righteous force and the threat of divine justice. Shortly after the massacre, the Banda Islands were re-populated with Chinese and Malay slaves and the nutmeg and mace trade once again flourished.

Robrecht watched the emerald waters of the tropical sea sparkle and sluice beneath the bow like silver ribbon cut asunder. At that moment, he had to admit that in all his travels, these were surely the most remarkable waters he had ever seen. But even as he thought it, from the corner of his eye, Robrecht spied a shadow dart beneath the boat. Looking deep into the clear waters as if hoping to divine what lay ahead in the near future—that is, the next few moments—he had turned his full attention to the shadow when another followed the first. At that moment, Robrecht knew it was not simply some mischievous sea nymph playing tricks on his eyes (for he had seen such tricks before). Another shadow streaked under the whaleboat. Then another and another. It could only mean one thing.

But as he let out the warning cry "Hold fast!" the shadows emerged in a maleficent mayhem of spiked teeth, thrashing fins, and beady black eyes. Robrecht felt the whaleboat beneath him rock, felt his weight pitch forward just as the firm hand of Dag clutched his sleeve. In that life-and-death moment, he clearly saw that one of the demonic beasts had its vile eyes set upon him, and in those eyes, Robrecht recognized something—something ancient and endless. There, a whole world of darkness opened up before him, an abyss that asked nothing more than simply letting go. Robrecht recoiled from the sight of it, and the enormous force of the beast's jaws snapping shut sent a shudder down his spine.[33]

---

[33] It should here be said that Robrecht's clear fascination with death stemmed at least in part from the fact that death seemed to follow him around. Or conversely, it could be said that he followed death around. Which proceeded which was unclear, and in fact, was somewhat of a moot point. The fact was wherever Robrecht went, death was there also. There was no satisfactory explanation for the phenomenon, at least not one that did not involve supernatural forces and the like. Quite simply, Robrecht had been around death for the whole of his life at sea. And thus had he acquired a morbid fascination with it.

One of his earliest recollections of death occurred near the lush islands of Riau, southeast of Singapore. It was a clear day and young Robrecht manned the Crow's nest. When the islands came into view, he shook himself from a trance-like stupor and sounded the warning: "Land ahoy!" As he rose and grasped the burnished rail of the crow's nest, he also noticed a small fleet of boats aimed directly for them. "Boats dead ahead!" said he then wiggled from the crow's nest and slid down to the spar deck. By the time he reached the ship's gunwale, the sampan boats were nearly upon them. Some of the seamen had flintlock rifles leveled at the dilapidated barges.

"*Orang laut*," said Captain Onderdonk.

"*Orang laut*?" said Jakob.

"Sea people."

Robrecht turned to his father. "What do they want?"

"They want to warn us away from their island." The Captain raised a spyglass to his eye. "Hold your fire, men. Steady as she goes."

Robrecht felt the breeze ruffle his hair, heard the tattered sails of the sampan lash and crackle. Then from larboard side came a howl, and a small brown man hurled a jute sack, which flew in a high looping arc before landing noiselessly on the spar deck. The sack churned and throbbed, until finally a black scourge of giant centipedes spilled from it. "*Duizendpoot! Duizendpoot!*" cried the men, scattering. The insects scuttled to the shadows and disappeared into the ship's cracks and crannies. Amid the clamor, a shot was fired. Then another and another. Robrecht watched a barrage of lead shred the sail of the sampan from which the jute sack had come. Moments later, two spindly oars poked from the barge. This followed by a frantic jettisoning of onboard possessions. A makeshift stove, pots, pans, a dog — which paddled alongside the boat, its head stiff and high. Then the brown man rolled something larger into the water, something alive. The fleshy lump flailed and bobbed on the surface as the sampan paddled away, but its frenzied attempts to save itself failed, as its movements grew heavy and finally halted.

By now, a group of men had gathered at the gunwale. The seaman who fired the first shot pitched a grappling hook into the water. After several attempts, he snagged the ill-fated flotsam and dropped it with a soggy thud onto the spar deck. Robrecht stared at the black-haired girl with no arms and no legs. She was nothing but a trunk. Her eyes were open and water drained from her mouth. Her hair lay plastered to the ship's timbers. Robrecht guessed her to be near his own age. Certainly no more. He gazed upon her almost longingly, infused as he was by such an uneasy mixture of emotions. Emotions that seemed not to end with questions (as was the case with his brother, Jakob) but with a set of underlying observations upon which he would later build a simple if brutal world view. It was the lank and scraggy seaman Dag who broke the profound silence. As the men of *Son of Batavia*

Captain Roorback, on the other hand, was less fortunate. When the foremost whaleboat rocked, the captain plunged headlong into the frothing waters. It was instantaneous, with no time for even a gasp or scream of terror. In the moment that it took for Robrecht to turn his gaze up, the swarm of sharks had shredded the man overboard into scraps. The sailors sat frozen, helpless, watching with trembling hands clutched to their idle muskets.

Moments later, the waters were still again and the air was heavy with the sickly sweet smell of death. A crimson cloud spread over the water's surface, washed up against the side of the whaleboats. By this time, Robrecht had found his sea legs again and, standing, cried "Onward Men! Before the demons drag us all to hell." As the whaleboat lunged forward, he glanced back at Dag. The sailor smiled and winked, making the prominent scar below his left eye pucker into a jagged seam upon his leathery flesh.

It became clear as the whaleboats neared land that Fort Belgica was rife with local *pribumi*. Robrecht instructed the men to fire at will. "Drive them from the Fort," said he. "Spare no force." The men grinned gritty smiles in anticipation. For in the first mate's words they heard the order to slaughter the locals. But with the boom of the first musket, the *pribumi* scattered. Hordes of brown-skinned Bandanese fled the fort and disappeared into the jungle. The sailors taunted them from the whaleboats, calling them cowards and daring them to return. But when it was clear that the *pribumi* had no intention of returning, the men of *Son of Batavia*, seeing their chances for a bloodbath slipping away, begged the locals to return.

"The cowards," said Dag. "There's only one way to deal with cowards."

"Perhaps you have an idea, Able Seaman Dag?"

"Ye know old Dag, sir. Always something up me sleeve."

They found the *perkeniers* chained in the fort's stockade. No sooner

---

stood around looking upon the poor discarded creature, the sailor nudged it with his toe and said "So, which of ye scoundrels will *fokken* it first?"

had they freed them, than a plump plantation owner fell upon Robrecht's neck.

"Thank God you've arrived! I thought the heathen help were going to starve us to death."

Robrecht eyed the *perkenier's* prodigious paunch. "You don't look to have missed a meal in quite some time," said he. "Did they refuse to feed you?"

"They fed us, yes. But I feared they were about to stop at any moment. The anxiety of it all has caused me to shed a few pounds."

Another plantation owner stepped forward. "I thought they were going to torture us. Flay us with red-glowing knives."

"You appear to have kept body and soul together," said Robrecht.

"Well, yes. But they carried long knives and tended to fires. Surely the thought was there in their minds night and day."

"And I thought they were going to ravage me," said the owner's wife. "As heavy with bosom as you can see I am, the barbarians were about to tie me up and take me over and over, again and again, in a most horrible and frightful manner."

"Not much chance of that," said Dag with a snarlish laugh that prompted a round of raucous hoots from the men.

Robrecht raised his arm and the ruckus stopped. "You are safe now."

"How do you plan to get the *pribumi* back into our orchards?" asked the portly *perkenier.*

"You needn't worry yourself about that. Now come, my men have a thirst for rum. And we have a dead captain to mourn."

"Yes, of course, whatever you need," said the plump *perkenier,* as if suddenly realizing that he had fallen shamefully short in his role as host to his countrymen. He led them to his plantation and to a cellar full of rum. Along the way, the *perkenier* related the story of how they had come to be captured by the *pribumi.*[34]

---

[34] The portly *perkenier,* himself, had called the meeting on the day in question at the small wooden church on Bandanaira—"admittedly, 'tis no more than a box with a flagging steeple," said he. The order of business was how to entice another parish priest to take up the good cause right there on

Bandanaira Island. "The previous pastor did not fare so well in this uncivilized realm and in this extreme isolation," said the portly *perkenier*. And isolation it was, to be sure. For the Banda Islands, a tiny speck in the Banda Sea, saw visitors no more than twice a year. Even then, it was only when the overlords of Batavia wanted something from them. And of course, that something was always the same: nutmeg and mace.

The Bandanaira *perkeniers* were second and third generation orchard owners; that is, the grandsons and great grandsons of those who had first benefited from the renowned largess of Governor-General Coen. They were died-in-the-wool islanders. The parish priest, on the other hand—whom they had seduced with promises of a grand stone church, complete with stained glass windows—was fresh out of divinity school in Berlin, the very heart of Prussian civilization. According to the portly *perkenier*, the young pastor sailed for Batavia with a head full of Calvin and a heart full of Erasmus, thinking he would preach the Good Word to the *perkeniers* while at the same time bringing the heathen *pribumi* to Christ. But it was not what he had expected. Not at all, as it turned out. "For, as you can clearly see," said the *perkenier*, "Bandanaira is no Ephesus and the pastor was no Paul."

Not a year after his arrival, the first signs appeared. Signs of discomposure. Signs of madness. So consuming was the pastor's sense of aloneness that he finally resorted to fashioning permanent houseguests with gourds for heads and bodies of twined-together bamboo. The "man," whom he had draped in a linen shirt and trousers, he called Herman and the woman, whom he had draped in a silk Ceylonese sari, he called Catherina. Most nights the pastor could be heard idly chit-chatting with Herman and Catherina, both of whom were perpetually seated in rattan wicker chairs.

Unfortunately, as these things go, the gourd heads of his house guests did not last long in the heat and soon shriveled to the size of the pastor's fists. This of course, did not keep him from his increasingly long conversations with Herman and Catherina. It was the scourge of swarming fruit flies that finally convinced the pastor to dispense with their heads. He hated to do it but knew it had to be done. Once Herman and Catherina were decapitated and disassembled, and only a heap of bamboo bones remained, he propped open the door and windows of his small abode hoping to get rid of the black cloud of flies that seemed intent on staying on indefinitely. For days and days, his windows and door remained open. "It was during this time that the banded krait slithered in and curled up in his bed," said the *perkenier*. "The pastor was bitten and died a day later."

The rum was retrieved and returned to the fort, where the men of *Son of Batavia* began their mourning in earnest. Robrecht sipped slowly from a tankard. He knew that he must keep his wits about him and wait for the right moment to make his play for power over *Son of Batavia*. As first mate, the mantle of leadership should rightly be donned by him. But Robrecht had been at sea long enough to know that things do not always happen as they should—especially in moments of disorder and chaos, not to mention in moments of extreme drunkenness.

Adding further to the tenseness of the present situation was the rivalry between the surviving officers—those being, Robrecht and the second mate, Meneer Bleeker. In such instances, circumstances often turn bad for one of the parties involved. And thus was Robrecht well aware of the fact that in a mutinous turn of events he could wind up hanged or keelhauled.

"See how the bastard Bleeker drinks with the men," said Dag.

Robrecht's sights were trained on the second mate.

"They weep 'n' wail over the captain in death. In life, they spat upon his existence. Ye must make yer move, sir."

"Patience, Dag," said Robrecht. "All in good time."

For the men, the night grew hazier thanks to the noxious

Of course, the *perkeniers* said nothing of the pastor's fate to any potential replacements. This was their little secret. And it would remain a secret. No need to mention this. In fact, these were his very words, as the portly *perkenier* adjourned the meeting in the small church. "There is no need to mention this," he had said. And the others nodded in agreement. "No need at all," said they one to another. Then together the *perkeniers* strolled from the church, bolstered in their renewed hope that they would find a man of God to complete their humble if far-flung community.

As they filed out into the bare and scalding sunlight, the *perkeniers* shielded their eyes with clammy palms. Before them stood a row of grinning *pribumi*, teeth gleaming in the shade of wide-brimmed woven hats. "We've been waiting for you," said one of them with brown pimples on his neck and a grin wider than the rest.

influence of the portly *perkenier's* red rice rum. A fiddle appeared and an able seaman sawed away on it, sea shanty after sea shanty. Helmsman Weidman jumped to his feet and executed a shaky jig, amid a gauntlet of sailors with hooked arms, swinging about in a sloppy reel and sending splashes of rum sloshing in every direction.

When this bacchanalian pageant at last drew to a close, Robrecht rose to his feet and raised his tankard. "Sailors, brothers! Let us drink to our captain. He lived and died for the sea. May his remains boil and burn in the bellies of those murderous demons who took him from us. *Santé!*"

A spirited "*Santé!*" rose from the courtyard of Fort Belgica. "And now to matters of business. We are without a leader. What say you to that, men?"

Taking his cue, Dag stood. "Old Dag says 'tis our first mate, Meneer Onderdonk, who must lead us now. Brothers, ye all know it is the natural order of the sea."

"Aye, it is the natural order," cried the seamen.

But not all present were in agreement. "There is no natural order of the sea," said Third Mate Buskirk. "For to say that some such natural order exists is to say that the death of our captain was natural." This prompted not a few puzzled looks among the men.

But it was Robrecht who was most puzzled by the third mate's apparent move against him. Why Meneer Buskirk should side with Second Mate Bleeker was a mystery.[35] It was at this point, after the

---

[35] There was, in actuality, a clear cause for the third mate's traitorous allegiance. For what Robrecht did not know was that Meneer Buskirk detested him. The reason for this enmity was the lisping manner in which the first mate pronounced his name—sounding more like /bɘthkɘrk/ than /bɘskɘrk/. For three long years, the third mate had endured this childish game. Although it should also be said that the mispronunciation may have been more imagined than real, as no one on the ship other than the third mate himself had ever detected a lisped pronunciation of /bɘskɘrk/ by the first mate. Real or imagined, Meneer Buskirk was greatly offended, nay enraged, by what he perceived to be a clear bastardization of his good name. For in the slight alteration from /bɘskɘrk/ to /bɘthkɘrk/, the meaning of the name changed from "wooden church" to "old lady church." But what was even

third mate's attempt to subvert Robrecht's authority as first mate of *Son of Batavia*, that Second Mate Bleeker made his move.

"Our captain was the worthiest among us to lead," said the second mate. "He who is to lead us now must be the worthiest to lead. What say you, men?"

Mouths mumbled and heads wagged in the affirmative.

In truth, Robrecht had expected resistance from the second mate and thus was he ready with a proposal. "So be it," said Robrecht. "Then I propose a simple contest between Meneer Bleeker and myself. The winner will assume command over *Son of Batavia*."

The men roared their approval. "Yes, yes! A contest" cried they in unison.

"What then is this contest to be?" said Meneer Buskirk.

"Simple. The first man to get the local *pribumi* back to work is the victor."

"Back to work is a foggy finish line." said Meneer Bleeker. "And what is to prevent you from employing some chicanery to achieve your desired end?" The crowd stirred, sensing an altercation.

But Robrecht refused to be goaded. "If it is a clear finish line you want, then a clear finish line you shall have. Fifty bushels of nutmeg. The first man who gets the *pribumi* to bring in fifty bushels wins the contest."

The seamen cried: "It is a fair contest!"

"Then I agree to the terms of your contest," said Meneer Bleeker. "May the best man win."

"Oh, he will," said Dag. "Ye can count on that."

---

more troubling to the third mate was how Meneer Onderdonk could possibly know that he came from a family of lispers and that he was the only one of his siblings to not exhibit the cursed speech impediment.

FROM A LETTER ADDRESSED TO
MEVROUW MARIJKE ONDERDONK,
LEYDEN, SOUTH HOLLAND

November 23, 1742

Dear Mother,

Father says I have been remiss in my duty to correspond with you. For that I am sorry, Mother. I suppose I have been so mesmerized by life at sea that I have had time for little else. There is much to see and do, and sometimes I feel that I may burst if I do not see and do them all. It is true that there are times when life at sea can be slow and monotonous, and routine breaks the back and spirit, both. But it is as an able seaman and friend aboard Son of Batavia said to me: "It is not the journey itself that so intrigues but the destination."

Yesterday we arrived at our destination—Macau. What a strange and wonderful place it is! The market is even larger and more exotic than the markets in Pulicat and Galle. There, for the first time, I watched two gamecocks do battle to the death. One flaming red and another black and white—they faced each other down and ruffled their neck feathers until they looked like two puffy flowers. The two pretty dandies circled and pranced about before finally pouncing one upon the other. My God! I could not have imagined a more frenzied and rabid spectacle. Minutes later, the victor, a black and white condottiere covered in the blood of the vanquished, strutted about like a nobleman at the ball. What a grand show it was, Mother! Like a poem or play of life and death. There were no leaders or followers, no rich or poor, no kings, knights, farmers or peasants, no gods, priests, saints or sinners. There were only two foes—one strong and the other stronger—in a contest that promised the conqueror life and the conquered death.

The master of the winning gamecock scooped the bird into his arms and pecked its bright yellow beak. The red gamecock lay broken and twitching in the dust, a blue vein from its neck squirmed and spat black blood. Finally the poor beast's bald master grabbed the bird by the legs and, swinging it like the clapper of a tolling bell, marched slowly away from the ring of men (some laughing, some groaning). I admit, Mother, that I was overcome by curiosity, and I followed close behind the bald master to see I knew not what. But soon enough it would become clear to me. For he walked to the edge of the marketplace and, without a second thought, threw the bird into a watery pit. *Just as I arrived at the pit's edge, two small water lizards (called alligators) snapped onto the gamecock and tore it asunder, each then gulping whole its share. It seemed like such a meaningless end, and I stood there for some time, sorting through it in my mind until finally I understood that to be victorious brings everything and to be defeated brings nothing, nothing but the end, which is nothing at all. Father says my observation is grim and Draconic. He claims that there are competitions in life but life itself is not a competition. Of course, I made no response to his shibboleth. For what does it matter? It means nothing — nothing at all.*

Robrecht

FROM THE JOURNAL OF JAKOB ONDERDONK

September 8, 1749

Father is out of sorts lately. It seems the crooked business he heard tell of on Dejima consumes him still. Today, while docked in Batavia, father called each of his officers to VOC headquarters to inquire about rumors and hearsay that may or may not be circulating about the ship. Being the captain's first mate, I was called last. When I entered his office, I found father slumped behind his desk and muttering in a state of deep consternation over the whole affair. For, as he soon revealed, the testimonies he had heard this day had led him to believe that someone of high rank in the VOC might be involved in the unsanctioned trading at Dejima. "And God knows where else," he added. However, this revelation still did not account for the apparent personal nature of my father's inquisition. When I pressed him to reveal all, he simply said that it was someone he was well acquainted with and someone whom he never would have expected capable of such dishonorable dealings—until recently. Father said he had no actual proof of anything—save for some words that had passed between him and the man in question—and thus, he felt that there was no action to be fairly taken at this time. I must admit to being taken aback at this uncommon reaction. For I had never known my father to retreat from a fight worth fighting and this, it seemed, was one such fight. Whether it was someone he knew well or not should have been of no consequence to Cornelis Onderdonk. For he would have gaoled his own son if in doing so he could maintain justice and order among the men. Furthermore, as he well knows, the reputation of the VOC is already in question back home, and there are those who would like to see the company's rule in the Dutch East Indies end. Thus did it come as a great surprise to me that father seemed so ready to quit the cause. Of course, I felt it was not my place to say anything of the sort but only took my leave of him. But even as I stepped from his office and strode down the hall, I felt there may have been something more to it, something that even father could not stand up to. Although exactly what that might be, I could not say. Perhaps time will tell all, as the saying goes.

EIGHT

The task of spying on Meneer Bleeker and his traitorous crew had fallen to Dag, as the able seaman was the only one Robrecht trusted. And seeing the number of sailors that had sided with the second mate, Robrecht became even more convinced that Dag was his most loyal companion—if not his only loyal companion. The two had been shipmates since Robrecht had first gone to sea. Back then, the able seaman had taken Robrecht under his wing while still a cabin boy answering to his father. Dag had watched the young protégé rise through the ranks at a truly nepotistic pace. Even as Robrecht rose, Able Seaman Dag had never asked for preferential treatment. He'd simply hoped to be included in whatever was afoot. And, of course, Robrecht always made certain that something was afoot, be it scheme, undertaking, adventure, or misadventure, Dag wished only to be there, to be included.

"What did you find out?" asked Robrecht.

"The fool tries to negotiate with the *pribumi*, even as we speak," said Dag.

"That will get him nowhere."

"Aye. He might as well be *fokken* a tree stump for all the good talking'll do. "

"We need something more convincing."

"Aye, sir. Old Dag has got just the thing."

They left the fort on foot just as the sun plopped red and yellow into the sea. The three men they had enlisted to haul barrels of whale oil huffed loudly, more by way of complaint about the present duty that had been thrust upon them than by actual exhaustion. The plan, as Dag explained it, was simple: they would send a wagon blazing through the *pribumi* village.[36] Dag flashed a grainy, tobaccoed grin as

---

[36] The blazing wagon was a simple variation on a recurring theme for Dag. And the truth was he always resorted to fire where plans of destruction and mayhem were concerned. For Able Seaman Dag, the power of fire was a force like no other upon Earth. The origins of this attraction—although *attraction* may not clearly convey Dag's clear obsession with fire—can be traced to the

he spoke, and the rum on his breath was a meridian not to be crossed. Nevertheless, Robrecht was pleased, for he believed that Dag's plan could work. A little unbridled terror might turn out to be exactly what was needed.

Dag returned to the outskirts of the village with a mule and cart. The beast brayed and kicked, to which the able seaman responded by knocking it senseless with a sizable stick.

"Hurry, ye scurvy dogs, for the night 'tis upon us," said he to the three sailors, who promptly dowsed the cart in oil. Raising a barrel to his own shoulder, Dag drenched the mule until the beast glistened in the moonlight. Then he held out a sulfur stick to Robrecht. "Ye do the honors, sir."

It was a touching moment, as touching moments go between sailors. Robrecht opened the lantern, ignited the stick, and tossed it onto the cart. The fire spread quickly: over the load bed and up the sides, down to the spokes and wheels, up the shafts. When the first flames jumped to the mule's swishing tail, the beast brayed long and loud. Truly, it was an unearthly sound. Robrecht did not believe he had ever heard anything like it before. Within moments, the beast

---

shores of the Ganges River in Calcutta. For it was there that he had once witnessed the widow of a powerful man in life throw herself onto his burning funeral pyre. The young seaman watched, wide-eyed and somehow aroused, too. The widow flailed for but an instant upon the pyre before abruptly springing forth onto the river's edge—apparently changing her mind about the level of devotion required of her—at which point the brothers of the dead man tried to force her back onto the pyre with pointed sticks. But their efforts were entirely unnecessary; for the flicker that still smoldered on the hem of her sari quickly grew high and hot, finally irretrievably engulfing her in flames. Soon her shrieks became peeps, and she laid her charred body down like a black sludge on the earth. Needless to say, the morbid experience kindled Dag's obsession with immolation. And in the years that followed, Seaman Dag set ablaze animals large and small, furry and feathered, ferocious and gentle, all with great relish just to relive that one rapturous moment on the shores of the Ganges.

was ablaze, kicking frantically, jerking the cart this way and that. Finally, it bolted off down the road—a sizzling inferno headed straight for the village.

It must be said that the smell was ghastly, and the sight, diabolic. The three sailors covered their noses and shielded their eyes in unison. Dag set out running, and Robrecht trotted close behind. They arrived at the single crossroads that quartered the village just in time to see the beast drop dead in its tracks and burn down to a smoldering carcass. All that remained of the cart was cinders and charred rivets. Dag stood before the ashes like some deranged shaman, wringing his hands, grinning from one ear to the other, clearly pleased with the results. By now, the *pribumi* had gathered around the ghastly spectacle. They watched, stunned and saddened. They shook their heads, wondering aloud who could be responsible for such barbarism.

Although the spectacle of the blazing mule was spectacular in a way that Robrecht had never imagined it could be, it failed to get the terrified reaction he had hoped for. If anything, it only served to strengthen the resolve of the *pribumi* to not bend to the will of the sadistic Dutch.

The village *leidsman*, an ugly man with brown pimples on his neck and wearing a long, coiling penis gourd, spat in the dirt at Robrecht's feet, calling him *lafaard*. Dag snarled at the *leidsman* and readied himself to reach down the *pribumi's* throat and rip out his windpipe. But Robrecht stayed the sailor's hand with an outstretched arm.

"That is your answer, then?" said the first mate.

"Go fuck your sister, Dutchman. That is my answer."

In the face of such hostility, it became clear to Robrecht that a more significant show of force was now necessary, especially if he was intent on intimidating the *pribumi* in true colonial fashion. The following morning, he returned to the ship with Dag and ordered anchors aweigh. An hour later, *Son of Batavia* positioned itself a hundred yards out from the coast with the *pribumi* village in clear sight and dropped anchor again. "Man the gun deck," cried Robrecht. "Prepare to take the village down."

Artillery hands skidded over the timbers and disappeared down the hatch. On the gun deck, they loaded twenty-four pound cannons with gunpowder and grape and chain shot.

"Fire at will," cried Robrecht. "Stop when nothing remains standing.

One after another, the cannons boomed. A haze of sulfurous smoke engulfed the ship, as it rolled and yawed in time to the deafening beat. The only reprieve was the eerie silence that prevailed as cannons were reloaded.

Robrecht witnessed the destruction with a spyglass pressed to his eye, the glorious mutilation. Chain shot ripped through the jungle, lopping off giant palm trees as if a scythe through wheat. Grape shot pulverized everything in its path to a milky mulch. At length, the last cannonball was fired, and Robrecht spied the ragged swath that scarred the jungle with great satisfaction.

But to his great astonishment, when he looked closer, the village remained intact, its huts defiantly erect. In the round glass eye, he could see villagers sauntering about—dazed, yes, but upright and unharmed. Some of them were sobbing. Some of them stared at the ground. But others pointed and laughed.

Robrecht swung the spyglass south of the village, only to learn that the assault had gotten slightly off track, and they had leveled a sizable orchard of nutmeg trees. The truth of the matter was the crew, still being drunk on rum from the previous night's debauchery, brought to bear a less-than-coordinated attack on the *pribumi* village. Given the order to open fire, the gun deck had fired more higgledy-piggledy than openly. The result was a slow, almost imperceptible, rotation of the ship southward toward the nutmeg orchard.

Robrecht's features grew hard and his fists tightened around the spyglass. The sourness of his disbelief pricked his tongue and burned in his nostrils. It was a bitter realization—to learn that his luck may have finally run out. It felt to him like a betrayal of the worst sort—far beyond that of the ship's crew who had sided with Meneer Bleeker. Of course, in actuality, Robrecht's luck had not run out (as we shall see), but it had simply taken a less direct route, as luck will sometimes do.

Returning to shore, Robrecht sent Dag to find out how Meneer

Bleeker fared thus far in the contest. In the meantime, he marched through the destroyed jungle to the village, where he was met by the *leidsman*. The look of amusement on the ugly chief's face caused the bile to squeeze from the first mate's gallbladder and boil in his belly.

"You wiped out a quarter of the nutmeg trees on the island," said the *leidsman*. "And half of your own men."

"This is no time for jocularity," said Robrecht, his chin protruding and defiant—but not for long. For much to his chagrin, the arrival of Dag at that very moment served to confirm the *leidsman's* claim. "He's . . . right . . . sir. I've . . . just . . . returned . . . from . . . the orchards." Dag huffed his foul breath in Robrecht's face.

"Spit it out, man!"

"Bleeker, the bastard . . . had his own men harvesting the nutmeg when we opened fire. Their body parts . . . are scattered from here . . . to Ceram. Not a single soul survives."

"And Bleeker?"

"Unknown, sir. Old Dag could find neither tongue nor toe . . . of the second mate."

"I can tell you about Meneer Bleeker," said the chief, his tone abruptly changing from derisive to informative, with just a hint of purposefulness. "He and I came to an agreement. I would get the locals back into the nutmeg orchards if he would bless my lineage."

"Bless your lineage?"

"Give me a grandson with Dutch blood running through his veins."

"But what about all the hated Dutchman nonsense?"

"Can't you see that hatred is the poison coursing through one who wants what he cannot have? Mixing Dutch blood with Bandanese blood gives me something I want—descendants who are not full *pribumi*—descendants who are above *pribumi*. It gives me status."[37]

---

[37] Although the ugly *leidsman* desired status more than anything else and believed that Robrecht could give that status to him, it should here be said that there was a time when simply being chosen *leidsman* was status enough for the *pribumi* previously known as Wibawa. Wibawa was just twenty-two

years old when he decided that he should be the next *leidsman*. After all, his name, which meant "authority," seemed to bear out his position. True, Wibawa was much younger than the others whom he found himself fiercely contending with, but it mattered not to him.

The contest for *leidsman* came about when the previous *leidsman* died without progeny, meaning, there was no son to whom the mantle of chiefdom could be seamlessly—or otherwise, for that matter—passed. Needless to say, this not unexpected void caused a stir among the villagers. For every man dreamed of being *leidsman*.

In the weeks that followed the *leidsman's* death, each contender vied for the villagers support. As was the custom, the one who garnered the most— that is, most *vocal*—support would be named *leidsman*. Predictably, then, there were shows of strength and feats of bravery. There were acts of kindness and compassion. There were promises made and blood oaths entered into. There were feasts—chickens plucked and goats slaughtered. And yes, there was backbiting and rumor mongering, plenty of backbiting and rumor mongering.

But Wibawa undertook none of these practical if predictable activities. Wibawa had decided to take a different approach. Having heard from Dutch travelers and Malay slaves about the fantastic penis gourds worn by tribes in Papua, he dispensed with his droopy loin cloth and donned a gourd he had made especially for the occasion. It was a long and twisting affair that curled up under his buttocks like an inquisitive snake. He painted the gourd with red stripes, and on the bulbous end, he drew two large black eyes. Wibawa paraded around the village wearing his snake-like gourd saying nothing more than the odd greeting to passing villagers. Such was the extent of his strategy to win the necessary support to be named *leidsman*.

The other contenders were at first stunned by such an unorthodox strategy, if it could truly be called such—a *strategy*. Then they were amused. Then they ridiculed Wibawa openly, calling him *tehnequsitoseptl* ("the one with a wondrous snaking cock sniffing his *aars*," but clearly intending *wondrous* to be understood in an ironic sense). But Wibawa paid no attention to their derisions. Instead, he wore his penis sheath more proudly around the village and began to call himself *tehnequsitoseptl*.

Many of the villagers were impressed with the confidence and composure exhibited by the young man with a wondrous snaking cock sniffing his *aars*, even in the face of his detractors. So much so, that many began to openly support him. Some of the men even donned their own penis gourds. And in an unprecedented move, even in Papua, some of the *pribumi* women also donned their own penis gourds. Soon, it seemed the whole village had

Robrecht's impatience manifested itself in the crossing of his arms and a slight lowering of the head in order that he might peer from beneath his brow. "That's all fine and well. But what, then, has happened to Bleeker?"

The chief paused, as if deciding how to best proceed. "Meneer Bleeker and my daughter were joined as man and wife yesterday. As tradition dictates, they were in the matrimonial hut in the jungle just outside of the village, about the business of making my grandchild, when your cannons leveled the jungle and the matrimonial hut with it. Meneer Bleeker was killed in a most unpleasant manner."

"What mean ye by unpleasant?" asked Dag.

"His *erectie* was shot off before consummation. The only blood to redden the marriage bed was his own. He bled to death in my poor Zeuga's arms."[38]

---

wondrous snaking cocks. By the time the other contenders went stumbling through the forest looking for penis gourds, it was too late. Wibawa, or *tehnequsitoseptl*, with his wondrous snaking cock, had walked away with the contest.

[38] Although the ugly *leidsman's* story was pleasingly tragic in its Aristotelian details, the truth was Meneer Bleeker was not about the business of producing offspring at the time of his death, as the *leidsman* supposed. In fact, minutes before, the second mate had quit the matrimonial hut in order that he might converse with Meneer Buskirk concerning an urgent matter.

"My God!" he said. "I've seen more attractive even-toed ungulates."

"Sir?" said Buskirk.

"Camels, pigs, hippopotami—even-toed ungulates."

"She is no beauty, to be sure."

"I guess one must ask oneself how desperately one wants to be Captain."

"Let me remind you that if you do not comply with this one condition, sir, there is a fair to middling chance that First Mate Onderdonk will win the contest. I hate to say it, but it seems to be the only way."

'The only way! The only way! I don't want to hear that." Bleeker was working himself into a lather.

"Remember, sir, the condition is only to wed the daughter and to sire a son. Nothing was said about staying on the island. As soon as the girl is with child, we can set sail from this cursed place."

"The bastard died *pik*-less." said Dag. "'Tis Music to me ears! The contest is over. Ye have won, sir."

"The contest for captain's rank may be over," said the *leidsman*, "but you are still without locals to harvest your nutmeg."

"But ye said yerself, Bleeker's dead as nits on horsemint. And how now's a dead Dutchman to give ye a grandson?"

"Not all Dutchman are dead," said the Chief, turning an eye to Robrecht. "I will make the same deal with you that I made with Meneer Bleeker. Bless my lineage and I will get the locals back in the nutmeg orchards."

Robrecht sighed. "Yes, yes. I will do it, then" said he.

The ugly chief clasped his hand and pulled him close. The first mate whiffed a pungent sweet odor of coconut oil and sweat. "Son! My Son!" cried the *leidsman*.

The crew was shamefully drunk, as was the ugly chief who now insisted that Robrecht call him *pappie*. Zeuga, coy in her pink and gold silk *kain kebaya*, made a corpulent bride. For his part, Robrecht had donned his officer's uniform—a token formality in order to get the locals back into the orchards, he'd told himself. Then his work here would finally be done.

This wedding feast was not as elaborate as the one that had taken place two days earlier. Still, the grilled goat in peanut sauce and the rice dumplings steamed in coconut leaves, if not an outright feast, comprised a succulent meal. And the *arrack* burned a hole in the gullet and sent its smoldering fumes to the heart. Robrecht could not

---

"Yes, there is that. Although I'm not so certain I want to leave my son in a place where he'll be forced to wear a gourd over his privates for the entirety of his mortal years."

"That will have to be your decision, sir. No other can make it for you."

After a few final moments of consideration, the second mate exhaled loudly and made his way back to the matrimonial hut. Of course, his timing could not have been worse. For it was more-or-less at that precise moment that the first cannonball blasted through the forest, shattering everything in its path.

eat another bite. Or swallow another drop.

After the celebration feast, a drunken crowd of sailors and *pribumi* ushered Robrecht and his bride to the matrimonial hut where the first mate wasted no time getting about the task at hand. For he had been on larger vessels before—rotund Polynesians prostitutes, Ceylonese whores of immense tonnage, even a lumpish Arab strumpet. The point was he knew what to do.

And so it was that in no time, Robrecht was vigorously taking his bride from behind. Zeuga's various squawks and yelps prompted cheers from the boozy revelers outside, and with her final climatic squeal came a mighty roar from the crowd.

Had Robrecht been more inclined to consider the situation objectively, he would no doubt have arrived at the conclusion that it was truly an odd custom, even by seafaring standards. Yet the only thing that mattered to him at this juncture was getting off the island. And whatever it took to achieve that end mattered neither drip nor droplet to him. He collapsed exhausted to the floor of the matrimonial hut and rolled onto his back. Zeuga flopped down beside him, her hands pressed to her bloody loins, and began to hum a tribal-sounding tune. This light, chirpy melody prompted another round of cheers from the crowd without.

"My son," blubbered the ugly chief. "My son!"

"Aye, sir. That's how ye get 'er done," said Dag.

From the Journal of Robrecht Onderdonk

January 13, 1748
Son of Batavia lies idly docked in the bay—a ghostship in the shimmering heat. I spent the day seeing to minor reparations on the vessel, for the ship's carpenter cannot be trusted to saw the leg from a table when he has been sniffing the vapors of tar and turpentine. In the end, Seaman Dag did much of the dawdler's work.

As we strolled along the docks that sprawl before VOC headquarters, Seaman Dag and I happened upon Captain Schoonhoven returning from his sailing vessel, Zwarte Zwijn. I came to an abrupt halt and bowed slightly to greet him cordially. To my great surprise, he swooped by us with only the most cursory greeting, as if he had never laid eyes upon me before. (To what do I owe such an apparent slight? I wished to ask him. But it was clear that the presence of Dag made the captain cautious and wary of engagement.)

Seaman Dag and I carried on our way to the north gate of Batavia and soon found ourselves in Glodok and the teahouse of the Chinaman Huīsè De (or "gray one" as I call him), where we drank warm baijiu and ate boiled jackfruit well into the evening. Finally, we rose and left with a mind to find some companionship—female or otherwise.

Out in the street, Dag asked me about my earlier encounter with Captain Schoonhoven, noting that something seemed amiss. I must admit that I was not surprised by the able seaman's keen observation, for he is not one to let things go unnoticed, especially where he senses opportunity. Of course, I told him nothing—or very little—but I decided in that moment that I would on some later occasion approach Captain Schoonhoven concerning our arrangement and see if we might put a trusted seaman such as Dag to good use. I did not tell Dag as much but only gave him a nod and a wink—as good a promise as you'll ever get from any man at sea.

FROM THE JOURNAL OF CAPTAIN CORNELIS ONDERDONK

August 16, 1749
Today, we drift on the Andaman Sea, where Notus and Eurus seem to
slumber without so much as a warm snort from their cavernous nostrils.
The men of Son of Batavia perform their tasks in the most rote manner, as if
to give some thought and meaning to one's work were to drop dead into
Hades' lap where a famished Cerberus lays waiting. Of course, Jakob is the
one exception to this. He goes about his labors dutifully and with due
diligence, despite the heat, and in spite of the prevailing tide of boredom that
has swept over the vessel.

When I look upon him, it is clear to me that a captain's stripes are in his
future. Yet, I am torn by such a realization, for I fear that a life at sea may
not serve him as well as he would serve it. Indeed, as of late, I have felt
overwhelmingly the urge to return to land and to drop anchor there for the
remainder of my time here on Earth. For although the sea itself has not
changed, the times have changed. The enchantment of the sea is no longer
adventure for the simple love of it but profit for the plain greed of it; and
many atrocities have been committed in its name—profit. One would have
to be deaf, dumb, and blind to not realize the truth of this. Perhaps therein
lies my dilemma; I can no longer remain deaf, dumb, and blind.

But beyond this, there is also the lure of a wife who longs for my
companionship day and night. For I know it is so, even though it would be
anathema for her to admit as much. To live out my remaining years by her
side, in her embrace, strikes me now as a most pleasing way to wander
toward my eventual end. She would certainly accuse me of being morbid for
mentioning the demise of my traitorous flesh—yet it is true that time
marches on, rigid and unflagging in its journey from the here-and-now to
the distant past. There is nothing to fear in this, and to turn a blind eye to it
does not make it any less so. Nothing makes it less so, and only a fool acts as
if there is no end to this day. And so it is that these thoughts churn and
percolate in my head, and I feel my spirit bending toward the setting sun,
west, toward my home and my love.

NINE

Jakob inserted a blue-burnished skeleton key into the padlock and twisted it. He pushed through the door and led Candide into the factory.

"This is it," said he, ". . . your place of employ."

Candide turned full circle, blowing a faint whistle. "But you are so young, good Anabaptist, to be one of such great wealth and power."

"Not great wealth and power. But perhaps I am more fortunate than many."

"This must indeed be the best of all places. For it brings you wealth and power, and it brings me the means whereby I might not perish. But if I might ask, good Anabaptist, how is it that you have come to make such exotic wares?"

"Just by chance, I suppose," said Jakob.[39]

---

[39] There was an element of truth to Jakob's simple explanation. However, in reality, it was not really by chance that Jakob had become a manufacturer of Dutch flat-weave carpets after the manner of Persia. The idea had been instilled in him years earlier, although back then he had not yet recognized it as such—an idea. It was only after he had returned to South Holland, determined to start life anew, that he recalled the experience and recognized it as a possibility. If there were indeed an element of chance involved in this particular episode of Jakob's life, it might be thought to have therein played a part—that is, recognizing the experience as a possibility in the first place.

The experience took place in Pulicat, in the Tamil Nadu state of South India, while Jakob wandered about the marketplace there. The heat was stifling on the day in question, and Jakob had removed his officer's coatee and loosened his collar. He stood before a stall of exotic looking musical instruments: drums of every shape and size, stringed instruments with long smooth necks, copper horns and wooden flutes. A man with a grizzled beard picked up the horn and blew out a single syrupy note.

"You like it? You like it? I'll give you a special deal." Jakob shook his head and moved to the next stall where another man, curled up on the ground, slumbered with an uneven snore. All around, carpets hung from bamboo rods, each with a unique intricate pattern. Staring at them made Jakob dizzy.

Jakob led Candide through the factory pointing to this and that: the dying room with its loose skeins of colorless wool, the packing and storing room with its bulky wooden crates, the production room with its still looms. He sat Candide at a loom and showed him how to string warps and wefts then how to tie the wool yarn in Turkish knots around the warps. After he had tied a row, Jakob packed the wefts with a comb and with great care trimmed the pile.

"Such noble work," said Candide. "Surely my Master Pangloss would approve."

"It may seem noble now but after ten hours of tying and cutting it's more likely to seem tedious and mind-numbing. But the job is yours for as long as you wish to stay."

"Who would ever choose to leave such noble employment, that this good fortune has fallen to me?" asked Candide.

He would never forget how looking at them was like looking into the mind of God—a beautifully cluttered yet perfectly organized space.

Stepping into the stall, Jabob caught sight of a cocoa-skinned woman (a Scythian from Gujarat) squatting over a floor loom, her feet stuck through the seemingly myriad lengths of hemp twine that ran from one end of the bamboo frame to the other. She weaved colored wool in and out of the twine with a nimbleness that Jakob had never witnessed before. He had known scores of dexterous seamen who could tie off a jib sheet quickly and cleanly with a bowline knot, but this was something quite different. Something quite incredible. In her meditative trance, the woman took no notice of his advance. Her movements were precise and practiced, like an elaborate dance, and it struck Jakob that here was a kind of worship. A reverence for balance and symmetry, beauty and simplicity. An act of creation.

Jakob glanced down at his own hands, as if they had suddenly sprung from the ends of his sleeves. He could recall no time in his life when he had created anything—made anything. He had been at sea since he was a young boy, and he had since come to the conclusion that there was nothing to be made at sea save ill-gained profits. With this in mind, Jakob had stepped up to the loom and dropped down beside it. The woman said nothing. Even as he reached out and strummed the loosely strung twine, she remained oblivious to his yearnful intrusion.

"That is another story," replied Jakob.

"I would like to hear it, good Anabaptist, if it does not tire or trouble you too greatly."

"It was my beloved Heleen who once sat at this very loom."

"What has become of your beloved Heleen?"

"She was called away to care for her mother's family in Lisbon. This senseless struggle for power has taken her cousins and left her mother's family helpless."

"Indeed it is senseless! I have seen with mine own eyes how it spreads throughout the land, ravaging and destroying all in its path. I, myself, still bear the hot stripes of war upon my back, and also my mind, it being lashed with so many painful sights and memories. I must ask Master Pangloss about war, should I ever behold his noble face again, for it seems that war does not at all fit into this the best of all possible worlds."

"I should say it does not, no matter what your wise master claims," said Jakob. "For I have also seen a bit of this world and I would certainly not agree that it is the *best* of all possible worlds. Only through Christ the Lord is one liberated from a destitute existence on this planet of dust."

"That is a noble thought, good Anabaptist. But is it not as my master says: all things have been created expressly to serve some end? Allow me to further extrapolate, using my master's example of the nose. There can be no doubt that the nose was formed to support glasses, for only on the nub of one's nose do glasses fit perfectly. Therefore, because the nose was formed to that end, we wear glasses. The same is true of legs. Legs were formed to bear stockings; thus, to that end, do we wear stockings."

"Does it follow, then, that because a hat fits perfectly on the head then the head was formed for hats alone and not for thinking?"

"That is an astute question, good Anabaptist. Oh, that I live to see Master Pangloss again, that I might ask him that very thing!"

"In the meantime, come," said Jakob. "Let's begin the day's labors with a cup of tea."

The day passed slowly, as thoughts of Heleen—and now Anneke, too—floated in and out of Jakob's head. Thoughts of Anneke were, of course, a recent development. Try as he might, Jakob was unable to keep them at bay and they stole into his head at idle moments. Although he found this slightly disconcerting, he in no way viewed the two young women as rivals. To his mind, it was impossible, as they were incomparable—that is, they were different as day and night. It was a point which he pondered while strolling through the commons with Anneke this very evening. The commons of Leyden was well known for its turning leaves in the fall, and the towering beech and oak stood consumed by exquisite reds and yellows of the season. Warblers lining the branches sounded their rapid chirp as the couple approached. Anneke was telling Jakob of her aunt's increasingly *eccentric*—she half whispered the word—behavior. Again, Jakob was stung by guilt. Mevrouw Schoonhoven's behavior came as no surprise to him. For he had witnessed men in the late stages of syphilis jump ship and drown in the sea.[40]

---

[40] Captain Roorback had once ordered a syphilitic sailor named Brusse to be bound and tied to a bed in sick quarters. This, only after Jakob had approached the captain and pleaded as much, fearing that Seaman Brusse may do harm to himself. "He is not of sound mind," Jakob said.

"Indeed," said Robrecht, stepping forward. "As third mate, sir, I feel bound to tell you that the seaman is a lunatic and haunts the spar deck like the emaciated ghost of some grotesquely rotting ogre. For once, I agree with my brother—First Mate Onderdonk. Seaman Brusse is a danger to himself."

At the time, Jakob wished to say more. About the scourge that had taken its toll among the rank and file of *Son of Batavia*. But he knew it would fall upon deaf ears. Captain Roorback was no disciplinarian. Not like their father had been. No, the Captain would do nothing. Of this, Jakob felt certain.

That night, as he slumbered in his berth, Jakob was awakened by the sound of a slamming door. He shot to his feet and rushed out of the cabin onto the spar deck. There, in a deep blue shadow set against a blackened sky, he saw Brusse walking unsteadily along the top of the gunwale with the ropes that had bound him fast to his bed still dangling from his wrists. Before Jakob could move, the sailor screamed "Land ahoy!" and dropped into the darkness, never to be seen again.

Anneke stopped to sit on a bench, and Jakob dropped down next to her. The sun was about to take the empyreal stage for an impressive finale, and they watched together in silence. Anneke's hand roamed over his knee and thigh, locating his hand and grasping it. Jakob felt the familiar swelling in his breeches. But today, it should be said, Jakob was well prepared for this particular eventuality. For, after displaying his all-too-apparent arousal during the ordinance of footwashing at the last meeting of the Anabaptists, Jakob had decided that some preventative, if not primitive, measures were in order. This came in the form of a Dutch flat-weave chastity belt, which he had woven the very next day with his own two hands. Although slightly bulky and coarse to the touch, the belt handily quelled any and all uprisings in the ranks below the beltline, despite the excruciating rash it left behind. But it should be said that the severe discomfort of the chastity belt gave Jakob's sagging spirituality an ascetic's boost. For who, he reasoned, knowing they are sanctifying the flesh, does not feel edified before God?

"I've been thinking," said Anneke. "I would like to be baptized, and I think that you should be too. We should do it together."

Of course, this came as a surprise to Jakob. He knew little of Anneke's religious background, if *background* was even the right word, but he had up until now assumed that organized religion was not something that interested the young woman. And it should be said that Jakob was largely correct in this assumption. However, being raised under the roof of a country gentleman, Anneke was not wholly ignorant of God and the Church that enshrines Him. What she had failed to see in the past was how God had anything at all to do with her life. As far as she was concerned, He was some faraway being that could scarcely muster the power to shift a single hair of her head should He wish to. That is not to say that young Meisje Schoonhoven was a non-believer. She simply failed to see the relevance of God in the here-and-now of existence, although she would never have put it in such heady, philosophical terms.

Despite her lapse in orthodoxy, Anneke was mindful of right and wrong, even believing herself to be somewhat of an expert in the area. In this sense, she counted herself a true Christian. But the meeting of the Anabaptists changed everything for Anneke. There, she had experienced for the first time what it felt like to be touched by God's Holy Spirit. Truly, it was as if something had descended upon the meeting hall, upon her. In short, she believed that God was among them—the Anabaptists. She had also never felt more accepted. It was the kind of acceptance that normally only her keen sense of social superiority made possible. In a word, Anneke felt at home among the Anabaptists. And to join them seemed the natural thing to do.

Jakob squirmed. "But this is sudden, is it not?" said he. "You have attended just two meetings of the Anabaptists."

"That is true. But you have attended scores of meetings over the course of five years. And what is different now from your first or second meeting? Anything?"

Admittedly, she made a good point, and Jakob knew it. Nothing was different. He felt then as he did now and every Sabbath day. But he couldn't tell her the real truth—that he wasn't ready; that he was plagued by sin. That his lust and his incessant habit of onanism held him back.

"You see," said she. "Your silence says it all. I am ready as I will ever be. And I want you there as the cleansing waters wash over every sinful inch of me."

An image of her in a sopping gossamer frock popped into Jakob's head. His hard *roede* bent painfully against the Dutch weave chastity belt. The sweet pain of purification caused him to bite his lower lip. How he wanted to say "yes," although he knew he should say "no."

"Let's give that some consideration," he finally said. "We'll consult Bonifaas concerning the matter."

Anneke leaned over and quickly pecked his cheek. Then she pulled his hand to her breast. "Do you feel that?" she said. "My heart beats with joy and anticipation."

"Yes, yes," said he. "I feel it."

Jakob left the commons and strode briskly through Leyden, hoping to burn off his desire as one burns off a too-rich meal of sauces and puddings. When Jakob arrived at his flat, he found Candide waiting.

The young man sat stiffly, fingers enmeshed on the table before him. "Good Anabaptist," said he, "a strange thing has happened to me this evening."

Jakob sat at the table and poured a glass of *bier*. "What is it?" said he.

"As I made my way from the factory to town, I came upon a beggar, a man in dire straits. The wretch was terribly disfigured and he wheezed and coughed upon me, much to my horror. Still, I was filled with compassion for him, and I gave him the two gulden that you gifted me, good Anabaptist."

"Yes, of course, that was the decent and Christian thing to do," said Jakob. "But what troubles you, then?"

"The wretch held the coins in his soiled palm and began to sob. He sobbed so long and loud that I, too, began to sob. Then he fell weeping upon my neck and asked why I did not recognize my master."

"Your master?"

"Yes, my Master Pangloss from the castle of noble Baron Thunder-Ten-Tronckh."

"But where is he now, your master?"

"Faint with hunger, he was scarcely able to stand. So I took him to your stables that he might have food and shelter for a spell."

"Of course, yes. That is well. But what has happened to him that he has been reduced to beggary?"

"After tasting the pleasures of paradise in the arms of the pretty wench Paquette, he fell deathly ill. It is a horrifying ailment with a long pedigree—one that has disfigured my master's kind visage."

"I know of the disease. It is the scourge of society both high and low." Jakob rose and tugged at the cravat around his neck. "Bring me to the poor wretch. We shall see about getting him treatment."

"Oh, good Anabaptist," cried Candide, "surely you are the best of all men."

Jakob followed his young guest to the stables and to his Master Pangloss, who lay curled up in a tight ball, nestled into a bed of straw as if an injured and badly suffering field mouse. Candide rushed to his master's side and, brushing away the straw, propped him upright. Candide had not exaggerated—Pangloss looked hideous. The philosopher may have appeared moderately youthful once, but as Jakob well knew, the disease ages one almost overnight. The nub of the master's nose hung by a thread. His lips were grizzled and not a blackened tooth remained in his head. His left eye was swollen and oozing pus. And a bulbous gumma protruded from the center of his brow. Uneven sprigs of gray were all that remained of his hair.

"Master, it is a miracle," said Candide. "I have found, in this the best of all possible worlds, a good man, an Anabaptist, who wishes for you to receive treatment for the disease that ravages you, body and soul."

"Body, yes," said Pangloss in a high quivering voice. "But not soul. For the soul is God's only to save or destroy as He in His almightiness sees fit."

Candide's jaw dropped in the same instant that his eyebrows rose. "But Master, how is it that the Almighty would be capable of destroying a soul? For is he not the maker of souls?"

"I have taught you well, young Candide. For God does not destroy men's souls but allows the Evil One to destroy men's souls, until such a time as the Almighty sees fit to destroy him, the Evil One. God's first act was creation and His final act shall be destruction."

Jakob stepped forward. "That may be true, but still, the body must be saved before it is too late. As you say, the soul is God's concern."

"This is he, Master, the best of all possible men," said Candide. "Jakob, the Anabaptist."

Pangloss executed an awkward courtly bow from his seated position. "I am in your debt, kind Anabaptist. And I trust that we may take up this discussion further in the future."

"As do I," said Jakob. "But now there is the pressing issue of getting you to the asylum to receive treatment."

"Yes, we must see to it now," said Candide.

Jakob and Candide circled around and each hooking a lanky arm, pulled the ragged, badly decaying philosopher to his feet. "Come, now," said Jakob.

"Perhaps this illness is my lot. For God has allowed it to ravage my body."

"How, then, can this be the best of all possible worlds," said Jakob, "if the Evil One is allowed to destroy souls and illness and disease are allowed to roam freely from household to household, family to family, father to son, mother to daughter, and so on?"

"But cannot evil bring about good? Cannot illness and disease bring about a happy and beneficial end to someone somewhere? I say yes, good Anabaptist, yes it can."

"How can this disease that ravages your body possibly bring about a happy and beneficial end to anyone?"

"It is the very origins of my disease that does so. You see, I received it from my fair Pacquette who received it from a learned friar, who received it from a countess, who received it from a cavalry captain, who received it from a marchioness, who received it from a page, who received it from a Jesuit, who while still in the robes of a novice received it from a companion of Christopher Columbus."

"But how does this strange genealogy bring a happy or beneficial end to anyone?" said Candide.

"Don't you see?" said Pangloss, pausing to hack a curdle of phlegm into his hand. "Had Columbus not caught the disease on an island of the Americas, we would have neither chocolate nor cochineal. Heavenly chocolate and carmine bleeding cochineal! Can you imagine a world without it? Thus, from my disease has come a happy and beneficial end to many." Pangloss's knees wobbled beneath his emaciated frame. "But on the other hand," said he, placing a hand to his brow, "perhaps the treatment is not such a bad thing. For God has allowed this disease to ravage my body, but God has also created the treatment that may cure it."

"Indeed it is so, Master," said Candide, "in this the best of all possible worlds."

FROM A LETTER ADDRESSED TO
CAPTAIN CORNELIUS ONDERDONK,
BATAVIA, JAVA, DUTCH EAST INDIES

December 2, 1749

My Dear Cornelis,

Perhaps I am a silly woman, but I cannot understand what business you could possibly have at the naval base in Surabaya. In your last letter you said that you had just returned from a month-long journey there, but you did not do me the courtesy of telling me why you had journeyed there in the first place. To be honest, Cornelis, I had to look up this Surabaya on the map you gifted me last Christmas. And I must say that it does not look to be the four hundred nautical miles away from Batavia that you say it is.

Nevertheless, I am overjoyed that you have returned safely to your hovel in Batavia, for I feel certain that a hovel is indeed what it is. My generous and long-suffering husband would certainly do nothing (least of all complain) to ensure that his quarters were suited to his station in life. He would, however, do everything to make certain that such was not the case for anyone and everyone else. A true seeker of justice, you are, dear Cornelis, for all others but yourself.

On a related topic, I must admit that I was surprised to hear that Captain Schoonhoven had decorated your flat in your absence. It strikes me as rather odd for men of your standing to be dilly-dallying with such womanly matters. Although I suppose your explanation does allow for a background setting that lends the unfolding drama a bit more conceivability. You are correct in assuming that I was unaware that you and Captain Schoonhoven were not on speaking terms; or at least you were not until he decided to have expensive paper applied to your walls in your absence. I can only guess that Mevrouw Schoonhoven is also unaware of this development, as she said nothing concerning it the last time we met (although she undoubtedly has more pressing matters, as rumor has it, with the kuiper she keeps in Amsterdam). However, once again, dear husband, you have told me nothing about the why of it—this falling out, as you call it. Such a secretive man, you can be, Cornelis. I can only assume that you two had a difference of opinion on matters of politics or some such ridiculous thing. Of course, I would not be able to comprehend such heady matters with my flighty female mind, so you undoubtedly thought it best not to say a thing about it to me. Be that as it may, I do hope that Captain Schoonhoven's recent gesture has made it possible for you two to bury the axe, as the Americans are wont to say.

But alas, I must go now, as Oma Onderdonk is prancing about the house with her dress pulled over her head. 'Tis a most puzzling and disconcerting practice which she has recently taken up. It began a fortnight ago at the mention of de haan. I know not what it is about a rooster that would bring on such an odd reaction. No need to worry, Cornelis. I'm sure it is nothing more than a passing fancy.

All My Love,
Marijke

FROM THE JOURNAL OF JAKOB ONDERDONK

April 5, 1748

Today, as we cut water in the Yellow Sea, I did something that I have not done since Sunday School: I took down the Bible from my bookcase and began to read. I turned to the Book of Mark and the story of Jesus calming the Sea of Galilee. It was a favorite of mine as a boy. "What manner of man is this, that even the wind and the sea obey him?" his stunned disciples wondered. And I have always wondered what it was that Jesus had been dreaming before they awakened him to the raging storm. He was, after all, half mortal and thus must have known the dreams of men. Did he dream of the kingdom he would one day inherit? Perhaps he dreamt of the world in all its iniquitous splendor, the same world that would soon spike him to a cross. Or perhaps like me, he dreamt of a calm cerulean sea, mother and mistress to us all, as it frothed and swelled beneath him.

At sea, my dreams float by blue and fluid. In them, I always find myself unable to speak and unable to act fleetly yet everything around me is imbued with a soft-shimmering grace that lubricates every movement so each moment slides effortlessly into the next. In short, in my dreams, it is as if the pleasing weight of the sea is upon me and my every action in this world. Perhaps it was a similar weight of design and deliberateness that filled the dreams of Jesus as he slumbered soundly on a skein of fishing net. Perhaps he, too, wondered at the meaning of those dreams yet somehow sensed it there just below the surface, a meaning understood only in the watery dream world from which he had just awakened. "And he arose, and rebuked the wind, and said unto the sea, 'Peace, be still.' And the wind ceased, and there was a great calm." A great calm. Surely this was more than the sea lying down obediently at his feet. This calm must have been a glimpse and glimmer of the great beyond. For the calm of the sea is but a fleeting moment, but the great calm that Jesus commands lasts an eternity. And this, I would do well to remember.

TEN

Ews of Bonifaas's vision spread quickly through the Anabaptist congregation, as did the rumor that Oma Onderdonk's blessed *aars* had been the source of the vision. Up until now, Jakob had done his best to ignore the idle chitchat. However, upon arriving at the next Sabbath day meeting of the Anabaptists, it became impossible for him to ignore it any longer. In the house of God, the idle chitchat was spoken in respectfully quiet tones, transforming it into a wave of sibilance that followed Bonifaas and Oma Onderdonk as the preacher escorted the septuagenarian up the aisle to the front of the hall and seated her there as a guest of honor. Lips buzzed with adoration. Heads bowed in reverence. Still, Oma Onderdonk was quite oblivious to it all. Anneke, on the other hand, appeared to find the unexpected attention pleasing—although it should be said that she remained blissfully naïve to the fact that she was not the intended recipient of said attentions and that her proximity to Oma Onderdonk was such that it became impossible for her to discern who was looking at whom, or who was *revering* whom, to be more precise. In her excitement, Anneke dug her lacey fingertips into Jakob's arm, immediately adopting a more regal—that is to say, unhurried—gait. For his part, Jakob flushed and reddened, as always. Needless to say, he had reservations about his oma's recent notoriety.

It would be fair to say that this Sabbath day, Bonifaas's dug deep into his repertoire and delivered an impassioned sermon on the evils of war—that is, the evils of war as they had come to him in his vision. And it would be no exaggeration to say that the preacher's righteous spittle rained down upon the front pews. When it was over the congregation sat quietly absorbing it—the sermon mainly but, unavoidably, the righteous spittle, too. There was no *Amen!* and no *Hallelujah!* filled the air. Just silent contemplation. Jakob also found himself moved to reflect on the words of Bonifaas Quackenboss. Even as he did, Jakob could not help but admire the preacher's unrivalled zeal this day.

Yet, a slight gasp of alarm hissed between his teeth when next

Bonifaas strode to the guest of honor and, splashing water into a basin, readied himself for the holy ordinance of foot washing. True, it struck Jakob as a spontaneous act, perhaps even an inspired act. Still, he could not help but fear the results. Discerning the gist of her husband's intent, Katrine Quackenboss left off her playing mid-hymn, leaving the chorus of "The Old Rugged Cross" stranded mid-refrain, as the notes of the fortepiano settled like floating snow upon the room. And if the room was still before, it was now a tomb of utter quietude.

The old woman beamed brightly—so brightly that Jakob very nearly did not recognize his own oma—as Bonifaas administered to her scaly, bunioned feet with their purple, corrugated toenails. That every gaze in the room was upon Oma Onderdonk was clearly evidenced by the row upon row of wide-eyed wonder that followed. The congregation waited with its breath collectively bated. And Jakob waited, too—although it should be said that the young manufacturer waited anxiously while the others waited hopefully. But neither he nor they would have to wait long. For soon Oma Onderdonk's eyebrows twitched faintly and a vague look of deliverance rippled over her placid gray countenance. There was a moment of hesitation, an instant of anticipation, before she discharged a pneumatic boom from her fundament.

Bonifaas flinched but remained steadfast upon bended knee. At first, the preacher sniffed cautiously through his nostrils, as a wolf for the scent of its prey. Then with much abandon, he breathed deep the soporific draught, foul and floating outward like swamp gas over the congregation. He rose and wobbled on two unsteady limbs rendered useless by the olfactory assault. Until finally, overcome by the fumes, he dropped to the floor and began to jabber. And just as he had before, the preacher twittered and quaked, vibrating to the glorious music of the spheres.

Katrine Quackenboss shot to her feet and cried "Hallelujah!" before herself succumbing to the edifying funk and immediately collapsing onto the floor. Then, like good Christian soldiers set all in a row, the members of the congregation began to drop one by one, each to his own spasmodic glory. To Jakob's great surprise, Anneke fluted a long leaky sigh from her delicate nostrils before sprawling out onto the floor beside him. Jakob watched her body writhe and listened to her moan. Her breasts swelled their corset as she arched her back, threatening to burst forth in seraphic glory. It was a vision to sear his very soul.

In the end, only Jakob and Oma Onderdonk remained upright and sentient. The rest of them wriggled orgiastically on the floor like snakes breeding in a snake pit. Oma Onderdonk grinned a dopey grin—the proud author of this holy chaos. Finally, Jakob rose to his feet, stepped over twitching Bonifaas, and led his oma from the meeting hall.

The carriage ride home was uncomfortable, with the silence sitting like a giant ogre between them. Yet is should be said that Jakob was not angry—although he was disappointed. Anneke sensed as much, and she held her tongue admirably. Once again, Jakob had been excluded, left in outer darkness. Every member of the congregation had been infused with the Holy Spirit—every member but him. What bothered him—nay, *troubled* him—most was even Anneke, a newcomer to the fold, had been gripped by religious enthusiasm. How, then, could Jakob not wonder if this clear exclusion was his punishment? Were his sins so grievous that God would deprive him—and him alone—of the spiritual manifestation that had taken place this day? For the plain truth was apart from the dreadful fetor of Oma Onderdonk's *scheet*, he had experienced nothing. Not a shiver, not a tingle.

When *Kanaalbrug* came into view, Anneke finally spoke: "Are you at all interested in my vision?"

"Perhaps later," said he.

"Even if I told you that you were in it?" She slid across the carriage seat until her thigh pressed against his.

Jakob puckered his lips in a way that suggested he was listening.

"You were dressed in a paisley patterned waistcoat trimmed with gold lace under a formal black coat complemented by black breeches, white silk stockings, and brass buckled shoes. Your long acorn-brown hair was tied back with a striking crimson ribbon."

"A dandified version of my true self, then."

"Oh, yes. You were dashing! Truly a gentleman's gentleman. And you held out your hand to me. It was terribly romantic."

In spite of himself and his earlier feelings of dejection, Jakob now found himself caught up in the cabalistic enigma of it all. "Terribly romantic, yes. But what does it mean?" said he. "What is the Almighty trying to tell you?"

"Oh, Jakob! Let me finish." said she. "I was dressed all in white satin and lace. A long flowing gown with a train of two yards or more. A veil obstructed my face, yet I could see the glint of a smile there. Certainly it was a smile! Surely it was the happiest day of my life!"

"My God!" said he. "That sounds like a wedding."

"Could it be true? Could I have had a vision of my own wedding day? But whatever could it mean?" Her breath felt hot on his neck.

"It seems clear that you are to be married."

"And why do you suppose *you* were in my vision?"

Before Jakob could fully consider the consequences of the words he was about to utter, he responded: "I suppose that the Almighty is telling you that you are to be wed to me." That this was meant to be something of a jocular repartee was lost on Anneke—to Jakob's great alarm, it should be said.

"Oh my! Do you really think it is so?"

He now felt like a rat with beady eyes darting desperately about the room looking for a hole to escape into. But clearly, it was too late. "Well . . . yes . . . I suppose it would seem that way."

With this, Anneke wrapped her arms around his neck and pulled him close. "Oh, Jakob! Yes! Yes! A thousand times, yes! I will marry you!"

By the time the carriage had reached *Kanaalbrug*, it was decided that both Mevrouw Onderdonk and Schoonhoven must be told posthaste. In truth, finding himself in a daze, Jakob contributed little more than the odd grunt and wag of his head to the decision in question. Nevertheless, the decision had been made—the engagement would be announced as soon as possible. And so it was that had any of

Leyden's faithful been idly standing about *Hooglandse Kerk* on this evening, they would have caught sight of Jakob accompanying his newly betrothed into the Onderdonk *herenhuis*, a little flustered and still rather bewildered by it all.

When he strolled into the sitting room with Anneke close by his side, Jakob thought he detected a trace of glee in the look that right then settled like a fat pheasant to its nest on his mother's pleased face. Jakob could not help but feel slightly annoyed. Perhaps it was the sunny eyes that beamed with excitement or the hint of a smile pushing up the corners of her mouth. A moment's consideration confirmed that, yes, it was the smile that vexed him so. For it was a smile that Jakob knew well—had come to know especially well over the past few years. Her all-knowing smile—the one that said *I know what you are going to tell me before you even say it.* Or as Jakob had come to think of it, her all-annoying smile.

"Mother, we have some news," said Jakob, rather too flatly, given the presumably happy nature of that news. "Meisje Schoonhoven— Anneke—and myself are to be wed in the spring."

His mother jumped up and clapped her hands. "Oh that is wonderful news. And what a surprise! Did you hear that, Oma Onderdonk? Jakob and Anneke are to be wed!"

The old woman raised her gray head and stared blankly at them like a fish facing a rock in an icy stream.

"We must celebrate!" said his mother. "Some *bier* and pastry. Perhaps even a glass of sweet wine. What do you say?"

Jakob suspected—rightly, it should be said—that much of his mother's delight at the news stemmed from the fact that she credited herself with the role of matchmaker in the union. Of course, he had not told her that the wedding proposal had been more a decree from God than an actual proposal. Neither had he told her that the decree had come in the form of a vision, one fueled by the foul *aars* fumes of their own Oma Onderdonk. As far as Jakob was concerned, that was something his mother did not need to know. He only hoped that she would be unable to divine as much for herself.

"Of course, yes, Mother." said Jakob. "Sweet wine sounds fine."

The following day, when Candide suggested that they travel to the asylum to visit Pangloss, Jakob eagerly agreed. This, he decided, would allow him to clear his mind. And his mind was indeed in need of clearing. Of course, most of those thoughts concerned Anneke and the impending marriage that he had somehow managed to fumble his way into.

The two arrived to find that the treatment had thus far had little effect on Pangloss. Gazing upon the unsightly philosopher was not a task for one of questionable constitution. Even so, the master's spirits were high. "Good Anabaptist," said he. "I shall never be able to repay your kindness. Surely you are the purest delight to our Creator." He wheezed and whistled in a decidedly unmusical way when he spoke.

"A kind exaggeration, but I thank you anyway," said Jakob.

"No, not an exaggeration, at all" said Pangloss. "I shall *never* be able to repay you for this treatment, for I have no money. After all, I am a philosopher. What use have I for Mammon?"

Just then a stiff-frocked physician swept into the room. He parted the patient's gown and plunged a needle into each of Pangloss's bony buttocks. The philosopher grimaced. "Quicksilver," said he. "Quite painful. But it could be worse."

"You cannot be serious. How could it possibly be worse?" said Jakob.

"The shots are only once every hour. And the cat *pis* and moose *poep* help ease the pain."

As if to illustrate this very point, the physician wound pungent smelling strips of gauze around the Master's head, leaving only a small opening through which to speak. Then he slathered a peppered brown paste onto the blotches that covered the philosopher's sunken chest.

Jakob addressed the physician: "What are his chances of recovery?"

"In my opinion," said he, "about ten percent."

"Ten percent? Is that all?"

"Give or take," said the physician.

"It could be worse," said Pangloss.

"Certainly it could," agreed Candide. "Ten percent is much better than no percent."

"Indeed it is. But let us speak of other happy matters. I am told, good Anabaptist, that you are to wed in the spring."

"Yes, it seems as if a wedding is in the cards for me." Jakob shifted his weight from one leg to the other, a habit he had only recently, if inexplicably, acquired.

"At the moment, I am blind but not deaf or dumb. You do not sound like one who is about to enter into matrimonial bliss."

"Well, yes. I mean, no. I mean, perhaps not."

"Ah, but let me explain. You see, the ring finger was formed precisely to fit and bear the wedding ring, thus by God's decree are we meant to wed. For every cause there is an effect and every effect there is a cause. All is for the best, and the best resides in all. It is as simple as that."

"I wish it were truly as simple as that." This was, of course, uttered with a liberal dash of irony, which, it must be said, went unnoticed by the philosopher and his disciple.

"He loves another—fair Heleen, the peasant girl," said Candide. "He pines for her, even as I mourn my defiled and departed Cunégonde. Quite the sorrowful pair we make."

"Ah, but there is a reason why circumstances occur as they do. The Maker knows every reason and every circumstance, and in accordance with those reasons and circumstances, he has created the best of all possible worlds. In this universal principle lies a universal explanation."

"Yes, it is so, Master Pangloss," said Candide, "though I am too quick to forget the truth of the principle."

Jakob was set to dissent when the physician returned with two silver syringes and jabbed them into the philosopher's rump. Pangloss yelped. "All is for the best," said he, with clenched teeth.

That evening, Jakob and Anneke were scheduled to officially share the happy news of their engagement with Mevrouw Schoonhoven. Jakob had arrived ten minutes early, as was his habit, and nervously fiddled with every piece of his attire that could possibly be fiddled with. When dinner was finally served, Jakob spooned *broodpap* into his mouth mechanically. "Matrimonial bliss," Pangloss had said. He wondered if such a thing were possible with fair Heleen always so near to his thoughts.

Jakob glanced at Mevrouw Schoonhoven. In the palsied grips of her disease, the poor woman fought to get a morsel of bread pudding to her lips. Her complexion was now splotched with unsightly blemishes and the gumma on her brow had grown to the size of a swollen plum.

Anneke rose to her feet, pulling Jakob up with her. "*Tante*," said she. "I—*we* have some wonderful news."

Mevrouw Schoonhoven raised two red bloated eyes and smiled painfully.

"Jakob has proposed marriage and I have accepted." Anneke clasped his hand. Jakob smiled weakly. "You have been like a mother to me these past years. And now, I—*we* wish for your blessing."

Mevrouw Schoonhoven rose unsteadily. "How could you? Look at me," said she. "I am hideous! You think only of yourselves!"

"*Tante*, no!"

"It is true. How shall I ever attend a wedding looking like a hagridden whore? I am hideous, so hideous when once I was so fair."

"But *tante*, you are still fair! Tell her, Jakob."

"Yes, yes, it is true. You are still fair."

"You lie! You both lie!" Mevrouw Schoonhoven brought a bony hand to her mouth and winced. Then her body buckled and she retched a spout of black slime across the table. Anneke shrieked in horror. But it was nothing compared to the horror that twisted the features of her syphilitic *tante*. What happened next occurred with such haste that Jakob was helpless to intercede. All he could do was sit by and watch as, in the space of that fleeting moment, Mevrouw Schoonhoven tore the wig from her head and baying like a moon-sick dog, threw herself at the nearest window. The crash of shattering glass that followed was deafening, heartrending.

Anneke screamed and smothered her face with two trembling hands. Jakob rushed to the window, where he saw the gruesome sight of Mevrouw Schoonhoven three floors down among the silver shards—broken, twisted, dead. And, yes, quite hideous.[41]

In the days that followed Mevrouw Schoonhoven's passing, Jakob took it upon himself to make all the necessary arrangements and to put things in order, as it is so euphemistically put in just such trying times. Family was notified—two distant cousins and an invalid great aunt. And of course, Jakob sent word to *Opperhoofd* Schoonhoven in Batavia, knowing full well that his wife would be long in the grave before the letter reached him.[42]

---

[41] What no one knew, or more specifically, what Anneke did not know— mainly because her *tante* had gone to great lengths to keep it from her—was after learning of her gloomy fate from a particularly morbid physician whose graphic descriptions of the disease were even more terrifying than the symptoms already manifested, Mevrouw Schoonhoven refused treatment in a sanatorium for fear of the shame it would bring upon her, her family, and her husband's good name. Instead, she vowed to suffer in secret, if not silence, and never leave the *herenhuis*. All she asked of the physician was that he tell no one of her condition and keep her amply plied with laudanum, which he did. Each week a corked brown bottle would arrive for her. And each day she would awake and pour twenty drops of the bitter tincture into a demitasse of strong French café and drink it with a slight grimace. On the night that her *nicht* and Jakob announced their engagement, Mevrouw Schoonhoven, having an especially bad day, had downed four cups of the bitter café.

[42] Six weeks later, when the letter finally did arrive in Batavia, *Opperhoofd* dropped down into his chair and set the letter on his desk. What struck him most about the letter was that it was written by Jakob—signed *Jakob Onderdonk* in a perfect hand: the "O" with a curlicue that breached the ink circumference then swooped upward, where it took squiggly flight; and the "K" supported by the loop of a piously bent knee. Why Jakob Onderdonk, whom he had not seen since the funeral of Captain Onderdonk, was the author of the letter *Opperhoofd* could not fathom. Perhaps being a family acquaintance and a former VOC man, reasoned he, Jakob had felt some residual sense of obligation to act as the man of the house in his stead. In fact, this seeming oddity consumed *Opperhoofd* more thoroughly than did the contents of the letter itself, almost to the point of exasperation. For what

The funeral service for Mevrouw Schoonhoven was an intimate one—that is to say, it was small. Unlike the casket in which the deceased was laid, which was an elaborate affair. And the slow and steady emaciation of Mevrouw Schoonhoven had left a corpse so slight as to scarcely put a dent in the satin lining of the hulking coffin. In the end, however, this mattered little, as it was decided that a closed-casket service would be best, appropriate—given the circumstances. Of course, it was generally agreed among social peers that Mevrouw Schoonhoven's fate had been a most unfortunate accident. There was no mention of madness or suicide. And certainly, the word *disease* crossed no one's lips. *Tragedy* and *misfortune* were the two words that Jakob heard most often at the funeral service.

When it was over, when the body was buried and her eyes were

Jakob had left out of the letter, deeming it to be in poor taste, was the news of his engagement to Anneke, *Opperhoofd's nicht*.

Finally, when he could think no more upon the point of authorship, *Opperhoofd* rose, uncorked a bottle of malt whisky, and filled a glass to the top. The realization that he was essentially alone in this world was unsettling but by no means debilitating. For his marriage had been neither happy nor unhappy. And in fact, he had never really considered it in those fallible extremes, and he doubted that Mevrouw Schoonhoven had either. The truth was their union had been satisfactory to both parties involved. A business venture that had brought together her family's wealth and his family's good name. The union had born no offspring. They had tried in the beginning. And *Opperhoofd* now believed that he would have welcomed a son or daughter and had on occasion even allowed himself to dwell upon that particular *what if*. But it was not to be. There would be no progeny. And over time, as that reality sunk in, he and Mevrouw Schoonhoven had spent fewer and fewer intimate moments together, until the their relationship could be described as simply cordial and nothing more. In fact, it had always been so. But in the beginning, attempts were made and airs were put on. But they soon after became impossible to keep up. And so it was that a young Meneer Schoonhoven stepped without regret onto a tripled masted East Indiaman and never looked back. It was twenty years ago that he left his wife alone in South Holland. And now, it seemed, she had responded in kind.

so sore they could not produce another tear, Anneke clung to Jakob. In the same way one might cling to a scrap of flotsam after the ship goes down. For his part, Jakob willingly bore her up, all the while offering her a shoulder to cry on. But even as he did, it occurred to him that the tragedy may well have cemented their future together. For if he had had any previous intention of extricating himself from his matrimonial obligations—nay, *entanglements*—the sudden passing of Mevrouw Schoonhoven had now rendered that intention a distinct impossibility. Quite simply, the callousness required to follow through with such a plan was beyond Jakob's emotional capacity, or *un*emotional capacity, to be precise. However, it should be said that he was not above trying—that is, testing the waters. And so, Jakob suggested that out of respect for the deceased, perhaps the wedding should be put off for a while. But he knew even as he uttered it that the suggestion made little sense.

"How can you say such a thing? For it is precisely the opposite of what *tante* would want."

"It's just that the tragedy has given us all—you and me—much to think about. Perhaps we should take some time to do just that."

Anneke teared up and cried into his neck. "Do you intend to abandon me now, my love?" She raised her eyes to his. "You do love me, don't you, Jakob?"

She pressed against him. Every hill and valley of her body found its complement on his. With his head swimming and his thinking muddled, Jakob still fought desperately. But in the end, he felt himself going under. And go under, he did. "Of course, yes. I do," said he. "After all, we're to be married, are we not?"

FROM A LETTER ADDRESSED TO
MEVROUW MARIJKE ONDERDONK,
LEYDEN, SOUTH HOLLAND

May 6, 1744

Dearest Marijke,

I received your most recent correspondence the day that we shipped out for Macau. How fortuitous! Of course, I am delighted that you and mother are spending so much time together. She does indeed enjoy her walks in the commons. Yes, I know that she can be stubborn and trying at times, but please remember, dear wife, that she has had a difficult life. (Yes a difficult life even by your family's stringent standards.) Losing her one true love on the very day of their union has, I'm sure you'll agree, had an indelible effect upon her mind. I fear that in her autumnal years, we shall see more of it. Let us hope and pray that, at that time, the disturbance in her mind manifests itself in nothing more than innocuous habits and petty annoyances.

Son of Batavia now returns from Macau loaded with slaves to be transported to various islands throughout the East Indies. The poor creatures whine and wail day and night, hoping for some intercession from their god or gods, whichever it might happen to be. As a good Christian man, I sometimes feel it is my duty to bring them to Christ the Lord, but as you can well imagine, this is no easy task. At times, I sit below and read to them from the Good Book in the hope that the truth of it will somehow be made known to them through God's grace. But they only stare back at me with the eyes of the damned—heathens condemned to occupy the fires below. Sometimes I cannot help but wonder if such will truly be the case. For the yellow man is not a beast, dear wife, he is as human as you or I. For are they not all mothers and fathers and children? Do they not fear many of the same things we fear—loneliness, betrayal, death? Why, then, would Almighty God wish to see them burn in the fires of Hell for eternity? 'Tis a mystery, to be sure, dear wife. And I cannot help but wonder if it is not God's wish at all but the wish of men with an agenda separate from His.

Of course, the godless deckhands of this ship do nothing to help the cause. They treat the slaves with less consideration than they would beasts of burden. When the yellow men below are brought above deck (which they are every day, in order that they might walk about and keep their spirits up), the deckhands sneer and spit upon them. Were my officers not standing there with loaded pistols, I feel certain the men would fall upon them. Who, I ask you, are the beasts and who the civilized men? Dear wife, at times, I cannot say with any certainty. But I suppose that is a question for another day. For now it suffices to say that the slaves are safely locked away in the ship's hold and they remain in their heathen state.

My dear Marijke, be well, and please see to Oma Onderdonk in my absence. I will write again soon and beg you to do the same.

Your Husband,
Cornelis

FROM A LETTER ADDRESSED TO
MEVROUW MARIJKE ONDERDONK,
LEYDEN, SOUTH HOLLAND

August 30, 1748

Dear Mother,

It has not escaped my attention that you no longer find it necessary or fitting to reply to my correspondence. For it has been better than a year since last I heard a peep from you. Despite this, your letters seem to easily find their way into the awaiting hands of my brother and my father, both. Perhaps they have been filling your head with fanciful tales. Perhaps you feel that the sea has stolen away your young and innocent son and left some wicked changeling in his stead. However, I assure you mother that no such shenanigans has taken place and that I am still the boy you once saw fit to suckle at your bosom.

It is true that my views of the world may have become slightly more focused and clear—but they have not changed. For how can a boy know the world of men? And now that I am nineteen years old and a man, am I to be expected to yet view the world as a boy? As the trembling twelve year old pup you turned over to father on the docks of Amsterdam? It is a preposterous notion, is it not?

And why is it, mother, that my brother's view of the world pleases you so? Is his clearly right and true and mine clearly wrong and false? Is there not room in this world for many views? For the one thing that I have learned in my years at sea thus far is this: ours is a wide and expansive world, a strange and wonderful world. So wide and expansive, in fact, that one view—your view—seems to me incapable of containing such a world with its rigid notions of right and wrong. Have you ever considered this, I wonder? You who have not stepped foot outside of South Holland.

Do you think the Mahometan or the Parsi or the Tantrist gives one whisker on a pig's snout about your view of the world? Let me answer for you—no, he does not. Why does he not? Because he has his own view of the world and, like you, has not given a thought to any others. Forgive my tirade—but you must understand, mother, that I am not Jakob, and I am not my father. If you cannot accept that then, yes, perhaps we have nothing left to say to each other. As much as it saddens me, I suppose that it is true.

I only hope that one day you may accept me, and not judge me. For that would be the happiest day of my life.

Your Second (Other) Son,
Robrecht

ELEVEN

Deciding he needed more rum to get the job done, Robrecht hoisted his tankard and drained it. "Dag!" said he. The sailor jumped to his feet. "How long have we been grounded on this godforsaken island. A month? Two?"

"Two, possibly three, sir. Old Dag can't be certain."

Robrecht sighed. One thing was certain—he had been unable to give the ugly chief his much-desired grandson. In the meantime, the fruit of the nutmeg tree rotted on the ground.

In those months in which *Son of Batavia* had been essentially grounded in the harbor of Bandanaira, Robrecht had grown to hate the matrimonial hut—nay, fear it. Not to mention that he now loathed his new bride, whereas before his feelings ran largely toward indifference. The reason being that despite all efforts, he had been unable to impregnate her. It was long past a point of pride for Robrecht. It would be fair to say that it was now a point of desperation.

The first mate had tried everything—every position, every orifice, every potion, powder, and paste. He had even slathered some foul smelling unction given to him by a blind albino shaman onto his privates, causing his *pik* to sizzle like a dog on a spit. But nothing seemed to work. Zeuga remained without child. He had come to think of her sizable womb was an unbroken plain upon which his seed could lever no purchase.

What Robrecht found infuriating about his all-too-apparent shortcoming was that he had never in all his years at sea encountered such a problem before. He had impregnated countless strumpets, harlots, and whores in the eastern hemisphere— effortlessly. He personally knew of thirty-two little scallywags with the characteristic beaked upper lip of an Onderdonk in thirty-two different port towns. How many other little scabs of life he had scratched into existence was anyone's guess.

All of this now led him to believe that his recent and painful bout of *pissen* blood was not so innocent after all. He cringed to think that it had rendered him a eunuch, if only of the symbolic sort. It was not that he wished to sire more beak-lipped bastards. He had not set his sights on begetting a legion of mongrels with which he would storm Delhi and slaughter the reigning Mughals. It was simply that one always wants that option should one ever be struck by such an ambitious whim. And for Robrecht, symbolic castration was so deleterious. He felt like he was marching into battle with a flintless flintlock. Without that very necessary spark that sent lead balls sailing over the battlefield. And so it was that Robrecht came to fear and loathe the procreative act—in particular, the procreative act with Zeuga. It was not pleasurable. It was humiliating and degrading. That is to say, it was heinous.

Dag held out a refill. "Here ye be, sir. Drink it down. Ye'll be needing yer strength."

Robrecht took the tankard and spilled it down his gullet. The truth was he'd lost track of how many visits he'd paid to the detested hut. "I need more than strength," said he. "I need luck."

"Aye, sir. But the drink has always been lucky for Old Dag. Drink it down, now."

Robrecht did. Then he stamped and stumbled through the village toward the matrimonial hut. But no crowd awaited him there. And the fanfare of the wedding night was no longer. In a word, the villagers had lost interest. Not only that, the men had now returned to the harbor to renew the battle for Fort Belgica.

Zeuga awaited his arrival this day on all fours, her squab buttocks elevated, revealing the flabby flaps of her *kut*. One look and Robrecht's stomach churned, sending him dashing from the hut, where he choked out a pint of rum. "Dag," said he, swiping at a dangling string of spittle, "you must do it."

"What, sir?—That? No, sir. 'Tis not possible. Ye know Old Dag is not of that ilk."

"Do you want to remain forever on this island?"

"No, sir. Old Dag does miss his Agnes so."

"Then it's time for you to stand up and stand in.

"But me old *pik* willn't stand up for the likes of her. And the island's not got enough rum on it to vary that one iota, sir."

Robrecht heaved another sigh, stood upright. As he was about to return to the hut, in this moment of deep desperation, he was struck by a novel idea—perhaps rum was not the answer, thought he, pausing just long enough to consider the details of the harebrained scheme that was presently taking shape in his head. Then he spoke confidently: "Let me worry about your *pik*. Wait five minutes then go into the hut. Hold your tongue, do not speak a word. Take no lamp and wait in darkness for my signal."

"What is the signal?"

"Rest assured, you will know it."

Minutes later, Robrecht returned with the ugly chief's goat in tow. He staked the nanny outside the hut, where she immediately buried her nose in the grass and began to munch. In the meantime, Robrecht found a switch and wasted no time laying it forcefully across the beast's rear haunches. As expected—nay, hoped—the cruel if necessary act elicited a long rolling bleat from the nanny. Robrecht stepped near to the hut and cupped his ear, hoping to hear the sweet sounds of procreation. When a soft whimper came from within the hut, he whipped the nanny again and again—with great glee, it should be said—until soon a chorus of howls and moans filled the hut, and Robrecht could clearly make out the frantic squawks of his *pribumi* wife. Rising and rising, louder and louder, came the squawks, matched only in their intensity by the tortured bleats of the nanny goat. It was a welcomed symphony of pain and pleasure. And at that moment, Robrecht was convinced that there could be no more pleasing sound in all the East Indies—nay, in all the world.

The following fortnight was a time for celebration, for he had done it—Robrecht had impregnated the ugly chief's daughter. Of course, he had done no such thing. However, to his mind, although he had not performed the actual impregnating act, the plan had been his and only his. But even more importantly, no one was the wiser. So as far as Robrecht was concerned, it would be his and Dag's secret, one of many that had accrued over the years, in fact.

An animal of every kind was slaughtered and stewed, boiled, grilled, or fried in a rainbow of exotic spices: *ayam percik, nasi kuning, otak-otak.* Fruits of all shapes, sizes, and colors accompanied every dish: *durian, mangosteen, rambutan*. Add to that an endless supply of red rice rum and black *bier*, and it equaled a feast unprecedented in magnificence and abundance. Like none ever before seen on the island.

The ugly chief was blissfully delirious from drink, gushing on anyone within arm's reach, whom it turned out, was mainly his own daughter. Zeuga gnawed on goat satay with one hand, while resting the other on the abundantly rolling flesh of her belly. Finally, she was pregnant. Robrecht allowed himself a controlled moment of joy. For tonight they would feast. And tomorrow the locals would return to the nutmeg orchards. Then he and his crew would weigh anchor and hoist sails for Batavia. Truly, this was a night to celebrate.

Robrecht caught the eye of Dag and gave him a clandestine nod. He planned to promote the able seaman to first mate as soon as bow cut water. And as far as Robrecht was concerned, that could not happen soon enough. For he was a dyed-in-the wool sailor, and being inland too long made his heels itch uncontrollably.

The pleasant thought of departing this wretched island, a thought which, it should be said, was at least in part fueled by the fumes of an especially strong *arrack* made from coconuts and palm sap, was interrupted by a long-nosed *pribumi* whose prominent proboscis looked to have been flattened more than a time or two by a battery of fists.

"I know what you did, white devil," said the smashed-nose *pribumi*.

Robrecht did his best to ignore the intrusion.

"I saw what you did. Or should I say you, the sailor, and the goat?"

A sudden gust of panic awoke Robrecht to the possibility that he had been spied whipping the nanny outside the matrimonial hut. He searched his memory for a clue as to who the smash-nosed *pribumi* might be and, more importantly, what he may have seen. But he could think of nothing.[43] "I'm sure I haven't a clue what you are

---

[43] Robrecht had been too preoccupied with his plan to impregnate Zeugma—via Dag—to notice the smash-nosed *pribumi* following him to the

referring to," said Robrecht to the smashed-nose *pribumi*.

"I think you do," said Smashed Nose. "How do you think the *leidsman* will react when I tell him that his grandson was not sired by a first mate—"

"Captain!" said Robrecht, clearly agitated with the whole scene that was playing out before his very eyes. "I'm the captain of *Son of*

---

matrimonial hut. The *pribumi*, who was named Bambang, had been reclining in his hut with a tankard of homebrew plum whisky never more than a martyr's plea away from his bloated lips, when he heard the bleat of a goat. He rose and cursed. Sloshing whisky on his toes, he peeked out his window and saw the white devil leading away the *leidsman's* goat—formerly his goat. For the nanny now belonged to Wibawa, the same who had cheated him out of his goat in a game of "This Way, That Way." In truth, Bambang had lost the game fairly—always lost the game fairly, which went a long way in explaining his badly beaten-down nose. The premise of the game was a simple one. A challenger ran at full speed toward the scrappy bole of a sizeable palm tree until at the last moment the challengee bellowed either "this way" (right) or "that way" (left), at which time the challenger then veered accordingly, without touching the tree. Paralyzed by indecision, Bambang typically ran headlong in the bole, and the game ended with his proboscis bloodied and another lost pig, chicken, or in this case, a nanny goat.

So, hearing his beloved and now former nanny goat, Bambang set down his tankard and followed the white devil at the safe distance of three donkey carts. He wondered what bargain the white devil had struck with Wibawa, that he now led the nanny away to some unknown fate. Perhaps the white devil had been the victor in a rousing game of "This Way, That Way," thought he. But the thought only fueled the fires of humiliation and made his smashed nose throb painfully. Bambang cursed under his foul breath.

When the white devil staked the nanny outside of the matrimonial hut and began to switch the poor beast, Bambang was scarcely able to refrain from falling upon him and beating him senseless. But then came a howl and moan from the matrimonial hut—louder and louder, until it reached a puling end. And much to Bambang's surprise, from out of the hut limped the white devil's confederate, a crooked grin plastered on his pocked mug. After several long and—and it must be said, faltering—moments of cognition, Bambang finally understood. More importantly, he had found a way to get his nanny back. And to get rich in the process.

Batavia now."

"Even better. How do you think the *leidsman* will react when I tell him that his grandson was not sired by a captain but by a lowly deckhand?"

Robrecht narrowed his gaze. The *pribumi* had to be kept silent, at least for the moment. He knew that. Later, he would take more permanent measures—that is, violent, lethal measures.

"What do you want?"

"So you admit to it, then?"

"I admit nothing. What do you want?"

"White devils! If you can't steal it, you'll buy it." Smashed Nose took a step back. "I want gulden, of course. A trunk full of them."

"I'll see what can be arranged," said Robrecht.

"Yes, you see what can be arranged. In the meantime, I'm going to share a drink with the *leidsman*. We're good friends, you know. So you should not wait too long. Who knows what might slip from my lips."

Smashed Nose slinked away into the orange glow of the fire that made his brown skin shine like wet metal. Robrecht watched him pick up a goat satay and shove it whole—and with no small amount of gusto—into his mouth. Then Smashed Nose held up his cup high to the ugly chief and said "To the health of your new grand—" but the final word snagged in his larynx like a hook in his throat. Smashed Nose gagged and gurgled, tried to cough out the offending syllable but nothing came. He clutched his throat. And when that didn't work, he clawed his chest. All of this was done while performing a herky-jerky dance in the warm coronet of light pulsing about the fire. Of course, for their part, the wedding crowd looked on, curious if not amused by this peculiar toast. Not least among them was the ugly chief himself, who waited patiently—that is to say, drunkenly—for this daftly entertaining mime to end.

Robrecht, too, stood by and watched silently, pleasantly distracted by the choking fool's antics. He marveled at how, once again, death had arrived on the scene—at least, it certainly appeared that way from where he was standing. So Robrecht raised his tankard and welcomed his old friend with a prodigious glug of *arrack*. No sooner had he done so than Smashed Nose stumbled over and fell into his arms. The *pribumi's* eyes were wide with panic, pleading with tears. A high-pitched squeak squeezed from the back of his throat and his long flat nose twitched like a rabbit's down the barrel of a musket. Of course it should go without saying that Robrecht had no intention of helping him. For he knew he could not rely on the discretion of the smashed-nose *pribumi*, even if he were to save the blundering *imbeciel*. For clearly, gratitude was a beast that these people knew nothing about, felt nothing for, save to slaughter and stuff it into their dripping muzzles. And seeing that Robrecht was not about to help him, the *pribumi* squinted his eyes and struggled, tried to speak, scream his hatred for the white devil. He struck his fists weakly against Robrecht's chest with what little remained of his strength. But the de facto captain of *Son of Batavia* held him tightly until at last Smashed Nose went blue and limp. Then Robrecht let the body fall to a heap at his feet.

"Must've got a bone," said the ugly chief with a slobber and a slur.

The ill-fated Smashed Nose was forgotten before the next round of *arrack* had been washed down the collective *pribumi* maw, and by morning the body had disappeared—to where Robrecht neither knew nor cared. Happily, he stood by and watched the ugly chief organize the harvest. Soon, the welcome sight and sounds of *pribumi* workers filled the nutmeg orchards. Fallen fruit was gathered and the precious brown core removed from its pulpy outer shell. The bright red mesh of mace was then peeled away from the nutmeg core before the fruit was sorted into baskets and hauled away by waiting donkey carts.

For Robrecht, it was all very interesting but not particularly compelling to spectate. So he decided to return to Fort Belgica to share the good news with the *perkeniers,* who, fearing an uprising, had remained there under the protection of the crew of *Son of Batavia.* When he arrived, Robrecht found the men slumped, curled, and sprawled in every construable attitude on the meticulously fitted cut-stone floor. Kegs of rum rolled onto their sides now rocked gently, extinguished. He located the third mate and roused him with a sound kick to the ribs. Meneer Buskirk rolled over and groaned. Seeing Robrecht hovering over him, the derelict officer jumped to his feet and his heavily stubbled jaw snapped shut.

"This is how you hold down the fort?" said Robrecht. "I ought to have you flogged."

"Sir, we thought you'd perished in the jungle. We've had no word from you in months. And we've been fighting off the *pribumi*."

"Well, I have not perished. And you will have no more trouble with the *pribumi*. I've negotiated a deal."

"Negotiated?" said Buskirk.

"Yes, negotiated. Normal tyranny and bloodshed have no effect on these people. I have been forced to resort to negotiating."

"And has this negotiating born fruit, sir?"

"As it happens, yes it has. The *pribumi* are harvesting the nutmeg as we speak." He pushed past Meneer Buskirk. "Where are the *perkeniers*? I have come to share the good news with them. They may now safely return to their plantations."

"They became . . . unruly, sir. We had to incarcerate them."

"Unruly? Do not jest with me! Those hen-hearted islanders lack the backbone to become unruly. Where are they?"

"In the stockade, sir."

Robrecht marched across the pentagon-shaped courtyard to the stockade. There, he found the plantation owners, stripped bare, their pale bodies beaten black and blue. The large-bosomed *perkenier's* wife lay staked to the ground, her legs splayed open, her breasts flopped in opposing directions. She moaned deliriously.

"They have become unruly, you say?" said Robrecht.

"Well, perhaps the crew also became unruly—and bored."

"Release them at once."

Meneer Buskirk moved from one *perkenier* to the next with great haste, opening locks and removing chains in a depreciative-cum-apologetic fashion.

"You are free to go back to your homes and plantations," said Robrecht. "The *pribumi* are back in the orchards, harvesting the nutmeg as we speak. You will have no more quarrels with them." Although he spoke matter-of-factly, Robrecht's proclamation was not without a certain whiff of pride. For it had—had it not?—been a great accomplishment, thought he. However, despite what he thought, and accomplishment or not, the *perkeniers* felt nothing resembling gratitude towards Robrecht and his crew.

"But I was pummeled by your men," said one of them. "And my teeth were knocked out." He stretched a stumpy grin as proof.

"They stamped on my balls like newly hatched chicks." said another. He proffered two squashed *testikels* as evidence of the misdeed.

"And they ravaged my wife, over and over," said the once plump *perkenier*, "despite her cries of displeasure."

"Yes, well, that is the cost of your freedom, then, is it not?" said Robrecht. "It is all in the past and all for the best. You are free to go now."

The once plump *perkenier* who had once before fallen upon Robrecht's neck fell again—this time not with tears of gratitude but with tears of rage. Robrecht easily fought off the feeble assault. "Has the heat scorched your brain, fool? I am your emancipator."

"And also my oppressor," said the *perkenier*. "For we have been tortured and abused at the hands of your men."

"Is in not better to be tortured and abused at the hands of Christian men than at the hands of heathen *pribumi*?"

"Christian? You are not Christian men!" The once plump *perkenier* threw up his arms, causing a ripple in the loose-hanging skin about his abdomen. "How is it possible that you are Christian men?"

"Look there, sir!" Robrecht pointed through the rusted bars of a window to the distant anchored ship. "*Son of Batavia* sails under the Dutch flag. Is there any nation in the world that is more Christian?"

"But would a Christian nation do to its own people what you have done to us? Would our Lord and Savior have done what you and your men have done to us?"

"Phooey! Even Christ was not immune to fits of rage. He cleared the temple with a whip, did he not?"

"That is different. Christ was filled with a righteous rage when he chased the money changers from the temple."

"Do you think the money changer whose back and legs were

bloodied by his whip cared one iota that it was a righteous rage?"
Robrecht paused. He dropped to a knee. "Do you think this tooth,"
said he, pointing, "cares to know if it was knocked out in a fit of
righteous rage or a fit of unrighteous rage?" He rose and walked to
the *perkenier*'s wife, gesturing to the dewy mound where her splayed
legs converged. "Do you think this *kut* cares that it was violated by a
righteous *pik* or a salacious *pik*? A *pik* is a *pik*. And rage is rage. It
makes us men. It makes us human. All men are subject to it, even
Christ, even Christians."

At this point, it was clear that the once plump *perkenier* would not
fall again upon Robrecht's neck in gratitude or rage. For the only
thing to fall in that pitiful moment was a profound silence over the
courtyard. The *perkenier* dropped his head and, seeing his shriveled
member beneath a flabby paunch, covered his shame and shuffled
away.

FROM THE JOURNAL OF CAPTAIN CORNELIS ONDERDONK

January 26, 1746
Today, I watched my sons each don the coatee of an officer in the VOC. 'Twas a proud moment, indeed. After the brief formality, Jakob quickly retreated to his cabin. Robrecht, on the other hand, pranced about the ship's spar deck as if he were the Papal Father in Rome. Some of the men cheered and others hollered their approval. But no one appeared more pleased than Able Seaman Dag.

From the start, the deckhand took a rather unhealthy interest in Robrecht's education at sea. Of course, not only as a captain, but as a caring father, I did my best to keep the two apart, but sadly, I have failed in this regard, for they are now thick as thieves. To my knowledge, Able Seaman Dag is a longstanding seaman with the VOC, and although more-than-competent in many respects, one who is unlikely ever to rise above the station of deckhand. Among the men, he is reputed to have vile and unhallowed appetites. And although I am not one to judge a man by the cut of his coat or the twirl of his moustache, by the look of Able Seaman Dag, it would come as no surprise to me to learn that the rumors were true. Perhaps the most peculiar thing about his look of him is his seemingly ageless quaility — by which I mean it is difficult to say with any certainty if he is twenty-five and a day or twice as much. At times, he seems young and sprightly, yet by the light of a full moon, he looks older than Adam's ghost. What it is about Seaman Dag that Robrecht finds so appealing is not clear to me. Admittedly, the man has a certain charm and seems to have no quarrel with the other men — that is, those who do not dare cross him. I can only conclude that Robrecht is drawn to the sailor's salt. Robrecht is the type of young man who wishes to know and see all — to experience it firsthand. I suppose he believes Able Seaman Dag is a worthy guide in that regard.

It would be highly untruthful of me to say I do not wish to be his mentor at sea. For I do, or at least, I did. What father does not wish to show his son the world as he sees it? However, it would seem that the world which Robrecht wishes to see is not the world in which I live. And the most tragic part of all of this is I am unable to stop him. It is too late, for he is a strong-willed young man who cannot be swayed this way or that. Whether I have contributed to his strong will or not, I cannot say (it is not an altogether undesirable trait in an officer), but I believe he comes by it naturally from his mother's side. Be that as it may, it appears that I am now helpless, destined to stand by and watch my son stumble down a path that leads to God knows where.

FROM A LETTER ADDRESSED TO
CAPTAIN CORNELIS ONDERDONK,
BATAVIA, JAVA, DUTCH EAST INDIES

April 1, 1741

Dearest Cornelis,

I know it has not been long since my boys escaped my matronly clutches, but I miss them more and more each day, it seems. You know that I am not one for tears and useless sentimentality, but I find myself increasingly at their mercy these days. They keep me occupied in the longs hours of these interminable days.

You ask how things are here in Leyden. Well, I will tell you, dear husband: the cows moo, the sheep baa and the pigs make whatever sound it is that pigs make (piggle?). What do I mean by this? Simply that nothing has changed and everything remains the same as it always has and undoubtedly always will. Leyden is a Cuyp landscape—stale and frozen in time. However, there is one bit of "news" that you are sure to find amusing: Pastor Hogarth came calling to the herenhuis a few days past. Such a blowhard and buffoon for a man of God! It would seem that the Almighty is not as discriminating as he may have once been (for the pastor could not be mistaken for a Moses, Peter, or even a Thomas). Oh Cornelis! 'Tis only a jest! But you must admit that the man and his tubby wife are a scourge upon this village. She is a crass saucebox and he is her only equal. And what did the pastor want from me? Of course, the premise of his visit was a "rather embarrassing emergency" which had arisen during a walk to calm his "colic constitution." (I ask you, what churchman calls uninvited upon parishioners in order that he might sully their indoor lavatory?) Soon after, however, the impromptu visit turned to concern for the state of my mortal soul. It seems Pastor Hogarth heard that I have been making secret visits to Hooglandse Kerk, where I sit in adoration at the Savior's feet for hours at a time. How preposterous! Me of all people! Why would I do such a thing, Cornelis? You know of my disaffection for churches. So I responded to this comment (accusation?) with a guffaw, and he suggested that I attend Mass the following Sunday. At this point, the real reason for his visit became clear: he wished to multiply the filthy lucre upon his collection plate. My God! Do these churchmen believe us all to be imbeciles? Do they think we cannot see through the pretense?

Not only that, dear Cornelis, the pastor clutched my hand as he bid me come to Mass and held it tightly for an immodest duration of time. I struggled to get my poor appendage free, to no avail. 'Twas as if he'd latched on to the Holy Grail with his pudgy paw and had no intention of giving it up in this lifetime. I swear there was a libidinous look in his eye! Finally he let go, and I snatched my hand away. He smiled, said God bless you, and took his leave with an air of entitlement that somehow made me feel as if I were not in my own home. But rest assured, dear husband, he has not put even the slightest chink in my armor. I will not be attending his or any other church this Sunday. I only wish you would have been here to set him on his way with a boot to his abundant backside.

But alas, you are not here. And now I have come full circle, back to my forlorn thoughts of you and the boys. It is a sadness that almost feels like a gloomy personage in the room, albeit one who offers nothing in the form of companionship. Take care of our boys, dear Cornelis. And please, take care of yourself.

Your Loving Wife,
Marijke

TWELVE

Organized and overseen by the ugly chief, the nutmeg harvest was well underway and pressing on towards a successful end. Wisely, Robrecht had let the *leidsman* lead. This, it turned out, was no small feat, as many were the times when he would wonder at the seeming folly of this or that particular course of action. Quite frankly, the *pribumi* baffled Robrecht in almost every way. As far as he could tell, their customs were senseless and their traditions a mockery of all things judicious. Yet somehow the harvest continued to roll forward—which baffled him most of all—like some colossal Trojan horse (which Robrecht felt certain must conceal at least one pesky Greek plotting for the sudden ruination of the whole endeavor) and so he did not wish to upset the natural disorder of things in this foreign, foreign land.

During this time, Robrecht could be found surveying the island from beneath a woven cane hat. He routinely traipsed from one end of it to the other, until he imagined he knew the lay of it, just as he knew the lay of the three-masted East Indiaman, moored and motionless in the harbor. One day near the end of the harvest, Robrecht hiked to the foot of *Gunung Api* and descended a rocky cliff to the white beach below. There, a group of *pribumi* boys had gathered in a circle. He approached and pushed his way in. In the center of the circle lay a young boy, perhaps the youngest in the group, thought Robrecht, rolling in the sand moaning and every now and then stiffening like a plank and grinding his teeth nervously. The other boys gasped then giggled at each convulsion. After several minutes of this, Robrecht finally broke the silence and asked what was wrong with him. A tall boy answered: "Sea snake," tugging on his big ears, then adding: "Many sea snakes are here in the waters below *Gunung Api*."

Once again, Robrecht was baffled. For why the boys would swim in waters infested with sea snakes was a complete and utter mystery to him. Finally, he asked the boy as much, to which he was given the response, "We all swim here, sir. It is a game we play."

"Swimming with sea snakes? A game?" said Robrecht.

"The sea snake does not attack easily. We must make it attack. But it is best to make the sea snake bite you here, sir." The boy pointed to his one of his bare buttocks. "For this bite will give you wonderful visions. Like drunkenness, but better." The other boys laughed in agreement. "But if it bites here . . . or here," said the boy, gesturing to his hand and foot, ". . . it could be very dangerous for you."

"So where was this young boy bitten?"

"Here." The tall boy grabbed Robrecht's forearm just above the wrist. "He will die soon, I think."

That night, Robrecht ate the local fare and drank *arrack*. News of the young boy's death earlier that evening had little effect on him. For Robrecht knew well that even the young were not immune in this world—to anything. Neither did the boy's death seem to dull the spirits of the *pribumi* workers who had gathered for a celebration. "The harvest is over," said the ugly chief, "just as the rainy season is set to begin. Tonight we drink like men afire with thirst." And this they did. But as *bier* and *arrack* flowed like the fountain of Peisistratus, the drink seemed to do nothing to quench the fire of their thirst. And so it was that the celebration went on into the wee hours of the morning.

Robrecht accepted a gourd of rum from Zeuga, and instinctively, his gaze dropped. Every time he laid eyes on the rapidly growing belly of his *pribumi* wife, he felt the need to escape—a need that swelled in him like a billowing mainsail. The ugly chief must also have been regarding his daughter's expanding girth at that moment, for said he: "When the boy is born we will build you a great hut of your own."

"Your generosity is much appreciated, of course. But I am a sea captain for the Dutch East India Company," said Robrecht in a mirthful way that stopped just short of a guffaw. "I cannot settle inland in a *pribumi* hut."

"Sea captain, ha!" The ugly chief paused to gulp rum. "How will the boy be raised to be a *pribumi* chief when his father is forever at sea?"

Of course, it should be said that Robrecht had never stopped to consider that his part in the bargain might not end with the birth of the child. Until now, that is. He wanted to protest but feared that displeasing the ugly chief might touch off another *pribumi* uprising, one in which he would be caught dead center.

To Robrecht's great relief, the weighty silence that followed was broken by the ugly chief's booming belch. The other *pribumi* men present responded with equally lusty belches. This prompted the ugly chief to jump to his feet. "Tonight we climb *Gunung Api*," said he, "to give thanks to the gods for a plentiful harvest." The men roared their approval and drank deep draughts to ready themselves.

When the time came, Robrecht was coaxed into joining them in the yearly male ritual. In actuality, Robrecht allowed himself to be coaxed into the yearly male ritual. For he was morbidly curious as to the bad end that would surely come to a group of drunken *pribumi* who felt compelled to scale the walls of an ill-tempered volcano in the dead of night. And so it was that he traipsed with them through the jungle in near darkness to the foot of *Gunung Api*, drinking and singing all the way.

Gunung Api, it turned out, was more volcanic hill than mountain, and it took less than an hour to ascend—even in the from-cupboard-to-wall and pillar-to-post manner in which the task was undertaken. At the summit, the ugly chief wasted no time in embracing Robrecht. "One day you will bring my grandson to this very spot so that he might see the island he rules over." A tear rumbled over the pimpled rind that was the *leidsman's* face. At least, it appeared to be a tear. But then Robrecht felt the splat of a heavy raindrop against his own cheek. Then another and another. And then came the deluge.

The *pribumi* danced wildly, primitively, in the downpour. Loud blasts of thunder rocked them back onto their heels; brilliant flashes of lightning blinded their eyes—intensifying the fierceness of their animalistic dance. Robrecht stood aside and witnessed this spectacle of pre-civilization, caught a glimpse of the primordial *pribumi*.

The ugly chief grunted and bellowed, crouched then bounded skyward. The others surrounded him, echoing his sounds and movements in what was clearly a well-rehearsed ritual. With every repetition, the ugly chief bounded farther and farther into the black sky, clawing at its celestial contents. The *pribumi* men around him grunted and leapt just as he landed. This went on for quite some time. So long, in fact, that Robrecht began to wonder at the impressive stamina of the podgy, yet seemingly indefatigable, *leidsman*.

Just when it appeared the ugly chief could go no higher, a dagger of lightning hurled from the darkest precinct of the heavens sizzled to Earth and split the ugly chief's skull open like a ripe melon. The precision of the strike was astounding, stupefying, lethal. Instantly lifeless, the *leidsman* flopped down onto the ground and the steaming contents of his brain bubbled from its cracked dome.

Here was the bad end Robrecht had predicted.[44] Thus did the *pribumi* men returned to the village with the now headless *leidsman* on their somber shoulders. They were met by a Zeuga, hysterical and screeching like a winged harpy. She wept and wailed uncontrollably. Robrecht watched as she beat her chest and yanked fistfuls of hair out by the roots.

As was the custom where great men were concerned, the dead *leidsman's* body was rubbed with coconut milk then covered with poisonous ground jequirity seeds in order to keep the village curs

---

[44] And at this point, Robrecht also correctly predicted that the harvest tradition would be indefinitely discontinued. More precisely, it was immediately abandoned. However, there was something fitting about the end of the ugly chief bringing an end to the tradition. He had, after all, begun the tradition only several years earlier during an especially energetic bout of drunken revelry. At the time, he'd been occupied with the customary temulent antics of harvest time—swigging *arrack* from his penis gourd and howling like a badly maimed dog at the moon—when he got it in his head that he could capture the unusually full moon in his grubby fist. It appeared to him to loom so very near overhead. So the *leidsman* jumped and jumped. And jumped some more—each time going just a little higher than the time before. The harvest tradition grew from this single act of idiocy by the *leidsman* to a group act of idiocy by all the pribumi men in the village. Still, as idiotic as it may have looked to outsiders, no one was ever killed while taking part in it. Until the ugly chief, that is.

from gnawing it clean to the bones. The next morning the corpse was humped to the top of Fire Mountain and tossed into the volcano. This was followed by a long session of public mourning, in which the *pribumi* men of the village drank copiously and blubbered tears into the hot lava below, a boozy performance which, Robrecht was informed, occasionally resulted in further death. The tears of the mourners were believed to quench the dead man's thirst as he dogpaddled the fiery lake to the center of the earth. Exactly what he did at the center of the earth was unclear to Robrecht.[45]

That whole night Zeuga stomped over the jungle floor like a wild beast in a fever of madness. Then at first light, she returned to the village. Robrecht heard her cry a mighty cry—a long single note of agony as if she were caught in the clamped and multiple jaws of Cerberus. Off-key mourning. Pure dissonance that tipped the universe one degree off in its unerring course of order. Robrecht rose from his cot and walked to the window. There, he witnessed the first tremor quake through her. This was followed by a shudder that grew in intensity and violence until blood poured from her nose, bled from her eyes, and dribbled from her ears. Finally, she collapsed into the dust. At that moment, Robrecht imagined her to be a Gorgon who had just then feasted upon the giant heart of Porphyrion. He had seen many things in his twenty-seven years on Earth. And it must be said that none of them had shaken him terribly. Yet, he was surprised by what he then witnessed—although to say that Robrecht was *transfixed* by this display of grief would be closer to the truth.

He retreated to his hut and eased down onto the cot. The truth was he was surprised but not saddened. Nor was he displeased. For he could not help but see this most recent development for what it really was: another bit of good fortune. And so it was that Robrecht

---

[45] Local mythology was frustratingly vague when it came to specifics concerning what was to occupy the dead once they arrived at the final destination. Suffice to say, it seemed to the *pribumi* to be an aptly courageous journey for a dead man to make, regardless of that one final detail.

rose resolutely and gathered his belongings into his seabag.

He slipped from the village as a crowd converged upon Zeuga, now lying unconscious in the dust. A volley of concerned calls for the blind albino shaman who lived near the top of *Gunung Api* echoed like cannon fire across the clearing. But Robrecht felt certain that by the time the old man hobbled into the village, Zeuga would be destined for the scalding hot stew that boiled at the bottom of the volcano, or however it was the *pribumi* disposed of the bodies of dead women, pregnant or otherwise.

In any case, it was no longer his concern. Not that whether his *pribumi* wife lived or died was ever his concern, really. Robrecht had long ago learned that a show of concern—along with its three ugly sisters: sympathy, empathy, and charity—was a waste of one's valuable energy, energy that could be better spent honing one's wits and priming one's instincts in order to better stay standing when death tried to lay one low in the grave. And death would try. Of this, he was certain, for he had witnessed it time and again in his years at sea.

When he arrived at the fort, he found the men in various stages of drunkenness, the worst dozing in and out of morphean slumber, with its blank dreams drawn like still black curtains over their eyes. Robrecht marched up the tower steps and looked out at the setting sun in a clear sky. He sniffed the breeze, tasted the sea on his lips. His senses told him that storms were brewing. And experience told him that it was too late in the day to weigh anchor. They would have to wait until sunrise.

He descended the stairs and found Dag. The inebriated sailor's state was such that he could not be roused by any means, lethal or nonlethal. Robrecht turned to Third Mate Buskirk. "We leave at first light. See to the provisions."

"What provisions, sir? We have none. With all due respect, is it wise to leave now?"

"What would you have us do, Buskirk? Stay here among the *pribumi*? Live off the land? Settle down and become inlanders?"

"No, Meneer Onderdonk, it's just that—"

"It's Captain Onderdonk, Meneer Buskirk. Or have you forgotten? Because I have not forgotten your traitorous acts on this island. But no one is here to protect you now. Your Meneer Bleeker is dead and gone. And you would do well to choose your side more carefully in the future."

The following morning, by the time the sun had fully arisen above the eastern meridian that separates sea and sky, *Son of Batavia* was cutting water for Batavia. The ship sailed on a west by southwest course, passing the southwestern tip of Celebes on the fifth day. But on the fifth night, a tempest arose and they were hit by a squall. When it was over, the ship lay well off course. Robrecht believed that the ship had been driven far up into Makassar Strait, and that the craggy tree-covered coast he could see from his cabin window was that of the Magkalihat Peninsula. A moment's calculations with pencil and rule, and he concluded that a south-southwesterly course would lead back to the Java Sea

As he contemplated the present predicament, a knock came to the door. Meneer Buskirk entered. The third mate spoke gravely: "Sir, the men are restless—anxious."

"Speak freely, Meneer Buskirk," said Robrecht with a sigh meant to demonstrate his growing impatience.

"The men grow weary of the storms and of our depleted provisions. How long can they be expected to eat bland beans and blackened bread? Especially when they see the cook daily throwing pounds of beef to flocks of awaiting seabirds."

Robrecht growled. If the point was a sour one with the men, it was doubly sour with him. For he, too, was frustrated by recent events, particularly those concerning the tins of beef. Still, Robrecht knew there was nothing else to be done.

"The beef sat in the ship's hull for months while moored at Bandanaira." Robrecht waved his hand angrily at the third mate. "It is tainted . . . inedible. It is that simple."[46]

---

[46] Robrecht had smelled for himself the odor that snaked through the mess deck and penetrated deep into his nostrils, until he felt as if a bloody

"I know that, sir," said Meneer Buskirk. "But the men, they—"

"The men will do as they are ordered."

"I must warn you that they are growing restless. There is talk, sir."

"Talk? Do you come here threatening me with mutiny?"

"No, sir. I come here to tell you that the men need some sort of . . . appeasement."

"I regret that I have neither whores nor beef shanks stored away in here. Tell them that."

"Perhaps it might be best coming from you. They are gathered on deck now. They wish to speak to you."

Robrecht raised his head from the charts. He was well aware of

---

gusher were imminent. It had to be disposed of, thrown overboard. And although the cook had been hesitant at first, fearing repercussions from the meat-starved sailors, Robrecht had insisted, knowing full well that the men could not be trusted to keep their grubby hands off the beef, despite the fact that eating it would make them deathly ill. And so it was that the cook had hauled a case of the beef up from below and opened the tins one at a time. Then leaning his bulging girth over the gunwale, he began tipping them into the choppy waters below. As he did, a flock of seabirds swept down from the patchwork sky and began to gorge on the rancid scraps. The trouble started when a passing seaman caught sight of the farrago of feasting birds and squawked loudly his complaint. Before long, a mob of sailors had gathered at the gunwale, where they cursed the seabirds with vile ejaculations. Then they turned to the cook and with menacing stares began to close in on him. Pinning the tins of meat between his soft and sweaty rump and the gunwale, the cook stood his ground admirably, while desperately trying to explain the how-come and why-to-for of his actions. But the sailors were not interested in how-comes and why-to-fors. They were interested in meat—in eating meat, in pressing it to their sallow cheeks, in slathering it on their wasted bodies. And if they couldn't have meat then they would have revenge. And, in fact, they would have torn the cook limb from limb had the crack of a pistol not right then shattered the sky. Robrecht climbed the stairs to the quarterdeck, reloaded, ratcheted the flintlock back, and leveled the pistol at the mob. "Proceed," said he to the cook. Trembling now, the cook resumed feeding the feathered frenzy of seabirds, while the men grumbled and growled and clenched their fists and chewed on their tongues.

the delicate nature of this situation. "Very well, then. I shall speak to the men myself." He tucked a pistol into his belt and marched for the door. But the moment he stepped into daylight, he felt the cold and deadly pressure of a steel barrel in his back.

"Not even a flinch," said Meneer Buskirk. The third mate reached around and slid Robrecht's pistol from his belt. The crew waited in a rag-tag half-circle on the spar deck, clenching their fists and growling their discontent. It was clear they wanted blood. Someone's blood. His blood. Robrecht searched the pocked and gray faces for the familiar mug of Dag. Finally, he spotted his trusted companion gagged and tied to the mainmast.

"The men want to know why you have put their lives in peril."

Robrecht stood straight and tall, responding with due authority. "Am I to blame for the rogue wave that battered our hull and drove us to the brink of destruction?"

"You are to blame for taking us to open seas in the stormy season," yelled Able Seaman Conklin, a senior deckhand with a ragged skull and bones tattoo carved into his forehead.

The men roared in agreement.

"Who among you begged me not to issue the set-sail order? No one. And who among you wished to remain on that godforsaken island? Again, no one."

The men shuffled their bare feet, roaring nothing this time.

Finally Buskirk spoke: "But we left Bandanaira without proper provisions. Now we are weak with hunger and our throats are burned by the salt air."

"You are men of the Dutch East India Company," said Robrecht, "and you are sworn to serve that company, not to moan like old men and weep like old women at the slightest inconvenience."

Confused by the imprecise nature of the captain's rebuke, some of the men half-roared in agreement until the third mate shouted: "Quiet, you idiots. You cheer when he calls you old women?" To this, the crew responded with a growl. "Now what are we to do with this so-called captain?"

"Hang him by the neck from the foremast, I say," said Conklin. The men roared in agreement. "Hang him, hang him!" cried they.

"As you wish, men. String him up, then," said Buskirk, stepping in front of Robrecht and nudging the pistol barrels into his chest. "I have chosen my side well this time, wouldn't you agree, Captain?" The third mate pried back the flint locks until each clicked loudly.

It was then, in the deafening silence that followed, that Robrecht heard it—an odd sound, indistinct but somehow familiar. A flutter from far above like a missed stay line flapping between masts. But when he rolled his eyes up, Robrecht saw no missed stay line but what appeared to be an albatross diving from a height of three full masts. Upon second glance, it became clear that the bird was not diving at all, but plummeting.

Robrecht followed the dropping bird until it landed like a downy white stone upon the head of the third mate. Of course, Buskirk stood dazed by the unexpected ornithological strike from the sky, and as his grasp on the pistols loosened, they too dropped. Each rattled to the deck and fired instantaneously, simultaneously. Moments later, Conklin's knees buckled and the seaman fell forward, blood gurgling from the precise midpoint above his clavicles where the lead ball had pierced him. A more direct hit would have been hard to imagine.

In the same instant, the sound of the ship's bell announced the ricochet and subsequent demise of Meneer Buskirk. The sound the lead ball made as it whizzed by Robrecht's ear was almost painful, although it happened with such speed that there was not even a split second to cringe. A moist black hole appeared in the center of the third mate's forehead and Buskirk's eyes opened wide then fluttered as a tiny rivulet of blood trickled down the bridge of his nose. He toppled over like a felled tree upon the deck. Beside him, the albatross lay dead and broken, twisted into some painful symbol of death. Robrecht stepped forward to examine the bird, noting the pasty brown mush of rancid beef now oozing from its crumbled beak.

FROM A LETTER ADDRESSED TO
JAKOB ONDERDONK,
BATAVIA, JAVA, DUTCH EAST INDIES

July 23, 1741

Dear Jakob,

Today, your oma and I were out for a walk and we passed by Hooglandse Kerk. From the outside, the stained glass windows looked dull and lifeless in the noonday sun. I was reminded of an occasion involving you and your brother not so long ago—I'm sure you have not forgotten it. Your father had just returned from a voyage and had brought with him two shepherd's slings from some Mediterranean country whose name I cannot recall (and probably could not pronounce correctly even if I could). I'm sure you know the name of it still (such a bright and agile mind you have), for it caused you boys tremendous excitement—to know that you had in your grip something from such a distant and exotic land. I do remember the long hemp twine and the smooth leather pouch of the slings. How could I not? You and Robrecht both slept with them under your pillows for months.

No sooner had your father given it to you than you, Jakob, went straightway into the forest on a brave little man's excursion and later that day brought home from the hunt a small hare for the pot, as they say. But Robrecht did not put his sling to such good use—instead he found a smooth stone and punched a hole through a south transept window of Hooglandse Kerk. As I recall the occasion now, what astounded me—nay stupefied me— was your silence in the face of your brother's accusation. For surely you remember that he accused you of the misdeed. I wonder if you know even now why you remained silent and said nothing in your own defense. (I imagine you are yet unaware that I knew from the start that Robrecht's accusation was a untruth, for someone I am well acquainted with—who shall remain anonymous—was in the church, silently worshipping at the foot of the crucifix, when the stone came rolling into the sanctuary).

I believe now that my inaction concerning the matter—I should have punished Robrecht and restored your good name—was a disservice to you both. Oh, Jakob! I feel so sorry and deeply ashamed about the whole affair! It was always difficult for me with your father forever at sea. It is difficult now, too, of course; yet, when one has two young boys to care for it seems that a missing father leaves a sizable rent in the family fabric. I hope that you can forgive me for this and all the other times I said and did nothing on your behalf, dear Jakob. Now that you are gone, the guilt is almost too much to bear. And I cannot look at Hooglandse Kerk without being haunted by the memory of it. I know that you believe me to be overreacting and I can hear you say that the incident was long ago. However, you will come to learn, as I have, that some things cannot be buried deep enough in the past. For they take root and grow of their own volition until one day you are strolling down a well-worn path on memory lane, only to walk headlong into the sprawling bole of it. Forgive my unwieldy trope (as you know, I am prone to them), but I do hope you see my point. Just as I hope that you can forgive me, dear Jakob. Forgive me, please. It would mean the world to me if you could.

Your Loving Mother

FROM THE JOURNAL OF JAKOB ONDERDONK

November 11, 1746

Tonight, I am unable to sleep, so I will write down some of my thoughts in the hope that doing so will help to ease me into a sound slumber. Since moving to the officer's cabin, I have not slept well, mainly due to the fitful sleep of my brother night after night. In the darkness, he cries out foreign words and mumbles incoherent phrases in foreign tongues. As it turns out, Robrecht has a gift for languages. He speaks the language of the Chinaman fluently, so I am told. He is also able to converse with shogunate officials on Dejima. I believe he also knows some Arabic and Indian and can make himself understood in a number of tribal languages from Papua and the Kepulauan Seribu. Perhaps it is because he spends much of his time ashore at the various destinations of Son of Batavia that he can speak their many languages. I, on the other hand, bide my time near the ship, tending to business or writing letters and keeping this journal.

The rumors aboard the ship seem to insinuate that Robrecht and his constant companion Dag frequent the brothels and opium dens that line the harbors of the Orient from one end to the other. Sadly, this does not surprise me. Nonetheless, it concerns me For I have twice stepped foot in an opium den (on both occasions looking for Robrecht and not finding him) and found it to be the most unwholesome of places. The men looked sickly and desperate, sleeping in filth with their open wounds gaping like the mouths of dying fishes. And the women reek of disease and dangers of the womanly sort. In fact, the very port town of which I speak is infamous for a priory, now abandoned by Portuguese priests, in which syphilitics who are in the final stages of the disease go to die. It is precisely the kind of place which I do not wish to see my brother end up. Yet, I am helpless to stop him, for he would sooner plunge into a sea full of tentacled sea monsters than listen to a word of advice from me. And I dare not tell father, for I fear it would break his heart asunder the way ice cracks open a stone. There is nothing to be done but watch, listen, and hope that I might be close by when my assistance is most beneficial. Yes, beneficial and necessary. But enough of that! For it seems that my ramblings now wane and I have found my way back to the netherworlds of sleep. So this, I hope, is goodnight.

THIRTEEN

After several weeks of hemming and hawing, Jakob finally agreed to again attempt baptism. When he and Anneke had approached Bonifaas together, the preacher seemed amenable to the idea, although Jakob could not help but wonder if he would not have been quite so amenable had it just been him, Jakob, alone. After all, his past record of conduct where rites of rebirth and redemption were concerned was decidedly bleak.

After some consideration—although it should be said that this consideration was neither lengthy nor exhaustive but was of the sort where the outcome is all but certain from the onset—Jakob decided it would be prudent to break the news to his mother with Anneke by his side. And of course, Anneke was more than happy to comply. Be that as it may, Jakob remained sensitive about the situation—him, a grown man, needing the support of another to stand before his own mother. He responded to this bit of nitpicking on himself—by himself—by drawing his own attention to the simple fact that Anneke was his fiancé, and as such, it was natural for him to want her by his side at the pivotal moment in question. But when this simple fact, which he came to view as a rationalization of the worst sort, failed to satisfy him, Jakob became even more self-accusatory and in turn more self-defensive. Somewhere in the midst of this tit-for-tat proliferation, he had thought himself a coward, finally responding to this blatant bit of self-accusation with a sudden vocal outburst: "I am not a coward, but rather a strategist." And in fact, living as closely as Jakob did to his mother, one had to be a strategist simply as a matter of survival. This, Jakob finally concluded, was an irrevocable truth. And in fact, it was a truth only arrived at moments before his carriage rolled to an icy halt before the *herenhuis*.

They found Mevrouw Onderdonk reading by the fireplace in the sitting room. Oma Onderdonk sat motionless by her side, mesmerized by the dancing flames. Jakob steamed by them both to the mantel, where he rubbed the cold from his hands. And although it seemed slightly awkward and a bit contrived (in that, it was cued by his anxious state), Jakob cupped his hands and blew warm breath into them. Anneke, on the other hand, rushed to *Moeder* Onderdonk and greeted her with an open and honest kiss upon the cheek.

"What a pleasant surprise," said Mevrouw Onderdonk. "What brings you out on this frosty winter's eve?"

"But we missed you, Mother. Isn't that reason enough?" Jakob stooped to shovel glistening brown coal into the fire.

"Missed me? Phooey!"

"It is the truth, *Moeder* Onderdonk. We missed you sorely."

"Dear girl, I fear my Jakob has coerced you into reciting such transparent pleasantries."

"Well, perhaps there is some truth in that, too," said Jakob. "Perhaps there is another reason for this unannounced visit." He now paced close before the fire—so close in fact, that the tails of his newly tailored cutaway coat very nearly broke into an unmitigated blaze.

"Indeed, there must be."

Jakob stepped to Anneke and took her hand. His gaze shifted from his fiancé to his mother.

"Good God! Such a production! What is it?"

Jakob sighed, smiled weakly. "We have decided to declare our faith in Christ the Lord and be baptized together—before the wedding."

A long moment of silence followed. Jakob noted how the room seemed suddenly drafty.

Finally, Mevrouw Onderdonk spoke: "But dear, do you really think the Son of God needs *your* vote of confidence? After all, he is heir apparent to the Kingdom, is he not? For none other, save the Almighty himself, is omnipotent, omniscient, and omnipresent. Who else can match those qualifications? The job falls to him by default, with or without your declaration. The Almighty Father will see to that, I'm sure."

It was just as Jakob feared—hopeless. And in that moment, he wondered why he had thought it could ever be otherwise.

"What he means," said Anneke, "is baptism is a public declaration of our faith. It is more for us and for the community of believers than it is for Christ the Lord."

"By all means, then, make your public declaration. Stand up in church, stand on a soapbox, if you must, but why is it always about baptism with you church types? Wasn't it baptism of this sort or that sort which caused the whole kerfuffle in Westfalen?"

"It is a ritual, plain and simple," said Robrecht. "No different than the ritual of marriage. Humans have need of ritual."

"And you have already participated in that particular ritual. Have you forgotten that a priest sprinkled water over your head when you were days out of my womb. Of course, I cared little for it. It was your father's doing. But it seems to have worked in your case. Sadly, it didn't take with your brother."[47]

"It was a christening," said Jakob. "And that is at the very heart of the matter. How could I possibly remember it—or more to the point—how could it possibly mean anything to me when I was, as you say, only days out of the womb?" He stopped to draw in a deep

---

[47] Here, Mevrouw Onderdonk had one of her convenient lapses in memory. For the truth was Jakob had not been christened, as he had always been led to believe. For Mevrouw Onderdonk had been vehemently opposed to it—but only partly on religious grounds. The infant boy was born blue as the frigid waters of the North Sea and Mevrouw Onderdonk was adamant that he, a sickly babe, not be removed from the *herenhuis*, even for a christening. For his part, Meneer Onderdonk saw the pallid hue in a more symbolic light: "He's meant for the sea, 'tis clear," said he, an utterance which prompted a scowl from Mevrouw Onderdonk. Despite Meneer Onderdonk's attempts to assuage the fears of his wife, Mevrouw Onderdonk remained staunchly stubborn concerning the matter until finally it was dropped.

Robrecht, one the other hand, was another story altogether. A hardy codling, there was no question of whether to christen or not to christen. But when the time came, the good pastor, who was well into his cups, made a critical misjudgment at a critical moment. That is to say, he sprinkled holy water into the infant's eyes and nose, a blunder that caused the babe to "scream blue murder," as Meneer Onderdonk put it. "'Tis clear he, too, is meant for the sea," said he with an amused snort. Of course, Mevrouw Onderdonk was not amused—or to be precise, she was unamused. And in fact, it would be fair to say that she was deeply upset by the whole affair and remained so to this very day.

breath then spoke more calmly. "Our baptism will be a believer's baptism. It is a ritual, yes, but it's so much more. It's a ritual to give us a sense of control over the chaos and sin of existence."

"And what about existence is so sinful and chaotic that you feel compelled to submit your mind and will to a charlatan posing as a man of the cloth? Sin! Chaos! Phooey! You get up in the morning, you eat, you work in your factory, you go home in the evening, you eat again, you go to sleep, and in the course of doing all of that, you avoid shedding the blood of innocent people and taking God's name in vain. What is so hard about that? Really, Jakob, what is so chaotic and sinful about that?"

Jakob walked to a chair and, tucking the tails of his coat neatly under him, sat down. It was a gesture that could only be construed as an admission of defeat. "As usual, Mother, you have reduced life's complexities to a single run-on sentence." Jakob bent forward and rested his elbows on his knees.[48]

---

[48] It was at times like these that Jakob's mind invariably returned to a particular episode from his youth in which his mother had also used the run-on sentence to her advantage. As a boy in boarding school, Jakob was often the brunt of practical jokes. As is often the case, the older boys who singled him out for abuse recognized Jakob as a sensitive boy. And although, in truth, he was not an especially sensitive boy, Jakob was an intelligent boy. To be fair, the distinction was a moot one as far as the bullies were concerned, and their choice of making Jakob the target of their injurious attentions was a gut reaction more than a calculated act.

Although younger, Robrecht tended to fare better than Jakob in boarding school, where bullies were concerned. Not because he was any less intelligent, but because he understood the bully mentality. Perhaps he was even a bit sympathetic to it. Although he would never participate in the bullying of his older brother, Robrecht would stand idly by and watch. In fact, so thorough was Robrecht's callous disregard that the lead bully, a squab young fellow named Wob Wubbels, was late to learn that the two Onderdonk boys were actually siblings. Wob Wubbels was not only surprised but also confused by this revelation. When he asked Robrecht why he said or did nothing while his brother was tormented so by the likes of him, Robrecht had simply replied, "It is no business of mine."

"But how can it be no business of yours?" said Wob Wubbels, "He is your brother."

"That we two were both sloughed from the same walls of the same womb wall is only a coincidence. He is he and I am me. That is all."

Of course, this response left Wubbels even more confounded than before—so confounded, in fact, that he felt the need to bully someone. And of course, that someone was Jakob. So, a plan was devised and put promptly into action. It involved morning prayer service and a cotton stocking full of boiled oats, which was fastened to the front of Jakob's breeches .

On the morning in question, the prayer service was already underway when the doors of the chapel burst open and in came Jakob—although to say *in came* he is to grievously understate the disruptive entrance. A rough hand pushed him so forcefully from behind that he actually careened down the aisle and toppled halfway down. Seeing this, the headmaster stormed down the aisle in a flutter of black robes and pulled the boy to his feet. As he did so, he caught sight of the sagging white stocking hanging from Jakob's breeches, that same white stocking that, it must be said, bore a striking resemblance a stallion's floppy *staf*. The headmaster growled: "What is the meaning of this?

Jakob muttered something to himself.

"Speak up! What have you to say for yourself?"

"Buggery, buggery, will someone please bugger me," said Jakob, with his eyes—one blackened—now fixed on the floor.

The headmaster, whose face had in the meantime turned a crimson red, not unlike the crimson red robe draped over Christ on the Crucifix, grabbed the stocking and, fueled by an unerring sense of righteous indignation, yanked with the strength of ten indignant men. As it tore free of Jakob's breeches, the stocking sent gray globs of oatmeal slopping through the air, spattering the Headmaster's robes and stuccoing his face with a pasty goo. The resulting grimace that contorted the old man's face caused a round of loud laughter to tear through the chapel and swell beneath its golden dome. And laughing loudest among the boys was Wob Wubbels, who could never have imagined that his ill-conceived prank would come off so brilliantly. Beside him, grinning widely, stood Robrecht.

Of course, parents were summoned, codes of conduct were invoked, and both Jakob and Wob Wubbels were suspended for a time. Later, alone with his mother in the carriage, Jakob fought back the tears and asked why God would allow someone like Wob Wubbels to exist in this world. To this she responded: "Evil is not something that can be avoided or changed, and it exists in this world so that it can kill itself, meaning, we don't have to do the

It was Anneke who moved to break the oppressive silence. She sat down on the settee and took Mevrouw Onderdonk's hand in her own. "*Moeder* Onderdonk, please, we do not wish to upset you so. We only hoped you would share in our joy."

"Forgive me, dear. I tend to go off half-cocked when religion is involved. But if I may ask one simple question of a practical nature: where and when is this baptism to take place?"

"We are to be baptized in the waters of the *Oude Rijn* in two weeks, on Christmas Day."

"Christmas Day! The *Oude Rijn*! You will catch your death!"

"We would love for you to witness the event," said Anneke.

"I'm sorry, dear. I have no interest in such matters, especially when they arise in the middle of winter. But if it's my blessing you want, then you have it. I only hope that one day you," here, she turned to Jakob, "will see the folly of this religious fixation."

---

unseemly job ourselves, for who better than evil to kill evil, so we just let evil kill itself and leave the rest of us alone. Do you understand?"

From the Journal of Robrecht Onderdonk

July 8, 1748
We have just cleared the southern tip of Formosa and Son of Batavia now
sails the open waters of the East China Sea. The weather is hot, humid, and
stubbornly still. And so it is that the sails droop overhead, and the men have
taken to the lower decks to avoid the heat. Today, as I stood drenched in
sweat upon the quarterdeck, I witnessed the antics of idle seamen with nary
a sensible thought in their heads. Their loud laughter rose to my ears like an
unhappy pestilence. Soon after came the plash and piddle of competing
cataracts, at which point I looked over the gunwale, only to see a stream of
pis arcing outward from the cannon portals below. A quick check to larboard
side confirmed my suspicions of a collective effort; that is, a stream of urine
escaped from every portal of the vessel. It occurred to me then that to one
looking on from a short distance off, it might appear that the ship had
sprung multiple leaks and was set to soon go down into the drink. But
before I was able to fully envision such a ridiculous spectacle, from the
portal directly below me came the peculiar sight of a white rump, which
proceeded to make the aggravated sounds that accompany defecation. It was
at this point that I felt the need to intercede, for, although the men have yet
to come around to the inherent wisdom of it, cleanliness at sea staves off
death and disease. Needless to say, I stormed below to the gun deck and
demanded to know what manner of foolishness this was. This of course, was
not an entirely perceptive question on my part, for the nature of the
foolishness was quite apparent to all present. After giving the culprits a
merciless dressing down, which included imminent threats of flogging, I
went in search of father to discuss some possible solution to the problem. Of
course, I knew full well how he felt about such horseplay on a vessel of the
VOC. And so, sitting in the stifling heat of his quarters, it was decided that
in future one portal, and one portal only, would be used for bodily
expurgations. The portal, it was decided, would be clearly demarcated by red
paint.
Thus was it with great satisfaction that I supervised the painting of the
foremost portal of the gun deck's larboard side red, in order that we might
keep filth and disease at bay while at sea. For I have come to learn that death
lurks near enough at every turn without bidding it come closer with acts of

human folly. I am not so oblivious as to presume that the men are grateful to me for this deed. I understand that they may be put off, even indignant about the whole affair. Yet, to hell with them, I say, for I did not do it for them. Aboard a ship, when one falls ill, all fall ill, including officers — including me. And one must do what he can to save his own skin. That is the first rule of the sea. For no other will see to your well-being if you do not. And that, I would argue, is the very crux of the matter.

FOURTEEN

Candide talked incessantly when he was excited. It was less of a nervous habit and more of a verbal compulsion surrounding the particular thing responsible for his sudden exhilaration of spirits. This was particularly true whenever the young philosopher spoke of his master. And so it was that today Candide was especially excited and especially talkative. For, as it turned out, Master Pangloss had been cured. The previous weeks of excruciating treatment had paid off. And although Candide praised and thanked the Anabaptist for leading Pangloss away from death's door, Jakob's modest nature would not allow him to take credit for saving the old philosopher's life.

They stood by the carriage, ankle-deep in snow, awaiting the appearance of the old philosopher outside the asylum door. When finally Master Pangloss's oddly proportioned figure emerged from the building, Candide rushed into his arms and wept. It was a touching scene, a tearful reunion, and Jakob felt his own eyes moisten.

Needless to say, Master Pangloss looked much better than when Jakob had first laid eyes on him. To say that the old philosopher looked to be a new man was to overstate it, certainly, but the sentiment behind such a statement could not be faulted. For his skin remained a waxy yellow hue, it was true, but the gumma on his brow had shrunk to a hard grape-sized bump. And his once swollen eye no longer leaked pus but had now withdrawn deep into its socket, like a small rodent that could not be coaxed from its hole. And although the nub of his withered nose had fallen off, leaving the remaining proboscis grotesquely truncated, the old philosopher's nose was intact and functional—at least, Jakob assumed that the glob of yellow mucus dangling from a cavernous nostril indicated as much. As if to complete this transformation, of sorts, the sprigs of gray that were once mere tufts of hair had now grown into long wispy vines shooting spottily from the old philosopher's scalp. Indeed, it was fair to say that Pangloss looked much better leaving the asylum than he had entering it.

"You look well," said Jakob.

"Thanks to you, my generous Anabaptist. I have lost hearing in only one ear and sight in only one eye." Master Pangloss flicked his bad ear with a finger. "Can't hear a thing," said he. Then he flicked his bad eye. "Can't see a thing," said he, winking with his good eye. "Isn't it wonderful?"

"Wonderful!" said Candide. "Truly, you could not have asked for a better outcome."

"Indeed, I could not," said the Master. "After all, it could've been much worse."

"We must mark the occasion with a libation," said Jakob.

"Indeed we must," said Candide.

They rode into Leyden with light snow drifting lazily down from a drab sky. Not wishing to break the muffled silence that presided over the countryside, they brushed their shoulders and marveled at the beauty of snow-tipped trees. At the tavern, they took a table next to the fireplace, and the three friends—two old and one new—warmed their bodies and raised their tankards high. Again and again, until the conversation flowed as freely as the *bier*.

They talked of Bonifaas Quackenboss and his vision. And of Anneke and her vision, and how it had led to Jakob's being engaged to be married. In truth, it was something that Jakob had said without real conviction, as if being engaged to be married were an everyday event that merited little more enthusiasm than a morning walk to the commons. Perhaps it was the *bier*, but at this point, Jakob decided to confide in his new friends about the doubts he had been experiencing of late. In particular, he expressed his misgivings concerning Anneke's vision and Bonifaas's vision, and what those visions may actually have meant—not to mention where they had come from.

"Surely, it is for the best," said Master Pangloss. "For if it were not so, God would not have created Oma Onderdonk's questionable constitution from which flow the rapturous *aars* fumes that whisper His will."

"Perhaps, yes," said Jakob. "But I can't help but wonder if my oma's *aars* really does discharge visions from God."

"But of course it does, for Bonifaas Quackenboss has attested to the fact. And so has your Anneke. What reason do you have to doubt them?"

"Maybe they are simply having visions because they wish to have visions."

"Who does not wish to have visions? Does wanting something to happen make it any less real when that something does happen?"

"What I mean is what if it's something that only exists in their own minds?"

"Of course, it exists in their minds. The mind is the seat of thought. From thoughts come knowledge. And God is nothing if not infinite knowledge."

"Perhaps you're right. Perhaps my doubts are unfounded. Perhaps visions from the Almighty do flow from my oma's *aars*. But I have been inhaling those malodorous oracular fumes for years. Why is it that I've had no visions?" Jakob realized, even as he posed this question, that this was at the very heart of the matter—he had had no vision himself. His doubts were nothing more than the protests of the uninitiated, the one left behind. At least, he now wondered if as much were not true.

"Only God knows the answer to that question," said Pangloss. "You must accept that He, with His infinite knowledge, has created the best of all possible worlds. That is better than any vision could possibly be, is it not?"

"Indeed it is, Master Pangloss," said Candide.

Jakob said nothing but raised his tankard and drank. Then in an attempt to move the conversation away from his oma's *aars* and the best of all possible worlds, Jakob brought up the more benign topic of work in the factory.

He remarked that since opening his factory, he had single-handedly taken care of the business end of things. At times, this meant taking on an assortment of different duties and working ridiculously long hours to keep the wheels of progress turning, where the factory was concerned. "There is wool to be inspected, dyes to be bought, carpets to be shipped, salaries to be paid, books to be kept—and the list goes on and on," said he. Of course, he pointed out that Anneke had not wasted any time making her presence felt in every aspect of his life, including this one. Soon enough, the issue of business came up, and she had made it plain to Jakob that she needed more of his time and attention. "For," she had told him, "you cannot be married to me and to your work, both."

And so it was that Jakob came full circle to arrive at the point of this particular detour in the conversation—to propose that Master Pangloss come to work for him. Of course, the old philosopher was "happy, indeed" to in some way repay the debt that was owed to the good Anabaptist. That is to say, Pangloss accepted the job offer, after which the three of them toasted the future of Onderdonk Manufacturing.

The following day, another desk was moved into his office, making quarters somewhat tight. The old philosopher sat slouched in his chair with a reading glass poised near to his face. His good eye moved across the ledger. Reaching the end of one line, it dropped down to the next. Then across and down, across and down, until he reached the bottom of the page, at which time he would lick his thumb and flip the page from the lower corner, mumbling to himself in a way that unsettled Jakob.

"Is everything in order?" he asked. "Is there a problem?"

But Pangloss remained absorbed in the task at hand. Jakob quickly realized that the desk had been placed in such a way that he now spoke directly into the old philosopher's deaf ear. Jakob rose and walked across the room to a cabinet where he opened a drawer then slammed it shut.

Pangloss pulled his head from the ledger.

"Is everything in order?" said Jakob.

"Yes, yes. Everything is quite in order. You have crossed all *T*s and dotted all *I*s."

Jakob turned to see Candide standing in the doorway with a tea kettle and three cups.

"Ah, come in," he said. "Let's take our tea together. I want to talk to you and Master Pangloss."

Candide poured tea then took a seat.

Jakob sipped at the edge of the cup, nodded his approval. "Now, clearly my flat is too small for the three of us. So, I have taken the liberty of finding you lodgings. It is above the tavern in which we shared a celebratory libation. Not fit for a king, but I think it will suit you fine. It is clean and it is large enough for two."

"That is good of you," said Candide.

"Yes, very good, kind Anabaptist. But can we afford such an extravagance?"

"I have paid your rent for the next fortnight. If you decide to stay on at the job, and you wish to remain in the flat, I will simply deduct it from your wages."

"It is truly the best of opportunities," said Candide.

"Indeed, it is," said Pangloss. "To labor for one's bread and butter, and in this case one's lodgings, is a most pleasing possibility. I accept your offer, good Anabaptist."

"And I also," said Candide.

"Good," said Jakob. With this, they finished their tea and each returned to his designated task—Candide to his loom, Pangloss to his ledger, and Jakob to his inventory.

At day's end, Jakob closed up the factory and led his new friends to the rear of the tavern, where they ascended some narrow stairs worn bare and creaking their complaint. He ducked under the low doorway into a single-room flat and lit a lamp, revealing the sparsely furnished lodgings—a table and two chairs, a single cot, a nightstand, a porcelain washbasin, a copper chamber pot, a single window, which when opened was within arm's reach of the adjacent building's chipped red brick. Jakob strolled to the wardrobe, opened it and produced a small bookcase. He set it next to the fireplace. "I had this made for you. It's not much but perhaps you will wish to fill it with philosophical works."

Candide grew weepy and smiled a tearful smile. "Surely you are the best of all men."

"Indeed, it is true," said Pangloss. He shuffled over the floor to the book case. "I shall cherish it. And these lodgings, they are indeed fit for a king. It is a palace, good Anabaptist." The old philosopher dropped his breeches, plopped down on the chamber pot, and made water. "Truly it is a palace on par with the castle of Thunder-Ten-Tronckh."

The mention of Thunder-Ten-Tronckh set Candide weeping in earnest. "Now, now," said Pangloss.

"But I miss my fair Cunégonde."[49]

---

[49] Although the gist of it had been conveyed to him, Jakob had was not privy to the conversation that had taken place between Candide and Master Pangloss in the stables shortly after they had been reunited. At that time, Candide had asked about his fair Cunégonde.

"Gone," was all Pangloss said.

"Gone? But where then has she gone, good Master?" said Candide.

"Why, gone to the great beyond."

"To the great beyond? But where is that?"

"That is the question, is it not?"

"But why, then, has my Cunégonde gone to this great beyond of which you speak?"

"She is dead, of course. That is why."

Candide faltered on his feet and began to weep. "Dead? My fair Cunégonde is dead?"

"Dead, yes. Very dead, indeed. I'm afraid."

"I beg you, Master, tell me of the fate my fair Cunégonde has met with."

"Her frail body was gutted from stem to sternum. That, only after several scores of Prussian soldiers took her in every way conceivable and some ways not so conceivable."

"Dear God! How horrible!" Great sobs heaved in Candide's meager breast. "What of the rest of them? The Baron and Baroness? The young noble master?"

"The Baron's brains were liberated from his skull with his own coat of arms when he tried to stop the soldiers from having their lustful way with fair Cunégonde. The Baroness was hacked into bite-sized pieces and scattered like feed in the fields. And the young noble master received the same treatment as his fair sister, perhaps with even greater gusto, he being a young and fair-haired boy."

"The castle of Thunder-ten-Tronckh is in ruins then?"

"Destroyed. Not one stone was left upon another. The Prussians burned the stables to the ground, executed the horses with a barrage of hot lead, sheared the sheep before slitting their bleating throats, slaughtered the ducks

Soon Candide's burst of tears slowed to a steady leak, and the young philosopher shambled to the bookcase and ran his hand along its smooth surface. Then he swung his head weakly towards Jakob. "Forgive me for asking good Anabaptist, but do you not miss her?" said he.

"Her?" said Jakob.

"Your fair Heleen, residing in Portugal."

A faint image formed in Jakob's head, rising like Venus from the calm waters of a not-so-distant memory. Jakob's heart expanded, beat a little harder and faster in that moment, pressing painfully against his rib cage. But the ache passed quickly. And Jakob, regaining control of his feelings, chose his words carefully.

"She is a peasant girl. I was once infatuated with her, it is true. But no longer. For I am betrothed to another," said he. But his words had the weight and timbre of a lie. He knew it even as he spoke them, and he knew that his friends knew it, too.

"Yes, that is well," said Pangloss, rising from the chamber pot and fastening his breeches. "I too loved a woman once. A marvelous thing, it was."

"But Master Pangloss, was it not the love of the pretty wench Paquette that caused you to lose your eyesight in one eye and your hearing in one ear?"

"No, no. Quite the opposite. It is the love of the pretty wench Paquette that suffered me to keep my eyesight in one eye and my hearing in one ear. Anything less than the love of the pretty wench

---

and geese and hung them from the trees, and then chopped down every tree within three furlong of the ruins."

"I pray thee tell me again, good Master," said Candide between blubbers, "how this is the best of all possible worlds."

"Oh it is indeed the best of all possible worlds," said Pangloss. "For our revenge came swiftly. I am told the Saxons did the very same thing to a neighboring barony, in which the master was a Prussian Lord."

Paquette and I would be blind as a mole and deaf as an adder."

Admittedly, it was all a bit much for Jakob. Thoughts of Heleen had unsettled him, despite all attempts to conceal it. And the old philosopher's logical train of thought had quite simply left him behind in a fog of confusion. So Jakob bid his friends a good night and left the tavern. But even the chilly carriage ride home, in which a bitter wind pricked his fingers and ankles and stung his eyes to tears, could not distract him from warm thoughts of his beloved Heleen.

The next two weeks passed quickly. During that time, Jakob managed—for the most part—to keep his thoughts focused on the blessed event of his and Anneke's upcoming baptism. Of course, the yuletide season brought with it its fair share of distractions, most of which were welcomed by Jakob. Finally, however, Christmas arrived, and the blessed day was sanctified by a fresh layer of powdery snow from the heavens—a profound whiteness that covered the world in a velvety blanket of purity. As far as Jakob was concerned, it could only be a hopeful portent of his imminent spiritual awakening.

He paused to scan the soft banks of the *Oude Rijn* and breathed in the cool air.

Bonifaas Quackenboss, on the other hand, did not see things quite so symbolically. For all his diligence and long-suffering, the preacher let slip a complaint while the two men shoveled snow from the river's icy surface. Jakob pretended not to hear it, and the truth was he couldn't blame Bonifaas. It seemed liked an inordinate amount of work to go to, especially given that precedence dictated there was a fair-to-middling chance that this could turn out to be another false alarm, another aborted attempt on his—Jakob's—part to become a bona fide member of the faithful flock.

Be that as it may, Jakob was determined to make this time different. He was prepared. He was ready. In other words, he had not succumbed to the sin of onanism for more than two weeks. That Pastor Hogarth's buxom wife had been away visiting family in North Holland did not fail to strike Jakob as a mitigating circumstance. Yet the interim had allowed him to strengthen his resolve, fortify himself against sin. It was precisely the kind of edifying breather he needed.

A part of him feared her return, it was true, but that wasn't going to stop him from publicly declaring his faith in the Lord Jesus Christ. Not this time.

In fact, the past weeks had allowed Jakob to reflect objectively upon his habit of self-abuse. He realized that his bursts of onanism were largely fueled by the pastor's wife and, more recently, by his own contrived mental images of a reposing Anneke. Yet he had also come to the conclusion that Anneke's touch was something of a double-edged sword. On the one hand, it put considerable strain on his Dutch flat-weave chastity belt—that is, it stirred up his base instincts to a whirlwind of painful desire. Yet, on the other hand, the ticklish touch of his betrothed shook loose giant boulders of guilt that rumbled down to a landslide of self-recrimination. It was the guilt that accompanies sin, certainly, but it was also the guilt that accompanies betrayal. For every time Anneke nuzzled her hand into his, or pressed her thigh to his own, or brush against him breast-to-chest, Jakob heard the loud crow of the cock squawking in his ear. It was betrayal, pure and simple, on all counts. He betrayed Anneke because he loved another; he betrayed Heleen because he desired another; and he betrayed himself because it would inevitably end in another heated session of self-abuse. For Jakob, onanism ruled the day. At least, it had ruled the day. He now saw it for what it really was, and this clearer perspective had helped him to forsake the sin, if not indefinitely, at least in earnest for a time.

Bonifaas Quackenboss retrieved an axe and began chipping at the hard sheen of ice. In an attempt to make conversation, Jakob brought up Bonifaas's most recent vision. The previous Sunday, at the bidding of Oma Onderdonk's now venerated *aars*, the preacher had toppled like a gassed Saul of Tarsus on the road to Damascus and had a vision.

"It was most amazing," said Bonifaas Quackenboss, suddenly animated. "I saw heaven, hell, and purgatory, and the souls who inhabit each sphere—all in the space of a few minutes. In truth, I must admit that hell was the most fascinating of the three spheres, heaven and purgatory being much less exciting. Hell boasted nine circles, each with a distinct punishment for a specific sin. There the wicked paid for their sinful lives in the most wretched and unpleasant ways. I think I may've even recognized a few faces among them."

"But Bonifaas, that sounds very much like the inspired work of a famous Italian poet."

"Why would God send me a vision of the inspired work of a famous Italian poet?"

"I don't know. It defies reason."

"Coincidence," said Bonifaas. "That is the only explanation."[50]

"Yes, I suppose."

The preacher handed the axe over to Jakob. Winding up with a wide-sweeping loop that boasted considerable angular momentum, Jakob took a mighty swing. Moments later, water gurgled through the breach. Another stroke and a fist-sized chunk of ice broke free. This seemed to lighten Bonifaas's mood. "Ah, there we are," said the preacher, "the cleansing waters to wash away your sins. The old man

---

[50] The vision that Bonifaas had as he lay gassed upon the floor of the meeting house was nothing more than a visual rendering of verse that he had heard as a young boy while in a somnambulist's trance in a monastery near Woubrugge. The reading of this verse was part of a bedside vigil undertaken by the Austin Friar who had found the boy wandering aimlessly about the monastery with a lump like a bloody goose-egg protruding from his pointed pate. When delirium set in, the friar, fearing the worst, sat stoically by Bonifaas's side, wiping the sweat from his brow and reading him verse in the Italian vernacular. All attempts by the friar to ascertain the unfortunate events that had precipitated the boy's injury failed, for Bonifaas was in and out of consciousness. Eventually, however, the prayers and devotions of the friar bore fruit, and Bonifaas recovered his strength little by little. Soon thereafter, the boy was able to piece together a blurred memory of the events that had led him there. It was then that the friar learned how Bonifaas had been working with his father as a blacksmith's apprentice when the mishap occurred. While striking hammer to anvil, the head of the hammer came unstuck and, bouncing off the anvil, looped through the air and cracked the boy's skull with a sound thump. Dazed, the young apprentice had stumbled from the forge. By the time his smithy father discovered he was gone, young Bonifaas was nowhere to be found.

enters and the new man emerges."

Jakob contemplated this. As he did, the voice of Anneke trilled his name. He turned to see her perched on shore, swaddled in a wool blanket, ensconced in the sisterly embrace of Katrine Quackenboss. A white gossamer gown peeked from beneath the blanket. She was ready.

A small crowd of faithful followers gathered on the riverbank, singing rousing hymns to warm the heart and stir the soul. Hymns to beckon the Holy Spirit come and light upon them.

Spirit of faith, come down, reveal the things of God . . .

Jakob saw the smiling faces of Candide and Pangloss among the flock—Siamese twins joined at the grin. Candide waved, his enthusiasm apparent in the choppy gesture.

. . . O that the word might know the all atoning Lamb!

Bonifaas slid into the icy waters, a slight contortion twisting his normally serene visage. The preacher took three deep breaths, as if to ready himself, then motioned for Anneke to join him. She dropped the blanket, and Jakob helped ease her shivering form down into the frozen current.

. . . Spirit of faith, descend and show the virtue of his name . . .

Anneke stood rigid as a post, a stiff blue smile upon her lips.

"I baptize thee in the name of the Father, the Son, and the Holy Spirit," said Bonifaas. Taking her by the wrists, he quickly submerged her in the waters of the *Oude Rijn*.

. . . the grace which all may find, the saving power, impart, and testify to humankind, and speak in every heart.

Anneke emerged with a fish-mouthed gasp. She squinted, trembled, wiped the water from her eyes before tipping her gaze upward to Jakob. In that moment, her countenance possessed an otherworldly glow. She had been scrubbed clean and buffed to a pleasing Christian luster by the grace of Christ the Lord.

"Hallelujah!" cried the faithful flock in unison.

"Hallelujah!" cried Jakob. His heart was full to bursting with admiration, if not love.

Jakob offered his hand and helped her from the water. And it was then, in that most blessed moment, that he caught a glimpse of the pert pink tips of Anneke's womanly charms, pushing through the sopping gossamer gown. The truth was Jakob had envisioned this very sight time and time again while in the throes of his shameful onanistic ritual, but it should be said that his imagination did no justice to the marvel that was Anneke's *boezem*.

Suddenly snagged by the sinful thought, Jakob's *roede*—unfettered by the Dutch weave chastity belt that normally held it fast—sprung like a tripped bear trap.[51] Katrine Quackenboss shrieked at the sight of it, stepping between him and Anneke as if to shield a virgin from the speedy advance of marauders and rapists.

Now desperate to conceal the mainmast of his arousal from the astonished faces of the faithful, Jakob plunged feet-first into the water. At which point, Bonifaas spoke with composed urgency, "I baptize thee in the name of the Father, the Son and the Holy Spirit," and dragged Jakob under with a forceful, determined hand.

The icy current poured into Jakob's nostrils and ears and tugged at his hair. All the while dowsing the burning desire that had only moments before raged as a heaped-high bonfire for all to see. Jakob's lungs squelched in his chest. His face stung. He flapped and flailed his arms like a drunken bird until Bonifaas at last pulled him to the surface and helped him gain a firm footing. Jakob coughed and spat river water. His lips and fingers were the color of the clear blue sky.

"Hallelujah!" cried the preacher, slapping a wet palm on his back. And it should be said that this was done with no small amount of enthusiasm—although *relief* would more aptly convey what Bonifaas was feeling at that moment.

For Jakob's part, it was not the quickening he had expected—at least, not a quickening of the spirit. It was, however, invigorating, and as if to prove that very point, he began to shiver uncontrollably. Yet somehow, he felt no different, aside from the obvious fact that he was colder, a lot colder. The involuntary shudders that racked his body were nothing like the rapture he had hoped for. And as he looked out over the faithful flock, it became clear to him that they felt

---

[51] Master Pangloss later remarked that it looked as if Jakob had grown a coat rack where his *geslachtsorgaan* should have been.

the same—he was no different now than before he had entered the waters of the *Oude Rijn*. In the profound silence that followed Jakob felt the faithful looking upon him with a saintly scorn—although it was in actuality something closer to an (uneasy) blend of reproach and incredulity that collectively swelled within them. To say that Jakob was ashamed would be tantamount to saying that Solomon's tent was cluttered with concubines—both being certainties after a kind.

Finally, just when Jakob thought he might slither back into the icy hole from whence he came and drown himself, a lone squeaky voice rose from the crowd and floated to his ear like a spring butterfly, timid and seemingly inconsequential. It was a small voice, yet at the same time, it was a lyrical and virtuous one. And at that moment, it could not have meant more to Jakob. "Hallelujah!" said Candide.

This was echoed by another voice—coarse and less virtuous than the first, but still infused with warm sentiment. "Hallelujah!" said Pangloss.

Jakob realized then that what he had been expecting—what he had hoped for—was some fanciful saint's tale. The magnificence with which he had once hope this moment would be imbued was not to be found in a euphoria that caused one to drop to one's knees and glow with goodness and grace. No, the magnificence of this moment was the acceptance and fellowship of friends—true friends. This, he felt, was God's gift to him at that moment. With this thought in mind, Jakob searched the faces of the faithful flock for Anneke, who had earlier been ushered away by Katrine Quackenboss. Spying her there, wrapped tightly in a wool blanket among the crowd, Jakob donned a contrite half-smile. He wondered if she could forgive him for turning their baptism into a fool's parade. But then Anneke smiled warmly, affectionately, and mouthed a single word: *Hallelujah!*

FROM A LETTER ADDRESSED TO
CAPTAIN CORNELIS ONDERDONK,
BATAVIA, JAVA. DUTCH EAST INDIES

January 22, 1742

Dearest Cornelis,

Your letter came just as I was feeling most despondent. How it delights me to read of your adventures! And your quiet times, too! And how pleased I was to learn that you have taken it upon yourself to personally tutor our sons. For it is as you say: they must continue in their studies in order that they may become gentleman officers of the VOC. Oh Cornelis! Surely there is no better father in all the kingdoms of the world! Perhaps if I had a father such as you, one who taught me Euclidean geometry and Latin, I would not now be struggling to understand what is meant by "Canis matrem tuam subagiget" or "Globos meos lambe." You say Robrecht has put his Latin to ready use and that he says such phrases to the deckhands. But dear husband, you neglected to tell me the meaning of them. Do you forget that I am the Lady of the house and nothing more? I am no scholar, although I have tried to deduce the meaning of the phrases. "Canis" I understand to be "dogs," and "matrem" is "mother," but the rest is unclear to me. Likewise "globos" is, I think, "globes" or perhaps the more general "balls." But that is as far as I have been able to proceed in deciphering the mysterious Latin phrases.

You will surely be surprised (and no doubt amused) to learn that after your letter arrived I took it upon myself to ascertain the meanings of these phrases. It became my mission, in fact, in a manner of speaking. And who is the only person in the neighborhood who speaks Latin? Of course, you have by now guessed it—Pastor Hogarth. I thought that I might kill two birds with one stone, as the saying goes, and visit the Pastor in the dismal abode of his Hooglandse Kerk, for I had no desire whatsoever to step foot in his home, where I would have to endure the most unpleasant presence of his strumpet wife. So, across the street I went, through a dusting of dry snow, under still gray skies, to the sprawling front doors of the church. The Pastor was, or course, taken aback, seeing me navigating the narrow aisle up the pews towards the sanctuary, where he was tending to some candles below the warmly glowing crucifix. To say that he was dumbfounded would be an understatement.

Once he had gathered his wits about him, he bid me come into his office, which I did, but not without some hesitation, dear husband, for the man in him is a lecher (I swear it) even if the pastor is not. Nonetheless, I was desperate to learn the meaning of the Latin phrases, so I handed him your letter (which I noticed him brazenly peruse before finally letting his eyes rest upon the phrases I had indicated with a pointing finger) and asked for a translation. No sooner had I done so than the Pastor's face swirled with color and his beady eyes opened wide, as if the second coming had right then bit him on his bountiful behind. He bellowed something about my son being a sinner and an infidel and not fit to be called a child of God. Well, Cornelis, my motherly instincts took hold of me, and before I knew what was happening, I had slapped his jowelled puss—twice—once with each hand. At this point, the stunned Pastor held up the Crucifix around his neck and began hissing Latin words at me, as if I were some evil spirit to be exorcised from the place. Not one to wear out my welcome, I turned and stormed straight out of the church, with Pastor Hogarth close behind me. His final words to me then were clearly spoken in the King's English: "Repent, repent and ye shall be forgiven."

Of course, I did no such thing, nor do I plan to. You of all people know, dear husband, that I have many faults and frailties, for I am human after all, and they may damn me in the afterlife, but I will not be damned for my actions on this day—oh no! For they were righteous actions, Cornelis. And I will never repent for being a mother—one who loves and protects her own, no matter what they may have said or done.

And so, I yet remain in the dark as to the meaning of the Latin phrases. Although I suppose, judging by our buffoonish pastor's reaction, it can be assumed that they are not fit for polite ears. Then it is just as well that I remain ignorant. No mother wishes to hear the idle curses of her son. And I hope, dear husband, that you will remember this in future and that you will not be tempted to do such a thing again. For you know how my curiosity unswervingly gets the better of me.

Your Loving Wife,
Marijke

FROM A LETTER ADDRESSED TO
MEVROUW MARIJKE ONDERDONK,
LEYDEN, SOUTH HOLLAND

October 9, 1748

Dearest Wife,

The sands of time funnel through the hourglass flipping end for end, over and over, until finally a lifetime has been measured out in minute grains. No, I am not so old as that, perhaps. Yet, sometimes I feel it to be so. Life is a web into which we are cast and become more and more entangled, and our pointless struggles against it only serve to entangle us further. In the end, we no longer have the strength to struggle and so we lie still in our old age and wait for the end to arrive. Yes, how bleak it is! I hear you say as much, dear Marijke. But at times, even as I drift farther away from the shores of middle age, I feel tired of life's struggles. You know that I am not one to quit—and I do not wish to lie down and die.'Twas only a trope, dearest, (three unrelated tropes, to be precise) and an unwieldy one at that. What is all of this leading to? you ask. Perhaps it is time to leave the sailing to younger men. Perhaps it is time for me to permanently take an office in the VOC headquarters. As luck would have it, that opportunity may well arrive soon.

Today, word around the scuttlebutt is that Opperhoofd Kunst is soon to retire his position and return to the Republic. Of course, there is a great deal of speculation concerning who will take up the position of opperhoofd of Batavia. Some of the other captains have suggested in not so plain terms that it should be me—that I am a likely replacement for Opperhoofd Kunst. Vanity, dear wife, is a grievous sin, one which can lead to even greater sins. And I am not so vain as to believe that I am the only, or even the best, candidate for the position, although I do believe that I am indeed qualified to lead the VOC in Batavia. And I must admit that the idea is not entirely unappealing—easing into my autumnal years behind a desk. I cannot help but wonder what you would say, dearest. Probably something witty and mildly acerbic, as you are apt to do on such occasions.

There was a time when I believed I would never leave the sea, would die with salt on my lips. No one knows this better than you, dear wife. For who but a dyed-in-wool seafaring man would leave at home a wife such as you in order to be tossed and turned upon every sea of the hemispheres. 'Twas like breathing to me then—being upon the water. But age, it seems, has a way of diluting one's core essence, watering it down to something more palatable, perhaps, until only a whisper of one's former self remains. And it is just such a whisper that sounds soft and low in my ears these days. Surely you will guffaw—or at least giggle—at my overwrought poetics. But it is nonetheless true.

I suppose we shall see, for nothing is certain yet. 'Tis only rumors and sighs at this point. But rest assured, I shall keep you informed, dearest Marijke.

Yours in Love and Longing,
Cornelis

FIFTEEN

"Come in, come in." *Opperhoofd* appeared genuinely pleased by Robrecht's presence there. "Sit down."

Robrecht hesitated, preferring to stand. However, when *Opperhoofd* Schoonhoven eased himself down into the seat behind his desk, he complied.

"You were successful in getting the *pribumi* back to work, I understand—and with a minimum amount of bloodshed. Well done, Meneer Onderdonk—Robrecht."

"Thank you, sir."

"And I also understand that we lost Captain Roorback on this expedition."

"He went overboard at a most inopportune moment."

"Yes, so it would seem. A gruesome death from the sounds of it." *Opperhoofd* placed both hands on the desk in front of him and, interlocking his fingers, began to knead his knuckles. "Yet, it does clear the decks, as we say at sea."

"Clear the decks, sir?"

"For you, Robrecht. Surely you haven't forgotten that I promised you a captain's rank."

"No, of course not."

"Well, then, *Son of Batavia* is now yours—officially—Captain Onderdonk." He opened a drawer, removed two sets of gold stripes and two gold braided epaulets, and slid them across the desk. "Wear them in good health."

"Thank you, sir." Robrecht rose and saluted.

"I must say that I'm curious as to just how you managed to get the *pribumi* back into the orchards—some surreptitious plan, no doubt." Meneer Schoonhoven sat up as if to listen intently then waved his hand as if to say it were best that he remain ignorant of the particulars.

Robrecht cringed, resisting the urge to reach out and slap this silly little man, make him eat his words—surreptitious plan! He of all people, accusing Robrecht of insidiousness. "No doubt, sir," he finally said. "Surreptitious, indeed."

The first voyage *Son of Batavia* was to make under the new command of Captain Onderdonk was to Pulicat, a port town on the Coromandel Coast overlooking the Bay of Bengal. In truth, official command of the vessel may have been new to Robrecht, but the voyage certainly was not. It was one undertaken over and over by countless VOC ships. At Pulicat, Robrecht would fill the ship's hold with kegs of gunpowder, a most important provision to be delivered to Batavia upon the ship's return. He would also take on significant amounts of the highly coveted trading commodity black pepper. Whatever room remained in the hold would be filled with slaves to be transported to Ceylon and sold to the *perkeniers* of cinnamon plantations.

The ship had barely cleared the harbor of Batavia when Robrecht sent for Dag. There was official business to attend to, and as captain of *Son of Batavia* he intended to take care of the matter promptly. A knock came to his cabin door.

"Come in, Seaman Dag. Sit down." Robrecht closed the cabin door and, stepping behind his desk, sat in the captain's chair. "How long have we known each other?"

He realized that this query, laden with a rare nostalgia as it was, would baffle the sailor. Dag ran three-fingers-and-a-half through his wiry beard, the missing half of his forefinger having been given up to a baby alligator in a fish market in Hau Ting.

"Why, sir, ye and Old Dag have been friends since yer head reached no higher than me old danglin' *snikkel*."

"Exactly right, Dag. I was but a boy when first we met. And you took me under your wing, and showed me the ways of the world — the real ways of the real world, that is, not the supposed world, exalted and apparitional, that my delusional father and brother imagine."

"Aye, sir. That old Dag did." A lopsided grin stretched beneath his mottled beard.

"And as I moved up the chain-of-command, and you endured as a lowly able seaman, you remained loyal to me, never bearing a grudge or wishing ill will upon me."

"Nay, sir. Never that."

"For your loyalty, for your unwavering friendship, I am promoting you to first mate of *Son of Batavia*. Now you will be my trusted companion both unofficially and officially. What say you?"

"Why Captain, old Dag be touched—touched as a *hoer* in heat on *Walpurgisnacht*. Thank ye, sir."

Robrecht removed an officer's coatee from his footlocker and held it out. "You'll be needing this."

Dag recoiled. "But Captain, old Dag couldn't."

"Go ahead, Dag. You're an officer now. It's only fitting."

Dag glanced down at the gray linen tunic that hung open to his waist and to the threadbare trousers rolled to his knees, below which poked two bare and calloused feet. Then he clicked his tongue and shook his head. "Nay, sir. Old Dag couldn't. 'Tis an honor, but old Dag surely could not."

"As you wish," said Robrecht, retrieving his tricorne hat.

Captain Onderdonk took his place on the quarterdeck with, it should be said, no small amount of satisfaction. For he had spent innumerable hours on this very deck, forced to listen to the blustery blatherings of lesser men than himself—first his own father, then Captain Roorback. He'd even mustered up a civilized veneer while held captive by his brother's high-flown discourses concerning life at sea.

Robrecht held the spyglass to his eye. Blue and more blue. The gold braided epaulettes trailing from the shoulders of his coatee sparkled in the sun. A porpoise stitched a silver seam over the warm blue cloak of the Indian Ocean. Robrecht swung the spyglass starboard and watched the northernmost tip of Sumatra disappear over the horizon. Back on high seas. As he always did at times like these, Robrecht wondered what new adventure awaited him, and as it turned out, he would not have to wait long.

His reverie was interrupted by a commotion on the spar deck, where two seamen were locked in a dangerous clutch. Robrecht collapsed the spyglass and called for order. He recognized one of the seamen as Dag, whom, refusing to don the uniform of a VOC officer, was virtually indistinguishable from the rest of the riffraff. And in fact, he was in every way indistinguishable from the ship's riffraff, officer or not.

"What is the meaning of this?" said Robrecht.

Dag stepped forward. "This brigand has stolen away me little vixen and does molest her with a scabrous *pik.*"

"Lies, lies!" cried the seamen.

"The little vixen you speak of—would that be the copper-hued laying hen?"

"Aye, sir. That's old Dag's little vixen. Everybody knows it." Dag turned to the crew in appeal.

"You, Able Seaman Van Dijk. It there any truth to these charges?"

"Sir, there is truth to the charge that the hen and I have relations— physical relations—same as those can be found in the Good Book. But sir, if it is a crime, then she be a willing accomplice. Stolen her away I have not, as this scoundrel suggests. She bid me come, sir, with a wanton eye. So I came."[52]

"Liar!" roared Dag, rushing the sailor.

"All right, All right," said Robrecht. "Here is my judgment. The hen in question is to be butchered and cut into two, that each man may retain a part of her to do with as he will, with a scabrous *pik* or

---

[52] Able Seaman Van Dijk had less *stolen* and more *lured* the hen in question away from Dag. On the night prior, while Dag lay in a drunken stupor beside the copper-hued laying hen, otherwise known as "the little vixen," with his shriveled *pik* having turtled its way back into his trousers, Seaman Van Dijk slunk from the shadows of the berth deck. With a foul desire tingling in his man-pouch, having for too long stood by and watched Dag and the little vixen flaunt their affections, and wishing to have his own way with the fetchingly fickle hen, Seaman Van Dijk set down pinches of cracked wheat on the berth deck, hoping to lure her away. Assessing the situation, the little vixen clucked, fluttered to her feet, and began to peck at the trail of wheat. All the while, Seaman Van Dijk watched and waited, one hand in his pocket rolling wheat and the other buried in his trousers plucking the heavy flesh of his foreskin.

otherwise. Does that suit you?"

"As you say, sir," said Van Dijk.

"No, Captain," said Dag. "I beg ye! Do not butcher me little vixen. Old Dag'll give her over to the brigand Van Dijk, just do not butcher me little vixen."

"That is evidence enough for me," said Robrecht. "But I will put it to you, good men of *Son of Batavia*. Which of these men does the wanton hen truly belong to: the one who would have her butchered and halved so that he may retain a piece of her, or the one who would give her over in order to save her life?" Letting his gaze wander from sailor to sailor, the captain waited in vain for a response. For there was only silence—a baffled silence that made it clear to Robrecht that the dilemma in question went beyond the rational capabilities of the crew.

"Well, the answer is clear to me," said Robrecht. "You, Able Seaman Van Dijk, are guilty of thievery on the high seas. What shall be his punishment?"

"Hang him! Hang him!" cried the crew.

"Perhaps the wronged in this case should choose the fitting punishment. What say you, Meneer Dag? What shall be his punishment?"

Dag hesitated but for a moment. "Keelhauling, sir."

The men roared their approval. They cried: "Keelhaul him! Keelhaul him!"

"Then justice has been served," said Robrecht. "Rig him up and keelhaul him."

Able Seaman Van Dijk was instantly buried in a crush of sailors. His hands were tied and the rope was passed beneath the ship's hull by a slender young sailor who went over larboard side and was moments later pulled up starboard side. The eager crew then tied the loose end of the rope to the condemned man's feet.

First Mate Dag took his place beside Robrecht on the quarterdeck and watched the crew cast Van Dijk into the sea and drag him beneath the boat. When they pulled the sailor aboard, he was conscious and still breathing.

"Again, Captain?" asked the crew, with great anticipation.

Robrecht turned to Dag. The first mate nodded. "And put yer shoulders to it this time," said he.

With this the men hurled the thief overboard a second time and with a grunt and groan dragged him forcefully across the hull of the ship. Robrecht recognized the sudden jolt of the rope as a death blow, the blow that snapped the sailor's neck as his head hit the keel.

When they pulled Van Dijk aboard this time, he was not breathing. His head hung at an unnatural angle—his neck kinked like a broken twig, and his back bloodied and sliced on the jagged barnacles that clung like armor to the hull. The crew formed a circle around the dead man, staring, as if somehow surprised by this outcome.

"A sailor's burial for this seaman," said Robrecht. "Wrap him in jute and give him up to the depths." Then turning to First Mate Dag: "I'd like a word with you in my cabin."

Dag followed the captain down the stairs of the quarterdeck, stroking the neck of his little vixen with great affection. It was clear to all that the first mate was delighted to be reunited with the impish-eyed hen.

"Come in and close the door, Meneer Dag." Robrecht stepped behind his desk and began to scribble in the captain's log, where he recorded the "accidental death by drowning" of Able Seaman Van Dijk. He flipped the cover closed and laid the quill pen beside a brass inkwell shaped like the Indian elephant god.

"When we arrive in Pulicat, I want you to personally see to the trunk of ducats in the hull. As before, you must get it past the harbormaster unnoticed."

"Aye, sir. Old Dag'll see to it. But if ye don't mind me asking, Captain—why turn ducats over for reals? Ducats trade same as reals. 'Tis a nonsense to Old Dag."

Robrecht rose and considered the consequences of what he was about to do—about to reveal to Dag. However, it took but a moment to conclude what he'd always known to be true—Dag was a trustworthy companion. "We do it for profit, plain and simple." Robrecht paused. "Since you are now first mate of *Son of Batavia*, I will take you into my confidence." He pulled a coin from his vest pocket and flipped it to Dag. "What do you see?"

"Why, sir, old Dag sees a Dutch ducat."

"Yes, but it is not the same as the ducats used in the Republic. What is different?"

Dag held up the coin and squinted. "Aye, could it be this stamp that ye are referring to, Captain?"

"Precisely. Gold ducats from the Republic arrive in Java. At the Batavia mint, they are counterstamped for use in our Dutch East Indies. But when exchanged for another currency, a counterstamped VOC ducat is worth more—about twelve stuivers more than a Dutch ducat. When viewed from a perspective of trade, that is a twelve stuiver profit on each ducat. But the ducats must be traded for another currency in order to collect that profit. So, we exchange the counterstamped ducats for Portuguese reals. Then we reinvest the profits gained into more Dutch ducats. Those ducats are then counterstamped and exchanged for more profit. Again, the profit is reinvested, and the cycle goes on and on. Needless to say, there is a small fortune to be made in trading currency."

The first mate stopped stroking his hen. "Old Dag will not try to fool ye, sir, and tell ye he understands the whole of what ye've just spoken. But sure as dragons *shijten* fire, old Dag understands 'small fortune' well enough. Aye, 'tis best to leave the head work to ye, Captain. But ye can count on old Dag to get yer trunk past the harbormaster."

Robrecht knew he could count on Dag, for the glint in the sailor's eye bespoke a hankering for schemes of an illicit nature. "Good, Meneer Dag. Then I'll leave it in your capable hands."

Robrecht stepped from behind his desk and extended a hand to Dag, an inclusive if clandestine gesture that conveyed a certain sense of gravity. But the gesture was interrupted by a shout from the quarterdeck. There came the shuffle of heals above them. "Ship ahoy!" cried the third mate. Robrecht exited the office and took the quarterdeck with authoritative calm. "Where," said he.

"Windward, sir," said the third mate handing over the spyglass.

"She's hull down," said Robrecht. "But I'm betting she's a frigate."

"Do they give chase, Captain?" said Dag.

"It would seem so. She's all in the wind." He dropped the

spyglass from his eye. "Fresh away, Meneer Dag."

"Loose topsails! Heave out staysails!" cried Dag.

"But Captain," said the third mate. "Our vessel will never outrun a French frigate."

"No, Meneer Closson, we can't outrun them. But we will lure them into a chase just the same, a chase that will prove to their great detriment and spell out their demise, with a bit of luck. Man the gun decks and prepare to engage."

Robrecht watched the frigate growing larger in the spyglass. Soon it was plainly visible to the naked eye. "Keep full sails, Meneer Dag," said he. "Keep to your luff, Meneer Oorschot."

At the helm, the coxswain gripped fast the wheel and trained hard his eyes upon the telltale. "Aye, Captain."

In the round eye of his spyglass, Robrecht could see the captain of the frigate standing tall and proud upon his vessel. "Ready about to drag anchor," said Robrecht to Dag.

"Ready about to drag anchor!" cried Dag in a raspy bluster.

"Drag anchor, Captain?" said the third mate. "We'll be sitting ducks to broadside fire."

"Do as I say, Meneer Closson. Follow my orders closely and it may be our good fortune to escape with hull and mast intact," said Robrecht. "Ready about to bring to."

"Ready about to bring to!"

He could now see with the naked eye sailors on the frigate toiling feverishly on the upper deck, loading the vessel's long guns. Shortly, the two ships were bow to bow, abreast, and within range of broadside fire. But Robrecht waited, anticipating the French captain's call to fire. Finally, when it looked as if engagement were inevitable he shouted the command: "Dowse sails! Heave to! Drag anchor!"

"Dowse sails! Heave to! Drag anchor!" cried Dag.

The sails came loose in the wind. Unfurling, they flapped loudly as the anchor plunged into the clear waters. Moments later, *Son of Batavia* jerked to a near standstill, sending the crew lurching forward in unison. Robrecht braced himself on the deck rail and watched the frigate—caught unaware—cut past the East Indiaman.

"Swing starboard the helm!" cried Robrecht. The coxswain spun the wheel to starboard and the ship yawed and rotated around her anchor. Moments later, she was perpendicular to the frigate and in a position to send a volley of raking fire at its stern. "Cannons, fire away!" said Robrecht.

The gun deck of *Son of Batavia* came alive with the boom and rattle of cannon fire. An acrid cloud of smoke wafted up from below. Robrecht breathed it deeply into his lungs and watched as cannon balls ripped through the fully exposed stern timbers of the frigate. He raised the spyglass to his eye and delighted in the look of horror upon the French captain's face. It was the face of a man who knew he'd been caught with his breeches down.

A barrage of chain shot blasted through the windows of the French Captain's cabin and ripped lengthwise through the frigate. The mainmast of the vessel teetered and finally toppled, its white sails flooded and tangled like some great winged bird caught in a net and sinking into the ocean's depths.

A mighty roar rose from the deck of *Son of Batavia* when the first mate of the frigate raised the white flag of submission.

"Hold fire. Prepare to board," said Robrecht.

He boarded the frigate with his flintlock pistol drawn and leveled on the vessel's captain, an elderly man with narrow shoulders and a sunken chest. The Frenchman looked quite ridiculous in his groomed periwig and polished leather boots. At least, such was Robrecht's view of his French counterpart.

"That won't be necessary," said the frigate's captain. "I am Captain Jacques Tresusé of the *La Royale*. We will yield peaceably while you ship your booty."

"Meneer Dag, take ten men and clean out the hold."

"Aye, Captain."

Robrecht lowered the pistol and slipped it into his belt. "Now, sir, tell me why a frigate of the French Navy has seen fit to give chase to a Dutch merchant vessel?"

"But, of course, you jest," said the captain. "Have you not heard? We are at war."

"*We*, sir, are not at war. The Dutch remain neutral and the war of which you speak takes place a world away from here. The only war that rages in the East Indies is the war of profits. Gold, silver, copper, silk, cinnamon, and slaves. That is the war which we fight. I care not a damn about stale battles of the old country. I fight for gain, plain and simple."

"You are nothing more than a freebooter, *un flibustier*."

"In the end, Captain Tresusé, we are all *vrijbuiters*. Why else would we be here, you and I, if not for the glory of gold?"

"For the glory of king and country, of course."

"King and country?" said Robrecht with a burst of derisive laughter. "And where is such glory to be found? Chained in what room, locked in what chest, might we find this thing called the glory of king and country? It is but a figment of your foolish imagination. A patriotic whim and fancy is what you speak of. And you, sir, are the king's jester and dunce." Robrecht dismissed the captain with a wave of his hand and addressed the frigate crew. "You men have a choice, upon which your lives depend, so think well on it. Those of you who will rise up in mutiny against your foolhardy captain and his officers will be spared. Those who do not will be stripped, shot, and thrown into the sea. The choice is yours. But know this—in any case, your captain's life is over."

"This is outrageous," said Captain Tresusé. "It contravenes all conventions of gentlemanly warfare."

Robrecht pulled his pistol from his belt, aimed it between the captain's eyes, and cocked the flintlock. "What, I put it to you, is gentlemanly about warfare—about mercilessly slaughtering one's enemies?" He paused before continuing. "Now, what is it going to be, men? Who will die for their captain and his conventions of gentlemanly warfare? And who will save his own skin?"

"Hang him! Hang him!" cried the frigate crew.

"Hang him! Hang him!" cried the *Son of Batavia* crew.

"As you wish. So justice has been served. Rig him up and hang him by the neck from the mainmast."

The frigate crew fell violently upon their captain. A rope was quickly fashioned into a noose and flung over the yard arm. Then Captain Tresusé was hoisted writhing and kicking above the spar deck. His eyes bulging and his teeth grinding. He jerked and twitched for a long minute until finally overcome by the stillness of death.

When *Son of Batavia* hoisted sails again, Robrecht counted four men dangling from the yard arm of the frigate's main mast. Some of the French crew cursed and shook their fists at their dead officers. Others drank and danced, happy to have been spared certain death.

"What will happen to them?" asked Meneer Closson.

"They will drift for two or three days, until it occurs to them that they are doomed to a slow and painful death on open waters. Some of them will be sacrificed, while the others drink their blood and eat their flesh in a futile attempt to prolong their own worthless lives. Most will die from lack of water. Some will throw themselves overboard in fits of madness. Others will die from exposure. But in the end, they will all die. That much is certain."

Robrecht returned to his cabin. He opened the captain's cabinet— its long black strap hinges rasping under the weight—and removed a bottle of rum. He poured the tawny brown liquor into a tankard and stood at the windows, sipping at it absently. He could not tell if it was his victory over the frigate or the spirits of the rum that now made his head bob and tingle. And the fact that this particular episode so closely resembled a much earlier episode with *Son of Batavia* and another French frigate had not escaped him. In fact, Robrecht could think of nothing else. But his response had been much different than his father's—much more decisive, more exacting. At least, so thought Robrecht.[54]

---

[54] The frigate had been following *Son of Batavia* at approximately one league for some time before Captain Onderdonk decided to take action. As a seasoned captain, he was well aware of the risks involved with direct confrontation, yet he also knew that the frigate could easily overtake the VOC vessel if it wished too. Trying to outrun it would be futile, and pretending to ignore it seemed foolish. "Dowse sails. Heave to, Meneer Horner," said the Captain.

"Dowse sails! Heave to!" said the first mate.

"Dowse sails! Heave to!" said the boatswain.

Jakob appeared at the Captain's elbow. "Why are we stopping, Father— Captain?"

"We are going to find out why the frigate continues to follow us."

Robrecht bounded up the stairs to the quarterdeck with a zeal that clearly called for action. "Father, should we not ready the cannons?"

"That is precisely the wrong action to take. It is a call to battle. And we do not want to do battle."

"But Father," said Robrecht, "the French are our sworn enemies. They are no better than pirates who aim to rob us on high seas. Does that not demand a call to battle?"

"It is true that leveling the flintlock and triggering the cock is the easier action to take, but easier is not always better. We will remain calm and allow the French officers to board. Then we shall see which is the most prudent course of action to take."

"Prudent? Prudent, Father?" said Robrecht. "Only a fool speaks of prudence when his enemies are upon him?"

"Robrecht!" said Jakob. "Hold your tongue!"

"The French are not our enemies. We are Dutch. We have no enemies. You would do well to remember that," said Captain Onderdonk, and then added: "And do not forget yourself, Able Seaman Onderdonk. You are a sailor in the Dutch East India Company, and I am your Captain. Impudence will not be tolerated." This was said with a finality that sent his son fuming away.

By now, the French frigate had positioned itself alongside *Son of Batavia* and its officers were about to board the vessel. Captain Onderdonk straightened his coatee and, descending the stairs to the spar deck, marched to meet them.

"I am Captain Achille LeBeau of *La Royale*," said the tallest among them.

"I am Captain Cornelis Onderdonk of the Dutch East India Company. We are not a military vessel. We have no quarrel with you."

"No, there is no quarrel. It is simply that we are in need of the cargo that sits so heavy in the hold of your ship."

"With all due respect, Captain, what would make you think that our hold is heavy with cargo?"

"Come now. Do I look like *un mousse*? You're course is north-northwest on the Indian Ocean. And the water line on the hull of your vessel bespeaks heavy ballast. Japanese copper and silver, is it not?"

"Let us suppose for a moment that what you surmise correctly. A captain yourself, you know that as captain of this vessel, I cannot possibly allow you to empty out the hold of this ship. A bloody battle would have to ensue for such a thing to happen. And let us be frank—neither of us wants a dead crew, or worse yet, an injured crew that would likely spread disease among those

Robrecht drained his tankard and set it down. As a young man, he had been baffled by his father's weakness. Now he was simply sickened by it. Unfortunately, his father was no longer, and thus was Robrecht—being unable to point out said weakness to him—overcome by the kind of restlessness that accompanies just such unfinished business, with its unsettling nuances of indetermination and irresolution banging futilely, noisomely about one's head like riotous prisoners in a cell. He tried to put it from his mind, focus on what lay ahead. For he knew he must not hesitate—that is, he must make his mark quickly as the new captain of *Son of Batavia*. Upon this, everything depended.

---

lucky enough to remain standing after battle. In the end, all that would be achieved by such an engagement would be two ghost ships drifting to nowhere."

"Be that as it may, you should know, Captain Onderdonk, that we are ready to do battle."

"And you should know, Captain LeBeau, that we are fully loaded with powder and lead. You may be fast, but we are forceful."

"What, then, would you suggest, that we might avoid such an undesirable outcome?"

"I would suggest that we offer you a gift, a token of our esteem for you and your cause."

"Half of all you have would be a greatly appreciated token."

"Half is far too generous for our humble vessel, sir. I would suggest that one-fifth is a reasonable sum."

LeBeau looked the Captain in the eye, and cocked his head slightly to one side. He spoke cautiously. "Yes, I do believe that one-fifth is a reasonable sum."

"Then it is done. Your first mate may oversee the transaction," said Captain Onderdonk. Then without turning his head, keeping his eye leveled upon the French Captain he spoke: "Meneer Horner, see to it."

From the Journal of Jakob Onderdonk

May 30, 1748

Today, two deckhands were flogged—one for stabbing another in a game of Landsknecht, and the other for inciting the stabbing by cheating during the game of Landsknecht. Father, it seems, is trying to make a point. He is trying to teach Robrecht an important life's lesson. My brother believes that the victim of a crime should be punished alongside of the perpetrator. Thus did father order Robrecht to personally deal out his distorted brand of justice to the victim; that is, Robrecht was responsible for administering twenty lashes to the cheating deckhand. 'Twas very nearly more than twenty, in actual fact, for had Second Mate Bleeker not stayed my brother's hand, who knows how long he would have flogged the poor fellow. His great relish, I'm afraid, was apparent to all, and his cruelty was clearly on display. Not surprisingly, then, the deckhands grumbled and griped under their breath about the merciless third mate.

Even father seemed openly aghast by this inhumane demonstration. He stepped stiffly down the stairs of the quarterdeck and retired immediately to the captain's cabin without so much as a word to anyone. Dag was, of course, grinning a dingy grin of admiration for his cold-blooded apprentice. The only person to utter a word was the ship's surgeon, who said to Robrecht, "You wish to maim a man over a card game?" or something to that effect. But my brother seemed unaffected by the comment, just as he seemed oblivious to the disapproving stares of the men.

Father stood with his back to me, looking through the clouded panes of glass to the shimmering blue world beyond. Even from that hindmost view, I detected an air of defeat about him that I had never before witnessed. It reminded me of the man in a brawl who has been beaten so badly that he no longer bothers to curl up protectively—he simply lies there numbly waiting for the black tide of unconsciousness to wash over him.

Perhaps it was something in his stance that made me think as much— there was something timid and cautious about it, and I had never known my father to exhibit either of those characteristics before. I wanted to say the words that would ease his mind, but I simply did not know what those words were or if they even existed, for that matter. I wished to stay with him but it seemed best to say nothing. So I sat in a chair in the corner of his cabin and waited, in the hope that he might turn his face to me.

FROM A LETTER ADDRESSED TO
MEVROUW MARIJKE ONDERDONK,
LEYDEN, SOUTH HOLLAND

December 3, 1748

Dearest Wife,

The land of the shogunate is an exotic land, one that I believe you would find delightful and intriguing. The people are tacit and mysterious in their ways; yet do not mistake this for weakness. The shogun is powerful and his warriors are mighty. It is said that the samurai can fell a tree with a single stroke of his razor-sharp katana. Improbable, yes, and an exaggeration, to be sure—however, there can be no doubt that the shogun's warriors are skilled with the sword. In fact, it was samurai who stood guard as the Shogun's men searched Son of Batavia upon our arrival at Dejima this very day.

Why would they search our ship? Are we not allied with the shogun in our quest for profits? 'Tis true that we are allies, and that the Dutch are preferred over the Portuguese by the shogun and his emperor. What the shogun's men were in search of was religious books and artifacts. For the emperor sees Christianity as a scourge and forbids the slightest whiff of it. 'Tis not my place to tell any man who to worship or what to believe, yet still I cannot help but take offense at such drastic measures. Do our Christian beliefs render us animals, barbarians, savages? Are we worse than pagans and infidels?

Thus it was that all religious books and artifacts (surprisingly few, or perhaps, not surprisingly few when one takes into account the number of godless deckhands that man Son of Batavia) onboard were put in a chest and given over the authorities the moment that our ship docked. In most cases, the search that follows is a formality lacking any real conviction or consequence. However, yesterday, the shogun's men made a thorough search of the vessel, even demanding to inspect the hold. What exactly it was they were looking for was not clear. What was clear, however, was they were looking for something more than Christian books and artifacts. When I demanded an explanation, they smiled and tipped their heads in the deferential way that only these people can do (deferential yet somehow superior, too, which may give you some idea of their enigmatic nature). In the end, they left the ship empty-handed, just as expected. The only thing they managed to find was the sore spot that raised my ire against them.

Forgive me, dearest, for I have allowed myself to be carried away by my emotions (an occurrence of increasing frequency of late, I'm afraid). Sufficeth to say, something was amiss with the inspection. Of course, this is a matter I will take up with Opperhoofd Jansen here in Dejima and Opperhoofd Kunst upon my return to Batavia. But now looking back over this letter, I see that I have wasted too much ink and paper on matters that will surely be of no interest to you. Allow me to remedy the situation soon. For at the moment, dear wife, I have more business to attend to in Dejima. It seems I owe you a lengthy letter of love and longing. Until then, know that I miss you.

> *Your Loving Husband,*
> *Cornelis*

SIXTEEN

The Pulicat marketplace was a wonder of vibrant colors, pungent odors, and entrancing sounds. Robrecht stopped to palm the ripe sunburst of a Banganapalle mango. Seeing his coatee and captain's braids, the merchant, a toothless Labbay Mahometan, bid him take the fruit. In truth, the merchant wanted only to be rid of the likes of Robrecht and the ruthless Dutch Christians who controlled all trade along the shores of Tamil Nadu.

Robrecht turned to find First Mate Dag among a crowd gathered about a long-limbed snake charmer. In a billowing white robe, the grizzly-bearded Sapera blew a nasally tune from his *pungi*, until out of a bamboo basket arose a snake brown and sleek, swaying to and fro with its menacing hood spread wide. Dag leaned over: "Say what ye will, sir, but if ye ask old Dag, this fool's a boot-full short of common sense."

Robrecht watched the charmer bend forward and kiss the snake on its flat, angular head. "Yes, I am inclined to agree with you," said Robrecht. "And that, Meneer Dag, gives me an idea."

Robrecht had decided that the first mate would accompany him to meet Barroso, for he well knew that it was always best to attend such meetings if not with a show of force, at least with some semblance of support. And Dag, he also knew, would prove to be more than enough support in the event of trouble.

Along the way, Robrecht told Dag what little he knew of the Portuguese slave trader's past—that he was apprehended on a Lisbon dock, a young man from Guarda province who had ventured to the city looking for adventure and that at the time of apprehension, he was lying unconscious, soiled and suffering the effects of his crapulous cups, in front of the *taberna* from which he had earlier been ejected for retching a meager portion of bread and goatfish onto the skirts of a barmaid. He had awoken the following morning to find himself in chains, part of a press gang on the *São Martinho*, a four-masted galleon in the *Armada Portuguesa* headed for the East

Indies.[55]

---

[55] What Robrecht did not know about Barroso was that his young, plump, and effeminately curved figure made the young Portuguese a sought-after commodity among the enlisted men. So much so, that he was buggered from continent to continent, from ocean to ocean, and from old world to new, until the ship at last reached the Indian Ocean. In fact, he was bent over a barrel in the ship's hold, in the clutches of a brute from the moors of Drenthe, when the *São Martinho* was involved in a squirmish off the coast of Sadras, in which twenty-three men were killed on the upper decks by cannon fire from a French frigate. To this day, Barroso attributed his state of continued animation to buggery—blessed buggery. He would be forever grateful that he was being reamed by the ship's coxswain when the cannon balls began to fly that fateful day.

Even so, Barroso quickly realized that life at sea was simply not for him, so when the ship docked at Pulicat, he disappeared out the backdoor of a brothel and into the marshes of Pulicat Lake, where he lived for six days on mud crab and storks' eggs. On the seventh day, he met Mohamed Ali Khan Wala Wala rah rah, the Nawab of Arcot—officially known as Amir ul Hind, Wala Jah, 'Umdat ul-Mulk, Asaf ud-Daula, Nawab Muhammad 'Ali Anwar ud-din Khan Bahadur, Zafar Jang, Sipah-Salar, Sahib us-Saif wal-qalam Mudabbir-i-Umur-i-'Alam Farzand-i-'Aziz-az Jan, Biradarbi Jan-barabar, Subadar of the Carnatic. Or more precisely, he met one of Mohamed Ali Khan Wala Wala rah rah's servants named Abhay.

Abhay befriended Barroso, eventually introducing the young Portuguese to the master and securing work for as him as an assistant. Since Abhay's duties centered on his master's slaves and concubines—mostly young Borahis captured from the Brahmaputra valley—so too did the duties of Barroso center on slaves. His main responsibility was that of "relaxer," a word which Abhay pronounced slowly and gravely. As the designated relaxer, Barroso undertook the task of easing the oil-slathered handle of Japanese *shinai* into the anuses of young Borahi men in order to coax their stubborn sphincters open, making them amenable to imminent penetration by the master Mohamed Ali Khan Wala Wala rah rah's sizable erection. Of course, Barroso's year of buggery at sea now turned out to be somewhat of a godsend, as his extensive personal experience in matters of forceful ingression made him a masterful relaxer.

Be that as it may, it was Barroso's simple modifications to the shinai that really caught his master's eye and, it must be said, his master's imagination, setting him apart as an innovator and a servant to be trusted. Finding the

Robrecht and Dag arrived at the bleached stone building and pushed through its massive oak door, complete with black cast-iron knocker. A short stout Portuguese who habitually licked his cracked lips until they bled greeted Robrecht with an embrace. The slave trader stepped back and grinned. "What is this? *Captain* Onderdonk is it now?" A lusty laugh whistled through Barroso's teeth.

Robrecht motioned to Dag and the first mate opened the trunk of ducats. "Counterstamped Dutch ducats," said Robrecht. "Six gulden, twelve stuivers per ducat in Portuguese reals. It's the going rate."

"Well, let me think on that," said Barroso. "Let us look at the merchandise first, shall we?"

Robrecht and Dag followed him to a clearing where an assortment of slaves—men, women, and children—stood chained to iron stakes.

"Eighteen men, all in their prime," said Barroso. The slave trader grabbed a young man and pulled back his lips, exposing a row of cracked teeth. "Just look at that—almost perfect dentition."

"Dentition, sir?" said Dag.

"Teeth," said Robrecht. "Barroso believes that using such words ups the value of his slaves."

---

shinai weapon long and unwieldy, Barroso had lopped it off at the *tsuba*, leaving only the handle intact. Then it was simply a matter of attaching the *shinai* handle—the *tsuka*—to a leather strap. Fastening the strap about his waist and thrusting with his hips, Barroso found the free use of both hands to be helpful in massaging the Borahi slaves' tense buttocks and ultimately expediting the whole relaxation process. Hearing word of Barroso's apparatus, the master demanded a demonstration. So impressed was he that he ordered Barroso to use the apparatus on his own puckered anus. So, drizzling olive oil onto the *shinai tsuka*, the young Portuguese fastened the strap about his waist and demonstrated the effectiveness of his apparatus to his deeply moaning master. The following day, the master Mohamed Ali Khan Wala Wala rah rah rewarded Barroso by entrusting him with the sale of several slaves. In this, too, Barroso proved to be exemplary. Within a week's time, he had a small stable of slaves to sell at the Pulicat market, which he did with ease. The following week his stable of slaves grew. And the week after that. Until Barroso was the largest slave dealer on the Coromandel Coast.

"Come now, Robrecht—Captain Onderdonk—let's not give away trade secrets." He continued down the line. "Eleven women, all impregnable." Barroso pulled open the sarong of a young woman and clutched her breast. "Look at those perfect mammiform." The Siddi woman spat in Barroso's face, prompting a swift and violent strike from the slave trader. "That one is greatly in need of impregnation," said the Portuguese, wiping his face and continuing on. "And here are the children. Seven in all. Each with a potential lifetime of servitude." Barroso turned up his lips into a blood-smeared grin. "That brings the total to thirty-seven slaves."

"Thirty-six," said Robrecht.

"What?"

"I'm sure you mean that brings the total to thirty-six slaves."

"Ah, yes. My mistake," said Barroso. "Thirty-six slaves."

"Fine. We'll take them all."

"Good. Come, let us strike a deal inside, out of this ungodly heat." The slave trader led them back inside where he picked up a ledger and opened it. "Since the merchandise I am offering you is of such high quality, I think six gulden, ten stuivers is a fair price for your ducats."

Robrecht had anticipated this. "The usual rate for a counterstamped Dutch ducat is six gulden, twelve stuivers. That is what was paid in Canton not three months ago."

"But that is Canton and this in Pulicat. Here, greedy *Mansabdars* breathe down my neck."

Robrecht nodded to Dag. "Perhaps this will help to convince you."

Dag produced a bamboo basket.

"What is that?" said Barroso, licking at his lips with a red-smeared tongue.

"What does it look like?"

"It looks like a Sapera's basket."

"Indeed it does. Meneer Dag, kindly show our Portuguese friend what is inside the basket."

Dag seized the slave trader's arm.

"No wait, please."

"You have something to say?"

"But you can't do this."

"Why not?" said Robrecht. He raised an eye to Dag. The first mate eased the basket lid open and jerked Barroso's hand closer.

"Okay, okay. Six gulden, twelve stuivers." said the slave trader with labored breath. "But not a stuiver more."

"Deal," said Robrecht. Dag released Barroso's arm. The plump Portuguese huffed and puffed and his face contorted. Then he keeled over at Robrecht's feet and began clawing at his chest with both hands.

"My . . . heart," said the Portuguese.

Robrecht removed the basket lid, turned it over, and let it drop to the ground, causing Barroso to jerk to one side, cringe, and stare wide-eyed into the empty basket.

"You . . . you . . . *bastardo*."

"Where are the reals?"

Barroso dug his chin into his chest. "Key."

Robrecht knelt and yanked a key from around the slave trader's neck. Turning to Dag: "Get the slaves back to the ship. I'll be right behind you."

"Help," said the dying man with a gasp.

"There is no help for you, *bastardo*."

With the slaves and provisions heavy in its hull, *Son of Batavia* weighed anchor the following morning and set a course for Ceylon. Once they had cleared the harbor, Robrecht took breakfast in his cabin. He scooped the last of a poached egg into his mouth and slurped strong green Chinese tea while glancing out the window to the Coromandel Coast. Soon they would round the cusp of Nagapattinam and encounter the brackish waters of Palk Strait. By following a south-southeastern course, *Son of Batavia* would avoid the unnavigable Adam's Gate that straddles Palk Strait and clearing Point Pedro would then coast along the eastern shore of Ceylon, circling the island to the Gulf of Mannār and Colombo city.

A metered rap came to the door, one he immediately recognized as Dag's. "Enter," said Robrecht.

The first mate stepped into the cabin. Behind him came a lumpish, bespectacled man in his mid-forties. Dag moved aside and let the ship's surgeon speak. "Captain, we have a situation." Robrecht understood that for Meneer Vrooman a *situation* lay somewhere between misfortune and quandary. In fact, he rarely saw the surgeon—only when a situation had arisen.

"What is it?"

"Ye'd better come with us, sir," said Dag.

"As you wish. Lead on." Robrecht followed the first mate and the surgeon to the ship's sick bay. There a sailor lay on his side groaning with every breath. "What ails him?"

Meneer Vrooman pulled back a bloody sheet. "I took these—" he raised a glass jar of lead shot, "—from there." He pointed.

"From his rectum?"

The surgeon nodded. "Thirteen balls, from deep within."

"Thirteen? How the devil did they get in there?"

"A slave girl, Captain," said Dag.

"What? A slave girl? How does a slave girl go about inserting thirteen lead balls into an able seaman's rectum?"

"While he was—" The surgeon pursed his lips and wrinkled his brow. "While they were—"

"While he was busy with his *pik*, Captain," said Dag.

"I see. Sit him up. I wish to speak to him."

"Up ye come." Dag propped the sailor upright.

"Now," said Robrecht, "what is the meaning of all this?" he asked. The sailor grimaced, saying nothing.

"Did you, or did you not, tamper with the merchandise?"

"Merchandise, sir?" said the sailor.

"The slaves," said Robrecht impatiently. "Did you stick your *pik* into my merchandise? It is a simple question."

"Yes, sir, I did. But I meant no harm. I was just looking for a wee bit of fun, Captain, sir."

"Some fun, I see. And were the thirteen lead balls in your *aars* part of the fun, too?"

"No, sir. Well, I mean, maybe, sir."

"Speak plainly, sailor, or I will have you keelhauled."

"At first, I believed they were, sir . . . part of the fun. What I mean is they felt . . . well . . . pleasing sir. I thought to myself that maybe the blackie . . . well . . . maybe she fancied me after all. So I did not concern myself with the lead shot, sir, until it was all over and the cramps set in."

"And how was it that the slave girl had access to lead shot?"

"I suppose our being on the gun deck at the time would explain that, sir."

"Indeed it would. So, you unshackled her and took her from the hold to the gun deck."

"And stuck yer *pik* in her," added Dag.

"Yes, sir."

"Do you know it is a grave offense to remove merchandise from the hold?"

"Well, yes, I suppose it is, Captain. But I returned her . . . the merchandise, I mean . . . to the hold when I was finished with her . . . it."

"But the fact remains that you are in breach of VOC code. In such a case, you must be punished."

Here the surgeon interjected. "Captain, if I may say a word—I think the able seaman is not fit to withstand the punishment you speak of. It may spell the end of him."

"That is your concern, Meneer Vrooman, not mine. My concern is keeping order on this ship." He turned to Dag. "Take the able seaman to the spar deck. Find the slave girl and bring her there also. Gather the men for a public flogging."

The sailor collapsed onto the cot and began to weep.

"Aye, Captain," said Dag then disappeared.

"But Captain—" said the surgeon.

"Your intercession on able seaman Courtlandt's behalf is of no use, Meneer Vrooman. He has broken the code and must be punished. It is black and white."

Robrecht stepped into his cabin long enough to retrieve the

Captain's Daughter.[56] He ran the seven frayed thongs of the leather strap over his open palm as he climbed to the quarterdeck. The crew were gathered below, forming a half circle around the able seaman who was already tied face-first to the mainmast. "For breaching VOC code, twenty lashes," said Robrecht. The crew cheered their approval. "Flog him! Flog him!" cried they. Then Dag appeared from below deck, dragging the slave girl behind him. Robrecht at once recognized her as the young Siddi who had spit in the face of Barroso.

"And for the unauthorized insertion of lead shot up an able seaman's rectum, twenty lashes for the girl."

The crew roared and began to chant. "Flog her! Flog her!" cried they.

Dag jerked the Siddi toward the mainmast and was about to tie

---

[56] The Captain's Daughter was not a traditional cat 'o' nine tails made from strands of plaited rope. It was much smaller, but considerably more painful. While a passenger aboard *Gulden Jager*, a sister VOC vessel bound for the Gulf of Mannār, Robrecht once witnessed a similar strap tear every last scrap of skin from a thieving sailor's back. He had been present when the kerfuffle over a plate of beans occurred, leaving one deckhand with a bruised cheek and the other with a nipped off pinkie in his teeth. The Captain of *Gulden Jager* was a staunch disciplinarian who believed that the seeds of insurrection resided in the heart of every sailor and must be trampled, lest they sprout and bring forth fruit (in this, Robrecht believed he and the captain to be kindred spirits). Thus, with the corners of his mouth moist with spittle and his eyes dry as firestones, the captain pronounced the verdict of forty lashes with "the daughter of no mercy."

Robrecht stood on the spar deck, mesmerized, transported, as the Captain's Daughter lashed at the seaman's back, lapping at the flesh like the black serpent tongues of Medusa. The screams of the deckhand stirred the blood deep within Robrecht, touched some newly exposed nerve that caused a sweet and sickly pain to twist the bowels of his lower gut. And Robrecht knew then, in that impenetrable moment, that there was no greater power in heaven or on earth than the supreme power over another's ravaged flesh. He also knew then that he must have one of his own someday—a Captain's Daughter.

her hands when she broke free. The fleet-footed slave sprinted for the gunwale and launched herself cleanly over it before falling into the depths of the sea.

Lest the stunned silence turn to disappointed mumbles, Robrecht tossed the Captain's Daughter to Dag. "Able Seaman Courtlandt will take the girl's lashes. Forty lashes." said he. "Let the flogging begin."

FROM A LETTER ADDRESSED TO
MEVROUW MARIJKE ONDERDONK,
LEYDON, SOUTH HOLLAND

August 3, 1741

Dearest Mother,

What a place is this Masqat! The sights—colors vibrant and arresting, architecture complex, yet deceptively simple as the Persians themselves are said to be. The sounds—the ethereal ring of the ud. And the sun! Mother, the sun! Oh but in my great excitement I get ahead of myself. Even now as I write this I hear the Mahometans mumbling their prayers in the street, facing the homeland of their faith. What a strange and wonderful country this is!

Today, while father and his officers bargained for slaves inland, I explored the famous souk of Masqat, where I was immediately drawn to the lightly fluttering odor of frankincense. A woman with a veil draped just beneath her eyes placed a box of golden nuggets before me and bid me handle them. Of course, mother, I being a young man with no more than a few gulden in my pocket was hesitant to do so at first. But soon enough I succumbed to the temptation to raise a single luminescent rock to my nose and breathe in its eternal fragrance. To say that it was magical does no justice to the Arabian jewel. Yet, despite my attraction to it, I was still cursed with a light money pouch—too light, dearest mother, to buy the box of frankincense that I so longed to give you.

Perhaps sensing my plight, the woman silently placed five nuggets in front of me and held up three fingers—a gesture which I could only assume was meant to refer to ducats. Feeling my cheeks warming, I picked a single golden nugget from the box and pinched it between thumb and forefinger, while at the same time offering a single gulden (all that was left of my meager cabin boy wages) in the open palm of my other hand. The Arabic woman plucked the coin from my hand and nodded gravely, as if it pained her to let the frankincense go.

And so it was, dear mother, that I left the market pleased with my purchase and determined to send it to you as soon as we again dropped anchor in Java. Needless to say, the thought of frankincense snaking through the air of the herenhuis delighted me to no end, as I slipped the nugget safely into my pouch. I hope you'll think of me fondly when you burn it, and know that I am thinking of you, too.

Your Son,
Jakob

SEVENTEEN

Three weeks passed, and Jakob had yet to return to regular Sunday meetings of the Anabaptists. Three weeks and no word from Bonifaas Quackenboss, either. The truth was the shame and embarrassment caused by his "irregular" baptism (as he had come to euphemistically call it) had kept Jakob away from the Anabaptists. And it should be said that for his part, Bonifaas had wondered about Jakob and had even been set to call upon his newest convert, until Katrine Quackenboss essentially forbid it. It turned out that the near unveiling of Jakob's *erectie* at the baptism had left a sour taste in Katrine Quackenboss's mouth, not to mention a salty image in her mind. And so it was that when Bonifaas had set a saddle upon his acceptably swaybacked mare with the intention of getting to the bottom of Jakob's prolonged absence, his wife had stepped to him and said: "Let him be, Bonifaas. Let him be."[57]

---

[57] Katrine Quackenboss had seen one before—an *erectie*—accidently, of course, while she and Bonifaas had been procreating in the condoned Anabaptist fashion—that is, fully clothed and one-atop-the-other in a room "dark like unto the womb." At the time in question, a gust of wind had blown the cottage door open and a ray of sunlight lit up Bonifaas's loins like a Babylonian sundial. For her part, Katrine had stifled a shriek (although it should be said that her gasp was clear enough) and dropping her head, squeezed her eyes shut and parted her legs in a stiff missionary position. Unfortunately, seeing Jakob's hard-pressed member at the baptism caused the whole disagreeable incident to surface again in Katrine Quackenboss's mind. Of course, Bonifaas, a devout but simple man, had not put the two *erectie* events together in his mind. In fact, he was unaware that the sight of his own *erectie* so long ago had caused such clear consternation in his wife. Furthermore, he had no idea that the womanly pains she habitually complained of were nothing more than a prevarication meant to spurn his advances, a kind of falsehood she hoped would spare her the rod (although it should be said that Katrine Quackenboss's sensibilities were such that they would never allow her to put it quite so crassly). And thus it was that Bonifaas saw nothing disingenuous in his wife's exhortation to let Jakob be. So he did just that—he let him be.

Jakob sat down at his desk and, dipping a quill into the inkpot, began to write. *Dear Heleen . . . .* He paused. Ink puddled on the paper, a growing blotch that bespoke his present indecisiveness. As before, he found himself unable to get beyond the opening line. There was much to tell—a death, a baptism, and a forthcoming wedding. Yet he seemed incapable of communicating the news. In fact, he had been incapable of communicating anything at all to Heleen. Sitting helplessly before the blank page, Jakob could only assume that his failed attempts had some deeper significance than previously imagined. It occurred to him then that perhaps he had been unable to correspond with Heleen because he could not say what it was he truly wished to say—that he missed her dearly and that he would hasten to her side if she would but only beckon him to do so. He crumpled the paper and rose from the desk with a momentum that caused his chair to squawk and skid over the floor. It also caused Pangloss, who was busily scribbling numbers into a ledger, to yawp out a complaint. "Good Anabaptist, does something trouble you?"

"No . . . yes . . . I don't know. Perhaps, a trifle. But there are other matters to tend to." He stepped to the window. In his frustration, Jakob rapped too violently upon the glass, drawing the attention of Candide. The young philosopher-cum-loom-operator left the factory floor and padded with the due deference of an underling to the office.

"Please sit down, Candide. I have something to ask you."

Candide slid into a chair and placed a blistered-tipped hand upon either knee.

"As you know, I am to be married in three months' time less several days."

"Yes, good Anabaptist, it is certain to be the best of all weddings." said Candide.

"Indeed, let us hope your wedding comes off as brilliantly as your baptism," added Master Pangloss.

Jakob flushed, despite detecting not a trace of irony in the old philosopher's tone. "Yes—well, let us hope for even better," said he. "As I was saying, I am to be married in not three months' time and I need a best man for the occasion. I was hoping that you, Candide, would do me the great honor of taking up that post."

"Oh, it is truly an honor," said Candide.

"Indeed, it is an honor," echoed Pangloss.

"But perhaps I am not the best choice, good Anabaptist, for my short time in uniform has aptly manifested my lack of skill in the deadly arts."

"Deadly arts? Whatever do you mean?" said Jakob.

"Is it not the best man's sworn duty to keep the bride's enraged family at bay until the ceremony has taken place?"

"That is a tradition of the distant past. There will be no enraged family, I assure you. In fact, there will be no family at all, now that her *tante* is gone."

"Forgive me, good Anabaptist. How quickly I have forgotten the sudden and tragic end that came to your betrothed's good *tante*."

"Indeed, it was a tragedy," said Pangloss, "but one that could've befallen no other. For God created the paned glass through which she burst and the Earth upon which she landed and the universal law of gravitation that caused her velocious fall."

"You mean to say that God was the author of her demise?" said Jakob.

"Of course not, good Anabaptist. God can do no evil—is incapable of such. He has created the best of all possible worlds, and thus whatever happens in this world is for the best. That is His only wish."

"But surely, God, abounding is grace and mercy as He is, would not wish for such a tragedy."

"Of course not. He wishes only for what is best in this world."

At this point, Jakob felt a tautological headache tightening at the base of his skull.

"But has your betrothed no other family?" said Candide. "No *broeder*? No *zuster*? No *oom*? No *nicht* or *neef*? No one at all?" said Candide.

Welcoming this timely interruption, Jakob paced behind his desk and spoke. "Some distant relatives, but none to speak of other than her *oom* who resides in Batavia. And I do not expect that he would wish to leave his post as *opperhoofd* to travel to a wedding halfway around the globe." Jakob stopped pacing and turned to Candide. "So, may I assume your answer is yes?"

"Of course, good Anabaptist. I wholeheartedly accept the call to best man. How could I ever deny you anything, you who have been so generous to me?"

"Good. It's settled, then. Let us leave early today and toast the occasion," said Jakob, marching to the coat rack and seizing his overcoat and hat. "For it is not every day that a man is fortunate enough to be wed to one as fair as—" Jakob stopped the air that bore this utterance like a bunged keg before he uttered the name poised on his lips—*Heleen*.

The tavern was warm and merry. Farmers, factory workers, butchers, blacksmiths, and merchants low and high all gathered to take the chill off with a social libation. The three friends huddled around a table where a sweet glowing peat fire lit one side of them or the other. They raised pewter tankards and drank *bier* the color of fading sunlight.

As regular patrons who took their residence above the establishment, Pangloss and Candide were well known to the proprietor and his wife. The barmaids, too, appeared to be friendly with the pair of philosophers from Westphalia. One by one, they approached the table and begged Master Pangloss to "do the trick" with his eye. Jakob was surprised to see the old philosopher plug his nose, cover his mouth, and then puff out his cheeks, causing his blind eye to poke from the recess of its socket like a dormouse from its hole. This combined with a feigned expression of shock made for a grotesque spectacle, one which evoked squeals of delight from the barmaids.

"There was a time, before this," said Pangloss, gesturing to his troll-like features, "when the ladies found me a more pleasing sight to set eyes upon."

This also surprised Jakob. Not because he believed there to be no truth in it, but because he had never heard Pangloss speak of anything other than philosophy and God's design. He watched the old philosopher drain his tankard, drop it to the table, and then grin a peasant's grin.

"Tell the good Anabaptist about the pretty wench Paquette," said Candide, who also appeared to be feeling the effects of *bier*. "I beg you, Master. Please do tell!"

"Yes, please do," said Jakob. "I would like to hear about this wench Paquette. It is, after all, a night for celebrating love."

"Ah, yes, the pretty wench Paquette." Pangloss squinted his good eye, as if gazing upon some distant prospect of the past. "She came to the castle of Thunder-Ten-Tronckh as a young lass of fourteen, a maidservant to the noble Baroness. I recall the day still; certainly, it was the best of all possible days. From the moment I saw her, I knew that pretty bud would bloom into a dewy-petaled maiden. The blossoming charms of her womanhood were a sight to behold — with her shimmering sable mane, the curvilinear slope of a maiden's gathering bosom, and a splendid derriere comprised of quadric surfaces to make Euclid weep." He paused to wipe an imaginary tear from his eye. "She was highly favored by the Baroness, a close second to the castle's own maiden, Cunégonde. And so was the pretty wench Paquette sent to me by the Baroness to be tutored in the classics." Pangloss stopped to slurp at his *bier*.

"The Baroness kept her maid servant close by, never allowing her to venture far from the castle. For what she surely understood was that the pretty wench Paquette was put here in this best of all possible worlds by God's design to test the moral fortitude of men."

"Indeed, the moral fortitude of men is in need of testing," said Candide with a slur.

"The first to fall was a lecherous monk who often called upon the Baroness at the castle of Thunder-Ten-Tronckh. On one occasion the ascetic believed he spied the witch's mark on the wench and gave her a pricking for it."

"What was this witch's mark?" asked Jakob.

"It was a small, insignificant blemish perched upon her clavicle.

'Twas no bigger than an insect clinging to a twig. The pricking of it provoked the monk to take more drastic measures, and he came to her one night thinking to *fokken* the sin from her with his holy *roede*.

"And did he?" said Jakob.

"Yes. And then some. The wench Paquette was not the first maid servant that the Franciscan had tried to *fokken* the sin from. And from him came the disease which has recently threatened my own life. For the Franciscan was the first to fall prey to the pretty wench's charms and I was the second."

"Surely you were not trying to *fokken* the sin from the pretty wench."

"No, no. Nothing of the sort. I was genuinely taken with her. Somewhere between the voyages of Odysseus and the battles of Jason, my own *roede* fell from my breeches and found its way into her pretty *kut*."

"My God, but was it not, then, a sin of lechery?"

"Oh no," said Pangloss. "Lechery is a sin of lust. And there was three parts lust but one part love in my heart when I lay with the pretty wench Paquette. Thus was it love, and all for the best."

"Indeed, it was," echoed Candide. "All for the best."

Perhaps it was Pangloss's story of Paquette or just the sea of strong *bier* that he had drunk, but at some point in the evening, Jakob decided that he would call upon Anneke this very evening. To that end, he bid his friends farewell and detoured on route to the Onderdonk *herenhuis* long enough to buy sweets from a confectioner. The idea to bring Anneke to live with his mother had been Jakob's. With the Schoonhoven *herenhuis* boarded up and the servants sent home, it seemed like the sensible thing to do.[58]

---

[58] There could be no doubt that Jakob's spirits were uncharacteristically high—although to say his spirits were high stops short of the peculiar elation that Jakob felt this night. For his part, Jakob partly attributed this elation to having successfully resisted the urge to sin the previous night. For when Pastor Hogarth's buxom wife had appeared across the way, he simply closed his shutters. As usual, the pastor's wife stood before the window in all her

Jakob's mother greeted him with a perfunctory kiss on the cheek, which was, quite frankly, more than he expected at this hour. "What brings you here in the dead of night?"

"Hardly the dead of night, Mother," said he. "I simply wish to say goodnight to my betrothed. Is she here?"

"Of course she is. But she has retired to her bedchamber—"

Before his mother could give voice to the impropriety which she believed the situation constituted, Jakob had rushed to the stairs and was taking them two at a time.

"But Jakob, it is not proper."

"Proper, Mother? Proper matters to you only when a stale aristocratic audience lingers nearby. Besides, she is to be my wife. There can be no harm in a quick call to her bedchamber." He turned away from his mother's continued protests and stepped lightly down the hall, past the portrait of his father in a blue coatee with gold braids and red lapels, a captain's blue bicorn hat resting in his lap. Jakob halted at the last door and rapped gently upon it. "Anneke, it is I, Jakob."

The door flew open and she fell into his arms. Under her thin cotton nightgown, Jakob could feel every contour, every depression

---

Junoesque glory. And as usual, Jakob was prepared to surrender to the sin of onanism. But on this night, the pastor's wife did something she had never done before—she turned her gaze outward and looked directly at Jakob. Then she smiled. And in that moment, the invisible barrier that had existed between them—actor and audience—the fourth wall came crashing down, collapsed. It changed everything for Jakob, although he was hard-pressed to say exactly what, or more to the point, *why*. In actuality, the cause Jakob found himself unable to identify was a simple one: he was no longer watching her in secret—she was performing. The spell had been broken. And suddenly, the excitement fizzled like a damp wick in his hand. Jakob rose, buttoned his trousers, and pulled the shutters closed. In this small but symbolic act, he had turned his back on sin. And of course, now he could only view it as a step forward on the path to salvation. In fact, in the aftermath of his victory, Jakob had purred the following to Gertrude: "Perhaps, I am not the worst of all men, after all."

and protrusion of her physical geography. The bag of sweets dropped from his hand.

"How I've missed you so, my dear," said she.

"And I, you."

Anneke pulled back. "You've *bier* on your breath."

"A celebratory libation. Candide has agreed to be best man."

"How wonderful! I simply cannot wait!" Her hands groped his face in the darkness. Finally her lips found his and they kissed. Jakob's eyes opened wide as her tongue slithered into his mouth in search of the prey that he could only assume was his tonsils. Then a snap vision of Anneke in a wet baptismal gown popped into his head. Jakob felt his herringbone hips pressing closer, his captive *roede* prodding the downy nest of her maidenhood. Anneke moaned softly in his ear. "I must have you," whispered she.

"But we must not," whispered he.

"We are betrothed," whispered she.

"It is a sin," whispered he. But his resolve had now all but failed, being pulverized like a dry clump of dirt beneath her naked heels. For Jakob felt certain that the weight of her *boezem* against him could have handily pinned mighty Moses to the altar of his own destruction. It seemed pointless to protest, hopeless to resist. So Jakob did something that he had never before done in his life, something that went well beyond the momentary surrender to whim that his previous sins (that is, onansim) amounted to—he let his inhibitions go, to run barefoot over the hills and vales of his desire, to wallow in the muck of his lust.

But as his hand crept down the small of her back, the door to her bedchamber creaked open. Jakob froze. Anneke went stiff. The oily glare of a lantern peeked into the room then in stepped Oma Onderdonk, wearing only the top half of a flimsy undergarment. Jakob clenched his eyes shut with a force that can only be described as herculean in might and desperate in measure, but it was too late— the image of Oma Onderdonk's knobby legs and flabby blue *kut* was seared into his eyeballs, branded unmercifully into the writhing midriff of his memory. He felt his stomach gurgle, and spittle poured into his mouth. It was all he could do to keep the earlier drafts of *bier* from spilling out of him in foamy protest.

Jakob stood motionless as the old woman doddered about the room and muttered to herself, unaware of his or even Anneke's presence there. Cracking an eyelid, Jakob glimpsed the pale cascading flesh or his oma's *aars* in the feathery moonlight, looking like the white cliffs of Dover an eon or two later. He winced, as if the sight of it caused him great pain. And the minutes that followed were an interminable stay in purgatory. Finally, mercifully, the senile septuagenarian shuffled from the room.

"She's looking for the lavatory," said Anneke. "It is a nightly occurrence, nothing to bother about."

"My God! I fear I shall never be able to look upon her again."

"Jakob! She is an old woman, not Venus de Milo"

"That much is certain."

"Jakob!"

"I'm a little shocked. That is all."

"Put it from you mind." She pulled him close and nuzzled into his neck. But even her hot breath could not revive the flames of his doused desire.

"My apologies, dear Anneke. I must go. I should not be here in your bedchamber at this hour. It is late. And I hate to say it, but mother was right."

Jakob rushed down the stairs and out of the *herenhuis*, without so much as a farewell to his mother, and followed his fast-moving footsteps home. There, Gertrude mewed a cackled greeting. The moonlight walk in winter had managed to calm his nerves, and Jakob bent to stroke the calico cat. Then he lit a lantern, started a fire, and put a kettle on for tea. Slicing a slab of crumbling cheese, he nibbled at it before tossing it on the floor, where Gertrude pounced. In a rare moment of decisiveness, Jakob pulled the kettle from the fire and retrieved a bottle of wine instead. Uncorking it, he took a long leaky pull.

Thoughts of Anneke's warm and inviting body filled his head as the wine trickled down his gullet. Even now, the mental impression of her *boezem* upon his own caused his *roede* to groan and stir in its pubis lair. But these pleasant thoughts were indiscriminately mixed with images of Oma Onderdonk's shriveled and pallid bottom half. Of course, it was an uneasy mixture that immediately extinguished any and all carnal appetites.

Jakob tipped the wine bottle to his lips just as a light appeared in the room across the way. Gertrude sprung onto the table, as if to get a better view. But Jakob launched himself upright from his bench and slammed the shutters shut. Then he splashed himself a goblet of wine and sat in silence, while every now and then trying to peek through the shutters' sloped cracks. This bout of half-hearted voyeurism was interrupted by the sound of Gertrude gnawing on an envelope.

He hadn't noticed it when first he'd arrived, but he now saw that clearly it was a letter. Shooing the feline away, he retrieved it and, straddling the bench, inspected the envelope. There, cursive curls like the golden locks of cherubs adorned his name. It could mean only one thing. Jakob's stomach shriveled to a tiny knot of anticipation as he tore the envelope open. To his great frustration, Gertrude's mindless masticating had left a substantial hole in the letter, making much of it illegible. He cursed the cat and read.

> *Dear Jakob,*
>
> *Perhaps I am being forward and presumptuous, writing to you in such a way. By that, I simply mean without having first received a letter from you. But I recall on our last meeting that you seemed so sincere in your wish to write. This remembrance alone gave me the courage to pick up*
>
> *Much has happened in*   *here. My father has*
> *died an agonizing death. I will*   *say that he is gone.*
> *And to make matters worse*   *with the promise of a*
> *generous dowry for*   *the only way that I*
> *can help my family*
> *Yet, I cannot*   *have often*
> *wondered if it was only*   *Or perhaps your*
> *attentions were something*   *I hope it was the*
> *latter—something more. My heart is heavy and my eyes sting with tears. Still, I hope this letter finds you healthy and happy.*

Sincerely Yours,
Heleen

Jakob set the letter down. His heart slowed to a mere drip, drizzling blood into his veins. The word *dowry* plunged like an anchor into a sea of despair. The room seemed to darken. Here was the news he had been dreading, if not consciously then subconsciously— somewhere locked in a dark gaol of his mind was the fear of another—a lover much stronger and more worthy than he—rattling the bars and screaming to be set free. And Heleen had found him— another. It was that simple.

Jakob rose and stepped to the fireplace, releasing the letter with a gravity that can only spell the end in one way or another. It floated on a warm current, sliding this way and that, before finally landing in a bed of flames. Then in an act of great abandon—although one not without undertones of equally great despair—Jakob flung open the blinds, slid a bench up to the window, and sat down. "The worst of all men is what I am," said he. Gertrude purred loudly, which Jakob, being in the frame of mind that he was, took to be concurrence on the part of his feline companion.[59]

---

[59] The unfortunate truth was Jakob would never know the whole story of what had happened to his beloved Heleen and her father in Lisbon. That Heleen was betrothed and that her father had died seemed clear enough. But, of course, there was much more to the story than that (as there always is). Funske Bonk, it could fairly be said, was killed by his second wife, Maaike Wulheizen, well after she had run off with her Dutch Flamenco guitarist who claimed to be one-thirty-second Gitano. As it turned out, Funske had a fat monk's appetite for *bier*; that is, it was prodigious and seemingly insatiable. As a result, he would often disappear for days, leaving Maaike, his daughter, and the twins to fend for themselves. Angered on one occasion by her husband's particularly long and indulgent *bier* binge, Maaike had dropped a perfectly round stone in his bowl of duck stew. Lapping up his meal with a slab of bread, Funske bit down hard on the stone and broke a tooth. Had he not still been feeling the effects of the *bier*, the sheep farmer may have screamed out in pain. As it was, he felt little more than a slight twinge. His left eye twitched and his tongue ejected a cracked brown molar. Between

thumb and forefinger, he pinched the poorly calcified mandibular stub which had just then been torn from its alveolar bone. Eyeing it suspiciously, he finally shrugged and tossed it over his shoulder, where it landed at the feet of his shaken, if disappointed, wife. She had hoped for something a little more satisfying, perhaps even more fatal. She grumbled as she bent over to sweep up the tooth. Little did Maaike know (and it should be said that she would never know) that the seeds of her husband's demise had been sown that day by her very own hand. The bloody crater in Funske's jaw soon became packed with putrefied meat and was inflamed within days. For the first five years, the infection was nothing more than a slight ache. In the next ten years, it turned to actual pain—sharp waves that crashed against the gray cliffs of his prominent malar bone. By the time he and Heleen had traveled to Portugal to live with his sister and her two sons, the wound had turned septic. The poison coursed through him like a flowing runoff of pain. He was often bedridden for days. Until finally, he gave up the ghost and left his ridiculously corrupted flesh behind. Of course, death by bad hygiene was not uncommon in the day and age.

And so it was that Heleen was left all but alone in this world. Her two idiot brothers were somewhere out there, wandering about the lowlands, singing hymns and speaking in tongues—which, she was always quick to note, they did even before they had converted—but she held out no hope of ever seeing them again. That left her *tante*—she still had her *tante*. But her *tante* had not been good company since her own husband had died and her sons had been dragged off to war by Fredrich's dragoons. The two of them were only just able to make ends meet by selling vegetables at market. It was there Heleen met the butcher, Gonçalo Madeira.

By matrimonial standards of the day, at thirty years and three months, Gonçalo was an old bachelor, although he preferred to think of himself as a seasoned man of the world. After all, the butcher shop was essentially his— now that his father was bedridden and not long for this world. To Gonçalo's mind, owning the butcher shop made him a "man of business," something which he was fond of saying. Not surprisingly, he felt it a much more dignified distinction than simply "butcher." And the truth was Gonçalo had not butchered anything in some years; that is, he had not bloodied his own hands with the cold pitted edge of the butcher's knife. He had underlings for that now. The business at hand was to find a suitable wife.

Gonçalo was well aware to the fact that he was no prince—far from it. He was not rich, but he was well enough off. It wasn't that which worried him. Simply put, Gonçalo was ugly. He knew he was ugly. Therein lay the real problem. One of his ugliest features was his nose, which had the shape, color, and texture of a jumbo *castanhas-do-Pará*, otherwise known as a Brazil nut. But perhaps his most unappealing feature was his neck. It was inordinately long, leaving a dullard's gap between head and shoulders. Also visually unsettling was the loose-hanging skin that seems to slop like a mudslide over his fist-sized Adam's apple. When he spoke, most people took a rather perverse interest in the way the laryngeal prominence bobbled up and down like a jettisoned keg caught under the docks at high tide. In fact, Heleen had been guilty of just such a gaffe when first Gonçalo had addressed her, saying: "But my, the *pimentão* are exquisite." His Adam's apple bouncing a mesmerizing triplet on both *pimentão* and *exquisite*. "Yes. . . yes. . . thank you, Senhor Madeira," said Heleen, her cheeks red and pulsing. "I will take the whole crate," said Gonçalo, smiling at the small and comely peasant girl.

And he did take the crate. That and many others. Over and over, throughout the entirety of the season. Crates of *pimentão*. Crates of *alho*. Crates of *azeitona*. Bags of saffron and coriander. He bought them all, week after week. Until he had become her best customer. Until finally Heleen felt obliged to accept his invitation for a carriage ride in the country. Not long after, she found herself entangled in a courtship she had no real interest in. Her *tante* encouraged her to beguile the butcher with her maidenly charms. With no men about the *casa*, someone like Gonçalo Madeira could amount to their salvation, their means of survival. But try as she might, Heleen simply could not put her heart into it. For what she knew but could not tell her dear *tante* was that her heart belonged to another—another who had promised to write but had not. And that silence felt to her like a broken promise. She could not—would not—marry the butcher without first knowing why. Why the silence? Why did he not write? Had his promise been an empty one? Was it nothing more than a whim? A fleeting fancy? Determined to find out, Heleen had sat down to the table and begun to write: *Dear Jakob*. . . .

From the Journal of Jakob Onderdonk

July 16, 1745

Today, Son of Batavia sailed from the Gulf of Mannār heavy with bark of the cinnamon tree. After delivering our cargo of slaves, we loaded the stripped branches and with our hands still sweating the sharp woody odor set a course for Batavia. No sooner had we done so than it became clear that the men were anxious about the female (a perkenier's wife) we had taken aboard at Colombo. The ship suddenly came alive with superstitious mummeries of every sort as the men tried to stave off the ill fate they felt certain lay ahead.

Father was at first reluctant to grant the perkenier's wife berth onboard, not because he is superstitious but because Mevrouw de Wit was clearly in flight from her husband, who we could only presume was unaware of her presence there on the docks and her plan to flee the cinnamon plantation. When father tried to reason with her, suggesting that he might attempt to intercede between her and her husband, Mevrouw de Wit broke down into tearful sobs and begged him to do no such thing, for her husband was a drunkard and a brute who cursed her barren womb and beat her with a horsewhip. True to his character, father respectfully bid the women go aboard; and true to his character, too, Robrecht openly guffawed at the woman's tale of hardship. I said nothing, not knowing what to say or even what to believe.

It was later in the evening that the truth of it would come out. Guilt-ridden, and in an apparent fit of remorse, Mevrouw de Wit admitted to the untruth she had earlier told about her husband. Weeping almost uncontrollably she related the story of her arrival in Ceylon and the hardships she had encountered as a perkenier's bride of sixteen-years-old. She simply could not bear it any longer, she said. As for her barren womb, she had refused to share a bed with her husband (whose pungent odor was a repugnance to her) and that alone was the only reason she had not born him a child.

With this revelation, Robrecht guffawed once again, more loudly this time than before. Father rose from his captain's chair and paced the length of his quarters, prompting Mevrouw de Wit to beg his forgiveness for her deceitful ways, claiming that desperation had driven her to it. But I could tell that father was not concerned with absolving the repentant woman, but instead was weighing his part in her escape and the consequences that might well rain down upon his head for such an unprecedented act. Yet, there was nothing to do be done for the time being. We could not set her ashore at the nearest port, for it would spell out her certain demise. Father left his quarters wringing his hands and Robrecht followed him, looking particularly smug. For my part, I stayed behind and, as kindly and tactfully as I was able, suggested that Mevrouw de Wit retire to her quarters and remain there for the entirety of the voyage.

FROM THE JOURNAL OF ROBRECHT ONDERDONK

November 4, 1748

The task of finding a suitable new slave trader in Pulicat has fallen to me (for the old one has been imprisoned and awaits hanging on a murder charge). Father finds it rather disagreeable business, wishing only to involve himself peripherally, and Jakob has no head for business (even father would admit to as much). To that end, I strolled purposefully through the market today asking questions. I was directed southwest of the village to a large estate whose architecture with its vaulted archways and cupolas exhibited a clear Arab influence. I knocked at the door and announced myself, only to be told by a servant that the master of the house was otherwise engaged and that I should return tomorrow. Of course, I would do no such thing and so brought to bear the necessary force to convince the servant of the urgent nature of my business. In fact, upon his return with his master, the servant collapsed into a heap and I and the slave trader, who introduced himself as Barroso, watched blood seep from the Sikh servant's head where I had made my will known to him with the handle of a Corsica stilleto.

A squat, rotund little man, there was nothing exceptional about Barroso. I had dealt with men like him before, men who viewed monetary gain as a kind of game with its own rules and winning was as simple as discovering and exploiting them. In truth, I am such a man also. But others panic when faced with losing, while I push on to the very edge of possibility, where failure becomes more and more obscured by will and determination.

Thus was I ready for Barroso's mindless bellows and brays, the same that were meant to intimidate me but served only to amuse and finally annoy me. I proposed an exclusive alliance that would be mutually beneficial to him and me and, of course, the VOC. He told me he would think on it then shooed me away like a pesky child and bid me return on the morrow. I stood calmly and walked to the door, turning there to take one last look at the slave trader and swearing to myself in that moment that one day, when he was no longer of use to me, I would slit the buffoon's throat from ear to ear.

EIGHTEEN

Nothing more was said about the intimate moment Jakob and Anneke had shared in her bedchamber, or of the unsettling arrival there of Oma Onderdonk in search of the lav. However, for Jakob, the moment in question was not an easy one to erase from his memory, and it, combined with his unceremonious if shameful return to onanism two nights previous, convinced him that he was badly in need of spiritual edification — that is, it was time to return to a Sunday meeting of the Anabaptists.

And so it was that Jakob followed Anneke into the meetinghouse, not, it must be said, without a small meadow-full of butterflies flitting in his stomach. A hush stifled the pre-meeting prattle and all eyes rolled their way. Spying the couple, Bonifaas Quackenboss pattered down the aisle to greet the truant couple. "Come in, come in. We've missed you, Jakob," said the preacher. Jakob took the hand of Bonifaas, who shook it eagerly. It was then Jakob noticed the fleshy festooned brow of the preacher, low-slung and wrinkled, a borderline physical abnormality which Jakob correctly assumed was meant to convey confusion on the preacher's part. "But where is Oma Onderdonk?" said Bonifaas.

Jakob stammered, looking for some appropriate response, but then settled on a lie — albeit a small one. "Oh, she is not well."

"Not well? Nothing serious, I hope."

"No. Just something seasonal. It will pass."

"Be sure to bring her along next week. The congregation is anxious to see her again. We are all anxious to see her again."

"Yes, certainly. As soon as she has fully recovered."

Of course, the truth was Jakob had not wanted his oma to accompany him this day. From the start, he had had his reservations about the Anabaptists' — and particularly Bonifaas's — reverence for Oma Onderdonk and her vision-inducing *aars*. That he was confounded by said reverence was apparent and, to his mind, entirely understandable. But there was more — somehow Jakob felt that his oma's presence there diminished the spiritual communion of the meetings. At least, for him it did. In short, the carnivalesque air that the meetings took on when his oma inevitably broke wind did not foster the pure, edifying experience that Jakob longed for. And now, more than ever, he needed that edifying experience.

Bonifaas led them to their seats in the front row. Katrine Quackenboss sat at the fortepiano, plunking out a mournful-sounding hymn. She twisted in her seat and smiled—in truth, it was a rather pained expression that made her eyes flutter unattractively. Clearly, she had not forgotten about the baptism fiasco. For his part, Jakob had hoped that they would be able put the whole thing behind them, but he now realized that he may have misjudged Katrine Quackenboss's capacity for understanding and forgiveness.

Anneke tugged at his sleeve. His eye followed her gesturing digit to the front wall. It was with equal parts amazement and shock that that Jakob gazed upon the imposing—that is, massive—portrait of Oma Onderdonk. Jakob wondered how it could have escaped his attention until now. There before him was a life-like and life-sized facsimile of his oma, painted in earth tones and heavily shellacked, giving it a saintly glare. The look on her face was one that could only be described as blissful relief. Even to the uninitiated, it was obvious that the painting was intended to depict the moment Oma Onderdonk had first shot a heavenly vision out of her blessed *aars*.

Jakob felt the blood pounding in his temples, his abounding embarrassment at that moment actually causing him physical pain. He let his head droop on a bowed neck. What he wished to say, he could not say. It had all been a mistake, a misunderstanding. For he had recently been reluctant beholder of his oma's blessed *aars* and it was anything but heavenly and far from saintly. To worship her and her blessed *aars* simply could not be right—that is to say, it could not be sane.

Anneke slid a reassuring hand into his. The music stopped and Bonifaas moved to the pulpit, slowly, thoughtfully—dribbling one languid foot in front of the other. It was then Jakob noticed the crazy prophetic air that seemed to have overtaken the preacher. There appeared to be a golden glow surrounding Bonifaas, which Jakob dismissed as an optical illusion created by the diffused light playing on the shellacked surface of Oma Onderdonk's *aars* directly behind him. Yet beyond that, there was something about Bonifaas that had changed. Something substantive, yet at the same time something not clearly identifiable. Something subtle but definite, as if another dimension had been added to his old flat self. As Jakob contemplated this very thing, it all became clear to him—or more precisely, when Bonifaas finally spoke it all became clear to him.

"I have had a vision!" cried the preacher. A murmur rippled over the congregation. "Yes, brothers and sisters, I have had another vision. From where did this vision come?" Bonifaas Quackenboss paused as if awaiting a response. "I will tell you from where it came. It came from God to me through mine OWN blessed *aars*!" A collective gasp sucked the stale wind from the meetinghouse. "Yes, brothers and sisters, it is true. Last night after hours of fervent prayer, I lay in my bed. And from my *aars* came a mighty gust of gas. I thought nothing of it, until I lifted the bedding and was overcome by a vision."[60]

---

[60] For all intents and purposes, it was true that the preacher had had a vision—of sorts. But the events of the previous evening remained somewhat muddled in Bonifaas's mind for reasons that will presently become clear. In actuality, when Bonifaas lifted the blanket the only overcoming that occurred was the overcoming of his wife, Katrine Quackenboss, who, kicking him savagely from the bed, declared him to "smell like the rotted carcass of Pan." Bonifaas, nearing slumber and barely sentient as he was at the time, soundly thumped his close-cropped dome upon landing.

There had been nothing unusual about the meal Bonifaas Quackenboss had eaten this night. No gastronomic anomalies. A bowl of *viszooitje*, a link of *metworst*, and a slab of ripe Gouda, all washed down with strong pale *bier* had resulted in the expected gastrointestinal exertions and their colicky byproducts. But by the time he had rolled into bed, Bonifaas was a swollen mass of methane set to explode. And explode he did, much to the chagrin of his normally long-suffering wife. Finally, less than impressed with her husband's foul expulsions, Katrine Quackenboss had forcefully ejected him from their bed.

And so it was that Bonifaas shuffled from the cottage, following the wilting flicker of lamplight down a well-worn path that led to the outdoor lav. Still dazed, he stopped and wagged his head, hoping to shake loose the pin pricks of light that yet spangled behind his eyes. As he was about to resume

Jakob cringed when Bonifaas uttered the word *vision*. Although unable to have one himself, he was still unable to rid himself of them—visions. Visions were everywhere, it seemed. All around him. For Jakob, visions had become the scourge of his life.

Bonifaas raised his voice sharply: "Yes, I have had a vision. A vision from God, ushering forth from mine own *aars*," said he. It was then that I knew mine own *aars* was a blessed *aars* too. And so it is, brothers and sisters, that I say unto you now, the blessed *aars* of our blessed Oma Onderdonk and the *aars* of Bonifaas Quackenboss are separate yet the same. They are one in purpose with the Holy *aars* of the Almighty. Mine is an extension of hers, and hers is an extension of mine. Ours is an extension of His, and His is an extension ours. Together, we form the Holy *Aars*head!"

"Hallelujah!" cried the congregation. "Praise Oma! Praise the Holy *Aars*head!" cried the faithful flock.

To say that Jakob was stunned by Bonifaas's manifestation would be tantamount to saying that a snake drags its *testikels* through the grass—both being apparent truths that one is willing to take on good faith. That is to say Jakob turned to stone, a pillar of salt. Unable to move, he sat staring at the portrait of his oma, swooning slightly. Until the hayward seated next to him tipped his *aars* to one side and let go a flatulent blast. "Praise Oma! Praise the Holy *Aars*head!" The hayward thrust his arms into the air with a kind of jouncing zeal that caused Jakob to flinch. Another blast came from the village dog

---

this midnight trek, he caught his big toe on the exposed root of a giant elm that flanked the cottage and, tossing the lamp, pitched headfirst into the bole of the tree. He felt his neck snap back and a trickle of blood immediately appeared on his brow. Bonifaas groaned and crumbled to the ground. A stillness, black and ethereal, infused all. His body went soft as his muscles released all attending tensions. The last thing he remembered was a thunderous bluster that flapped and fluttered beneath his night shirt. And a smell, an odd smell—sharp and sweet—unpleasant but somehow enticing. It was the smell of change, the odor of a life about to go wrong—momentously wrong. Bonifaas inhaled it deeply and flopped back onto the grass, where he dreamed of a giant *aars*.

whipper on the other side. "Praise Oma! Praise the Holy *Aars*head" Before long the entire meetinghouse had erupted into an ataxic fit of flatus. Even Katrine Quackenboss let ring a stout rip without missing a note of the accompanying hymn. "Praise Oma! Praise the Holy *Aars*head," cried she, spouting tears.

"Praise Oma! Praise the Holy *Aars*head!" cried Bonifaas. Then he raised his arms and brought the congregation back under his spell. "And what was this vision?" said he. "God has told me to build an *aars*. Yes, brothers and sisters, an *aars*. For let us not forget the words that the Almighty spoke to Moses: 'And I will take away mine hand, and thou shalt see my BACK PARTS: but my face shall not be seen.' Thus did Moses see the Holy *Aars* of God, which is one with Holy *Aars* of Oma Onderdonk, and one with mine own Holy *Aars*. The *aars* that God has told me to build is to be twenty-five cubits high and thirty cubits across, that we may praise and venerate God and Oma Onderdonk, whose *aars* is God's chosen vessel, within its hallowed buttocks. For God has commanded it!" He slammed an exclamatory fist down onto the pulpit. "Will you help me, brothers and sisters, to build the giant *aars*, the holy of holies?"

"Yes, yes. We will help you build the giant *aars*, the holy of holies" cried the crowd.

"Then let it be so," said Bonifaas.

FROM A LETTER ADDRESSED TO
MEVROUW MARIJKE ONDERDONK,
LEYDEN, SOUTH HOLLAND

May 6, 1748

Dearest Marijke,

It has been a busy month. What with another trip to Dejima and a short stop in Macau I've barely the time to write! (Yes, dear wife, I hear you hiss indignantly at this.) Yet, I would feel forever remiss to not convey (awkwardly) in words my undying love for you, my Marijke. But first, you will certainly be interested in our latest "adventure."

Our stop in Dejima was predictable in every way, from arrival to departure. However, our stop in Macau presented difficulties we had not encountered before—one difficulty, to be precise. The harbormaster who greeted us was not the same Chinaman we had done business with in the past. This harbormaster spoke no Dutch, at least that is what he led us to believe. He and Jakob grunted and gestured until it was clear that the Chinaman would only do business with us if we had someone on board who spoke his tongue. When Jakob protested, claiming that the former harbormaster spoke fluent Dutch, the little man tucked his beaded counting device (a suanpan, Robrecht later called it) under his arm and dropped his ledger into one of the myriad pockets in his silk cloak (a changshan—again, according to Robrecht)and shuffled from the docks.

It would have been an unmitigated disaster (as our hold was top-to-bottom with Japanese silver) had Robrecht not at that very moment stepped forward and intervened. Yes, dearest wife, 'twas Robrecht who saved the day! He strode down the gangplank and overtook the diminutive Chinamen. Then the two began to converse. Yes, converse! 'Twas an astonishment to me, my Marijke, I assure you. At first, I believed that the Chinaman had lied about his ability to speak Dutch. But when I cocked an ear to the wind, I distinctly heard the unpleasant nasally sounds of the Chinaman's tongue. When and where Robrecht had learned to converse in Cantonese was and remains an utter mystery to me. Nevertheless, before long, the two men were making their way back to the ship and the Chinaman looked more than appeased by this new development. He bowed to Robrecht, who returned the gesture in kind, and removed his ledger and readied his suanpan. Robrecht boarded the ship and ordered the men to begin offloading the silver. 'Twas an amazing sight to behold, dearest wife, and I believe it may have been one of the proudest moments of my life.

No, I have not forgotten about your misgivings concerning our second son, and this letter is no attempt to try and win you over. You must believe me when I say it is simply a story I thought might interest you. Still, I must add that perhaps a more dispassionate view on your part would reap great familial benefits where Robrecht is concerned. Please keep it in mind, or even better—take it to heart, dear Marijke. It would mean the world to me if you would.

Your Loving Husband,
Cornelis

NINETEEN

Captain Schoonhoven commenced poisoning his on-again-off-again friend shortly after their falling out over the former's scheming ways. Cornelis had been enraged when Hendrik suggested that they capitalize on the inflated value of Dutch ducats stamped at the newly opened mint in Batavia. What Captain Schoonhoven neglected to tell Captain Onderdonk was he and Robrecht had already started trading the stamped ducats at all the major trading posts in Asia and the East Indies.

"Come now, Cornelis," said Captain Schoonhoven. "The opportunity presents itself to us now, and it will not last long. It is not unlawful—not explicitly. But we must act quickly, for the authorities will soon discover how easily such an ill-conceived policy can be abused."

"Precisely," said Captain Onderdonk. "It is an abuse. It is not your God-given right as a captain in the VOC to follow any avenue—lawful or not—that reaps a profit. I will not hear of it. And I will not stand for it."

And thus did their friendship come to an abrupt and bitter end.

It should here be said that Captain Schoonhoven did not actually do the poisoning himself. He had arranged for it when it became clear to him that Cornelis was going to seriously complicate matters. After their talk—or argument, as it were—he knew steps had to be taken, something had to be done.

Captain Schoonhoven recalled once hearing tell of a certain green wallpaper that was rumored to bring about sickness and eventually death in those exposed to it for extended periods of time. He set out in search of the mysterious paper, finally locating an Arab merchant who, holding up a whorling leaf-patterned swatch, whispered to him that the green dye contained arsenic. "Death by poisoning," said the merchant, "although it looks to be death by cholera, even to the trained eye."

So under the pretense of making amends, Captain Schoonhoven had the wallpaper hung in Captain Onderdonk's quarters while he was away on business to Surabaya.

"This is your solution," Robrecht had said with a sneer, inspecting the wallpaper. He stepped close and sniffed it. "To redecorate?"

"It is odorless but deadly, I assure you." said Captain Schoonhoven. "And no one will be the wiser. I will be promoted to *opperhoofd*, and nothing will stand in our way. Your father grows suspicious at the seemingly endless inspections of shogunate, and it is only a matter of time until he finds us out. So let us move forward with our plan without delay."

In the weeks that followed, Captain Schoonhoven watched his oldest acquaintance in the VOC grow weaker and weaker until finally bedridden. The company physician could do nothing for Captain Onderdonk. No one could. On the day that Cornelis Onderdonk died, Hendrik Schoonhoven entered the sick man's quarters and found his two sons at his side. At that moment, an unexpected stab of remorse caused his stomach to sink, and inwardly he winced at the grim outcome of his traitorous deed.

He stood with his gazed locked on Robrecht. For the longest time he stared at the younger of the two Onderdonk sons, looking for something, some fitting sign of contrition—some look of shame to share between them, some morsel of regret. But there was nothing. Robrecht stood stock still with his jaw clenched tightly. When finally he tipped his head toward Captain Schoonhoven, it was clear that his eyes were dark and dry.

And in fact, Captain Schoonhoven—even in the years that followed, well after he had been promoted to *opperhoofd*—would never see anything other than a dark, dry void in the eyes of Robrecht Onderdonk. Although it was true that his dealings with Cornelis's son had been and continued to be strictly business—the very business that Cornelis himself had condemned—*Opperhoofd* Schoonhoven sometimes wondered if there were not also a human side to his young associate. Even now, as he reclined behind his sprawling desk listening to Robrecht recite the sums and tallies of their shady business in Pulicat and Ceylon, he wondered it. Yet still he saw nothing.

"To a successful voyage," said *Opperhoofd*. "Keep it up, Robrecht—Captain Onderdonk—and you'll make us both very rich men."

They raised their sterling silver tankards and drank.

"I intend to do just that," said Robrecht

"Yes I believe you do," said *Opperhoofd*. "To that end, load up the reals and depart at your earliest convenience for Amsterdam. We must trade the reals for more ducats or our thriving business will soon grind to a halt."

"I anticipated as much. The ducats are already loaded. We depart at first light."

"Good. There's one other thing." *Opperhoofd* walked to the window and clasped his hands behind his back. "I need you to take care of some business for me in Leyden."

"What sort of business?"

"Family matters. My wife has recently passed away. And I need you to deliver a letter to my attorney there."

"My condolences, sir."

"Yes, well, no matter really. We have been strangers for some years now." *Opperhoofd* placed a letter in Robrecht's hand. "Will you do it?"

"Of course. I will deliver it, as you wish."

"And one other thing. I have recently learned that my *nicht* is to be married in Leyden. Should you arrive by spring, I need you to attend the wedding and give the bride away in my stead."

"I am inclined to refuse this request. The truth is I'm not one for weddings."

"I see." *Opperhoofd* paused, as if considering a risky yet ultimately irresistible tactic. "You may be interested to know that my Anneke is to be married to your Jakob."

"Jakob?"

"Yes, Jakob. Perhaps that will make a difference."

"Perhaps it will." Robrecht brushed the sleeves of his coatee in a manner that suggested nonchalance. "I will do it on one condition."

"I have a feeling I may not like this condition. What is it?"

"Equals shares, you and I."

"You want to split the profits evenly? I would have to be mad to agree to that."

"Mad? No. I do the work, take the risks, while you sit in your stuffed leather chair counting your shekels. With all due respect, *Opperhoofd*, you are paid well for doing nothing. Too well."

"Nothing? Now it is you who are mad!"

"Forgive me. Perhaps I have been rash in suggesting that you have done nothing. You did after all arrange for a certain venerated captain to fall ill and die. That is something."

"While you stood idly by and watched without the slightest objection."

"Ah . . . perhaps you are tormented by your conscience."

"You may not believe this, Robrecht, but I have been in my own way."

"No matter. He was a fool. Anyone who would refuse such a windfall of profits is a fool."

"He was a fool, but he was also your father, and an honorable man. You would do well to remember that. You could learn something from him."

"And you as well. For did he not once count you a friend? The blood on my hands is the same blood that stains your hands. Do not forget that."

"Are you threatening me?"

"Not a threat. A simple trope."

Opperhoofd dropped down into his chair. He exhaled loudly. "All right. Equal shares. But do not let me down. For I have brought you up through the ranks and I can bring you down. Do not forget that."

"Now who utters threats?"

"That is not a threat, Robrecht. That is simply business."

The ship departed the following day. *Son of Batavia* crossed the Indian Ocean and rounding the southern tip of Ceylon entered the waters of the Arabian Sea within two weeks' time. There, the East Indiaman followed the Indian coast north to Persia and, turning south-southwest, continued along the Arabian Peninsula until the Dark Continent finally came into view. It was a welcome sight, indeed, although it did little to alleviate the bloody flux that had recently gripped the collective bowels of the ship's crew.

From his cabin, Robrecht could hear the groans of agony. One after another and interminably, it seemed. Being captain of the vessel, he had escaped the torments of the ailment whose provenance was a gritty meal of tainted pork in beans.

An urgent rap came to the door. He'd been expecting the call. "Enter, Meneer Vrooman."

The ship's surgeon stepped into the cabin, hat in hand. "Good afternoon, Captain."

"Yes, Meneer Vrooman, what is it?"

"Well, sir, I'd like your permission to raise the water rations to three cups a day. As you know, most of the able seamen have a serious case of *buikloop*, and because of this, many of them are dangerously dehydrated."

"Very well, Meneer Vrooman. But only for those most serious cases. You know as well as I what will happen should our water supply be depleted before we reach the Cape Colony."

"Yes, sir. And thank you, sir."

Robrecht followed the surgeon out, the two parting ways on the spar deck, where the captain climbed the stairs to the quarterdeck. Seamen lined the ship on either side, hanging their exposed rear ends over the gunwale with their trousers tight about their ankles, their faces long and washed-out. Some of them saluted weakly and spoke through a grimace: "Afternoon, Captain."

"Stay about it, men" said Robrecht.

Dag skidded down the ladder from the poop deck. "Quite a sight, Captain, don't ye agree?"

"A sight? Yes it is, First Mate Dag."

"Haven't seen such a number of braying brown *aarses* in donkey's years. 'Tis got the sea creatures in a stir."

"Sea creatures? What do you mean?"

"Sea creatures of every kind, Captain. They follow the ship looking for tasty morsels of sailors' *stront*."

Robrecht stepped to the gunwale and peered over the edge. A drove of creatures large and small, finned, tentacled, tailed, and scaled, frothed in the ship's wake. "My God, you're right. I've never seen anything like it before."

"'Tis Poseidon's Curse, Captain. Old Dag has heard tell of it before."

"As have I, Dag. Although I have never seen it with mine own eyes until this very day."

Dag moved in close. "Captain, if old Dag may have a word with ye in private."

"Yes, of course." They drew near into a huddle at the telltale.

"Old Dag's heard rumors that Able Seaman Courtlandt wishes to extract some measure of revenge from ye, Captain."

"Courtlandt? The sailor who had shot stuffed in his rectum? What would possess him to attempt such foolishness?"

"Not six months ago ye had him flogged, sir."

"Yes, I remember. Took forty lashes did he not?"

"Yes, sir. And broke down weeping like a wee girl," said Dag.

"Yes, I believe that's true, as I recall it," said Robrecht.

The truth was Robrecht recalled it well, and he was not surprised that Able Seaman Courtlandt had gotten it into his head to extract some measure of revenge. He had seen Courtlandt's kind before—a fool with a meager portion of sense but a lion's share of pride. Too dunderheaded to understand his place in the ship's hierarchy—or the world's, for that matter. Too blind to see that some were meant to lead and others to follow. For such was an inescapable law of nature. It was this that Courtlandt did not grasp. And that was precisely why Courtlandt and his kind always ended up at lash's end, or worse.[61]

---

[61] The severe flogging that Courtlandt suffered had very nearly been the death of the able seaman. Of course, his inflamed lower gut—the dirty work of thirteen balls of lead shot—had not helped matters much where the sailor's condition was concerned. With a torn and bloodied back, and with his colon seeping from his anus, Courtlandt had laid for weeks on his stomach, enduring feverish fits and convulsions. When finally he recovered, the folly of his earlier infraction was made manifest to all by the thirteen lead balls that hung fastened to a chain around his neck, they being the same pistol shot that had been both inserted into and extracted from his rectum. Under threat of another flogging should the seaman not comply, the chain was to be worn at all times.

Able Seaman Courlandt quickly became the butt of all jokes on the berth

"With yer permission, Captain," said the first mate. "Old Dag would like to look into the situation—quietly—ye understand, no questions asked, before 'tis right out of hand."

It should be said that Robrecht was well aware of Dag's murderous intentions. There were other proper ways to deal with such matters, but Robrecht had never been one for such judicious bunkum. For in the end, the proper ways were much less effective than a simple show of brutality. As Robrecht considered the matter, the helmsman suddenly let go the wheel and rushed to the gunwale, dropping his breeches and sliding his *aars* over the sea.

"Sailor!" said Dag. "Don't ye know 'tis a lashable offense to lower yer breeches before the Captain?"

The sailor puffed and a frown turned down his pale face. "My apologies, sir."

Robrecht climbed down from the poop deck. "Do as you see fit, First mate Dag. I trust your judgment. I'll be in my cabin."

No sooner had he closed the door and sat down than he heard the cry of "Man overboard!" Stepping to the window, Robrecht saw a sailor bobbing in the sea amid a frenzy of sea creatures. Sharks

---

deck. His single escapade with a slave girl had made him infamous at sea, a kind of infamy from which there was no escape, a kind of infamy that drives sailors mad. And Courtlandt was certainly no exception. However, at the center of his madness—at its very core—was a seething resentment for the man who, to his mind, was responsible for the shame, the intolerable humiliation that now mocked him at every turn. It was upon this man—none other than Captain Onderdonk—that he would come to seek his revenge.

It should be said that the sailor, for all his stewing and scheming, sought a rather unimaginative revenge—that is, he hoped to lay hands on a flintlock and blast a bloody stuiver-sized hole in the Captain's chest. In fact, he had said as much to another deckhand while trying to gain possession of said firearm, no small feat when one considered that only officers had access to pistols aboard the ship. Had Courtlandt been less forthcoming with his plan, had he kept his chops muzzled, he might have succeeded. As it was, every sailor with half an ear and a morsel of wit was aware of Courtlandt's deadly scheme. And of course, word of it got back to First Mate Dag.

gnawed on the poor sod's skull and tentacles popped out his eyeballs and probed his proboscis, while schools of rabid fish made quick work of his chest, midriff, and privates.

A knock came to the door and Dag entered. "Captain, there's been an accident. Able Seaman Courtlandt has fallen overboard," said the first mate. "By all accounts, the sailor slipped while hanging his *aars* in the wind."

"Gather the men for a public flogging, and bring up the cook." Robrecht tossed the Captain's Daughter to Dag. "Give him a taste of this. Perhaps he will think twice before bringing such a plague upon the ship again."

And so it was that another sailor was flogged upon the thirsty timbers of *Son of Batavia*. What Robrecht knew well was that public floggings—seemingly against all reason—boosted morale among the crew. Perhaps it fed the fundamentally cruel-heartedness of the sailors, or perhaps it was simply a matter of them counting themselves lucky to have skirted an unpleasant encounter with the Captain's Daughter. In any case, as far as the men were concerned, a good old-fashioned flogging was an event not to be missed. In fact, many of the crew lived to witness just such events. Floggings kept them going, working, focused during the long months at sea. And the flogging of the ship's cook was just what the crew needed to keep their minds occupied until the ship arrived at its next destination: the Cape Colony.

The cheer went up long and loud—that is, as long and loud as the parched and burning throats of the seamen could sustain, when *Son of Batavia* glided into Table Bay. The vessel had been without fresh water for three days. The shortage, made worse by the heat of the season and a persistent salty breeze, had all but turned the men mutinous. Robrecht had sensed this like a hind in the forest senses danger. Most of the men had been hording their own *pis*, just in case, and the resulting odor now barricaded the lower decks with stifling severity.

Dag climbed to the spar deck from below. Then, ascending the stairs to the quarterdeck, he removed the wooden peg that pinched his nostrils. "Smells worse than oma's *kut* below."[62]

"Air out the ship," said Robrecht. "Give the men three days reprieve. But warn them to stay within the settlement."

"Yes, sir. 'Tis very generous of ye, Captain."

"And tell them to avoid confrontation with the blackies. We are not here to worsen the situation."

"Yes, sir. Will ye be joining old Dag for a drop?"

Robrecht let his eye roam to the shore. "Yes, I believe I will."

The inn was a smooth stone and plaster affair behind the Cape Coast Castle, a step up from the wooden *bordeel* on the docks where the crew would soon sit wobbling in a senseless stupor. Robrecht and Dag drank warm *bier* on a cramped veranda facing Table Mountain. The green plane ascending the mountain to its flattened peak faded to grey in the weakening light of dusk. It was a land as vast as it was mysterious. But then, Robrecht cared little for mysteries. And the only sort of vastness he truly appreciated was the vastness of a Ceylonese slave girl's tabular bottom. There, thought he, was something to be appreciated.

---

[62] More than just a turn of phrase, Dag, in actuality, quite literally knew the smell of his oma's *kut*, having sniffed it from an early age. A rambunctious rapscallion with "neither a whiff of sense nor a whisper of conscience," young Jos Dag, if left to his own devices, would slaughter everything in sight and burn it down to brown cinders. Having the responsibility of rearing the boy thrust upon her, Oma Dag had tried to "straighten the boy out," meting out every possible rendering of corporeal punishment imaginable, only to find them all ineffectual—all except one. The boy Jos, it turned out, had a strong aversion to the odor of the old woman's *kut*. (Just how Oma Dag knew this was another story, even more incredible than this one, as we shall see.) And so it was that when young Jos was caught diddling a hen or reducing a neighbor's shack to ashes, Oma Dag would grab the boy by the neck and, pulling his head under her skirt, clamp her thighs around his ears and force him to sniff the gamey scent of her long expired maidenhood. At first, Jos would squirm like the proverbial bear with its head caught in the honey jar, but soon he would fall still and silent, docile as a newborn calf.

And in fact, Robrecht was appreciating just such a mental image when a knock came to the door. A Dutchman named Breed, the proprietor of the establishment, entered the room, followed by a young Hottentot *hoer*. Her thin black neck glistened in the heat and a row of golden hoops swung from either ear as she dropped her head in a show of deference—although it should be said that the young *hoer's* deference, like the deference of all blackies of the colony, was one fueled more by economic need than by some misplaced sense of inferiority felt deep down within their savage bones.

"This is Elisabeth," said Breed.

Although Robrecht doubted that her name was Elisabeth, he was pleasantly surprised by this Khoikhoi beauty. He smiled and greeted the girl with a nod.

"And for Meneer Dag," said Breed, "your companion awaits you in the courtyard."

In truth, the courtyard was nothing more than a dusty parcel of bare earth below the veranda. Nevertheless, Dag grinned and rubbed his hands together in a distinctly sinister way.

Now overcome by curiosity, Robrecht's rose and sidled up to the veranda. "And who or what exactly might that be?" There, he looked down on a pair of feathered colossuses below. "You intend to *fokken* an ostrich."

" 'Tis a fantasy, Captain. Old Dag's got a hankering for a big bird." He swilled his *bier* and belched loudly. "Ready, then," said he.

"Proceed with caution, Meneer Dag" said Robrecht. "It is a wild animal, after all."

"Aye, 'tis that, Captain," said Dag over his shoulder. "'Tis that."[63]

---

[63] Robrecht was not surprised by Dag's admission. As a young cabin boy on *Son of Batavia*, he quickly learned of Dag's rather singular preference where bedmates were concerned. And the truth was that from a very early age, Jos Dag had exhibited a predilection for shaggy quadrupeds and ornithoid bipeds. This predilection manifested itself in a long parade of deviant acts perpetrated upon unsuspecting animals about the cottage, or more precisely, about the sty, coop, and pen of the place. Oma Dag was convinced that this unseemly behavior had all started when the boy was still

When they were finally alone, Robrecht turned his attention to Elisabeth, who stood rigidly awaiting his instructions. He let his eyes

---

an infant, after having been abandoned by his mother. Since the paps of Oma Dag had long since outworn their usefulness (jute bags stuffed with sawdust would have been more likely to lactate), baby Jos was suckled on the teat of a nanny goat. Quite simply, there was no other female within miles of the valley, save for the hirsute bovid. In a fit of desperation, Oma Dag set the infant to gumming on the goat's hind teat. The attraction baby Jos felt towards the nanny was apparent from the start. So much so, that at the age of four, when the toddler should have been off the teat, he was more on the teat than ever. He refused to eat solid food and spent most of his days and nights with the nanny. It was clear to Oma Dag that the situation called for drastic measures.

The first thing the old woman did was to slaughter the nanny goat. But this only set the boy off on tearful rampages that typically ended with something being thrown, kicked, or bitten off. It was clear that something more needed to be done. So after no small amount of silent deliberation with herself, Oma Dag devised a plan. Inspired by the Biblical story in which Jacob deceives his blind father, Isaac, Oma Dag lay down in the goat pen at dusk and covered herself in goatskins. In doing so, she hoped to wean the toddler by deception. However, the plan began to unravel when the boy nuzzled into Oma Dag, looking for a hind teat on the old woman. Before she knew what was happening, little Jos had his head buried in her loins and was lapping at her *kut*. Here it must be said that Oma Dag wanted him to stop, she truly did, but admittedly, she let it go on too long. For something moved in her that had not moved in a very long time, like an old rusted waterwheel stirring the stagnant green waters of sex. Soon enough her juices began to ooze and flow—although *trickle* would be a more apt description—and with those juices came the smell. It was overwhelming. More than just an odor, it was a stench-worthy sign, a reeking dispatch. It was nature's grimmest warning. This became clear to her when Jos suddenly stopped lapping and began to shriek. She sprung to her feet (as well as an old woman is able to spring), sending goatskins flapping in every direction like furry flightless birds. In that moment, Oma Dag stood naked before her infant grandson, shameless in the dusty beams of light that sliced through the pen. But then, his shrieking stopped, just long enough for him to scamper away in a tearful retreat. And so it was that the old woman never again tried to rid the boy of his shameful predilection for beasts.

roam over her figure beneath a tightly wrapped, brightly colored garment. "Do you speak?" he said.

"Sir, yes, I speak," said the young Hottentot woman through a thick accent.

"Would you have some *bier*?"

"No."

"A Mahometan, are you?"

The girl dropped her head again, this time not in deference to Robrecht but in deference to her prophet.

"It means nothing to me. Christians, Buddhists, Hindus, Mahometans—I've had them all."[64]

---

[64] This was no overstatement. In his years at sea, Robrecht had indeed had them all. And he had begun to have them all from a relatively early age. A month short of his sixteenth birthday, Robrecht had his first black women. He was still a deckhand at the time, and he had bought the *hoer's* services in a Calcutta brothel. She was Sentinelese, an infidel, a savage. To Robrecht's surprise, in the realm of coition, she was anything but savage. He still recalled how after a short-lived but spirited bout of intercourse, she had pursed her pink lips, almost sadly, and kissed his drooping *pik* as if it were a wilted flower.

Over the years, Robrecht had been with a number of Japanese *jōrō*. As always, they waited for *Son of Batavia* within the walls of Dejima, porcelain jugs of rice wine at their feet and transcendent smiles lighting upon their faces. With the Japanese *jōrō*, it was the whole of the experience that counted, from start to finish, not simply the climax. In was something akin to a ritualistic act with many ascending stages. Robrecht attributed this to a Shinto and Buddhist mystique that infused all life on the islands. It was on Dejima that Robrecht also first encountered an *onnagata*. In fact, he hadn't known that the young male prostitute was male at all until he reached down and grabbed and handful of loose genitilia. It was a startling but at the same time exhilarating discovery, one that he would experience again and again upon his return to Dejima.

But it was from the *biǎo zi* of Macau and Hong Kong that Robrecht learned the art of lovemaking. So enchanting were the Chinese *hoeren* that they made sailors fall helplessly in love by simply disrobing before them, letting layer after layer of silk float to earth. The way they moved—fluid, buoyant, yet somehow deliberate and chock-full of intent—was something to behold.

Robrecht slid onto the bed and propped his head up beneath an elbow. "Come stand before me." The *hoer* Elisabeth hesitated a moment then obeyed. He tugged at her garment and it dropped to the floor. His eyes were drawn to the small breasts with chinked nipples and areolas like eclipsed moons at dusk. Then he let his gaze drop to the mat of black hair between her legs.

"Is it pleasing to you, sir?" said she.

"Oh, yes. It is pleasing," said Robrecht. "Very pleasing, indeed."

Many a sailor found himself awash in his own *zaad* just being privy to such a rare spectacle.

In Barawa, Robrecht had his first Mahometan. She was as tall as him and twice as wide. Her black skin, scrubbed and oiled, gleamed like Armenian obsidian in the low lamplight. In a husky voice, she growled out her pleasure, as Robrecht took her from behind. After spending the better part of the night working up the courage, he finally braved a full frontal assault, which ended well enough, save for several dark bruises on his buttocks, hips, and thighs.

Of course, Robrecht had seen the inside of virtually every European brothel within a thousand English lugs of shore. The Christian *hoeren* were not especially well favored by him. He found them to be insipid and aloof, their gold coins jangling in dowlas pouches tied into their panniers even as they worked a man's *pik* with their small, delicate mouths. To Robrecht, it was abundantly clear that they were only there for the money. Of course, all *hoeren* were all there for the money; there could be no mistake about that. And Robrecht had no qualms about paying for companionship of an illicit nature. Yet there was something brash about the Christian *hoeren*, something deceitful that Robrecht did not care for. And so it was that whenever he found himself stuck in Europe on VOC business, he longed for the brothels and opium dens of the Orient, with their arcane mysteries and their untold treasures.

FROM THE JOURNAL OF JAKOB ONDERDONK

April 23, 1748

Yesterday, we dropped anchor in Canton. Against his better judgment, father allowed the men two nights' shore leave. I remained on the ship and kept father company, although my underlying motivation for staying behind was an uninterrupted opportunity to look over the ledgers for our excursion thus far. Not surprisingly, Robrecht disappeared with Able Seaman Dag to unknown destinations, leaving Second Mate Bleeker to oversee the assignations of night watch upon the ship.

All in all, it was an uneventful night, and father and I shared some bier, after which I retired early to my cabin and slept deeply for the first time in weeks (perhaps it was the lulling bump of the vessel against its berth). However, today was something of a different story, as it brought with it a most peculiar encounter. I had just completed my morning ablutions, when I heard a commotion on the spar deck. There, I found Second Mate Bleeker in heated discussion with a Chinaman (who spoke Dutch tolerably well). I dismissed the second mate and asked the Chinaman his business on Son of Batavia. He said his name was Kwon, the proprietor of an establishment (a seedy one of ill-repute, it turned out) near the docks. Kwon went on to explain how the third mate of Son of Batavia (a "Mena On'e'dong," as he pronounced it) had patronized his establishment yesterday evening and had left sometime early this morning without paying. I asked the Chinaman Kwon exactly what services had been rendered, thinking that perhaps they were unsatisfactory and thus had Robrecht refused to pay for them. However, it was immediately clear that the proprietor was reluctant to divulge that information. When I pressed the issue further, he finally blurted out "ho" and "opum,"which although uttered awkwardly were clear enough. In fact, the words rang out over the spar deck like a ship's bell, causing me to instinctively turn and scan the works to see if anyone was idling about. Fortunately, Meneer Bleeker had retreated to his quarters and father was below deck inspecting a small leak in the hull of the vessel.

Gripping the Chinaman's arm tightly, I escorted him down the gangway without a word. On the docks, I took two ducats from my money pouch and placed them in Kwon's hand. He grinned a dingy gray grin and turned to leave. However, before he could get away, I clutched his silken sleeve and, giving him a third ducat, told him to say nothing more about the incident to anyone.

FROM THE JOURNAL OF ROBRECHT ONDERDONK

January 3, 1747

Today I experienced a torment from Hell right here upon a three-masted vessel drifting aimlessly upon high seas. My God, the pain! It was as if the cloven-hoofed beast himself had shat fire into my blood-filled mouth. The devastation was complete and thorough! That, even after quaffing every bit of father's private stash of Scots' whiskey. The ship's surgeon, Vrooman, held up the blackened stub of a tooth before me and in my drunken state it looked like the claw of Satan. More to the point, it felt like the claw of Satan coming out. When Vrooman clicked his tongue and inquired as to how long the tooth had hurt, I spat blood then spat the answer "years." Vrooman—a tolerable boob who is not often guilty of sanctimony, like most of the officers who surround me—rose and spoke rather timidly his reply: "Perhaps it is the just deserts of your foul deeds." Had my tongue not been otherwise engaged trying to stem the flow of blood from the sizeable hole in my jaw, I may have given him a tongue lashing. As it was, I simply guffawed and wondered how this odd little man had mustered up the courage to carry out such an affront, mild as it was. Then I thought on the matter of what he had said, and there was no miscalculating as to his meaning, for clearly the surgeon knew well the rumors that swirled all about me on Son of Batavia. The thought that the Almighty would retaliate in such a trivial way struck me right then as highly amusing, and I chuckled and coughed my delight until the surgeon, alarmed by the bloody show, splashed water into a tankard and handed it to me. The omnipotent God of this universe, the great Elohim above, the same who created heaven and earth in six days, has seen fit to inflict a toothache upon me, a sinner! Priceless! What then when the Pope suffers from a bad case of buikloop? Perhaps it is Satan punishing him for his good deeds. Or perhaps God has mistaken him for some other infidel in robes. Amused as I was, I continued to chuckle and cough, finally waving the surgeon away, determined to now happily surrender to my drunkenness. He rose and, looking half perplexed and half frightened, shuffled to the door and left me alone.

TWENTY

Robrecht was awakened the following morning by the sounds of rattling chains outside his window. His left arm had breached the bed netting during the night and now itched with a preponderance of insect bites. He sat up and raked his nails over the burning red bumps. The room was bright. The salty air blowing in off the harbor seemed to awaken him to some distant seafaring adventure. It was then he noticed that Elisabeth was gone. And gone with her was the smell of samp and sugar beans that had bled from her every pore.

He held her pillow to his nose and inhaled deeply. He ran a hand over the dried pool of blood on the sheets. A pleasant surprise, to be sure. There was something not unlike a look of terror upon her face when he had first penetrated her, and he should have guessed then that she was a virgin. It quite simply had not occurred to him. But now it was clear.

Easing his thin, angular body from bed, Robrecht slid two lazy (and occasionally creaking) feet over the wooden floor to the window. He watched slave traders below herd blackies into Cape Castle's dungeon doors. Then finding his breeches, he pushed his legs into them with a lack of urgency that attested to a sleepless night. For it had been a long and vigorous bout of pleasure-seeking. What Elisabeth may have lacked in experience, she had made up for in an abounding will to please.

He pulled on his shirt and fumbled with the buttons. Outside, a slave trader screamed obscenities. Robrecht was not opposed to obscenities and he was certainly not opposed to slaves, but it was simply too early in the morning for such mental turbulence. The swine should himself be lashed, thought he. Then thinking to make his displeasure known to the slave trader concerning the racket at this ungodly hour, and wondering which ungodly hour it was, exactly, Robrecht stuck a hand into the pocket of his coatee and went in search of his watch. But after several puzzling moments, he realized that his pockets were empty. Believing his foggy state to be responsible for a muddled cogitation, he checked again. But there was no mistake: his pockets were indeed empty. "I have been robbed," said he matter-of-factly then wagged his head in disbelief. Robrecht dropped down onto the bed and chortled softly, somehow amused by the situation. But the more he thought about it, the more his amusement turned to anger, as it is wont to do in such cases. Finally, overcome by said anger, he rose to go after her, but he next discovered that she had also taken his boots, along with the stash of ducats that he kept in either toe. "That little Hottentot bitch," said he.

Robrecht was about to rouse the proprietor, when a shrill screech echoed across the courtyard below. This was not the broken groan or welted cry of a battered slave. This was the unmistakable squelch of death's arrival. Robrecht peered over the veranda and saw a young woman who he immediately recognized as his young *hoer* lying in the dust. Dag and Breed were crouched over her lifeless body.

He ascended the stairs of the Inn with great haste and was very nearly run down the moment he stepped into the courtyard by an ostrich trotting to and fro in a highly agitated state. Robrecht pushed the proprietor aside and rolled the dead girl over, retrieving his watch and boots. A sticky red halo oozed from her head and a glob of his *zaad* dribbled down her blood-smeared thigh. A scrap of black scalp clinging to the jagged edge of a stone near her head clearly attested to the cause of the girl's death. The stone looked to be unmoved, and Robrecht could only assume that she had fallen upon it, and not the other way around.

As if to affirm this assumption, Dag spoke: "The big bird ran her down, Captain. The *hoer* fell upon the stone's edge and 'twas the end of her in an instant. Old Dag'll swear to it on a heap of burnin' Bibles."

Breed seconded the first mate's word. "I've never seen anything like it before. The bird was half-crazed. And to look at it now you'd have to agree that it is still half-crazed."

"What has caused the creature to behave in such a way?" said Robrecht.

Dag stepped forward. "Well, Captain, old Dag's been tryin' to get on that bird all night. But she's a stubborn vixen. I nearly had me *pik* in her when she bolted like a spooked horse."

Breed gasped loudly, held up a rough knuckled hand. "Wait! Wait! You mean to say you tried to *fokken* this bird?" said he.

"Aye, she's a big one. 'Tis no pygmy, to be sure. But old Dag had to have her."

"But it is not a *she*. It is a *he*, poor fellow. The smaller brown one is the lady."

"You mean old Dag's had neither wisp nor wink of sleep for trying to stick me *pik* into this one's *aars* all night?"

"Yes, I'm afraid so."

Dag huffed and grunted then turned on his heels, raising a small dust storm at his feet as he set off over the courtyard.

"Where are you off to, then?" said Robrecht.

"To find that lady bird," said Dag, calling over his shoulder. "She's a wanton one she is."

Scarcely had Robrecht returned to his room and gotten himself properly dressed when a knock came to his door. Believing it to be the local authorities come calling about the death of the *hoer* Elisabeth, Robrecht momentarily entertained the thought of ignoring it—saying nothing, in the hope that it would pass. But when the knock sounded again, he beckoned the caller in. A man in military uniform entered, introducing himself as Lieutenant Mesick of the local militia. Robrecht invited him to a share a glass of *bier* on the veranda, an offer which Mesick refused, stating that he was "duty-bound to remain clear-headed." Acting as if he had not heard the lieutenant's response, Robrecht poured two glasses of *bier*. He emptied the first then picked up the second. "What is it that I can do for you?"

"As you know, we have had trouble with the surrounding blackies of late. They prey upon colony stock, steal food, and refuse to move." Mesick had an off-putting nervous tick that caused his left eye to blink involuntarily. Robrecht wondered if a stiff sock to the lieutenant's pointy chin might not eliminate the problem.

"Move? But the land is theirs, is it not?" said Robrecht.

"I have orders from the *Staten-Generaal* to expand our territory outward, whatever the costs may be."

"I see. And you wish to enlist the help of me and my men."

"You and your men are VOC men. The mandate of VOC, as a chartered company, is to assists the colonies, is it not?"

Again the question of a stiff sock to the chin arose in Robrecht's head. "Having not read the charter, I wouldn't know. However, it would seem that I too am duty-bound." Robrecht drained the second glass of *bier*. "I assume that the assistance you are referring to is military assistance."

"Yes, Captain Onderdonk. We are gathering the militia now to launch an assault on their village."

As far as Robrecht could tell, he had no alternative but to agree to the lieutenant's request, although he was hesitant. It should be said that Robrecht was not one to shirk his duties. In fact, in most areas of VOC life he was compellingly duty-bound. It was simply that he personally had no quarrel with the blackies and killing them seemed to him like a blatant waste of resources—on both sides of the gun. Be that as it may, in this case, there were simply no exceptional circumstances to excuse him from this call to duty.

"I see," said he. "Then you may count on the men of *Son of Batavia*."

The following morning, he found Dag in a pen, slumbering soundly beside the smaller brown ostrich, which had folded itself into a compact mass of feathers. Rousing the first mate proved to be a task, as the ostrich took every opportunity to swipe its blossom-pink beak at Robrecht. In the end, a bucket of water achieved the desired result.

"Captain?" said Dag. He sat up and sputtered. "Old Dag must've dozed off, sir," said he, turning his grinning mug toward the big bird. "She's a spirited vixen. But Old Dag got the job done, eh me pet?"

It was an image that Robrecht did wish to conjure up. "Gather the men at the ship and arm them. We've a job to do."

"Aye, Captain. But if old Dag might say so, the men aren't going to be one bit keen on it."

"Tell them it can't be helped." Robrecht turned to walk away then halted. "No," said he, swinging back towards Dag, "tell them murder and mayhem, plunder and rape, are the order of the day.

That should be more to their liking."

Within the hour, he had set out for the outskirts of the colony, where the crew of *Son of Batavia* were already gathered. Despite the early hour, the men looked prepared and eager to force the blackies farther inland. Each leaned a flintlock musket against his shoulder, and the officers had pistols tucked into their belts and Walloon swords hanging at their sides. As best he could tell, the militia, on the other hand, consisted of a ragtag band of farmers, merchants, and Hottentots, armed with pitch forks, machetes, and the odd blunderbuss.

As they began their advance, Robrecht matched Lieutenant Mesick stride-for-stride. Before them marched a young Hottentot blackie carrying a shredded Dutch flag with a distinct lack of ceremony. The boy's marked indifference, as exhibited in his sloped shoulders, bare feet, and grimy fists, amounted to a kind of subversive defiance that stopped just short of disrespect for his colonial rulers.

Early in their conversation, Mesmick made a point of telling Robrecht that he was the local brewer when not on duty as a militia man. Although Robrecht found Mesmick an unextraordinary man in every regard, he had to admit that he did enjoy the fruits of the brewer's labors. "My compliments on your work. And I'm sure I speak for my men as well."

"Thank you, Captain."

As the advance continued, Robrecht could not dismiss the nagging suspicion that there was no well-thought-out strategy behind the present offensive. To that end, he inquired thusly: "If I might ask, what is the plan?

"The plan?"

"Yes, the plan of attack."

"Oh, there will be no attack," said Mesmick. "The Bushmen are a lazy and unorganized people. The sight of you and your men will be enough to scare them off."

"I see. My men may be disappointed with such an outcome."

"Ah, yes. Well, let them fire at will, then, if it will lift their spirits. A dozen or two less blackies isn't going to make a difference to anyone, I assure you."

"That is a generous gesture, Lieutenant Mesick." Robrecht turned to Dag. "Tell the men to fire at will upon the enemy."

"The enemy, sir?"

"The Bushmen, the blackies."

"Yes sir." Dag boomed the order, "Fire at will!" which was met with a spirited roar of approval. No sooner had he done so than a smattering of Bushmen huts appeared in the scrub grass up ahead. Women rushed from the village with their arms full of wailing children. Robrecht spied a group of Bushmen who appeared to be holding their ground.

"You are certain there will be no attack?" said he. "The blackies do not seem to be running."

Mesmick was about to respond but the moist thump of a deadly straight arrow piercing cleanly through his neck was the only sound to leave his throat at that precise moment. The lieutenant folded in half and fell face-first into the dirt.

"Take cover!" boomed Dag. But as the men tore about in the knee-high clumps of shrubland, it became obvious that there was very little cover to take. Some of them threw themselves at the mercy of this austere vegetation. Others rolled into tight trembling balls. Still others turned and ran. All of this, while a shower of arrows tapped out the drag and flam of a death roll all around them.

For his part, Robrecht cried "Retreat!" then spun on his heels to make a speedy escape. It was then that two black arms seized him from behind in a chokehold. "You kill my sister," growled a youthful voice in his ear. "Now I kill you." Robrecht quickly surmised that it was the young flag bearer who was now trying to squeeze the life from him. Death, it seemed, was advancing upon him from all corners of life's battlefield. Never one for an ambush, particularly one in which death played a part, Robrecht bent at the waist and, hoisting the boy onto his back, sprinted as best he could down the dusty road with the blackie riding pick-a-back.

"Run, coward! Run!" cried the boy, tightening his grip.

Robrecht tried to speak but was unable to draw the breath to do so. His chest burned for air and his legs felt like two York hams soaked to term in saltpeter. The scrub that slid by his peripheral vision slowly began to spin and swirl into a sun-scorched vortex, and Robrecht thought his head might drift off into the ether. But as the darkness threatened to consume him, there came a hiss and a thud. Then another and another. The next thing he knew, he was stopped and gasping for air in a near panicked state, with the boy's arms dangling loosely around his neck. Robrecht breathed deep. And in this vivifying act of dispelling the darkness, he thought he heard the screaming of souls in some far off netherworld.

His legs had now regained a portion of their former strength, so he set out running again. The dead weight of the boy now felt double what it was only moments ago. When finally he was safely away the Bushmen's fierce arrows, Robrecht stopped and let the boy slide from his back. It was then that he noticed the flag bearer's striking resemblance to the *hoer* Elisabeth. The slight tilt of the eyes and the perfectly round ears. "Elisabeth," said he, as if to call her forth from a grassy grave.[65] Robrecht paused to look upon the boy with the

---

[65] Had Robrecht known how the boy despised the name so—Elisabeth— he might not have spoken it aloud. Or perhaps he would have anyway, for he had never been one to bend to the will and wishes of others. And in fact, in this way, Robrecht and the boy may have been kindred spirits, after a fashion. For Dakarai had seen the name as precisely that—bending to the will of others. And when he would ask his sister why she must abandon her tribal name—Farai (a beautiful name, he thought, which meant "rejoice")—her answer would always be the same: "The Dutchmen prefer it."

"Why must you work for them anyway?" asked Dakarai, but he knew the answer, felt it like a dagger in the pit of his stomach. Since their mother died, there had only been Farai to watch over the boy. Their father and mother had been caught in an armed confrontation between the Dutch militia and the Bushmen. The drunken Dutchman who killed both parents with a single blast believed them to be Bushmen, not Hottentots, although their traditional dress should have made clear their tribal affiliations. The death of their mother and father strained the already tenuous relations between the settlers and the Hottentots, who generally tolerated the presence of the Dutch in their traditional lands. Some of them, like Farai, had even tried to benefit from the clear intrusion. But these attempts, more often than not, did not end well.

What Dakarai could not have known was the night before her death, Farai

same cold cruelty that he had always believed excused him from feeling anything for anyone. For the blackie was dead, and there was nothing more to be said or done.

From the corner of his eye, he spied Dag. The first mate trotted up to him. "Old Dag was beginning to worry about ye, Captain."

"Yes, well, I had a spot of trouble back there," said he. "But it's taken care of now." He again dropped his gaze to the dead body at his feet. It appeared as if a small grove of arrows had inexplicably sprouted from the blackie's back. It struck Robrecht then that the boy could not have been older than he, himself, when first he had gone to sea.

"Who was the star-crossed lad, sir?"

"I've never seen him before in my life. The heat in this ungodly land must have finally driven him mad."

---

had finally agreed to lay with the Dutchmen for ducats. The tavern owner, Breed, a short and sweaty man whose incessant wiping of his brow with a cotton kerchief had caused his skin to patch and seemingly melt away in the African heat, had made less-than-subtle overtures to that end since the day she walked through the door of his establishment. To Farai's mind, it was a sacrifice that had to be made, for she could see no other way to attain that for which she secretly longed. With the Dutchmen's gold, she would take her brother to Paris or Brussels, where he would receive a white man's education, a proper education. And they would live together in this or that grand palace eating chocolate and sipping strong coffee from the new world. It was all that she lived for. And if it meant selling herself—her body, her virginity—then so be it. Farai would do whatever was necessary.

News of her death traveled quickly throughout the Hottentot village. That morning, mumbling voices and the patter of bare feet in the dirt outside the hut awoke Dakarai. He was still sitting upright, still awaiting his sister's return. When he saw her bedding undisturbed, exactly as he'd made it for her, he knew something was wrong. He felt a tightness in his head and a burning behind his eyes. Dakarai knew, even before the tribal elders filed somberly into his hut, that the Dutch had killed his sister, too. And so he had vowed to take his revenge on the white devil responsible—for who but a devil would wish to extinguish the beauty that was his Farai.

FROM A LETTER ADDRESSED TO
MEVROUW MARIJKE ONDERDONK,
LEYDEN, SOUTH HOLLAND

March 2, 1750

My dearest Marijke,

How this life at sea makes me weary, for weary is what I am. Although I must be forthcoming and tell you that I have not been to sea for the better part of a month. Perhaps, then, 'tis not life at sea alone that makes me weary. 'Tis true that under circumstances more typical, I would be climbing the walls, anxious to take my place upon the poop deck and watch the world come and go in redeeming shades of blue. But these, my dear, are not normal circumstances, for I have taken ill. Yes, ill. The surgeon tells me 'tis cursed cholera that nails me to my bed, even as I write these lines. Do not concern yourself, I pray thee, dearest, for I am stout and sturdy of constitution, and it shall take more than tremors and a fever to usher me into the Great Hereafter. Although I must admit that the constant companionship of our sons is cause for consternation; 'tis as if they know something I do not, and they lurk about in such proximity as if to suggest my next breath might be my last.

I hesitate to tell to tell you of the mishap that occurred on the poop deck of Son of Batavia prior to my taking to my bed. Yet perhaps "mishap" is to overstate the incident, for 'twas only a fall, albeit one that took place at a most unfortunate time and place. Suffice to say, it took the wind out of my sails and I am now forced to take to my bed day and night. Fear not, dearest Marijke, for the worst of it is over; of this I feel certain.

But now I must return to the realm of Morpheus. Trust that I shall write again soon in a state of renewed health and wellbeing. 'Tis a promise I make to you, my dear wife. Until then, be well and happy.

Your Loving Captain,
Cornelis

TWENTY-ONE

After the death of his father, Jakob returned to Leyden with no clear idea of what he would do there. Of course, he knew he had to do something. The truth of this had been made aboundingly clear with each passing day. For each day was an exercise in restraint, with his mother pushing the limits of his restraint by uttering a continuous stream of poorly guised gibes and barbs. In short, she was driving him mad. By the time Jakob had come around to the idea of manufacturing carpets, he was very nearly fit to be tied, as the saying goes.

He traveled to Tabriz, where he took up the ascetic's life and studied the art of weaving for eight months. There, he proved to be an exceptional student, and by the time he left, Jakob had devised and developed an innovation to the Senneth knot, which he rather unimaginatively called the Dutch knot. It was this very knotthat would later be the foundation for his Dutch flat-weave carpets after the manner of Persia.

The first order of business upon his return was to find a suitable home for his fledgling enterprise. This he did by securing a sizable abandoned structure once used by the VOC for shipbuilding. His next order of business was to buy the necessary looms for his factory. He had heard tell of a new innovation to the traditional hand loom — a flying shuttle that was reported to speed up the weaving process considerably. Thus did he sail to England, where, convinced that the new loom could be used to weave Dutch flat-weave carpets after the manner of Persia, he bought ten such flying shuttle looms from a manufacturer in Lancashire.

In the months that followed, Jakob hired and trained ten weavers. Then, precisely thirty-two months after his return to Leyden, he filled his first order of fifty carpets for a merchant in Stockholm. The day the carpets were loaded onto wagons destined for Amsterdam (then onto Stockholm by merchant ship), Jakob packed his belongings and left his mother's *herenhuis* for a flat on *Herengracht*. At the time he offered his mother the decidedly unelaborate and equally unimaginative excuse, "I am in need of some place to call my own."

The truth was he simply did not possess the will to devise an excuse that might be more pleasing—that is to say, more palatable—to his mother.

Jakob stopped to dislodge a pebble from the sole of his shoe. Even as he did, he recalled his mother's recent instruction concerning the acquisition of a "less horrifying pair," as she had put it. "You are to be married. It's time to give up the ascetic's life. Spend a little money, for God's sake. It is no sin. And it's not as if you have none. You are a successful manufacturer," said she. "Or is that a sin now, too—making money?" At the time, Jakob had made no response, believing it wiser to conserve his energy for fiercer battles with graver outcomes.

He set out on his way home again, feeling that the void left by the stone had now also left a slight defect in the sole of his shoe. He could only presume that he had been walking for such an unusually long period of the time with the stone buried in his sole that he had become accustomed to it, to the point where its absence felt almost as if a part of him had gone missing.

As usual, dinner in the Onderdonk *herenhuis* this evening had been a trying affair. The pleadings of his betrothed Anneke not to antagonize his mother had had him holding his tongue the entire evening. At one point, Jakob feared he may've bitten the tip of it cleanly off. When he thought about it now, he could not help but feel somewhat troubled—although *vexed* may more accurately convey what Jakob was feeling this night as he cut through the cool spring air with a course set for the warmth of his flat. In fact, so consumed was he with the matter that he had failed to properly prepare himself for the eventuality of an encounter with Pastor Hogarth.

"Onderdonk, is that you?" A familiar voice boomed behind him. Jakob considered burying his head farther into his collar and walking on as if it had been a simple case of mistaken identity. But then a hand gripped his shoulder. He turned to see the ruddy complexion of Pastor Hogarth.

"Ah, hello, Pastor. I didn't hear you."

"If you did not hear me, then how are you aware that I said something?"

"What I mean to say is I didn't hear anyone approaching."

"Never mind that. I understand that you finally damned yourself to the eternal fires."

"You are referring to my recent baptism, I presume."

"Precisely, although a baptism it was not, for that must be performed by one invested with the proper authority from God. Yours was nothing more than a frigid dunking in the *Oude Rijn*."

"As always, I suppose we shall have to agree to disagree, Pastor."

The corpulent man of the cloth snorted as if such an agreement were unthinkable. "I understand that your preacher—what is his name . . . ?"

"Brother Bonifaas Quackenboss."

"Yes, Quackenboss. I understand he has gone completely round the bend."

"Round the bend, Pastor?"

"Yes, round the bend—loony, mad, whatever you wish to call it."

"I was unaware of any such development," said Jakob.

"Well perhaps, then, you are also unaware that he is building a colossal *aars* as a place of worship with the help of his misled flock. In fact, they are putting the finishing touches to the thing, even as we speak."

"I must say that I am surprised that you would even trifle with such matters, Pastor. They seem beneath you."

"It is my business to know the state of all souls in my parish, even those who have yet to find their way to the truth. And speaking on behalf of my parish, I must say that this *aars* is an affront to God and His true believers."

"Ah, but God works in mysterious ways, Pastor, does he not?"

"There is mysterious and there is lunatic. What kind of man of God, even though he be a self-proclaimed man of god, does such a thing?"

"The Bible is full of such men. What about the great man of God who kills two hundred men to gather their foreskins? Or what about the man who curses a mob of children and then stands by to watch them be mauled by bears, all because the youngsters have mocked his baldness. Or most famously, what about the man who builds an ark on dry land in the middle of a drought."

"Your Quackenboss is no Noah. Nor is he a David or Elijah. Let's be clear about that. And you can rest assured that the civil authorities will be hearing about the abomination that he has seen fit to raise to his false god."

"Surely, good Pastor, you have more pressing issues to attend to than bringing down a giant *aars* on the outskirts of town."

"If one turns a blind eye to a giant *aars* then what is next? No, there is no more pressing issue. Now good day, Onderdonk. I pray that God may forgive you for your part in this abomination."

It should be said that the pastor's fixation with bringing down the giant *aars* was a rather recent development. After all, nearly eight weeks had passed—during which Bonifaas and the faithful Anabaptists had with great spiritual momentum begun to raise their monument to God, that is, to build the giant *aars*—before Pastor Hogarth was even aware of its existence. Even then, he had only stumbled upon it by chance.[66] Nevertheless, Pastor Hogarth was

---

[66] On the day in question, the pastor had decided to take a brisk stroll in the countryside. The preponderance of Edam and Gouda cheese he had consumed at lunch had had a stultifying effect on his gastrointestinal system. That is to say, his lower gut felt like the sun-hardened sludge in an abandoned country *kanaal*. And in fact, it was to the country that the pastor often took this all-too-frequently occurring malady, as a spirited bout of perambulation never failed to mollify his gut and ease the fast clench of his fundament.

And so it was that Pastor Hogarth marched purposefully along over hill and dale of South Holland, waiting to hear the blessed call of nature. Ten furlong out of town, he began to wonder at the efficacy of this ambulatory remedy. At twenty furlong, when cramps set in, he began to curse in a way unbecoming a man of the cloth. "Sweet Mother Mary," said he. "I'd give up this Godforsaken parish for but a moment's *schijten*." It was at that precise moment that the giant *aars* came into view. Rising above the horizon like a stark white moon in the heart of day, it was a sight so baffling, so puzzling, that the Pastor pulled up from his rigorous gait and stood staring at the oddly portentous edifice. As if in response to the sight of it came a gurgle and a groan from within his gut. He paused and wiggled his midriff just to be sure. Before he had time to utter the words "Sweet *aars* of Abraham," the Pastor

determined to bring the giant *aars* down, just as the Almighty had brought down the abomination in Babylon, just as Jesus had brought down the Kingdom of Satan upon earth. The pastor would not let this idolatrous act of trickery go unpunished. This he vowed with a curse most vile.

The following morning, Jakob rode behind the alternately rising and falling rump of the ball-less wonder to the site of the giant *aars*. In the past two months, he had watched the building take shape and

---

was squatting in the ditch with the holy robes of his employ slung over his shoulders, *poepen* with real intent and making foul the lilies of the field (had they actually been at that time in bloom, that is).

He emerged as Lazarus from the tomb—newly alive and having shed at least some portion of his mortal coil. Again, he beheld the giant *aars* and could not help but wonder at who was behind its construction, for upon a closer look he now saw scaffolding and men moving to and fro about the structure like busy ants. He also wondered how the prospect of the giant *aars* had seemingly cured his previously mummified prat. Clearly, it had moved something deep within him. Yet he had no ready explanation, no blustery decree that might put the episode in some Church-sanctioned perspective. Thus did the pastor contemplate the conundrum, standing on a twisting clay path through *Grote Polder* with his eyes locked on the giant *aars*. However, in the binary, twofold world in which the pastor existed, where there was only Good and there was only Evil, there was in the end only one possible conclusion to be reached where the pastor was concerned: the *aars* was wrought of Evil. For, reasoned he, no good man authorized by God to act in His behalf would construct such a crass monument. Only an evil man driven by Satan himself would dare make a mockery of God's greatest creation—or at least, a fundamental part of God's greatest creation. The pastor could only conclude that the Great Deceiver himself was testing him in a way that alarmed him on one level, yet at the same time, delighted him on another. For what the pastor knew well was Satan tested only the Jobs, and Jacobs, the Adams and sometimes even the Jesuses of this world. And thus, Pastor Hogarth concluded that he was in good company indeed. The Son of the Morning had placed the idol before him and bid him worship it. But not unlike the Son of Man, Himself, the pastor would not be tempted by such an abomination. "Get thee behind me, Satan," said he then retreated abruptly down the path, marching to the deafening beat of his own righteousness.

rapidly expand at an almost unheard of pace (due largely to the unbounded enthusiasm of the congregation and, it must be said, a will to make their mark on the surrounding religious community). However, Jakob, himself, had done little to expedite the realization of the giant *aars* within the realm of the real. As much as he believed in the goodness and sincerity of Bonifaas Quackenboss, he simply could not put his heart into an effort that he felt may have been misguided from the start. As a result, he found himself making excuses—not that Bonifaas had ever confronted him about his scant level of involvement in raising the giant *aars* (an omission that led Jakob to wonder if the excuses he had been stewing over may have been more for his own benefit than anyone else's).

As his carriage approached the building, Jakob marveled at the daring dexterity of an Anabaptist brother who hung from a rope into the deep crevice between the building's two buttocks, there, installing a Castilian-red stained glass anus. Below him, two Anabaptist brothers scaled either cheek of the structure with brushes sopped in paint poking from their fists and a spirited hymn wet upon their lips. Jakob paused to watch the gray plaster exterior disappear beneath a layer of white. It was only then, upon closer inspection, that he noticed the two brothers were more than simply brothers-in-Christ—they were actual brothers-in-family, for clearly the two young men were identical in look, carriage, and manner. A few steps closer was all it took for Jakob to realize that not only were they twins, they were the previously infamous Bonk twins, Erwin and Filibert—the half-brothers of his beloved Heleen.

It was this last point which, strung like emotional twine across the already treacherous road to his past, tripped Jakob up. He had not thought about Heleen since receiving her letter, the same in which she revealed that she was betrothed to another. The truth was Jakob may have stopped thinking about Heleen, but she had remained in his mind. It was simply that her continued presence there had become a backdrop upon which all other scenes in his current life played out. Thus was she always there, if only in the background, and if slightly out-of-focus.

Jakob heard footsteps behind him. "You've come to help."

He turned to see the lightsome face of Bonifaas. "Well, yes, I suppose I have come to help in a way." He paused and looked at the brothers again. "Are those two not the Bonk twins who were converted by Emil Gygax and his congregation?"

"Yes, they are one and the same. Gygax gave them to us on loan — permanently, it turns out. They will stay for the remainder of the week, until construction is done. We shall see what to do about them then," said the preacher. "It is a beauty, don't you think? An inspired work, to be sure. Thanks to Luuk." Bonifaas gestured to a man whose waif-like body and oversized head gave him a top-heavy look. Barefoot and stocking-less, the architect furiously mucked mortar with his feet.

"As far as giant *aars*es go, yes," said Jakob. "I would have to concede that it is a beauty."[67]

---

[67] Jakob was aware that the architect Luuk was in some circuitous way connected to a famous artist of several centuries earlier. And in fact, the famous artist in question was none other than Hieronymus Bosch. After receiving the heavenly decree to construct a giant *aars*, Bonifaas Quackenboss had set out for the Duchy of Brabant in search of a sculptor who was reputed to be a descendant of the famed Bosch, the same who had centuries early composed the profanely surreal triptych *The Garden of Earthly Delights*, a painting which Bonifaas had once seen and admired as a tapestry in the manor of a wealthy Luxembourg lord who had been seeking the other Lord and so had called upon the preacher to intermediate. Locating Aloysius Bosch, Bonifaas was pleased to learn that the sculptor was indeed a descendent of Hieronymus. However, he was equally disappointed to learn that Aloysius was a drunkard and a talentless pretender, who had for years been shamelessly taking credit for sculptures created by his apprentice, Luuk. Fortunately for Bonifaas, not only was Luuk a talented disciple of Hieronymus Bosch, but he had grown weary of his Master Aloysius's proprietary ways and was highly amenable to the preacher's overtures concerning the design and construction of a giant *aars*.

The two men retired to a tavern, where between hearty gulps of *bier* they discussed details from Hieronymus's sprawling masterpiece — the phallus-like fountain of the triptych's left panel; the giant mussel shell of the middle panel; and Bonifaas's personal favorite, the naked pig-in-a-habit of the triptych's right panel. When talk turned to designing the giant *aars*, Bonifaas

"I hoped we might have a moment to talk." Jakob phrased the utterance halfway between a statement and question.

"Of course, yes. Come in," said Bonifaas. "There is something I wish to discuss with you, also."

Jakob followed Bonifaas into the modest cottage that sat like an afterthought behind the smithy forge. Katrine Quackenboss stood before the stove and a blackened cast iron pot, stirring. "Brother Onderdonk," she said coolly, with a slight tip of her blonde bonnet-less head.

"I was about to sit down to a meal. Would you join me?"

"No, no. I don't want to impose," said Jakob.

"Come now. It is no imposition. A simple meal of boiled beans, stewed cabbage, *metworst*, and *bier*. Please sit."

"All right. It does sound appetizing."

"Appetizing?" Bonifaas chortled. "Perhaps. But more importantly, it is sustenance to keep the gases churning within. That, my friend, is of paramount importance. I must be vigilant in keeping up my gasses. For no man can know the hour and minute when God will again see fit to speak to me through a blast from mine *aars*."

"Of course, yes, that's true," said Jakob. "It is difficult to know, as you say."

"And that brings me to the point I wished to discuss with you. It would mean a great deal if Oma Onderdonk could attend the ribbon-cutting ceremony this Sabbath. She is, after all, the inspiration behind the giant *aars*. It has been better than two months since we've laid eyes on her blessed *aars*. Has she regained her strength that she

---

brought up the giant torso of the tree-man in the right panel, in the hope that Luuk could design the giant *aars* in a similar vein. "Sir, yes," said he. "I will erect a brick and plaster sanctuary to make Master Hieronymus swoon in the heavenly spheres. It shall be an *aars* like no other, an *aars* to match the mosque of the Mahometans in Mecca"

The following morning, Luuk cursed his Master Aloysius, calling him "a turd that floats and bobs upon the River Vile," and departed for South Holland with only the clothes on his back, a sketch pad under arm, and visions of a giant *aars* rising over the horizons of his mind.

might venture out?"

"Oh . . . yes. Her illness now wanes." Unprepared for Bonifass's request, Jakob found himself unable to conjure any satisfactory excuse short of a transparent lie. "I believe it may be safe to bring her along this Sabbath."

"Praise be! That is good news" said Bonifaas. "I have devised a special performance for the two of us—her and I, and our blessed *aars*es. A kind of duet. A call-and-response sort of number accompanied by my dear wife on the fortepiano. Perhaps you can make an early appearance, so we might set down our parts and practice a time or two before the congregation arrives."

Jakob's knee began to bounce nervously beneath the table. "Yes, I suppose that would be fine."

"It's a glorious thing, don't you think, Jakob?"

"Glorious? The duet? Yes, I suppose it will be."

"Not the duet—my visions. They waft to my nose like scented dreams from God. Although I've yet to have another since the giant *aars* vision. Not for lack of trying, mind you. I've had my head between my legs, sniffing around for the slightest whiff of divination ever since. But nothing yet. Everything in its time, as the Good Book says."

"Yes, I'm sure something will come soon enough." Jakob scooped a spoonful of beans into his mouth. Then he looked at Bonifaas with what he hoped was a serious expression. "The real reason I'm here today is to warn you."

"Warn me? About what?"

"Some of the other church leaders in town see the giant *aars* as an abomination. They aim to report it to the authorities in an attempt to bring it down, I'm afraid."

"Bring it down? Impossible! It is situated on my land. And it is an affront to no one, least of all God, who has commanded it."

"I understand that, and I am firmly at your side in the matter," said Jakob. "I simply thought you should know."

"Enough about that. Let's finish up the meal and go pick up a paint brush with a spirited hymn in our hearts. The giant *aars* awaits."

As his carriage rolled away from the giant *aars* later that evening, wheels bouncing over the hard clay road, an unseen hand plucked a guilty chord of dissonance somewhere inside Jakob. He could not help but feel that he had not tried hard enough to warn the preacher about the pitfalls that may well lie ahead for him and the Anabaptists. For Jakob knew well that Pastor Hogarth was a blowhard in most every respect—there was no denying it—but the man of God was not one to utter idle threats where his authority was concerned. And the presence of a giant *aars* on the outskirts of town was an infringement upon the pastor's God-given right to lead the people of his parish in righteousness. More than a droll distraction, the architectural anomaly was an affront to the pastor's powers of jurisdiction. Thus did Jakob believe that Pastor Hogarth would stop at nothing to destroy Bonifaas Quackenboss and his giant *aars*.

Jakob awoke the following day feeling much the same—guilty. Even as the day wore on, he was plagued by a rather vexing unease about the whole situation, an unease that would soon spread to other areas of his life. The scratching quill and gruff hum of the old philosopher stooped over the furry pages of a ledger only served to make him feel more ill at ease, more guilty. For although it looked as if trouble may lie ahead for Bonifaas Quackenboss and the Anabaptist brothers and sisters, things could not be better for Jakob—on the business end of life, that is.

In short, business was booming. There could be no doubt about that. It was an incongruity in more ways than one, and Jakob had spent much of the morning grappling with it. For when he examined his life closely, it seemed to him that all aspects of it—other than business—were in shambles. In matters of the heart and soul, Jakob felt that things could scarcely have been worse. He was betrothed to someone he did not love (although he liked her well enough) and his long-awaited (and hard-wrought) baptism had been anticlimactic, to say the least. Now there was the possibility that Bonifaas Quackenboss and the Anabaptists—for whom it should be said Jakob had had nothing but admiration and respect since the day he first set foot in the modest meetinghouse—had been led astray by the foul gastric offerings of his own oma's *aars*. This, in contrast to his booming business made no sense to Jakob. None at all.

Even so, there were incongruities on the business end, too. Why in these politically precarious times—in the midst of wars and rumors of wars—the demand for Dutch flat-weave carpets should so surge he could not say. What he could say was this—if business continued on in this manner, he would be a rich man before he had reached the age of thirty years. A very rich man, indeed. But as soon as he thought it, he questioned it. For who was he, Jakob Onderdonk, that he should be a rich man? This is the question he kept returning to over and over again.

When he took a moment to step back and look upon his life as others might look upon it (he being a well-to-do young manufacturer betrothed to a fair maiden of good name), he wondered why he wasn't happier. Much happier. More content, more fulfilled. For he had more than most, a great deal more than some. But even as he wondered it, he felt the icy stab of an abysmal void pierce his being. It was an ache that he had not felt since the day his beloved Heleen departed for Portugal. And in this emptiness, he recognized something more—his dismay, even dissatisfaction, with the state of his mortal soul.

When five years ago he had turned his life over to Christ in the shadow of *Hannekes Boom*, he had expected a transformation. As far as Jakob could tell, this had not happened, despite his recent baptism into the Anabaptist fold. Somehow his transformation had not been full, total, for he still felt himself to be a summation of many parts— both good and bad—rather than a pure, unvarying soul basking in the goodness of God. Thus had Jakob's thinking come full circle, back to the sorry state of his heart and soul. And so went his thinking, on and on, for the whole of the morning.

"I hear tell of a giant *aars* on the outskirts of town," said Pangloss. "Is there any truth to this most peculiar rumor?"

Jakob sighed. "Yes, it's true. There is a giant *aars* on the outskirts of town."

"And what, if I might ask, good Anabaptist, is the purpose of this giant *aars*?"

"It is a place of worship."

"Ah, it is a fine thing to worship God. The Almighty Maker made our knees to bend for that very purpose."

Jakob paused to consider the implications of this claim. He leaned forward in his chair and tugged the ripple from his waistcoat. His mood on this particular afternoon was ripe for contradiction, if not contention. "But then, Master Pangloss, are goats, cattle, and swine to worship God on bended knee? For they, too, have been given knees that bend by the Almighty Maker."

"Of course not. They worship the Almighty by simply existing in this world. The knees of a goat bend that it might drop and rest in the grass. The knees of a swine bend that it might locomote through the bog of its own filth. The knees of cattle bend that the bull might heave its bulk onto the unsuspecting heifer. A purpose for each and a purpose for all. It is the order of God on Earth."

"But if God made man's knees to bend that he might worship the Almighty Maker, why is it that all men do not worship? And why, if all knees bend similarly, do not all men worship similarly?"

"But all men do worship, good Anabaptist, and in the selfsame manner, too. The simple bending of the knee to sit, walk, or ride is veneration for and a reverence to the Maker who made it thusly. To worship or not to worship is not a matter of will, just as to worship this way or to worship that way is not a matter of preference, it is a matter of design. To worship is part of the human design, for the Almighty Maker has made it so."

"If to worship is part of the human design, is to sin also part of the same design? Are we, then, born to sin?"

Pangloss jabbed the quill into the inkwell. "The Almighty Maker could make no such flawed design. For sin is the result of evil. And in this the best of all possible worlds, God could no more create evil than he could winged swine."

"But God could create winged swine, should he wish to."

"Why would he wish to? That is the question."

Although convinced that this juncture might be the most likely place to bring the present conversation to an unsatisfying close, Jakob felt compelled to ask: "Who, then created evil, if God did not?"

"Evil grows spontaneously within men. As with maggots that spontaneously appear in rancid meat, so does evil appear in the rotting souls of men. It is neither created nor destroyed, but it lives like a parasite moving from soul to soul." Pangloss picked up his quill again and turned his attention back to the ledger. "But what all this has to do with a giant *aars* I cannot fathom. Mine was but a simple question."

"I suppose, I'm having some doubts. That is all."

"About the giant *aars*?"

"Well, yes, I do have my doubts about that."

"And what might these doubts be, good Anabaptist?"

"I'm having some doubts about the state of my own soul. But I am also having some doubts about the path Bonifaas has chosen to go down. First with the visions, and now, with the giant *aars*. He's even preaching about a Holy *Aars*head."

"*Aars*head? I must admit that in my case, simply uttering the word brings back troubling childhood memories, and there was nothing holy about those, to be sure. But what is it that troubles you so about this Holy *Aars*head. "

"It has made clear the fact that I don't know my friend Bonifaas anymore. Something in him has changed, I fear."

"It is always wise to regard change as the mark of a troubled stasis. Perhaps caution is in order, good Anabaptist. It could be that the maggots of evil now writhe in the preacher's soul."

"Yes I suppose anything is possible." Jakob leaned forward and propped his elbows on the desk. It was then that an idea occurred to him. "Master Pangloss, have you any plans this Sabbath?"

FROM THE JOURNAL OF ROBRECHT ONDERDONK

April 13, 1750

Son of Batavia now nears the waters of Bengal Bay. Soon we shall weigh anchor along the Coromandel Coast, where we will conduct VOC business. There I will also conduct some business of my own, although "my own" is only wishful thinking, as Opperhoofd is careful to take his exorbitant cut at every turn. All is grist that comes to the mill.

Son of Batavia is now under the command of Captain Roorback, a sniveling husk of a man who does not know a cat-head from a monkey-pump. His ignorance has been otherwise useful, however, as conducting clandestine business is considerably less complicated now that he is at the helm. He could not be more deaf and blind to what takes place right under his nose were he a moss-covered stone in Abel Tasman's forest. Father, on the other hand, is quick to spot the slightest irregularity in company procedure. In fact, his attentiveness nearly spelled the end of me and my business in Dejima. Had it not been for the welcome interference of the shogunate, which distracted him from his watchful state, father may have found me out. As it was, the shogunate's unprecedented searches served to perturb him — nay, consume him like a jaguar gnawing at the carcass of its kill. Nevertheless, those worries are behind me now — behind us, Opperhoofd and I, for father's inhospitable disposition has been rectified — inhospitable to making money, to living grandly. And inhospitable to me.

As for Jakob, he sees and knows even less than before (which was very little indeed). Since father has taken ill to his bed in Batavia, my brother wanders the ship alone and distracted. Surely some storm brews within and will no doubt burst soon enough. Who knows what peculiar behavior such an emotional storm may give rise to? Until then, I wait and watch with the patience of a stillborn saint. Perhaps in this way I am my father's son after all. (For the truth is a red-hot dagger, cauterizing the wound even as it inflicts it).Oh irony of ironies! Such terrible irony would surely send father weeping to his grave again and again. Of this, there can be no question. For such is the pain that only a son can inflict.

TWENTY-TWO

The stirrings of spring were clearly perceptible in the colorful buds that burst from the trees and the sprigs of green that mottled the hills and valleys. The vibrant sights and scents caused Anneke to grasp Jakob's arm tightly and whisper: "Spring has finally arrived." This he understood to be an allusion to their spring wedding. "Indeed it has," said Jakob. Then, he abruptly changed the topic: "How are you faring back there?"

"Very well, good Anabaptist," said Candide.

"Yes, Oma Onderdonk appears to be quite delighted to have some company along for the carriage ride," said Pangloss.

Jakob twisted in his seat. Oma Onderdonk possessed the faint smile of someone whose lucidity has long flickered low in a breeze of senility. "Yes, I think you're right."

The ball-less wonder labored up a long sloping hill, finally gaining the height of it with a whinny and nay of objection. There, from the highest hill in the county, the giant *aars* came into view. The double-domed buttocks rose above the trees in a clearing that stretched a farthing or more behind the forge. The stained glass anus flashed and winked in the sun.

"My goodness!" said Anneke. "It really is a giant *aars*."

"Surely that must be the best of all possible *aarses*," said Candide.

"Indeed, it is a fine *aars*. A sight to please the eye and warm cockles of the heart," said Pangloss.

The old gelding stubbornly fought the push of the overloaded carriage as it lurched and pitched down the hill. Even Jakob's repeated switches were to no avail. Following a winding road to the forge, the old gelding delivered them to the door of the giant *aars*. Bonifaas, who was eagerly awaiting their arrival, rushed to the carriage and, with only a cursory greeting, led Oma Onderdonk away.

At this time, Jakob took the opportunity to show the others around the awe-inspiring gluteal edifice. Candide and Pangloss appeared to be duly impressed, as they circumnavigated the new meetinghouse, stopping to contemplate various contours and slopes.

When the architect Luuk appeared, grinding a belly bowl pipe in his teeth, the pair of philosophers eagerly shook his hand. Meanwhile, Jakob and Anneke stood at the main doors, which were tucked into a nook at base of the *aars* crack, looking upwards at the dual intrados of the interior.

"Quite amazing don't you think?" said Anneke.

"Stirring, yes," said Jakob, sounding more impressed than he really was.

At this point Pangloss and Candide joined them and the old philosopher jumped in. "And to think that all of this was inspired by Oma Onderdonk's little *scheet*."

"Not so little, as I recall," said Jakob. "Truth be told, they never are."

Inside, hardwood covered the floors and the smell of beeswax rose from every crack and cranny. Above them, a web of wooden beams and trusses propped up each vaulting cheek. On the front wall above the pulpit hung a wooden cross with the painting of Oma Onderdonk on one side and a painting of Bonifaas Quackenboss on the other. The painting of the preacher was new. Jakob found the pose struck by Bonifaas to be an unflattering one, in which the foreground of the composition was overwhelmed by his protruding *aars* while the background was underwhelmed by the pensive gaze he had cocked over one shoulder. Jakob clicked his tongue quietly, a sound that bounced back and forth from cheek to plaster cheek, seeming to pick up intensity with each reverberation.

"My God!" said Candide. "The acoustics in here are amazing."

"Indeed," said Pangloss. "It is a cathedral of sound."

"And smell," added Jakob, "as you shall learn in due time."

Before long, the Sunday congregation began to trickle into the giant *aars*. Startled gasps and reverent murmurs of approval echoed in the giant *aars* like boisterous declarations of the divine. Here was what the faithful flock had toiled over day and night through the long winter months. Here were the fruits of their labors, the offspring of their devotions.

Jakob spied the Bonk twins standing at the rear of the left buttock, barefoot and dressed in ill-fitting breeches and waistcoats with the sleeves of their linen shirts being excruciatingly short. It looked as if some of the beeswax on the floor had been spared for their stiffly straightened manes. And as always, their favorite hymn burst as silver bubbles of spittle upon their lips.

At length, Bonifaas and Oma Onderdonk appeared—two-thirds of the Holy *Aars*head. Bonifaas wore his usual fustian coat and trousers, but with a pair of new black shoes—leather soled and brightly buckled. Oma Onderdonk was cap-less in an Antwerp blue gown and white *fichu*. Together, the unlikely pair marched in slow deliberate steps up the aisle, keeping time to the bright and melodic hymn that Katrine Quackenboss coaxed from the keys of the fortepiano. Jakob could not help but see a kind of perverse wedding march in the procession.

As they reached the front of the giant *aars*, Bonifaas spun ceremoniously around to face the congregation and Oma Onderdonk, apparently missing her cue, remained standing with her back to the congregation until the preacher gently prompted her to turn about-face. At this point, Katrine Quackenboss seamlessly segued into a somber piece in a minor key and a lower register. It was music both grave and conciliatory. All eyes fell upon the bearded complexion of Bonifaas, who with a slight grimace and a twitching lip let go a voluminous *scheet*. The holy flatus drifted heavenward and siphoned out of the open stained glass anus. Before the congregation could respond in kind and utter the first *Hallelujah*, Oma Onderdonk replied with a holy blast of her own. Scarcely two bars later, Bonifaas sent a long pneumatic zephyr bounding from cheek to cheek in the glorious rump. To which, Oma Onderdonk responded with a sequence of staccato boofs and booms. After several minutes of this volleying back and forth, Bonifaas raised his voice and cried, "Brothers and sisters, please join us now!"

Jakob felt as if he were standing outside the walls of a kingdom born of the bizarre, some empire of the outlandish whose floodgates of flatulence had right then swung wide before him. From all around, it seemed the rumble, sputter, and squeak of enthusiastic worship bid him enter. Then came the cries of "Hallelujah!" which were in due time punctuated by the thud and groan of brothers and sisters crumbling to the floor, overcome by holy fumes and dreaming fanciful dreams. Several interminable minutes later, Jakob and Oma Onderdonk were the only ones left standing—again, and as always, it seemed.

Bonifaas lay in a contorted heap against the podium, like a black and twisted branch that had suddenly come twitching to life. Katrine Quackenboss was bent at the waist and face down on the ivory keyboard. Beside him, Anneke sat slouched over in her chair, murmuring trance-like incantations, slobbering great cataracts of twaddle. Even Pangloss and Candide seemed caught up in the enthusiastic spirit; however, is should be said that Jakob was uncertain from which end of the prostrate old philosopher a raspy wheeze ushered.

The young manufacturer looked around the room and shook his head—in disbeliefrather than disgust. Oma Onderdonk smiled her most befuddled smile and let go one last gusty blast. This time, Jakob eased his weight down onto the wooden pew and waited for the odor to hit him. And hit him it would, like a runaway dogcart of warm wet *schijt*. Jakob inhaled deeply, again and again, but nothing came, save for a rallying heave of bile.

Anneke was uncharacteristically silent on the carriage ride home. Unlike Pangloss and Candide, whose lively prattle bristled the spring calm of hill and vale. "I had the most incredible dream while prostrate on the floor of the Giant *Aars*," said Pangloss.

"And I, too," said Candide. "Surely it was the best of all dreams. I stood as a tall and giant oak tree, where among my many limbs climbed whole lineages of white-faced monkeys."

"I was being licked up one side and down the other by an enormous tongue," said Pangloss.

"An enormous tongue?" said Candide.

"Yes, an enormous tongue."

"But whose tongue was it?"

"No one's, as far as I could discern. It was simply an enormous tongue and nothing more. Quite extraordinary. And somewhat arousing, too."

"It does sound quite extraordinary, Master," said Candide. "And arousing."

"What, then, was your dream, good Anabaptist?" said Pangloss.

"My dream?" Jakob's chest tightened. He carefully weighed his response, but in the end opted for the truth and the awkward humiliation it brought with it. "I had no dream," said he.

"You mean to say you were not overcome by the holy *aars* fumes of the Holy *Aars*head?" said Candide. "But it is impossible, is it not?"

"Surely it is impossible, for the fumes were thick and rancid as carrion porridge," said Pangloss. "How could one not have been overcome by the holy *aars* fumes of the Holy *Aars*head?"

"Two-thirds of the Holy *Aars*head," said Jakob. "And I don't know why I wasn't overcome, but I wasn't." This, he realized, was said with discernible resentment.

"What do you make of that, good Anabaptist?" said Candide.

"Truthfully, I don't know what to make of it. Perhaps I am immune to the holy *aars* fumes," said Jakob. But what he really wanted to say was, "Perhaps they are not holy *aars* fumes at all but simply putrid gaseous emissions." Wishing to escape from this unwanted attention, he said: "What about you, Meisje Schoonhoven. You do not seem at all immune to the holy *aars* fumes. What did you dream?"

Anneke fidgeted with the ribbon tied beneath her chin until she had transformed it into a hopeless knot. "I dreamed again of my wedding day," said she.

"How wonderful," said Pangloss.

"Indeed," said Candide. "Surely it will be the best of all possible wedding days."

Anneke turned her gaze to Jakob for the first time since they had rattled away from the giant *aars*. "But it was not as before—in my earlier dream."

"What do you mean?" said he.

"This time it was not you dressed in a formal black coat and breeches, with white silk stockings, and brass buckled shoes. Nor was it your long acorn-brown hair tied back with a striking crimson ribbon."

Jakob was surprised by this new rendering of her earlier vision and could not help but show it in his rather stunned visage. "I don't understand. If it was not me at our wedding then who was it?"

"It was the Lord and Savior of us all," said Anneke.

"You are to marry the King of Prussia?" said Candide.

"Not that king," said Pangloss. "The King of the Jews."

"But how is that possible?" said Jakob.

Anneke placed a hand upon his shoulder. "I was mistaken about the identity of the groom in my first dream. It was not you I saw. It was our Lord and Savior, Jesus Christ."

Jakob turned his gaze forward and gave the ball-less wonder a sloppy switch with the buggy whip. The gist of what had just been related to him remained obscured in a fog of incredulity. "But what then does it all mean?" he finally said.

"Do you not see?" said Anneke. "It is God's will that I become the bride of Christ and serve and honor our Lord for the rest of my life."

"You mean you are to become a nun?" Somewhere in Jakob's soul, a piercing ray of hope burst forth through a door just then cracked open by the sure hand of Fortuna.

"Yes, dear Jakob, I am to become a nun."[68]

---

[68] As surprising as this revelation may have been to Jakob, it was considerably more surprising to Anneke. For as a young girl, her exposure to the Church had been limited to regular calls from the local pastor in order to "square accounts" between the Almighty and his fold. She recalled how her father would slip a leather pouch of gold coins into the waiting hands of the pastor, who would then respond with a gravely uttered "God bless you" and a rigidly drawn *signum crucis*. To this, her father would add with an impious grin and a wink of sarcasm: "Salvation secured for another six months, eh pardre?"

Anneke had seen nuns before—often, as it turned out. Not far from her father's country manor stood an abbey with imposing gray walls and a single soaring spire that yearned heavenward. So much so that young Anneke felt certain that the spire must snag the cloaks of God whenever He should choose to pass this way. And pass this way He must, for, as it was told to her by her father, the Lord and Savior had many "goat-faced brides to tend to" within the walls of *St. Lidwina Klooster*.

The news that Anneke was now to be a nun resulted in a night of fitful sleep for Jakob. He tossed and turned, and dreamed of a foppish Savior in silk stockings, breaches, and a macaroni jacket. Then all morning, he sat idle at his desk as the manufacturing of

---

Aside from believing that the Lord and Savior had a puzzling preference for plump and unlovely maidens, Anneke inferred that the God of Christianity must surely be the most spotless of all Gods. The provenance of this inference could be traced to the nuns' daily routine of hauling wooden buckets of water several furlongs from the village spring to the abbey upon their spare shoulders. As young Anneke watched the Sisters of *Lidwina*, she assumed the water was drawn for the Lord's morning ablutions, He being the undisputed Master of the House.

One spring morning, overcome by curiosity, the young girl stole into the abbey to catch a glimpse of the immaculate Almighty but instead found nuns living a simple existence of devotion and toil. She heard their prayers, heard their choruses seeping through damp stone walls and taking flight like doves to the sky. Then she saw the crucifix hanging from the chapel wall. Young Anneke boldly approached it, noting that this particular Lord was not spotless at all. His flesh was torn and his body leaked blood everywhere. Why the goat-faced brides of Christ would leave their master in such a state was beyond her childish comprehension. Anneke sat on the ground with her legs pulled to her chest. She felt the coldness of the stone. She wondered where the living Lord was to be found, for it seemed He was nowhere within *St. Lidwina Klooster*. And she wondered where all the water went—the many buckets trudged daily by the nuns to the abbey—if not to keep the Master immaculate.

As she sat wondering this very thing, from out within the walls of the cloister, she heard the rasp of spade and hoe and the song of spring. Following the sounds, Anneke watched silently from the squat dense shadow of a pillar, nuns ladling water onto narrow rows of green. And finally she understood—it was here that the buckets of water were spent. The reverence with which each sparkling ladle was drizzled made her believe that the nuns knew something no one else did, something the pastor did not know, something her father did not know. And in the pure light of spring, it became clear to her that the brides of Christ were not goat-faced at all. They were young and fair, and about the work of their Master. Wherever it was He might be.

Dutch flat-weave carpets went on without him.

He rubbed his eyes and sipped his tea.

The slight upon Jakob which Anneke's resolve to enter the nunnery amounted to did not result in an abject surrender to fate on his part. On the contrary, he had come to see it as a relief, although he would dare not say such a thing to any living soul. It would be fair to say that Jakob felt in some way delivered from hapless circumstances. What concerned him most were the many visions of late that seemed to be arising from deep within the bowels of Oma Onderdonk. Her phantasmal gasses had even provoked metaphysical reveries in Pangloss and Candide. And clearly, the dreams of Bonifaas had become more and more cabbalistic in nature.

Jakob set his cup into a saucer and spoke to Pangloss. "Not long ago you warned me that the maggots of evil move like parasites among men and that those maggots of evil may even writhe within Bonifaas Quackenboss. After attending yesterday's meeting of the Anabaptists in the giant *aars*, do you still believe it to be so?"

Pangloss cocked his head to one side and Jakob could see a gusty utterance building within the old philosopher. "Like religion itself, belief is not something someone does or does not do," said Pangloss. "It cannot be founded on one or two or even three experiences, even if those experiences be visions from Oma Onderdonk's holy *aars*. True belief is recognition—recognition and acceptance of God and His perfect order—"

"—in this the best of all possible worlds. Yes, I am quite aware of that." Jakob picked up his tea cup and put it down immediately when he realized that the slight tremble with which he held it was a clear indication of his growing impatience. "Let us disregard belief for a moment. And let me rephrase my question. Do you *think* that evil may lurk within the soul of Bonifaas Quackenboss?"

"Oh yes, of course. Evil may lurk within the soul of any man. It is, as I said, a parasite, and a parasite may live undiscovered until such a time as it manifests itself in a malady of the soul. Only then can one know with any certainty that evil lurks within."

What a malady of the soul was, exactly, Jakob could not say. But clearly, something had changed in Bonifaas Quackenboss. At length, he decided that the only way to settle the matter would be to speak plainly to Bonifaas about it. In fact, he decided he would do it now, for to wait any longer, Jakob realized, would do nothing to restore his peace of mind. To that end, he took his jacket from the coat rack and slipped it on. "I will be out for the rest of the afternoon," said he. "Please tend to any matters of business that may arise in the meantime, Master Pangloss."

The gray sky threatened to rain on him, as the ball-less wonder loped lamely through sprouting fields of *Grote Polder*, approaching the forge. Jakob felt the first drops of rain, wet upon his face, and soon water was pouring from the low-slung clouds. When he reached Bonifaas's forge, a quick survey of the building turned up nothing. It was empty and the stove cold as a river stone. Jakob turned and trotted to the giant *aars*, where, pushing past the doors, a rivulet of rainwater sluicing down the great buttocks' crack doused him.

Inside, the room was sweltering. A dry heat made his lips stick to his teeth and his tongue raked across the back of his throat. Scanning the place, Jakob found the source of the heat to be a fierce blaze in the fireplace. He immediately began to pant. Staggering up the aisle, he found Bonifaas shirtless, prostrate, and glazed in sweat. Even as he approached, Jakob could see that the preacher's eyes were closed.

"Bonifaas, are you all right?" said Jakob.

"Yes, yes, fine," said he, sitting upright.

"What are you doing in here?"

"Thinking. I think best in here."

"In this heat?"

"Heat?" The preacher's eyeballs rolled to one side and his head followed immediately behind. "Oh, that. I may have put an excessive amount of coal on the fire."

"Since when do you buy coal for the fire?"

"It is for the special prayer meeting that is to take place on the day after tomorrow."

"A special prayer meeting? On Wednesday?" Jakob helped Bonifaas to his feet. "Has something happened to prompt this special prayer meeting?"

"Nothing that is not God's will," said Bonifaas.

"But what exactly is it—God's will—that it would require a heat like unto Hades."

"It is nothing, nothing at all."[69]

---

[69] What Bonifaas meant by "nothing at all" was not actually nothing at all but instead another vision—the strangest and most vivid yet. On the previous night, following the meeting of the Anabaptists, Bonifaas had retreated to his bed, burning with fever and complaining of abdominal pains. In fact, his gut was home to a flourishing colony of parasites—not uncommon among his class. Bonifaas had been host to the protozoan *Giardia lamblia* for some time now—not coincidentally, since about the time that he first began having his visions. (And it should also be remembered that Bonifaas was mildly epileptic—a condition which was triggered by the methanethiol and hydrogen sulfide present in his *scheeten* and resulting in his seizures-cum-visions.) Of course, the parasites would explain his present infirmity; it would also explain his excessive and particularly foul flatulence of late. But this night, as a slightly tainted *makreel* stew made its way into Bonifaas's lower intestines, mixing and mingling with the protozoan colonists in a celebratory fashion on par with Carnival, flatulently speaking, it was one for the books. Katrine Quackenboss, unable to brave the palpable stench that now mired the cottage, essentially abandoned her home and husband for the shearing shed. Alone in a mephitic haze of his own making, Bonifaas had another of his visions—that is to say, seizures—this one being like none other before. In it, he is walking down a path that quickly transmogrifies into a long, black tongue squishing between his toes when he walks. The tongue is weaving this way and that, rising and falling over the familiar landscape of South Holland, which is suddenly littered with people, naked people, and animals, and people-animals all broken and twisted in a carnage of sin and desire. He follows the tongue for what seems a very long time, passing a pig-in-a-habit in fond embrace with a magistrate or politician, a commoner being gored by dogs in centurion uniforms, a rabbit-monk jousting with a barbed spear, and many other unnatural spectacles. At long last, a giant white *aars*—the giant white *aars* that he has built—appears on the horizon. As Bonifaas reaches it, he sees the tip of the black tongue circling the anus, licking and lapping at the red stained-glass window. Then the earth quakes beneath his feet. When he looks down the black tongue is now a ribbon of black smoke funneling into the anus of the giant *aars*. Bonifaas enters the building and finds it full of his followers. It takes him a moment to realize this, as the followers all have

Jakob helped the preacher to his feet and out of the stifling heat of the giant *aars*, which it should be said was no small feat given that Bonifaas was glazed and slippery as carp in a bucket.

"Bonifaas, I must confess that I am somewhat . . . well . . . worried about you," said Jakob. "You are not yourself lately."

Bonifaas cranked his head up—slowly as if he were toiling to turn the gears of a drawbridge. "It is true," said he, finally. "I've not been myself, lately. Not myself, at all. Nor shall I ever be myself, again."

---

white *aars*es where their heads should be. He lifts the skirt of one follower, only to discover the head of Aloysius Bosch where the buttocks should be. The faux sculptor is softly singing a familiar hymn, but the words are all wrong. Bonifaas bends down closer and listens. *Come all ye faithful to the warm and tender seat of the Almighty Aars . . .*

Bonifaas's eyes flipped open and he shot up in his bed so violently that his neck popped loudly. He sat wide-eyed, as if awaiting further instruction. And in that moment, it became clear to him what he had to do next. In fact, it could not have been clearer. Bonifaas Quackenboss stroked his kinked silver beard and spoke aloud to no one: "It is time to bring the flock home."

FROM THE JOURNAL OF JAKOB ONDERDONK

March 1, 1750

Today is a day sinking with sadness. Father has been relieved of his duties as captain of Son of Batavia. Even now, he lies near lifeless in his bed, and I wait for what seems his inevitable end from afar, on the South China Sea. When we shipped out two weeks ago, I promised him I would return, yet even as I promised I held out little hope that he would live long enough for me to set eyes upon him again. At the time, Robrecht said nothing, just stood by father's bed and stared out the window at nothing. Nothing! It is a word that sums up my brother well: he fears nothing, believes in nothing, cares about nothing. The truth is he does care about something—gold. For I have heard rumors that he collects gold for himself at every port, although I know not what he does to deserve it, I am willing to wager that it is not something father would approve of. But then, that seems to matter little now, for father will likely never return to the sea. And I myself now entertain the very same possibility. It is true that I was never enchanted by the sea in the same way that father was, or the same way that Robrecht still is. Captain Roorback is a personable enough fellow, and to sail at his side is not an unpleasant task. Yet, something has changed, something in me, I suppose.

On his deathbed, father, in a fit of fever, bid me return to land before it is too late. And I must admit that the thought weighs heavy on me still. For the sea no longer strikes me as alive and teeming with life but as cold and dead, the bringer of death and destruction to the lives of all who devote themselves to her. These days, I can scarcely bring myself to leave my cabin. And when I do, I walk the timbers with little feeling for anything I see. The only person I care to converse with is Meneer Vrooman. There is something about him that I find comforting. All the others seem to have a touch of madness about them. And perhaps it is this touch of madness that is necessary to keep one at sea. In any case, it is something that I must think long and hard on. I only hope that father may live long enough to hear my decision regarding the future, my future.

TWENTY-THREE

Bales of tea leaves and yards of Chinese silk were unloaded at the *Oost-Indische Compagnie* boom in Amsterdam. Raw nutmeg and mace, weighed and loaded into waiting boats, were transported to warehouses along *Wittenburgergracht*. First Mate Dag humped a hefty dome-top trunk of Portuguese reals from the ship's hold and loaded it into a trolley. He called out to the captain: "Ready when ye are, sir."

Robrecht descended the gangplank to the dock. He stepped up to the bench seat and took the reins into his fist. "Now is the time when our efforts pay off," said he, snapping the leather and clicking his tongue.

Following *Prinshendrikkade* to *Prinsengracht*, they rode alongside the canal to *Noordermarkt*, where finally the trolley arrived at a narrow four-story building beset by brick and chalky mortar on all sides. Robrecht scanned the height of it, noting the pair of cross-hatched windows on each floor. Behind him, a row of budding poplars obscured the muted grandeur of *Noorder Kerk*. The sky above was gray and shifting.

Robrecht climbed to the third floor of the building and knocked at a door. An elderly man with a silver diadem of hair and wire spectacles hanging from the tip of his nose appeared, still chewing a sizable morsel of fatty worst. "What is it?" He stopped to jab a fingernail between his teeth.

"It's business," said Robrecht.

"Business? What kind of business. Can you not see that I'm sat down to a meal? Come back later."

Robrecht produced a gold coin and, pinching it between thumb and forefinger, held it out as if it were a secret password between them. "Perhaps this will interest you."

The elderly man pushed his spectacles up snuggly to the bridge of his nose and leaned in close. "Real." He straightened up. "What am I to do with it?"

"I'm told you are a trader of currencies. I would like to trade it."

"Who is it, Leo?" An old woman with a knit shawl looped over her sloped shoulders swung the door open wide.

"It's no one. Go back to your meal," said Leo.

"But who is it?"

"Give me a moment's peace! I said go back to your meal."

"Perhaps I was misinformed," said Robrecht. "My apologies to you and your wife," He turned on his heels and made a long stride for the stairs.

"Wait." The old man Leo stepped into the hall and closed the door. "Follow me."

Four flights of rickety backstairs led to a windowless cellar beneath the building. In the darkness, Robrecht could smell the coke-hardened steel and bitter black powder. Leo quickly located a lamp and lit it. As the light flickered to a steady glow, Robrecht found himself standing in the middle of an armory. Rows of *haakbus*, English flintlock muskets, and American long rifles. Piles of socket bayonets. Swords and spears of every shape and size. Stacks of body armor.[70]

---

[70] Leo Krantz was more than simply a trader of currencies. This, Robrecht could certainly attest to. But the truth was the old Jew knew exactly what it was that Robrecht wanted the moment he laid eyes on him. More importantly, he knew exactly *who* Robrecht was. To be clear, he did not know Robrecht's name. Names were not important in Leo Krantz's world—in fact, names were shunned like houses of the plague. No, Leo Krantz did not know the name of the man who stood before him. But he knew the nature of man that stood before him—precisely so, in fact. For Leo Krantz had dealt with every ilk of man in his lifetime, particularly the lowest kinds. Murderers, rapists, sodomites, coprophiliacs, cannibals, and so on. Much of this he had witnessed as an infantryman during the succession dispute between Philip of Spain and the Habsburgs, a dispute that ended up being over a decade-long war. But for Leo, the war had not been all bad. It was during the war that he discovered that a young man with a nimble mind and ready hands could turn misfortune into opportunity—others' misfortune, his opportunity. That opportunity turned out to be a lucrative business in trading currencies and selling arms.

As the allied forces of the Holy Roman Empire pushed through Europe, Leo liberated various currencies and arms from any and all sources available to him. In some cases, that meant liberating an *épée de cour* or a Brown Bess

Robrecht stepped forward and picked up a truncated blunderbuss. "French. An *espingole*," said Leo. "Tell me, Captain. What would you like to trade the reals for? English pounds? French francs?"

Robrecht slowly, deliberately loaded the *espingole* with powder and lead before swinging his arm around so that the pistol was aimed directly between Leo's eyes. "I want Dutch ducats, of course."

Leo went stiff. "But I have no ducats. No one has ducats. The wars have spread our neutral currency all over Europe. There are no ducats to be had in Holland—nor in all of the Netherlands, for that matter."

---

from the brittle fist of a dead man. In other cases, it meant snatching a small booty from beneath the quilted warmth of a cold and dead woman's petticoats. In all cases, it meant following behind the bands of marauders that followed behind the rapists and murders that followed behind the Emperor's forces (usually all one in the same). But from whence the arms and currency came mattered not, for they all ended up in coffers of Leo Krantz.

Leo quickly realized that there were many advantages to not committing exclusively to one side or the other in the dispute, to not limiting himself to this or that battalion. The freedom to roam unhindered behind the rising tide of destruction was the key to amassing a small fortune. For the armies marching through Europe were many and mongrel, and allegiances were obscured by a myriad of factors and complex circumstance. With a collection of jackets, facings, and caps, Leo found seamlessly slipping in and out of the ranks of almost any battalion to be a relatively easy undertaking. Doing so, of course, allowed him to collect a wide range of currencies and arms, and to collect a tidy profit in the process.

By the end of the war, Leo had four mercenaries and six burros—each burdened with full coffers of gold and silver coins—in his employ to protect and transport his interests back to Amsterdam. There he opened a curiosity shop called *Wonderkamer* to front his thriving arms and currency business. And it was to *Wonderkamer* that Avigail would one day come. Standing among the stuffed exotic birds and twisting sea shells, among the cracked whale's teeth and the smooth ivory tusk of an arctic walrus, Leo found his future wife holding up an awkwardly dangling *banraku* puppet. A keen sparkle in her eye clearly attested to her fascination with the Japanese curiosity. When she asked him the price of it, Leo made a show of hemming and hawing before finally bidding her keep it. "After all," said he. "One cannot put a price on such a thing."

"I need ducats." Robrecht cocked the flintlock. "Are you quite certain you have none? Perhaps you are hoarding them for yourself."

"No, no, sir. I have no ducats. I swear it. If it is Portuguese reals you wish to trade, then you must travel to Lisbon to do such business. The Portuguese will gladly trade ducats for reals."

"You are certain of that?"

"Yes, certain." Leo puffed and whimpered softly.

Robrecht returned to the trolley shouldering the chest of Portuguese reals. In his absence, Dag had drifted off to sleep. He gave the first mate a nudge and handed him an iron fist-load weapon. Dag gripped the wooden handle in one hand and ran the other over the sharp iron nubs atop the knuckles. A grin surfaced from under his sleepy mug.

"It's called a *tekko*," said Robrecht. "Courtesy of the old man."

Having set aside the business at hand, it was time for pleasure. To that end, Robrecht steered the trolley to *De Wallen*, where the narrow streets thrummed with seamen. He waited while Dag teetered on the edge of a canal, pissing a stream into the oily brown water. "Old Dag loves spring in the city," said the first mate, inhaling the brackish scent of sewage and rotting fish.

"Perhaps you've a touch of spring fever," said Robrecht.

"Yea, Captain. Ye may be right. Old Dag must call upon a wanton sheep who awaits me return on the farms of *Velds Polder*."

"Yes, you do that," said Robrecht, bidding farewell to the first mate. Then thinking to procure company of the womanly sort, with all its frills and favors, he left the wagon and ascended the stairs that flanked a faded-red brick building to the second floor. Even in the waxy lamp light, the sparkle of his officer's coatee caught the attention of the *hoerenkast* proprietress.

"Ah, good evening, sir," said she. "Welcome." She fanned her arms wide, inviting him to choose from among the assortment of young women who sat with rigid backs and smooth crossed legs on stuffed chairs. "Something special for you tonight, sir?"

"Something special? Yes, why not?" Robrecht gazed around the room, his parched eyes drinking in the lacy form of each girl. It had been three years since he'd had a white woman. His gaze smeared over their creamy glabrous skin, lapped at their blossom pink nipples and golden mounds of hair. He felt his *pik* thickening. Robrecht pointed at two *hoeren*.

"Two of our finest, good sir." said the proprietress. "I assure you."[71]

---

[71] In truth, the proprietress could assure no such thing—"two of our finest"—for she was hardly acquainted with the young women Robrecht had chosen. It was only yesterday that Myrthe Naaktgaboren carried the *hoeren* from *Zeedijk*. She loathed having to scour the opium dens of the city in search of *meiden* to fill her brothel. Unfortunately for her, it was somewhat of an occupational hazard. The girls who frequented *Zeedijk* were all *maniaken*— addicts of the worst sort. And the Chinamen were difficult to deal with. Everyone in the trade knew it to be true. But what choice did she have? She had lost two of her best within the space of one week. One had been swept away by a golden-maned English poet who, brandishing a rattan cane with a silver eagle skewered on its handle, fancied himself a gentlemen's gentleman. The other girl had miscalculated in womanly matters and, finding herself with child, had died trying to rid herself of the unwanted burden of motherhood.

   Motioning with more of a look than actual movement, Dame Naaktgaboren had ordered Joris to wait outside while she slipped from the cobblestone street to a dark entrance and down a flight of randomly warped stairs. A man whom she knew only as Fong stepped quickly into her path, demanding to know her business there.

"You know my business here," she said.

"Yes, I know your business," said the Chinaman. He stood firm before her, holding his ground, but refusing to hold out his hand.

Dame Naaktgaboren grabbed Fong's sleeve and locating limb's end beneath it, dropped a handful of gulden into his palm. Fong stepped aside and stabbed a long pale finger into the darkness, pointing to the farthest corner of the room. She swept by him, pressing a handkerchief to her face in order to dull the olid odor of lives lived there in the shadows. Navigating the broken rows of men stretched out on mats, she inspected the listless faces lit up by opium lamps, until finally she saw the unlikely features of two *meiden*, asleep and facing each other. Experience told her they were young, perhaps fourteen or fifteen, although they looked much older—an illusion that she would use to her advantage. Strays, she concluded, and *maniaken*, too. She

The proprietress waved her hands and snapped her fingers. The two girls rushed to Robrecht's side, immediately cooing and fawning.

"Pay now, please," said she.

Robrecht extricated himself long enough to remove a pouch of gulden from his coatee and drop it into the *powdery* palm of the proprietress. "Enjoy yourself, Captain," said she.

"I intend to."

He followed the *hoeren* down a hallway and up a narrow staircase to a small room on the third floor. Within minutes, all was a tangle of flesh. Thrusting, nudging, prodding, tingling, incontinent flesh. Robrecht ejaculated three times before his *pik* finally tipped over like a fence post in wet sand. He rolled from under them. Then pushing the *hoeren* aside, he rose from the bed. "I'm in need of a proper bath," said he. "See to it."

He eased himself into a cast iron tub and a Chinaman brought alternating buckets of hot and cold water until the warm accumulation reached Robrecht's neck. Steam shimmered off the dingy suds. Robrecht raised a red hand and splashed water to his face. "Civilization," he said, swinging his gaze to the *hoeren*, who had in the meantime lit a paktong opium lamp. He closed his eyes and

---

tried to imagine them dressed in lace, with their hair piled high upon their heads, rather than sweating in soiled peasant gowns with their stringy hair falling across their faces like dry and tangled foliage. They would do, thought she. They would have to.

Moments later Dame Naaktgaboren returned with Joris, who swooped down and scooped up both *meiden* in a single motion. She would take them to *De Wallen* and wait for them to awaken. Then she would clean them up, feed them a decent meal, and listen to their unhappy stories. But she knew them already—the stories. Stories of how they had come to the city to escape the unbearable circumstance of their former lives. Dead parents, two-fisted brothers, lecherous uncles, no food, no money, no work. It was all the same, or at least it always ended the same. Then after listening to their stories, she would hum a warm melody in their ears and transform the two peasant girls into two *hoeren*.

soaked up the water's warmth.

Just as his mind was set to drift over the seductive horizon of sleep, a sharp odor stung his nostrils—an odor not at all like the sweet and pungent scent of opium. Robrecht coughed and sat up with a start, only to find the room swirling with smoke and a wall of flames clawing its way across the wooden floor. He tried to stand, but the flames were all but upon him. With no escape, he slid back into the water and submerged, until only his nostrils stuck from the surface. Through a lens of soapy water, he watched the inferno rage, felt its voracious hunger all around him. Then bubbles began to spring to the water's surface, turning the cast iron tub into a boiling cauldron. Bright red skin tightened over his softening flesh and bones, and he feared he might be cooked alive.

From the watery precinct of the cast iron tub, Robrecht could hear the room collapsing all around him. The infernal shrieks of the two *hoeren* being burned alive sounded dull in his ears. Then a black hand clutched the edge of the tub and a charred face appeared, the flesh sliding from it in oily black chunks. He saw a sizzling hollow where a nose had once been and two eyes steaming in their sockets. The roots of the *hoer's* teeth clung to a charred jaw. It was a startling sight, yet Robrecht could not take his eyes from it. He breathed deeply through his nose, determined to remain calm, until finally the fiendish specter disappeared, withered away before his very eyes. He could smell burning hair and scorched flesh, incinerated lace and silk—and smoldering wood, plenty of wood.

When it seemed there was no hope and that he too would suffer a similar fate, the floor crackled and snapped. Robrecht felt the tub shift, as a leg broke through the hardwood, sending a wave of water sloshing sloppily over the tub's edge. He coughed and sat up. No sooner had he done so than the floor gave way entirely and the bathtub plunged. It was a strange sensation, "like dropping from a boiling uterus," he would later describe it. The impact of landing sent Robrecht twisting into the air in a tide of flung water. He landed face down on the floor and, coughing, slowly rose to his feet with his skin tingling and his *pik* erect. He gazed up at the sizable hole in the ceiling, looking much like the work of cannon fire, while all around him, *hoeren* were screeching and slipping and sliding for the door. It was then he noticed two limbs protruding from beneath the blackened tub, a silken arm and a lacy leg. Robrecht crouched to inspect them before prying his pouch of gulden from the clawed hand of the proprietress. He stood and tossed the pouch into the air then caught it firmly in his grasp, as if to test the weight of it. "A bit of good fortune, that was," said he to no one.

"Does something trouble you, good Anabaptist."

The voice of Candide sounded far away. Jakob looked up and stared blankly for a moment. Finally, he spoke: "How hot is it today?"

"How hot is it?"

"Yes, how hot is it outside?"

"It is more than warmish but less than stifling," said Candide.

Pangloss jumped into the conversation. "I am familiar with the Swede Celsius's thermometer, good Anabaptist." The philosopher stood and strolled to the open office window. He licked his thumb and stuck it out into the open air, sweeping it back and forth. "My scientific guess would be that it is a warm eighty-six degrees outside today."

"I must admit to knowing nothing of the Swedish thermometer. But I would say that it is too warm for a fire inside, is it not?"

Both the philosopher and his student nodded in agreement. Pangloss grunted. "Indeed, only a lunatic would have a fire on such a temperate day."

"A lunatic, indeed," said Jakob. With this, he disappeared out the factory door, without a word of explanation. Walking with an odd kind of restrained urgency to the Onderdonk *herenhuis*, he was aware that such antithetical impulses produced a gate that could fairly be called overdone—that is, with a skip and a hop breaking unevenly between long purposeful strides.

He recalled how at the previous night's dinner, Anneke had spoken of the prayer meeting, the special meeting Bonifaas had called for this very evening. He had thought nothing of Meisje Schoonhoven's remark until today, until this morning, when he arrived at the factory at 7:20 and realized that today was a day to open windows and let the springtime in—not a day to start a fire. Then he recalled how Bonifaas had purchased a load of coal especially for the prayer meeting. Jakob had tried to tell himself that it was nothing more than a seasonal miscalculation on the part of the preacher. But the incongruity of the act held Jakob hostage to the endless imaginings of his unsatisfied curiosity for the entire day. To make matters worse, Pangloss's assertion that the maggots of evil may lurk within any man tolled in his head as if it were eternally high noon. Finally, Jakob's restless mind converged on one inescapable conclusion—something was not right. What exactly that something was, he could not say. But he felt certain of it. In fact, he had never been more certain in his life.

Jakob burst through the doors of the *herenhuis* and found his mother in the conservatory—as she liked to call it, although it was nothing more than a room with a sizable glass roof lantern—watering her exotic pink pogonias from the Orient.

"Where is Anneke—Meisje Schoonhoven?"

"Why Jakob, do I not deserve even a perfunctory greeting?"

"Mother, there is no time for that. Where is Meisje Schoonhoven?"

"Were you not sitting at the same table as I this past evening? Did you not hear her say she would be attending some meeting in the enormous buttocks? Or whatever it is you Anabaptists call it."

"She is gone, then?"

"Yes, of course. She took Oma Onderdonk and left not an hour ago."

Robrecht emerged from the carriage with a canvas seabag in hand. He tugged at his collar, in an attempt to relieve the irritating rub on his yet red and tender skin. He glanced down at his hands, on each an archipelago of tiny white blisters. Then pausing, he scanned the landscape he had not seen since a boy of twelve. Much had changed it seemed, although he would be hard pressed to say exactly what. He and Jakob had played leapfrog together in these very streets. They had raced whittled toy boats down the cobbled banks of the *Oude Rijn*. But these were not necessarily happy memories for

Robrecht. They were simply recollections stirred by an old and almost forgotten familiarity with the place.

He walked in the direction of *Hooglandse Kerk,* swerving in an out of carriages and crossing *Kerkbrug* to the tree-lined lane of *Hooglandse Kerkgracht.* Soon the cathedral rose triumphantly above the reach of spruce and elm. He crossed the street and climbed the stairs of the Onderdonk *herenhuis.* Then, without a moment's hesitation, he knocked upon the door and was presently met by the Lady's maid.

"I am here to see Mevrouw Onderdonk. Is she in?"

"Yes, she is in. May I tell her who is calling?"

"You may tell her the captain of *Son of Batavia* is calling."

"Just a moment, sir. Please wait here." The maid disappeared and returned shortly with Mevrouw Onderdonk following closely behind, muttering: "A young captain, you say? Who could it possibly be?" Then she came to an abrupt halt before him.

The missing years of his youth appeared there in the lines that marred his mother's once near-perfect beauty. For that is how he recalled her still. But this was not the woman Robrecht had expected to lay eyes on. Clearly, he had forgotten that time marches on and ravages all. "Hello, Mother," said he.

"Robrecht? But what are you doing here?" Mevrouw Onderdonk dismissed her maid with an absent wave of her hand. Robrecht could discern little from the jumble of emotions that swelled beneath her stormy countenance.

"Does a son need a reason to call upon his own mother?"

"He does when he's a scoundrel who lives as a sinner and an infidel upon the high seas."

"Ah, I see Jakob has been filling your head with tales."

"Not Jakob, but everyone else who knows the sea from a spoonful of salt. What is it you want?"

"May I come in for a proper visit?"

Mevrouw Onderdonk paused to consider this proposition. Finally, she sighed and stepped aside. "As you like. Come in. I'll have my maid lock away the flatware and candlesticks. And you should know that I have no ladies of ill-repute for your pleasure and amusement under my employ."

"Mother, you surprise me. Such hostility for one's own flesh and blood." Robrecht removed his captain's tricorne and followed Mevrouw Onderdonk into the sitting room.

"Flesh and blood means nothing. Certainly not to you. I realized that long ago."

"You mean to say that I am not like you? And not like my father?"

"You are nothing like your father, God rest his soul. And you are nothing like your brother, either."

"I am nothing like my brother, you say? How can that be? Our flesh and blood is the same. But for the year that separates us, we are almost mirror images of one another."

"You are like your brother in the same way that a shark is like a porpoise."

"Is that so? A shark and a porpoise? A shark rules the sea and all fear it. But the kindly porpoise does not truly live in the sea, for it cannot give up its constant longing for the world above. And so it must return to the world above again and again. And therein lies its weakness."[72]

---

[72] It is fair to say that Robrecht was somewhat of an authority on the matter. For over the years, he had had his fair share of dealings with both sharks and porpoises. It was not uncommon for sailors at sea to stave off boredom with feats of onboard sportsmanship. One such feat was firing upon porpoises. Robrecht was known not only to take part in such sport but to relish in it. When he recalled these occasions, one episode in particular always came to the forefront of his mind, one that aptly illustrated the weakness of which he spoke.

In his recollection, Robrecht stood at the rail of the quarterdeck and watched a flurry of lead shot perforate the ocean calm. A groan and a volley of curses rose among the men as the glassy gray and white hide of a porpoise arced above the water before slicing a clean return. "See how the beast taunts you," said Robrecht to the sailors. "Let us hope you level your sights on our enemies with a great deal more precision."

"Why must you torment the beast?" said Jakob. He turned to their father in appeal. "What has it done to deserve an untimely death?"

"What has it done?" said Robrecht.

"Yes, what has it done?" said Captain Onderdonk.

"Clearly, it mocks us, sir. The fish that breathes as we breathe yet is

Mevrouw Onderdonk frowned. "Porpoise, shark—make of it what you will. You are nothing like Jakob. He is a good son."

"And I am not."

"How am I to answer that? You have abandoned your roots here in South Holland. Gone to the sea. I have not seen you since the day I bid you and Jakob farewell for the first and last time.[73] And what of

---

seaworthy without sail and helm."

"And for that it deserves to die?" said Jakob.

"There is an arrogance in the beast. Men have died for much less, brother." Then, as if to demonstrate the point, Robrecht removed his hat, knelt at the rail of the quarterdeck, and leveling a long rifle at the sea, squinted down the barrel, waiting. When finally a dorsal fin poked from the blue, he squeezed the trigger. A blast echoed over the water and a white cloud of sulfurous smoke drifted up into the mizzenmast. This, followed by a lusty roar from men as the sea beast bobbed to the surface, trailing a red ribbon of blood.

[73] When her sons joined their father, Mevrouw Onderdonk could not have anticipated the effect that losing her two boys to the sea would have upon her. Marijke Onderdonk had been a widow to the sea since the day she married a young officer in the VOC. The daughter of a naval officer, this lonely life had come as no surprise to her. For as a girl, she had watched her mother, Jacomina, don of the black veil of solitary longing, never to remove it again. Now she, too, wore it stoically, almost heroically. But losing her boys was something she had not bargained for, something she was not prepared to do. So when she learned the news that Jakob and Robrecht would ship off to sea in less than two weeks to there take their place beside their father on *Son of Batavia*, she wept as she had never wept before.

Oma Onderdonk was unable to console her, and her husband's assurances seemed hollow. During that time, Mevrouw Onderdonk could unfailingly be found at the side of one boy or the other, as if she half expected the tide to sweep them away before the designated time.

The night before their departure, she stayed up to watch them sleep. Two boys, still babies in her eyes, fast asleep, unaware of the grand adventure that lay before them. They would come to know the vastness of the sea, the depth of its mysteries. Just before sunrise, Jacomina Onderdonk rose and folded her sons' clothes for a second time, a last time. Linen shirts, cotton underclothes, velvet breeches, silk stockings, all in two neat piles. For she knew that soon they would wake, and soon they would carelessly stuff their things into a

all the rumors I've heard?" said Mevrouw Onderdonk. "All the depravity, the debauchery, the treachery. A mother knows when others speak ill of her own."

"And if they were all true, would that make me any less your son?"

"It is as I've said—flesh and blood means nothing."

"I see. Well then, it is best that I get to the business at hand. For it seems that this household is sorely lacking in hospitality."

"Yes, let us cut to the chase. What is this business you speak of?"

"I have come at the request of *Opperhoofd* Schoonhoven. He has sent me in his stead to give away his *nicht* on her wedding day."

Mevrouw Onderdonk sat down, transformed from defiant to sullen at the mention of the wedding. And Robrecht could not help but note his clear advantage at this point. And, as always, he intended on using it to lever his own desired ends.

"I'm afraid you have come in vain," said Mevrouw Onderdonk. "There is to be no wedding."

"But *Opperhoofd* Schoonhoven received a letter stating as much. His Anneke is to wed Jakob."

"She has called it off. The details have not been made clear to me, but I'm sure it has something to do with those Anabaptists. I warned Jakob not to get mixed up with them."

Inwardly, Robrecht smiled—although *beamed* would be closer to the truth. For the fact that Jakob had turned to religion in his time of need was a clear manifestation of weakness. The porpoise, thought Robrecht, comes up for air. He had seen it before—grown, hardened men turned to simpering pups by tragedy and loss then turning to God as if there were some supernatural remedy to be had, some cosmic balm to spread on their deep ontological wounds. Himself, Robrecht did not have the stomach for it. As far as he was concerned, it was a flaw in the very grain of a man's makeup.

---

seabag. Then they would be gone and she would be left alone. Alone and awaiting word from them. Any word. Or stories. Stories passed around among the sea widows like morsels of nourishment, scraps of hope. These, she knew, would have to sustain her for the rest of her life.

"The Anabaptists, you say? It seems the landlubber's life has caused my brother to take leave of his senses. And where is he now?"

"He is not here. He has just left."

"But where has he gone, Mother?"

"He has gone to them, of course."

"Them? The Anabaptists?"

"Yes. He left in a fuss."

"But it is not even the Sabbath? Good God! Does he worship day and night?"

Mevrouw Onderdonk narrowed her eyes and frowned at Robrecht. "It is better to worship day and night than to sin day in and day out, is it not?"

So frustrated was Jakob with the beast's leisurely loping that he removed his shoes and tossed them at the ball-less gelding (who was, incidentally, also shoeless). The first grazed its chinked ears and the second landed a soft blow between them. Still the assault provoked nothing more than a trifling whinny. And thus resigned to defeat, Jakob slumped down onto the carriage bench, waiting for the giant *aars* to come into view.

He was agitated. But more than that, he was confounded. Why his mother would allow Anneke to take Oma Onderdonk to the giant *aars* without him was nothing short of perplexing. He understood that Oma Onderdonk was an integral part of the Holy *Aars*head, and as such, Bonifaas would want her present at the special prayer meeting. He also recognized that Bonifaas had likely prevailed upon Anneke to bring the septuagenarian along. (Such was the sway that the preacher had over the young convert who was now convinced she had been called to wear the bridal veil of Christ, a conviction which, it should be said, Bonifaas had supported from the very beginning, proclaiming that "only the righteous will of God ushers forth from the *aars*es of the Holy *Aars*head.") What he did not understand was why his mother would allow it to happen. It was this detail that perplexed him so.

Jakob spied the giant *aars* in the near distance, rising in all its gluteal glory above the awakening trees. From a distance, it appeared as if some egg shell giant had been folded in half and buried up to his haunches. For Jakob, the structure's impressive appearance only emphasized its underlying perversity—a perversity that yet went unspoken among the Anabaptists. The truth was Jakob had begun to seriously question to Holy *Aars*head and its tenuous place within the true worship of God. Having said this, Jakob's faith in Christ the Lord was intact and as firm as ever. It was Bonifaas's giant *aars* and the edifying fumes of Oma Onderdonk's *winderig scheeten*, along with the visions they produced, which he now questioned. Jakob sincerely believed that God worked in mysterious ways. Of this, he felt certain. However, the recent pageant of all things flatulent struck him as going well beyond mysterious— beyond cabbalistic, even. And Jakob could not dismiss the idea that something more sinister was now at work among the Anabaptists.

The giant *aars* was surrounded by empty carriages. Other than horses shifting from one haunch to the other and swatting aimlessly at flies with soft-swishing tails, Jakob could discern no movement around the giant *aars*. All was quiet. Too quiet, thought he. Even the normally ubiquitous jangle of Katrine Quackenboss's fortepiano was absent.

He tugged at the reins, bringing the ball-less wonder to a stuttering halt. A rapidly rising sense of urgency sent him vaulting from the wagon and hop-sprinting for the entrance. But when he reached the door and made to yank it open, it would not give way. Summoning the strength of his inner Hercules, he yanked again, but it was to no avail. "Locked. Locked. Locked!" cried he. Jakob banged on the door with both fists, blow after blow, until he had worked himself into a kind of gentle rage—which, it should be said, was the only kind of rage Jakob was actually capable of. Finally, he dropped his fists to his side and heaved a sigh—one part exhaustion, two parts frustration. Now Jakob felt certain that something was amiss— clearly, all was not as it should be here at the giant *aars*.

He turned, dug the toes of his shoes into the soft earth, and burst into a lanky gallop. At the forge, Jakob's search ended quickly with the locating of a prisebar. Returning with it, he executed a mighty

thrust—again summoning his inner Hercules—that popped the front
door off its hinges.

No sooner had he done so than a black cloud of smoke poured
from the open doorway. Jakob buried his face in his sleeve and
stepped inside. The room was dark, save for a ruby red pillar of
sunlight hovering there in the smoke below the stained-glass anus.
His gaze then turned to the glow of the coal fire with its sputtering
spent flames and heavy fumes. And these fumes, Jakob quickly
noted, were not the edifying sort that resulted in rapturous visions—
they were the noxious sort that resulted in death.

The reality of this became clear to him as he tread carefully
through the tangled sprawl of the faithful flock looking for signs of
life. His eye seized upon two barefooted figures—the Bonk twins—
curled up and face-to-face, one the precisely inverted image of the
other, both equally still. Jakob buried his face deeper into his sleeve
and pushed on. Among the faithful lay Luuk, flat on his back, with
one hand flung above his head and the other clutching his crotch (a
detail Jakob tried not to read too much into). Farther up the aisle, he
saw the hayward and the dog whipper, the butcher and the tinker.
All of them slumped on the pews or sprawled upon the floor. It was
as if some unseen hand had simply flung them there—their bodies
strewn about like the bones of a diviner. There was no writhing, no
snapping and snarling, no speaking in tongues. The enthusiasm
which he had previously witnessed was now gone, extinguished. For
the giant *aars* had been transformed into a giant sepulcher. This grim
realization made his hands and knees tremble, not for fear but for
helplessness. Standing there among them, Jakob felt helpless to help
them—for he had not the powers of life and death, and he could not
bring them back.

He found Oma Onderdonk near the pulpit, slouched in her chair.
Bundling up the septuagenarian and slinging her spare frame over
his shoulder, Jakob packed her out to the carriage. A thousand things
spun around in his head, like a sky fuzzy with blackbirds—circling,
diving, swooping upon his exposed soundness of mind. Not
surprisingly, foremost among these troubling things was the
browbeating that he would take at his mother's hand, so to speak,

should his oma die there in his arms. A panic within fused his liver, spleen, and pancreas into a venom spitting viper that stirred him to hasty if medically unsound action. That is, Jakob thumped his oma upon her frail chest. When this did not have the desired result—or no result at all, for that matter—he thumped again. First the old woman's eyes flipped open then her mouth, from which came a smoky belch. Jakob let go a long leaky sigh of relief, and the sky of circling birds suddenly decreased by one. Several hacks and coughs later, and the old woman was conscious but confused (and now bruised, too).

With the initial shock receding, Jakob now began to think more clearly. And the first thing that occurred to him was there may be others alive in the giant *aars*. Perhaps he could bring them back, after all, as he had brought Oma Onderdonk back. With this in mind, Jakob rushed back into the giant *aars* and went in search of Anneke. He found her face down at the foot of her chair, looking as if she'd simply slithered from it into a fashionable heap on the floor. Jakob scooped her up and bore her to safety. At the carriage, he thumped her on the chest with his fists, just as he had done with his oma. When, again, this did not have the desired result, he tried another equally unsound tactic. Jakob dealt out a series of bracing slaps upon the young woman's pale complexion. These, it turned out, did have the desired result, eliciting a moan from his once betrothed. Then Anneke's eyes fluttered and opened. "Jakob?" she said. "What are you doing here?"

"Saving you," said he.

"But we were to awake lovingly ensconced in the warm and tender seat of the Almighty *Aars*."

"Lovingly ensconced? Who told you that?"

"Why, Bonifaas, of course."

It was Jakob's turn to be slapped in the face—and the name *Bonifaas* landed a sound blow. He had forgotten about the preacher, his friend—and the architect of this tragedy. Jakob sprinted back into the giant *aars*. He simply could not believe that Bonifaas—his spiritual mentor, his friend—had been the mastermind behind such destruction, behind such fiendish perversion. Truly, the maggots of evil did writhe within him. Jakob saw it clearly now—a malaise of the soul, as Pangloss had said. For how else was he to view this slaughter of the innocents, this mass gassing?

Jakob found the preacher flat on his back behind the podium. Stark white, his face looked to be a death mask cast in Indian ivory. But a serenity now smoothed the once furrowed brow of Bonifaas Quackenboss and death, it seemed, had somehow made him appear youthful, perhaps even more alive in death than life. It was a paradox not lost on Jakob. As he gazed upon the tranquilly loosened features of the preacher, a wheeze and cough ushered forth from the preacher's lips. Startled by this Lazarean trick, Jakob very nearly ushered forth his own vision-laden *schijt*. Dropping to one knee, he propped up the head of Bonifaas Quackenboss. "You're alive," said Jakob.

"No, friend Jakob, I am a dead man. Off to join the Almighty *Aars*."

"You've brought death upon the congregation, upon your own fold. Why, Bonifaas? Why?"

"Not death, life. Life lovingly ensconced in the warm and tender seat of the Almighty *Aars*."

"So I have heard."

"Then you must also have heard that it is all for the best. For everyone. For the Almighty *Aars* has commanded it."

"How am I to believe such a thing, Bonifaas? Life is to be lived, fully, to its very end, though undignified that end may be. Life is not to be sacrificed according the fetid whims of a fusty old woman's gastric emissions."

"Truth is that one came from deep within my own bowels." Bonifaas smiled, a weak but contented smile. "This one too," said he with a pained grimace, blasting one final gusty *scheet* before expiring. The sour smell of spoiled beets awash in rancid *bier* cut through the acrid smoke of bituminous coal and rose to Jakob's nostrils, clinging there like bats in a cave, all the while wringing a handful of tears from his stinging eyes. Jakob felt his head begin to tingle and his knees to wobble. Thinking to rise and regain his constitution, he straightened up and took a deep breath. But the odor filled his mouth like Aerico's kiss, rendering him blissfully faint, as if he were on the verge of a monumental orgasm. It was then that Jakob dropped to his knees and flopped onto the floor. And it was then that he began to writhe and gnash his teeth, the same as Bonifaas had done. The same as Anneke had done. The same as all the others had done. And somewhere amidst all the writhing and gnashing and speaking in tongues, Jakob began to dream. Finally, he dreamed.

From the Journal of Jakob Onderdonk

January 4, 1748
*Today was clear and breezy upon the Andaman Sea. On such occasions, one
can see the curve of the Earth with the naked eye—the horizon receding,
dropping off into certain uncertainty. As I stood upon the quarterdeck
pondering such things, as I often do on such uneventful days, a ship came
clearly into view on the horizon. I ordered the coxswain to steer for it and
sent a deckhand to fetch father. I suppose Robrecht heard the commotion
that normally occurs on the occasion of such a sighting because he was soon
making his way up the steps, followed shortly thereafter by father and
Meneer Bleeker.*

*Second Mate Bleeker believed the ship to be a Spanish Galleon. Robrecht
guffawed, claiming it was an English Man-of-War. Finally, father put the
telescope to his eye and said, "It is neither Spanish nor English; it is
Portuguese, and it appears to be unmanned."*

*As we drew nearer to the ship it became clear that it was indeed
unmanned. The ships sails hung torn and ribonned from the ship's boney
yardarms and no flag flew over the mainmast. It was impossible to say how
long it had been adrift—weeks, months, perhaps even years. It was equally
difficult to say what had happened to the men aboard it. As we together
contemplated this, father pointed out that there appeared to be no signs of a
military engagement. The cannon portals remained closed and the ship's
hull was fully intact. It could only mean one thing—plague.*

*It occurred to me that the right and Christian thing to do would be to
board the ship and see if anyone had survived, but father rightly pointed out
that even if there were survivors we could not risk bringing them aboard
Son of Batavia. It seemed a rather callous stance to take, especially for father,
yet I knew that he was right and that the welfare of his own men was his
first priority.*

*Robrecht had other ideas. He wished to board the ship and raid its hold
for gold and silver and its gun deck for gunpowder and shot. "Who knows
what other treasures we may find there," said he. Robrecht believed we must
act on such fortuity, and to not do so was an absurdity of the highest order.
Of course, father's rebuke was swift and merciless. Calling Robrecht a
despicable pirate and unconscionable looter, he forbade it. "Some things in*

this world are better left alone—unknown, undiscovered, untried and untrue," said he. And it was clear to me—and to Robrecht, too—that father's remark went far beyond the present circumstance.

There was a moment in the throes of this heated exchange when I believed Robrecht may fall upon father and beat him with his fists—such was the look of fury in his eye. And such was the distance that had come between them, like separate continents, each of them firm and unmoving, and kept apart by a sea of misunderstanding. How could I not feel inconsequential in their blatant shows of might? How can I not think myself small and meaningless in their war of wills? For in truth, father is consumed with concern for Robrecht—with guilt and shame, too. And so, I sometimes selfishly believe my brother has gotten the better part—the largest part, yes, but also the greatest part—of my father. But how can I ever let such a thing be known? I cannot, will not.

The Portuguese ship soon came up on starboard side of Son of Batavia. And we—the three of us—stood and watched it slide silently by, lifelessly by, leaving it to drift for an eternity towards who knows where.

TWENTY-FOUR

Jakob had made a promise to God and to himself that he would never again set foot on a vessel bound for the sea. In this, he had literally and symbolically turned his back on his former life—the life of a godless seaman, the same life that had taken his father and destroyed his brother. He had believed that living his new life on land was God's will, God's wish for him—to live far away from the lure of the sinful sea. At least, he had believed it until now, until the dream.

In it, he stands upon the deck of a ship. He feels the hard timbers beneath his feet, pushing up his heels, hears them creak as the sea squeezes the vessel in a tight blue grip. He sees the seemingly chaotic web of sails and lines above him, brazen in their quest to steal the breath of Zephyrus and Notus. He smells the sea, the brine of its essence, the scent of its hidden desires. It is all so familiar to him, and Jakob cannot help but feel a kind of hazy ecstasy at again being upon the sea.

Up ahead in the distance, land appears. Soon after, a harbor then the boxy buildings of Lisbon with their clay tile roofs baking in the sun. He knows it is Lisbon, not because he has traveled there before (which he has), but because he feels that it is Lisbon. Just as he feels that his beloved Heleen awaits him there. It is a feeling that blooms warmly in his chest, a gush of understanding which then courses through his whole body like an ocean breeze winding through the voodoos of Formosa. But there the dream ends. Not a long dream, as dreams go, but a short, potent vignette, unfinished but not unattainable.

Even as he considered this, a pleasant smile lit upon his lips. For finally a dream, Jakob thought. A deathbed gesture from his friend Bonifaas, whose final utterance in this life was an inarticulate blast from his holy *aars*, a sour flatus that had caused Jakob to dream.

He hunkered up to the table and gazed out the window of his flat, still amazed at how real the dream had seemed. Even now, days later, he could still clearly recall how his heart gurgled in his chest like a boggy spring at the prospect of seeing Heleen again. Jakob now believed that he had been wrong about the Holy *Aars*head and about the dreams. At least some of them. (For, wondered he, who in his right mind could believe that Bonifaas's final dream of utter destruction had come from God?) He had been wrong to question the truth of others' dreams. And he believed that sin and bitterness had kept him from experiencing his own dream. For Jakob was convinced that his dream had indeed come from God, having been carried forth from that heavenly provenance on the foul anemic wings of Bonifaas's final *scheet*. And that dream was a message, God's way of telling him to seek out his beloved. (Unfortunately and, yes, ironically, as we shall see, Jakob's dream was—like the others' dreams—only the result wishful thinking. For unbeknownst to him, he had circuitously arrived at that final destination where people simply believe that which they wish to believe.)

He recalled the letter from Heleen and its familiar lines . . . *the promise of a generous dowry . . . the only way that I can help my family. . . .* For all he knew, it may've been too late. This had occurred to Jakob before now. Perhaps she had already wed another for a generous dowry. But even if it were the case, he reasoned, she must not have loved him—could not have. For Jakob had read as much between the lines. Over and over, he had read them in his mind's eye. And over and over, he arrived at the same conclusion: she had acted to help her family, and nothing more.

Even so, thought he, in the eyes of God and man, Heleen belongs to another. That was the simple truth of the matter. Still, his mind kept returning to the dream, his dream. He, Jakob, had had a dream. God had finally seen fit to bestow upon him a rapturous vision. How could he deny it? He could not. For did this dream not trump all? God would not send him such a dream if God did not wish him to go. That seemed clear enough. And if it were true, then he would go, must go. Because it was God's will that he go, because it was God's will that he seek out Heleen. And when he found her, he would open his heart to her, and like an un-bunged spigot, it would flow rivers of love.

Jakob slammed his fist upon the table, his resolve now firm. The violent rattling of the table sent Gertrude arcing across the room in a single skittish bound.[74] Yes, he would do it! He would go to Lisbon! Jakob felt relieved and somehow proud of his decisiveness. But then it occurred to him that his decision, even for all its decisiveness, was not going to please his mother—an understatement to be sure. In that moment, Jakob felt his resolve beginning to waver, grow flimsy as the legs of a newborn lamb. For he knew his mother would decry his plan and humiliate him. Surely, it would be another massacre of the innocents. Or in this case, the innocent—himself, Jakob.

He took a moment to ponder this, to imagine the unpleasant encounter. As he did, Jakob found himself growing increasingly angry. Admittedly, it was an uncommon reaction for Jakob. But the truth was the idea of his mother lording over him made Jakob angry, very angry. For was he not a grown man? A man capable of building a thriving manufacturing business from nothing more than a simple idea? Was he not a man capable of seeing to his own personal affairs? At that moment, something stirred in him, and Jakob imagined that this is how his Savior must have felt when He found the moneychangers in the temple. Jakob grew angrier and angrier, until finally there was nothing left to do but face her, to stand up to his mother for the first time in his life. To tell her that he was going no matter what she said. For God had commanded it.

Of course, it goes without saying that he would not fall upon her with a whip in hand, as Jesus had fallen upon the moneychangers. And, upon second thought, he decided to omit any mention of God, believing that nothing God-like or God-related would be prudent in this case. And certainly, nothing would be mentioned about Bonifaas Quackenboss's holy *aars* or the Holy *Aars*head. To say such a thing would be insanity, pure and simple, as Bonifaas Quackenboss's was not a name to be bandied about at this particular juncture. For his mother was well aware of the tragedy that had befallen the Anabaptists within the giant *aars*. The truth was all of South Holland

---

[74] It should be said that Jakob was aware of his recent habit of banging his fists on things—doors, tables, people's chests—but he had come to find it liberating in some way and could not help but associate the act with good outcomes.

was well aware of the tragedy. And two-score and seven deaths was nothing if not a tragedy, despite the fact that Anneke and his own oma had survived.

Of course, Jakob knew his mother would not admit to being relieved that Bonifaas Quackenboss was gone and that the preacher no longer held sway over him. No, she would not say such a thing, although Jakob felt certain that very thing had crossed her mind — numerous times — within the last few days. He was still waiting for the inevitable "I told you so." But this, Jakob felt certain, would come in due time. And it was for this very reason that he had not called upon his mother since depositing Oma Onderdonk, alive and still hacking, at the door of the Onderdonk *herenhuis*.

And so it was that Jakob decided to say nothing about God or visions or flatulence of any kind to his mother. The nature of his trip to Lisbon, he would tell her, was business and nothing more — a delivery of carpets to the Portuguese capital, to be specific. He would even take Candide and Pangloss along to lend the whole taradiddle some credibility. "It just might work," said he to Gertrude the cat. And as he did so, Jakob felt his resolve grow stiff again. He would do it. In fact, so certain was he about his course of action at that moment that he grabbed his hat, flew out the door, and marched straight for *Hooglandse Kerkgracht*.

Jakob had scarcely removed his hat when his mother began her verbal assault, one which, it became readily apparent, she had spent days planning.

"Word of this devil's business has spread over the whole county," said Mevrouw Onderdonk. "Really, Jakob! Did I not warn you?"

Having failed to strike first, Jakob now found himself on the defensive. "What devil's business are you referring to, Mother?"

"Now is not the time for one of your unfortunate spells of idiocy. You know the devil's business of which I speak. The deaths of those poor fools in the immense buttocks, or bottom, or whatever it is you lunatics called it."

At this point, it became clear that to deny any knowledge of "the devil's business" of which his mother spoke was futile. "All right! Yes, you warned me. But I had no idea that it would come to such a tragic end," said Jakob, unwittingly proffering a lowly if crude pun. He grimaced.

"What normal God-fearing person rolls around the aisles of an immense buttocks or bottom speaking gibberish? Is it not enough to sit respectfully in the pews? And what is this I hear of breaking wind? "

Jakob grimaced again, more thoroughly this time. "Is this really the time for *I told you so*s?"

Mevrouw Onderdonk smoothed the pleats of her dress with a hand grown more feeble than delicate in recent years. "Jakob, dear, it is always the time for *I told you so*s."

Jakob began to pace. "Sometimes you can be so infuriating!"

"Infuriating? Indeed, yes. Now tell me this Jakob—what would have happened to your Oma Onderdonk if you had been a moment later? If you had not arrived in time to save her from this buttocks or bottom when your Bonifaas Quackenboss revealed himself to be the devil's minion?"

Jakob dropped down on to the settee, resting with his arms wide, his palms up, now resigned to this thorny bloodletting. Finally, he spoke: "She would have perished with the rest of them."

"My God, Jakob. You willfully put your oma's life at risk. For what? For a thimbleful of solace in this already treacherous existence we call life?"

Jakob ventured one final defensive blow, admittedly a weak one, which he immediately regretted. "But mother, you forget that it's you who sent Oma Onderdonk off with Anneke to the giant *aars*, not I."

"How was I to know that she had been so fully deceived? And since we're about the business of laying blame, whose fault is it that she was so fully deceived? And whose fault is it that she has called off the wedding?"

"I grow weary of your jabs. The fault is mine, all mine. I am to blame that Oma Onderdonk very nearly perished. And I am to blame that Anneke—Meisje Schoonhoven—has decided that we two shall not be wed." Jakob rose and retrieved his hat. "I did not come here to quarrel with you or squabble about the giant *aars*. I only came here today to tell you that I must travel to Lisbon—on business."

Mevrouw Onderdonk froze. Her previously narrow gaze grew wider, opened up and became more earnest. For what Jakob knew well was his mother hated to be left alone. And ever since, as a full-fledged landlubber, he'd opened the doors of his carpet factory, Jakob had not so much as stepped out of South Holland for more than a day. "How long will you be gone?" said she.

"I'm not certain. Two months. Perhaps longer."

"So long? What is this business that requires your undivided attention for two months?"

"It is just business, Mother. That is all."

"Just business! What sort of business?"

"Since when are you interested in the affairs of my business? I am a manufacturer of carpets. Were you even aware of that?"

"Don't be absurd. Of course I was aware of that you make some kind of flat-weave carpet fashioned on the wares of infidels from the Orient."

"Dutch flat-weave carpets after the manner of Persia."

"Persians, infidels. What does it matter? You make carpets. Need I know more?"

"Apparently not."

"And this business is more important than me?"

"Of course not. It is business, and business must be attended to."

"Is it more important than your marriage?"

"There is to be no marriage. Must we revisit this? Anneke—Meisje Schoonhoven—has called it off."

"Yes, yes. I know. She wishes to be a nun. As if Christ needs another barefoot virgin withering away in his harem of spinsters."

"Mother! Such blasphemy! And the truth is she has changed her mind about being a nun. Now she believes she was deceived by Bonifaas, somehow tricked into it. She does not know what she wants. She only knows that she must travel to Batavia to be with her *oom*, *Opperhoofd* Schoonhoven. He is the only real family she has left."

"And that is precisely why you must not be off gallivanting to God knows where."

"Lisbon."

"Yes, Lisbon. You must convince her that she was indeed deceived by your Bonifaas and that she must again agree to take your hand in marriage. You must not let her go, Jakob."

"I cannot convince her. I shall not." Jakob walked to the window and looked out at the spine-like branches of an ash tree clawing at the sky. "Since we are talking so freely about the truth—the truth is I do not love her, and she does not love me."

"Love! Love! Don't be a fool. Love is not some treasure you find, a crown you stumble upon then place upon your head and parade around as if you are a sovereign among serfs. It is nothing so grand as that. And nothing so real. Love has little to do with marriage."

"Say what you will, I leave on the first VOC ship that sails from Amsterdam."

The mention of the VOC caused a deep crease to slice across Mevrouw Onderdonk's brow. She lowered her head and sniffled. This sudden change caught Jakob off guard. All he could think at that moment was that she could not be weeping, surely. He had only ever seen her weep once, and that was upon hearing the news of her husband's untimely passing.

"Mother, what is it?"

The sound of his voice caused her to go stiff. She raised her head and swiped at a tear upon her cheek. "Then if you must go, there is something you should know. The first VOC ship leaving Amsterdam may well be your brother's."

Jakob rocked back on his heels. It was now his turn to go stiff. This was not news that he had expected to hear—not today. "Whatever do you mean?"

"Exactly as I say. Your brother has come home on business."

"Robrecht? Robrecht has come here?"

"Yes. He paid a visit here not three days ago, while you were out saving Oma Onderdonk from the immense buttocks or bottom, or whatever it is you lunatics called it."

"But what did he want?"

"He said that *Opperhoofd* Schoonhoven had bid him come to your wedding to give away the bride in his stead."

"Robrecht sailed halfway around the globe on an errand? It is impossible. There must be more at stake. And what did you tell him?"

"The truth, of course." said Mevrouw Onderdonk. "What else would I tell him?"

"It is all for the best, Mother. To hear that the wedding has been called off will suit him fine. I am sure he was delighted to hear of my failure. But his opinion no longer matters to me. I travel to Amsterdam tomorrow."

Robrecht drummed his fingers on the arm of the captain's chair. Between his teeth was clamped a meerschaum pipe, into which a Turkish craftsmen had carved a male and female figure committing an impossibly nimble lascivious act. Clearly, Robrecht's nerves were on edge, although not inexplicably so. Ten days on land was more than enough for any seafarer. He was anxious to cut a path for the wide open sea. A quick stopover in Lisbon to trade the Portuguese reals for Dutch ducats and it would be clear sailing to Batavia.

Robrecht exhaled a gray fog of tobacco smoke and rose to look out over the Port of Amsterdam. The dawn boiled like a ball of molten metal in the silver waters. Detecting the bellowed croak of his first mate outside the cabin door, Robrecht called out, "Enter, Meneer Dag."

The door rattled open. "Captain, landlubbers've overtaken the spar deck. They claim t'be seeking passage to Lisbon. And they'll pay."

"How many?"

"Three men in all and a woman. But old Dag'd best tell ye that one of 'em's yer brother."

"My brother? How odd."

"Shall I send 'em in?"

"Yes—no. Tell them I'll be out to speak with them presently."

Robrecht slipped into his captain's coatee and set his tricorne on his head. Then in a manner which can only be described as rigid with a touch of the theatric, he strolled out onto the deck and stood directly before Jakob. In the long, silent moment that followed,

Robrecht inspected his brother—although, it should be said, what precisely he expected to find was not at all clear to him.

Perhaps he had hoped for more apparent signs of weakness— regret, sorrow, nostalgia, or the likes. Anything that might afford him some advantage. But he found nothing. Jakob looked the same as he always had—unexceptional. The same plain features (unfailingly straight nose, slightly beaked upper lip, milky blue eyes, shoulder-length brown hair, prosaically rounded chin) that rendered him sufficiently ordinary so as to wholly and completely disappear into a crowd.

It struck him that Jakob looked ordinary in much the same way that his father had looked ordinary. Even standing stately upon the quarterdeck in his captain's coatee, tricorne hat, and glimmering epaulettes, Cornelis Onderdonk could not have been thought an arresting figure, any more than a distant star could be mistaken for the sun above. Jakob and his father bore none of the striking features for which Robrecht had always been known. It took but a glance to realize that the resemblance Robrecht bore was to his mother, not his father. It could be said that he was handsome in a way that a Caesar was powerful.

"Hello, Robrecht," said Jakob. "I imagine this comes as quite a surprise to you."

"I couldn't be more surprised if Poseidon rose up from the sea wearing a Turk's turban," he said, with not a hint of jocularity. "I presume you have not come in the hope of returning to a life at sea. For you look so thoroughly to be a landlubber."

"Yes, life upon land suits me well. And I see life at sea also suits you well—Captain Onderdonk."

"Indeed, yes, it does." Robrecht brushed a hand over the four gold rings on the sleeve of his coatee. "But enough idle chitchat. What brings you to *Son of Batavia* this day?"

"We are seeking passage to Lisbon."

"The four of you? Yes, I think that can be arranged." Robrecht turned his gaze to the young woman, whom he immediately noted wore too fine a gown for a voyage at sea.

"Where are my manners?" said Jakob. "Allow me to introduce my traveling companions. This is Master Pangloss and his student Candide. They work in my factory. And this is Meisje Schoonhoven, *nicht* of the *opperhoofd* of Batavia."

"So this is your Anneke," said Robrecht, ignoring the unsightly philosopher and his twiggish sidekick. "Your betrothed, is it not?"

"As I understand it, you are already aware that she is not—no longer—my betrothed."

"Ah, you've spoken to mother, then." Robrecht circled the young woman, as if inspecting one of Barroso's slaves. "And does Meisje Schoonhoven also have business in Lisbon?"

"Meisje Schoonhoven wishes to sail on to Batavia to be with her *oom*."

"Is that so? *Opperhoofd* mentioned nothing of this to me." Robrecht touched a golden curl that had escaped from the young woman's calash bonnet.

"It was something of a last minute decision. I'm sure that *Opperhoofd* Schoonhoven would be indebted to you for such a service." said Jakob.

In this last utterance, Robrecht detected the intended warning against any impropriety.

The porpoise surfaces again, thought he. Robrecht grinned.

"Of course, I am obliged to deliver Meisje Schoonhoven to her *oom*. She may take up residence in the first mate's cabin. The rest of you, I'm afraid, will have to bunk below with the men."

For his part, Jakob had felt nothing unusual in seeing Robrecht again. But then, there had never been much of a filial bond between them. They had been playmates for a time in their youth and that was all— never mates, never friends, and certainly not confidents. They had been and remained essentially strangers in their adult lives.

Being back on the deck of *Son of Batavia*, however, stirred some long forgotten feelings within Jakob. Aside from all the sensual delights that being at sea stimulates within the seafarer, there is the much more subtle (although in some ways more obvious) sense of movement. Jakob had become aware of this sense very early on, even as a cabin boy, and had developed it to acuity. He recognized that the moment one set foot upon a ship was the moment one entered a world of movement. There were the tiny movements, the sways and tips of the wind and waves upon the ship, most readily noticed by those not accustomed to life at sea. But there were also the larger movements—great bodies of water shrugging their shoulders and the constant cycling, shifting, and mixing of one sea into the next. There was even the wobble and slosh of the globe as it turns from one day into another. These were the movements that went unnoticed by most, even the saltiest of sailors. All of these movements, Jakob had become acutely aware of. But the movement that had always struck him as deeply satisfying was the movement from one place to another, from departure to destination—from beginning to end. This was the movement that, although most trivial in the grand scheme of universal flux and fluidity, Jakob found to be truly meaningful.

The clanging ship's bell signaled *Son of Batavia's* departure from the Port of Amsterdam. The day was clear and the winds crisp. The deckhands got about their nautical tasks with a renewed vigor, one that bespoke the conclusion of an extended shore leave. The sight of Robrecht upon the quarterdeck, now captain of the vessel, brought to Jakob's mind their father, Captain Cornelis Onderdonk, although the two captains could scarcely be thought father and son. Robrecht's steady and proud stance was the antithesis of their father's unassuming slouch, particularly in the months of the latter's decline.

Jakob recalled how on one occasion before he was bedridden their father had lost consciousness while standing upon the quarterdeck and, falling upon the binnacle's edge, had badly split his brow. The captain remained unconscious in his cabin for days. The ship's surgeon declared that there was nothing to be done and, for wont of any better remedy, bled a quarter pint from Captain Onderdonk and fed him spoonful's of castor oil. As first mate of the vessel, the ship's command fell to Jakob, and he immediately ordered *Son of Batavia* to return to home port. For his part, Robrecht remained largely unaffected by the event. But then, as Jakob well knew, his brother's seeming indifference in any situation was no real indication of anything he may or may not be feeling. Be that as it may, their father never again took his place as captain upon the quarterdeck of the ship. When *Son of Batavia* was safely moored in Batavia, he was removed and returned to his quarters, where he would expire not long after.

Jakob and Candide lugged a leaf-patterned Saratoga trunk between them into the first mate's cabin, releasing it with a careless clatter. Candide placed a hand at his waist, as if to fold himself in two, and lowered his own reedy trunk in a gentlemanly bow before taking his leave.

"Well, we're on our way," said Jakob. He brushed invisible dust from his breeches and started for the door. But as he did, he spied the twinkle of a tear on Anneke's cheek. He halted his retreat and placed a hand on her shoulder. Had he known the melancholic response that this harmless gesture would instigate, Jakob may have refrained from doing it. For Anneke fell into his arms, sobbing great heartfelt sobs into his gray Guernsey frock.

"Oh, Jakob!" said she.

"What is it? What troubles you?"

"I'm afraid. I've never been away from South Holland. And I feel so alone—so adrift."

"You have nothing to fear. You will be safe. Robrecht will see to it. And you are not alone. Soon you will be with your *oom* in Batavia. There, you can begin a new life. That is what you want, isn't it?"

"Yes, I suppose it is." Anneke stepped back and looked into his face. "You have been so good to me. And I have been so horrible to you."

"Nonsense," said Jakob too emphatically.

"Can you ever forgive me—for my foolish visions, for—everything?"

"There is no need to even speak of such things. It's all behind us now."

"But you saved my life. How can I ever repay you for that?" Anneke pressed her body to his and placed her head upon his shoulder.

"There is nothing to repay." said he. "Your life was in peril, and I was to blame, for it was I who brought you into the Anabaptist fold.

It is only right that it should be I who saved you from them."

"Good, kind, Jakob. I will never forget you."

He felt her hot breath huffing on his neck. Then her lips brushed his jutting jaw before latching on to his mouth. Jakob whimpered like the dog that piddles in fright as her tongue, a sweet moist flame, burst into his mouth. By now, his *roede* was awake and prowling. To the casual observer it may have looked as if he had right then stuck a fishing gaff down his breeches. There could be no doubt that the impassioned kiss of Anneke was an irresistible enchantment, and, it should be said, he was at this point in time vulnerable to it. But as he was about to succumb to her trembling flesh, an image of his fair Heleen shearing sheep in a peasant's gown formed like a cotton cloud in the blue sky of his subconscious, floating softly into his head. The image had the effect of waking him suddenly from a dream with a sound open-handed slap.

Jakob reared back and pushed Anneke away so forcefully that she dropped down hard onto the trunk and very nearly toppled over backwards.

"I'm sorry. This is not right," said Jakob. Then, following the promontory point of his *roede*, he rushed from the cabin.

Two uneventful weeks passed at sea. Jakob made it a point of avoiding close encounters with Anneke and to steer clear of Robrecht, as much as either was possible in the close confines of the ship. For as he often reminded himself, the purpose of the present journey was to seek out his beloved Heleen. And thus was Jakob largely successful in his attempts to remain focused on the larger goal, until one evening in the mess hall. It was then that everything changed.

"My God!" said Pangloss. "These sailors eat like kings." The old philosopher scooped a spoonful of gritty beans into his mouth. A lantern swung over his head, making the dark circles around his eyes slosh in and out of two deep sockets like black water in a blowhole. It must be said that in the dim light of the galley, the master was quite a shocking sight to behold.

"Indeed," said Candide. "Surely this is the best of all possible meals."

Jakob picked at the shredded beef on his plate. It was black and inedible.

"And thank you again, good Anabaptist, for allowing Master Pangloss and myself to accompany you on this most exciting adventure."

"Yes, and exciting it is." A half-masticated bean gurgled from the corner the master's mouth and plopped into his tankard of *bier*.

"It is my first time at sea," said Candide, "but I hope not my last."

"For my part, I have sailed the seas to England a time or two, there to trade philosophies with a Scots philosopher of great renown," said Pangloss. "A highly intelligent sort, he is, although a naysayer and a bit of a sourpuss."

Just as Jakob had plucked up his courage and was about to place a morsel of the canned beef upon his tongue, the sailor seated behind him spat and swore loudly. "This meal isn't fit for a worm-riddled cur with a bleeding *aars*hol."

"By the stinking crotch of Loki, you are right!" said the sailor's companion. "The cook must be in league with the captain, trying to poison us all."

The word *poison* seemed to float in the air, a sibilant bubble that burst over Jakob's head. He crooked his neck and spoke. "Excuse me. I couldn't help but overhear something about poison and the cook and the captain. What do you mean by that?"

"It was nothing," said the sailor. "Just a bit of fun."

"No, please. I am curious. What did you mean by that remark?"

"'Tis only a rumor," said the companion. "Nothing more."

"And what is this rumor?"

The two sailors eyed Jakob suspiciously.

"Surely, if it is nothing more than a rumor, what can it hurt to recite it?"

"All right, then. I suppose it can't hurt to simply recite it." The sailor snorted as if he'd said something amusing. He leaned in close. "Rumor is the captain—*a* captain, I mean, and I'm not saying which one, you understand—a captain of the VOC had the first mate—*a* first mate, I mean, and I'm not saying which one, you understand— poison his own father."

Needless to say, Jakob was stunned by this. He felt a heavy darkness closing, encroaching like a shadowy specter in a fluttering black robe. Or like some unfathomable beast bursting from the lowest depths to hoist open an abysmal maw. "But why would this captain do something like that?" said Candide. "Poison his own father?"

"Why? Greed of course. Money," said the sailor.

"What money? What do you mean?" Jakob was speaking loudly now.

"Calm yourself, *domkop*. 'Tis only a rumor. And doubtful there's any truth to it. Rumors come and go at sea like a bad case of the clap."

Jakob ascended to the spar deck, thinking to get some fresh air. The white cliffs of Dover glowed pale in the moonless night. On the opposite coast, Cape Gris-Nez was near invisible. A cool breeze whistled through the ship's rigging and strummed the brown locks of his hair. Had his thoughts been less muddled and had he not been so thoroughly nonplussed he may have taken the moment in as if it were a breath of salty sea air.

But Jakob knew sailors and their rumors. Rarely were such rumors utterly false. They always contained some grain of truth, some nub of possibility. And it was this realization that gnawed at him. All he could think about was his father's slow and painful demise, one that had transformed him from a man of sound physique to one infirmed and not long for this world.

Jakob still recalled how he had followed his own slow-shuffling shoes into his father's quarters. The weather that day was unseasonably hot, even for Batavia. His father looked as white as the sheets on which he lay dying. Jakob noted how the flesh of *vader* Onderdonk hung from his frame like loose fitting clothing. He took his father's hand, a meager semblance of the thick hand of a VOC seaman and captain. For although his father had never been a stately or sturdy sort, neither was he soft. He was a sailor through and through, as once manifested in the hardness of his hands. Jakob watched his father's eyes open, cloudy and red. "The rewards of a seafaring life," said he, coughing then wincing. "Save yourself, *zoon*.

The salt in your brother's veins runs thick, but you—you can be saved. Go ashore." *Vader* Onderdonk's eyelids slid closed and his breathing rasped like the pull of a saw through dry timber.

The VOC physician had said cholera. And at the time, there was no reason to suspect anything else. But now Jakob scoured his memory looking for clues—anything to suggest that it might not have been cholera. But there was nothing. Still, how could he know for sure? He had heard tell of such things happening before—poisonings. Although he'd never believed them. But then, the truth was he no longer knew what to believe.

At length, after going in mental circles to the point of dizziness, Jakob asked himself the question that had been hiding in the shadows just beyond the well-lit although largely void realm of probabilities: Was Robrecht capable of such an act? It was this very question that lay at the heart of the matter. Five years ago, Jakob would have replied "no." But those passed five year now afforded him a more objective prospect, particularly where his brother was concerned. Jakob knew that the seafaring life could change a man, turn him into a scoundrel. Even a murderer. He had seen it happen before, many times to many men in the VOC. And back home, the company and its reputation was increasingly being called into question. "An antiquated, unethical charter," it had been called by certain people in high places. "Warmongers and pirates" he had heard VOC men called. And when he heard these things, Jakob could only shake his head because he knew they were right. He knew it was true—all of it.

Finally, unable to bear it any longer, Jakob marched with a kind of reluctant determination to the stern of the ship, there halting at the door to the officers' quarters. The air outside was heavy and wet, and Jakob recognized the signs of a coming storm. He turned his gaze up, where darkness swirled about the vessel, black as the devil's hooves. But other storms were brewing too, and Jakob knew there was only one way to dispel them: he must find out if the rumor was just that— a rumor.

As he entered the officers' quarters, the ship rocked beneath him, very nearly knocking him from his feet. Jakob rapped at the captain's cabin and waited. When there was no response, he swung the door open and stepped inside, only to find it empty. He groped through the darkness to a lantern and lit it. As the cabin flickered to life in the yellow haze, Jakob could not resist the temptation to look about — that is, to snoop. He opened the captain's log and flipped through it, stopping randomly to run a finger down the page. It all appeared to be in order. Then he shuffled through some loose parchment piled on the corner of the captain's table. It should be said that he had no clear idea of what he was looking for. And he was not so naïve as to think he would find drained vials of Cadet's fuming liquid, but he hoped to find something — some scrap of evidence, some shred of proof, one way or the other.

At first, while pacing absently upon the spar deck, Jakob had hoped the rumor was not true. He hoped that his brother was not guilty of patricide — the most heinous of crimes. But the more he considered it, the more convinced he became that Robrecht was capable of such a crime. Deep down, Jakob knew he was; moreover, he had always known it. Even in the innocent games they had played as boys aboard the ship, Jakob recognized something in his younger brother, something that made him uncommon — although *uncommon* may lack the sense of *ominousness* that Jakob later came to sense in many of his brother's actions. Back then, Jakob had simply believed it a mischievous strain in his brother's elemental makeup. Now he saw that it was something much more dangerous, malignant. He wondered if perhaps their father had recognized it, too.

Jakob staggered slightly as the ship swayed to starboard side and the first drops of rain pelted the window panes of the cabin. Opening the captain's wardrobe, he spied a dome-top trunk at the foot of the cabinet. A trunk in the captain's cabin was commonplace — certainly nothing out of the ordinary and in itself proof of nothing. But a trunk hidden away in the captain's wardrobe did arouse his suspicions to the point that Jakob squatted and cracked the lid open. Inside, he found a small fortune in gold coins. There was no doubt in Jakob's mind that these were ill-gotten gains. But this was no revelation. For Jakob well knew that the VOC was rife with corruption, especially among its officers. And again, this was proof of nothing — certainly not proof that Robrecht had poisoned their father. Jakob stalled at this thought, which seemingly amounted to a deductive dead-end, long enough to squint at the coins and consider another possibility. However, reasoned he, if their father had found out about these ill-gotten gains, Robrecht would have had to take action. For Jakob well knew that the incontrovertible truth was their father would not have stood for such corruption, particularly in his own son.

He plucked a coin from the trunk and rolled it between his thumb and forefinger—a Portuguese real. Finding the coins explained the trip to Lisbon. It seemed certain that Robrecht wished to exchange the reals for ducats. But why Robrecht was collecting reals in the first place was the real question, the question that Jakob had no ready answer for. Reals were easy to come by and accumulate in the East Indies. But the question remained—why reals? Or more to the point—why not ducats? For it was a well-known fact that ducats were generally favored above reals.

As Jakob pondered the question, a flash of lightning burst through the cabin windows and the gold flashed before his eyes, blinding him momentarily. Then the sound of footsteps making a stealthy approach sounded behind him. This, followed by the gruffly uttered, "Did ye find what yer lookin' for?"

First Mate Dag gave Jakob a shove and ground the flintlock pistol into his back. "Ye may've been first mate of this vessel once—but that particul'r position now belongs ta Old Dag. So, get ye goin', ye cod-tongued landlubber."

When they entered the first mate's cabin, Robrecht's fists were full of lace and his undulating hips were eliciting primpish whimpers from Meisje Schoonhoven, who was at that moment bent at the waist before him. Dropping the gown, Robrecht pushed the young woman onto the cot and pulled up his breeches. As he did, he could not help but note the surprised expression that registered upon his brother's face at the sight of Meisje Schoonhoven, lying disheveled and flushed upon the cot. It was all there in his eyes. A sadness that Robrecht recognized, a kind of dull longing that had always been there, ever since they were boys. A longing to be more like him, more like he was, Robrecht. But then his brother's eyes narrowed, pulled tight by hatred into two spherical knots of enmity. Robrecht had seen this look before on the face of many men. This was a look he knew only too well.

Robrecht sighed. "What is it that requires you to burst in unannounced? Please tell me that the main mast is ablaze, or that a giant sea monster is about to submerge our vessel."

Right then, the ship rocked under the sea's swell and the first mate reeled and stumbled. "Excuse old Dag interrupting yer fun, Captain. But yer brother the landlubber was makin' mischief in yer cabin, sir."

"What sort of mischief would that be?"

"He found the reals," said Dag.

"Yes, I found the reals," said Jakob. "Profiteering is an indictable offense in the VOC. You could lose your stripes. But then, you are fully aware of that."

"Fully," said Robrecht. "And you are fully aware that every captain in the VOC is guilty of profiteering." The ship pitched and Robrecht braced himself against a beam. Meisje Schoonhoven squealed.

"Captain," said Dag. "Perhaps now 'tis not the time to take up the matter. We'd best see to the ship. A white squall sits nigh upon us."

Robrecht ignored the first mate. "Show me one officer who does not set aside a few gold ducats for himself."

"Our father did not," said Jakob. "He was not guilty of profiteering. He despised the very thought of it."

"Captain!" said Dag.

"Our father . . . yes perhaps you're right. He was not guilty of that particular offense. Come to think of it, he was not guilty of any offense. Self-righteous old fool."

"You ungrateful bastard!" Jakob shifted his weight forward, made ready to lunge, but the gun barrel pressed to his spine kept him at bay.

"Captain! 'Tis no time for— "

"Bastard— me?" said Robrecht. "Yes, it would seem so, wouldn't it? After all, what do we have in common, you and I, brother? About as much as father and I had in common. Yes, perhaps I am the bastard. And perhaps he was not my father at all."

"That would suit you fine, wouldn't it?" Jakob's face was full, red and ripe with hatred. Even in the gathering darkness, Robrecht could see the rage tugging at the corners of his older sibling's countenance. "That would make it easy for you," said Jakob, ". . . easy for you to murder him."

A burst of thunder rattled the ship's timbers. The sound of rain beating down on the quarterdeck above them was almost deafening. Only a clamorous flurry of shouts and footsteps on the spar deck and the furious flapping of sails proved louder.

Murder. The word sounded so peculiar on his brother's lips. It was not because Jakob had accused him of such a thing. That did not make it strange. He'd been accused of murder before. In fact, he was well aware of the fact that he probably was just that—a murderer. But the word clearly meant something more to his brother than it did to him. Coming from Jakob, it was infused with a morality that Robrecht found ridiculously emotive, not to mention irrational. For killing was the very foundation of the natural order of things. Robrecht wondered how Jakob could not see that, how anyone could not see that. To kill another was not evil or immoral or even despicable—it was something much more sinister than that—it was *natural.*

"Murder? What do you know of murder," said Robrecht.

"I know that you murdered our father. Did he find you out? Some scheme? Your booty? Your corruption? Your reals? What was it?"

"It is not so simple as that."

"It is as simple as that!" Jakob raised a hand and pointed. "And I shall see you hang for it!"

Son of Batavia rolled violently and Robrecht clung to the cabin's central beam, while his brother and the first mate were thrown to the floor, where they slid over the timbers and hit the wall with a clatter and crash, causing a shower of glass to rain down upon them. The two men scrambled for the flintlock. Just when it looked as if Dag were about to prevail, a small white hand snatched it up. Meisje Schoonhoven pulled the pistol tight to her chest and pointed it at Robrecht.

"Anneke! What are you doing? Give me the pistol," said Jakob.

"He . . . he forced himself upon me," she said. "You have to believe me, Jakob."

"I do. I do believe you. Now give me the pistol."

Robrecht let go of the beam and spread his hands wide. "If that is really the truth, if I did force myself upon you, as you say, then fire away, Meisje Schoonhoven." Robrecht detected a tremor in her wrist, a quiver in her lips. Her finger chattered on the trigger. And he knew she would not shoot. "It's just as I thought. You and your *oom* are a cowardly pair," said he, reaching for the pistol. "Captain Schoonhoven—*Opperhoofd*—there is your murderer, brother. It was he, not I."

Meisje Schoonhoven jerked the pistol to arm's length, clutching it tightly now. "What are you saying? You are a liar! You demon!"

In that critical moment, in an unforeseeable twist of fate, Robrecht realized he had misjudged her—Meisje Schoonhoven. For it was there in her eyes, and he saw it as if he were gazing into a future where she had already fired upon him. Robrecht braced himself for the excruciating pain of fiery hot lead. He braced himself for death, for the end, the same pitiless end that he had seen come to others so many times before, the same that he had so many times himself eluded. But as the trigger released and the flintlock scraped towards the frizzen, from the corner of his eye, he saw Jakob lunge. The pistol's report felt like a solid swat upon his ears. And the acrid smell of spent gunpowder boiled in the cabin.

Despite how things may appear at this juncture, when the smoke finally cleared it was not Robrecht who lay dropped by Meisje Schoonhoven's rage but his brother. Jakob felt as if his ribs had been beaten with a white-hot poker. Instinctively, his hand dropped to his side, where he quickly ascertained that the wound was little more than a bloodless graze. With his feet set firmly beneath him, he made to rise, but was caught with a fist under the chin. The force of it sent him slamming back onto the timbers. He rolled onto his back, just in time to see Robrecht clambering for the door and the first mate crawling upright to his feet.

He saw Dag coming at him full on but was unable to avoid the blow. Just then the ship heaved hard to starboard and the contents of the cabin scuffed over the floor. Jakob caught Anneke by the arm as she rolled by, headed straight for the windows, where a wave crashed through the few remaining panes of glass. He scrambled to the central beam, dragging her with him.

Outside, thunder boomed like cannons one after the other. Jakob cried out to Anneke, bidding her hold fast to the beam, telling her she would be safe.

"Don't leave me!" she said, clinging to his leg.

But it was too late. Jakob felt the sinewy crook of the first mate's bicep tightening around his neck. He reached back and yanked out a fistful of hair, which hung like a bloody beet top in his hand. Dag loosened his grip, cursing loudly. The ship heaved again and the two men burst from the cabin and rolled out onto the spar deck. There, lanterns swung and rattled, sending their crooked light shooting this way and that. Some deckhands clung for their lives to fallen rigging and others had seized the gunwale. The mizzen-mast, now snapped, hung like a broken branch over the quarterdeck. Jakob spied Pangloss and Candide hugging the downed yardarm. He called out to them just as a colossal wave beat the vessel's larboard side and drowned the decks with black foam.

Jakob took hold of the gunwale and pulled himself to his feet, and then turning, spied the first mate's hard, wiry frame charging him again. But this time, Jakob stepped to one side and watched his assailant flip over the gunwale and disappear, save for two white fists gripping the top edge of the vessel. Jakob grabbed hold of the first mate's arm and tried to heave him aboard, but the fiend snapped and snarled like one of hell's own, and seizing the collar of Jakob's frock with both hands hauled him overboard. Jakob had almost cleared the gunwale when a sudden jolt stopped him from tumbling into the sea. A rush of pain shot up his leg and he knew his foot had caught a rig line. The first mate swung below, twisting his weight, pulling savagely, until finally Jakob heard his leg snap and felt himself plunging for the tempest below.

The water was cold, colder than he would've expected for the season. But the pain in his leg burned with a fury never known to him before. In those few dark moments, he felt certain that his broken limb was hot to the touch. But the tightness in his chest bespoke more pressing matters—he was badly in need of air. Which way was up or down, he could not tell in this timeless black womb, the same that some claim to be the cradle of all life. So he did what he used to do as a boy—a game in which he and Robrecht jumped from the gunwale into the sea to determine who could hold his breath the longest. It was a game that Jakob invariably lost, as his full lungs would inevitably float him to the surface like a soggy bole of driftwood. Jakob let his body go limp, waiting, until he felt himself slowly drifting up from the depths. Unable to wait any longer, he kicked his legs, biting back the excruciating spasms of agony it caused, until he reached the water's surface.

The ship had split at the seams and was taking on water. Jakob knew it would not be long before it disappeared into the sea, and *Son of Batavia* would take its final place on the ocean floor. Another shipwreck, another jewel for Poseidon's crown.

A short distance away, he spied the first mate, hanging on a powder keg, his beard dripping like a sopping mop from his chin. Even amongst all the death and destruction, the fiend's grin was evident, unfolding before him like an ageless story, one that Jakob now felt would be told over and over until the end of time. For Jakob had lost, and he had won. The fiend knew he had won. And Jakob knew it, too.

He thought about his father, and the waves just kept coming. And he thought about his mother—his poor, spiteful mother. And the waves kept washing over him. Pushing him under. Until Jakob could no longer keep the water from rushing into his lungs. It pried his mouth open, forced its way in. And in those final moments it struck him that this mortal wrestle with death was more a violation than assault.

He felt his lungs fill with water. He was weary now. And, no longer able to sense his arms or legs, was unaware that he had stopped kicking. Until he felt himself dropping, drifting down. Farther and farther. Until in the depths below, all was finally calm.

The stem of the ship had fully submerged and the foremast was quickly disappearing, causing the quarterdeck to rise in opposition to it. Robrecht held fast to the ship's wheel. Beside him, the coxswain began to sob, watching the ship's sailors trying to claw their way up the spar deck, but all failing in their futile attempt. One by one, they dropped into the sea, where they floundered and thrashed each upon the other as if crabs in a bucket, until finally they were all dragged under.

The rain had now let up and the moon reappeared. The thunder and lightning of thirty minutes past proceeded did its dirty work somewhere over the horizon. Robrecht cursed the malevolent gods of the sea. It was only then that he noticed the squall had driven *Son of Batavia* into the harbor of Lisbon. The lights of the city, tiny orange drips on a bleak night canvas, were clearly in view. He felt as if he could reach out and touch them. The irony of this was not lost on him. For the ship and its crew would meet their fate not a furlong from shore.

The water grew suddenly calm, eerily still. Save for the desperate froth stirred up by drowning sailors. Robrecht let his eye roam over the wreckage—the flotsam bobbing and flashing in the moonlight— looking for the familiar figure of his trusted companion. He had witnessed the battle between the first mate and his brother. And he had watched them both go overboard. But it was the last he had seen of either of them.

Then his eye snagged upon a lacy figure, bobbing among the splintered timbers. Meisje Schoonhoven's hair floated like a tangle of golden seaweed just below the water's surface, her gaze downward into the blackness below. Yet Robrecht felt nothing—except perhaps regret that she had not lived long enough for him to spill his seed into her maiden's *kut*.

An immense bubble exploded from the hull, and the ship began to slide more quickly now into the sea, like a blade going deep into the heart of it. When the water drew near to the quarterdeck, the coxswain leapt in and fluttered like a bird with wings too small to fly. Still Robrecht held fast to the wheel. Determined. Destined for the ocean floor.

It seemed to him now that there could be no other ending, just as there could've been no other story. No other story than the one he had lived. A parade of the dead passed before his eyes—some long dead, some recent: the harbormaster, the samurai, the ugly chief, the Dutch *hoeren*, the Hottentot Elisabeth, Barroso the slave trader, Captain Roorback—all of them. But the final face to appear was that of his father. And still Robrecht felt nothing. For what was he to do now? He was no deathbed Christian. The very thought of it sent a guffaw belching from his throat. What was done was done—and, yes, he had done it. For now the hour was late and the time of his death upon him. Robrecht knew it to be true. This time there was no escape. Yet he did not curse this dark fate. He did not curse death, for death was nothing if not a worthy opponent; Robrecht was intimately aware of just how worthy. And so was there nothing left to do but laugh in the face of death and scoff at humanity.

And laugh he did, and scoff, too—at death and humanity, both. Even with his final breath did Robrecht laugh. And scoff. Even until the very end.

TWENTY-FIVE

Pangloss and Candide were wrapped around the downed yardarm on the spar deck when they witnessed Jakob's final battle with the sea—or more accurately, Jakob's final battle with the sea *and* the first mate, who, it must be said, was clearly on the side of the sea. When it looked as if Candide might attempt a rescue, Master Pangloss restrained him.

"It is not for you to question God's will," said the Master.

"How can it be God's will that the good Anabaptist should perish?"

"God's will is God's world. And this harbor is a part of God's world. Every drop of water and every grain of salt that chokes the good Anabaptist—even now as we speak, before our very eyes—was created expressly for that purpose. By extension, then, this harbor of Lisbon was created that the good Anabaptist should perish here. Were it not so, he would not be here now, sinking into a watery grave, never to return again."

It was true that Candide held his Master in the highest esteem—this could not be disputed. Yet the young man's emotions were running high and he was not convinced, in this instance, by his Master's reductionist logic. And thus was he was still contemplating a rather reckless rescue attempt. Candide loosened his grip upon the mast, only to redouble his efforts at self-preservation when a bolt of lightning atomized the ship's crow's nest. While Candide considered again braving another rescue attempt, a most violent shudder and crack split the ship asunder and spilled it contents like a broken egg scrambled into the stormy waters. The nose dive into the blue beyond that followed, caused the the vessel's mizzenmast to snapp and it, the philosopher, and his devoted pupil were pitched into the sea.

Sucking air and rubbing brine into his eyes, Candide said: "It seems that the harbor of Lisbon was created that we too may perish here."

"Not so," said the Master. "For this glorious pole to which we now cling was created that it might keep us from the depths of the sea below."

"But is it not also the same pole that was created to propel the vessel which would ultimately bring the good Anabaptist here—to his final destination, to his earthly end? Thus, can it be said that the pole is both destroyer and savior at once?"

Pangloss smiled, as if in this just uttered realization the young Candide had finally gained some long-strived for intellectual summit. "The Almighty is perfectly capable of authoring such complexities. For His world is full of just such antinomies. Do not forget that things which seem opposed are still joined in their opposition, and the point at which they converge is God and His grand design, His purpose."

Candide stared blankly over the water, not bothering to hide the fact that he was no longer listening. For right then was he startled by the sight of the sinking ship, with its captain laughing and grinning as he was, standing solid at the wheel, as if to steer the vessel safely into the underworld below.

The two philosophers drifted among the flotsam until dawn. Candide awoke to find Pangloss gnawing through the yardarm. "The Almighty may have had yet another purpose for this post," said the philosopher. "Nourishment."

Candide swooshed away a copper-red laying hen, bloated and floating on the water, for fear that his master might geek the lifeless creature on sight. It was then that, twisting his trunk in an attempt to stave off a cramp, Candide spotted land, big as life, spread out before him (behind him, actually) like an earth-brown oasis in a desert of blue. At the sight of it, he cried out: "Land!" But it sounded more like the honk of a thirsty goose than the exultation that it really was.

They set the post adrift and swam ashore, where they spied the first mate, the same who had spelled out the demise of their friend and benefactor, the Anabaptist. The fiend was trotting for town, whistling a lighthearted tune, shrill in its delight and floating on the breeze to their ears.

Candide began to weep in his characteristically feminine manner.

"How is it that the Almighty has allowed my benefactor to perish and yet spared such a murderous scoundrel?" He stopped blubbering long enough to remove the sopping stockings that had flopped down to his ankles. Wiping a tear with one of them, he flung it to the sand.

"The Almighty has not spared him," said Pangloss. "It is simply that the harbor of Lisbon was not created that the scoundrel should perish here."

Candide stopped his sobbing and, with the characteristic audacity of youth, puffed up his chest and said: "Perhaps my two hands which fit perfectly around his throat were created that I might squeeze the life from him."

To this, Pangloss responded only with a chuckle and a whinny. And Candide, feeling foolish, began to blubber again.

As they reached the outskirts of Lisbon, a slight tremor tickled the bottom of their feet.

"'Tis Hades again, stomping a raucous reel in the pits of Tartarus," said Pangloss. "No good can come of it."

Then a quake tore the earth asunder, cleanly up the main street of Lisbon. Buildings on either side of the chasm crumbled into heaps of stone and slid into the precipice. Shops disintegrated into billowing clouds of dust. Cathedral spires, lopped off by some unseen scythe, tottered and tipped, as their walls cascaded down onto the unfortunate faithful below. And as the boats moored to the quay slammed together into waterborne chips and slivers, off in the distance, Mount Pico spilled its filthy seed into the sea and spewed a foul yellow fog from its molten maw into the sky.

It lasted nigh an eternity, or so it seemed to Candide. In truth, the calamity was over in moments.

"It seems destruction is the order of the day, where the Almighty is concerned," said Pangloss, with a coarse dry cough that had his bad eye bulging in its socket.

"Indeed it does," said Candide.

"Come, we must apply some Christian charity," said Pangloss, "and do our best to give some fitting explanation for this tragedy."

Thus did they make their way through the cluttered street,

stopping to comfort those poor souls who had lost an arm, a leg, or worse, by telling them that it was the best of all possible outcomes in this the best of all possible worlds, all the while being careful to avoid the snarls and snapping teeth of the injured, who, it became readily apparent, did not see it that way.

Candide bent to help a man whose brow was bleeding and whose beard was a pasty glob of whiskers, blood, and dust. Only when the fellow jumped to his feet and brushed the ash from the two strips of cloth that were once his trousers did Candide recognize him as the first mate.

"You . . . again! You have not perished in this disaster, either?" said Candide. His disbelief cracked in a high register.

"Ha! 'Tis no disaster, boy," said the fiend. "'Tis a bleeding godsend. Now step ye from old Dag's path so's he may make the best of it."

Candide watched him hop and limp with a most awkward gait down the street, stopping to pour half a broken bottle of wine into his gullet then bending over to inspect a silver candlestick, which, finding it less than sterling, he tossed away in disgust.

When next they happened upon him, the first mate had his trousers at his ankles and was positioning himself at the dung-bearing end of a mortally wounded, three-legged nanny goat.

"By the locks of Lucifer, man!" said Pangloss. "Have you no common decency? Have you been robbed of all reason? There are good Christian folk here who are in need of your charity. But you only indulge your most unnatural desires."

The first mate cranked his head to one side and spat blood into the dust. "Old Dag's a sailor, birthed in Batavia—four times to Japan, and four times stamped upon the crucifix there," said he, jabbing four fingers into the sky. "So, get ye to hell with yer reason and yer charity, ye fool's philosopher."

And so it was that Pangloss and Candide continued on their way among the ruins with sad and heavy hearts at the inhumane and unnatural display they had been witness to, hoping to find some good and decent folks farther down the road in this the best of all possible worlds.

Mevrouw Onderdonk's initial reaction to the shipwreck was to say, "I told you so." Unfortunately, no one was around to hear it— certainly not Jakob. To her abounding chagrin, her maid tactfully (and most annoyingly) refrained from comment when Mevrouw Onderdonk explained how she had pleaded with her son not to leave Leyden, adding the requisite, yet not wholly satisfying, "I told him so" in a stern, matronly tone. Through it all, Oma Onderdonk only smiled vacantly, blissfully, as always, as only one who has lost every last wit of her mental capacity can smile. As it turned out, for Mevrouw Onderdonk, the destruction of *Son of Batavia* was a hollow victory indeed.

After a time, upon realizing the true and lasting effects of the tragedy, Mevrouw Onderdork fell victim to a paralyzing bout of melancholia. She refused to eat or bathe (even in the most cursory manner), and she haunted the halls of the *herenhuis* all night, every night, then proceeded to sleep upright on the settee through what are normally designated as the waking hours of the day. So frightened by this unseemly habit was the lady's maid that she one day quit the premises, never to return again. At this point, if one were to walk into the *herenhuis,* one could easily locate the lady of the house by following one's nose to the sitting room, where one would be shocked and appalled by the musky odor that had descended upon it, an odor otherwise found only on the berth deck of a merchant's ship three months out to sea, an odor emanating from the very persons of the lady of the house and her windy *schoonmoeder.*

Just when it looked as if Mevrouw Onderdonk might vanish into a filthy sinkhole of her own making, something extraordinary happened. Her former maid, who had since taken employment in another *herenhuis* with another prominent lady in Leyden, having there stumbled across a handwritten manuscript of poetry concerning love and loss, and believing that that poetry might ease the suffering of her former lady, anonymously delivered the bound copy of *Poems for the Solemn and Lovelorn* by Gérard Jambon Shirley to the Onderdonk *herenhuis.*

Needless to say, the manuscript struck a chord with Mevrouw

Onderdonk, and within a week's time, she could recite the contents of the entire manuscript by heart. Forced to name a personal favorite, she would, with no small amount of difficulty, have cited the oddly lyrical elegy *Drubbed by Death, Succored by Love*. So taken was Mevrouw Onderdonk with the poems that she sought out the poet behind the bardic gems.

At length, her expansive letter writing campaign paid off when she received a reply from the poet himself, who as he put it "would soon be visiting the sights and sounds of the Lowlands." In actuality, his itinerary centered mainly on the *hoerenkasten* of Amsterdam's *De Wallen* district, where he intended to seek out more young and adoring *hoeren* to add to his collection back home in Merrie Olde England.

As the day of Gérard Jambon Shirley's arrival drew near, Mevrouw Onderdonk (who had again taken up the necessary habits of eating and bathing) found herself primping like a peacock in springtime. When the day finally arrived, the very sight of him set her to swooning. For to her great delight, the English gentleman and poet was as pleasant to look at as he was to read. And equally to her delight, although perhaps a decade her junior, the gentleman poet made no secret of the fact that he was quite taken with her, the lady of the Onderdonk *herenhuis*. Thus were the two immediately married (a rather common occurrence for the poet, in actuality, whose collection of wealthy wives across Europe kept his fiscal boat afloat and financed his prodigious whoring and drinking habit).

Mevrouw Onderdonk lived happily with her new husband— listening to the verse gurgle from him, while combing out his golden mane and braiding it into the silken plaits worn by the Gaels of Northern England (the people of his "heart and might," as he had told her)—until such a time that he was called away on business. "A worldly matter that would only rimple and ruck up the ivory brow of a lovely creature such as you," said he by way of explanation.

So she let him go. And she let him return again some months later. Just as she would let him come and go for the rest of their married life together. When he was gone, Mevrouw Onderdonk would take solace in the quiet if flatulent residence of her *schoonmoeder*, Oma

Onderdonk (whom she was convinced would live on indefinitely to "behold the glory of the Second Coming"). When he returned, she would fawn on him and live happily in the life-giving rays of his blinding poetic presence. Thus was she happy for a time and sad for a time.

And so went the cycle of Mevrouw Onderdonk's life—up and down, over and again. Happy and sad. Until, in time, the sadness all but consumed the happiness, like a shadow moving over the floor. Like a realization creeping into the mind. And she was left lonely and alone, and sitting upright on the settee of the sitting room.

News of the disaster moved like a ripple over the water back to Batavia. *Opperhoofd* Schoonhoven, not a callous man, was moved to tears for the loss of his *nicht*. But he was soon over it, and so set about the task of finding another partner—or perhaps more accurately, a pawn—with whom he could recommence his Dutch ducat scheme. As luck would have it, First Mate Dag of the downed *Son of Batavia* miraculously found his way back to VOC headquarters and one morning reported for duty. *Opperhoofd* knew the moment he looked upon the shifty-eyed sailor that his search was over. He immediately promoted Dag to captain and, in a portentous gesture, handed over the command of a three-mast fluyt, aptly named *Goude Reael*.

As expected, *Opperhoofd* profited greatly from his scheme—for a time. But when prominent shareholders in Amsterdam caught wind of it, they promptly shut down the mint in Batavia. They also took the opportunity to remove *Opperhoofd* Schoonhoven from his post on an unrelated charge and offered him a position on the docks as a warehouse clerk.

Broken but not defeated, Meneer Schoonhoven took the position, determined to regain his high-ranking post as *opperhoofd* of Batavia. And to that end did he toil for thirteen long years on the docks and in the warehouses, living in the barracks among the dark-skinned *pribumi*. But he would not live long enough to realize his dream. Meneer Schoonhoven was found dead on his back in the barracks, within eyeshot of headquarters and the blue-bubbled window panes of his former glory. A stake sharpened from the branch of a cinnamon tree lay planted in his heart, the blood like viscous sap grown thick and heavy on his chest. There were rumors of a boy, a Bandanese boy, who had come looking for his Dutch father—a gentleman and a captain in the VOC—but instead found the man whom he believed responsible for the slavery of his people on Bandanaira Island.

Ironically, the father for whom the boy searched was captain of the very vessel that had brought him to Batavia. Standing on the quarterdeck, looking down upon the boy, Dag had not seen the resemblance. He saw only a bastard—worse, a mongrel bastard— part Dutch, part Bandanese. For what the captain of *Goude Reael* did not know was the ugly *leidsman's* daughter, Zeuga, did not die of a broken heart on the day she learned that her father had been rendered headless by a spectacular but cruel bolt of lightning upon to the top of *Gunung Api*. Instead, she had won the support of the other villagers, primarily on a platform of sympathy, to take her father's place as *leidsman* of the tribe, which she did admirably.

Nine months later, when she bore a blue-eyed son, she sang soft and sad songs into his ear about a father who was lost upon the sea and could not find his way home. A father whose whistle could be heard blowing in the breeze that swirled over the waters of the Banda Sea. When the boy's pubescent parts had sprouted and turned into a young man's more prominent parts, he secured passage on the next VOC ship bound for Batavia.

In the beginning the boy spoke freely of his captain father. But he quickly learned that such claims were not well received by the Dutch deckhands. For a Dutch *pribumi* was unheard of, unthinkable. And the seamen's disbelief quickly turned to disgust and then to fury— until they would beat him with their hard Dutch fists. So the boy learned to hold his tongue and to say nothing about his mixed lineage.

In Batavia, he worked on the docks, weighing, sorting, and stacking nutmeg seeds and cinnamon branches in the VOC warehouses. It was there that the boy heard tell of the clerk's plight, the same who lorded over him and the others—the *pribumi*—with an incongruous air of self-importance. The clerk, he learned, was once the *opperhoofd* of Batavia. This revelation meant little to the boy at first, for he was only working the docks that he might continue his search for his lost father. But in time, the boy became disillusioned. He finally gave up on his search after hearing the tale of a captain who had gone down with his ship years ago off the coast of Europe. He became convinced that the captain was his long lost father. He felt it in his heart; that is, he wanted to feel it in his heart. He even produced a tear or two to prove it, mainly to himself.

Seeing this, and hearing the boy's story, the clerk, Meneer Schoonhoven, laughed derisively. "That is madness, boy. Robrecht Onderdonk could not possibly have been your father." He sat up on his cot and spoke with authority: "For as *opperhoofd*, I personally sent Captain Onderdonk to the Banda Islands to quell a brewing revolt there. And I know firsthand of his disdain for the *pribumi*. I think it no exaggeration to say that the captain would have been more likely to lie down with a goat than with your mother."

Understandably, the insult stuck in the boy's craw, and he silently vowed to exact his revenge. So that night he crept out to the warehouse and chose his instrument of destruction. He sawed off a sizable stake from a cinnamon branch and stripped the bark from it, before sharpening it to a precise point with the clerk's own machete. Then stuffing it inside the leg of his trousers, he returned to the barracks, laid down on his cot, and waited.

When the sun poured into the barracks the next morning and the *pribumi* had gathered around the body of the dead clerk, the boy was already at the docks. Standing in a morning breeze that whistled slightly in his ears, with his *pribumi* eyes as blue as the sea—he was waiting. But no longer was he waiting for the imminent arrival of his father there at Batavia. What to believe about his father was unclear to him now, and would forever remain so. No, he was no longer waiting for his father or for anyone. Instead, he waited calmly for the next ship to take him away to the sea, to grand and mysterious places. To take him away to anywhere—anywhere but back to his island.

ABOUT THE AUTHOR

Gary A. Anderson

Gary Anderson is from the prairies of southern Alberta. After living for a time in Korea, he now resides in New Jersey with his wife and two children.

He is the author of the highly crtically acclaimed debut novel, *Animal Magnet*, voted among the "Best Novels of the Decade" and "Best Literary Books of All Time" by *Goodreads*.

+ + +

WORDSWORTH
GREENWICH
PRESS

Lightning Source UK Ltd.
Milton Keynes UK
UKOW04f1929190715

255458UK00001B/45/P